"*D*on't you want me?"

His face flushed with emotion. "You know I do." He caught a loose lock of her hair and rubbed it between his fingertips. "It's all wrong for us."

"Because you're a rich lawyer and I'm the granddaughter of an Indian?"

"Damn it, Rachel," he flung back. "We're past all that, you and me. I'm a soldier. I have to go back to the war, and you . . ." He swallowed. "There's no place in your life for a Confederate—"

She was trembling from head to foot. "I'll not ask you to give up your cursed war, Chance Chancellor. I ask only that you love me for a little while. Until you have to go. Can't we accept our fortune and enjoy what time we have?"

"Do you know what you're saying, Rachel?"

By Judith E. French:

FORTUNE'S BRIDE
FORTUNE'S FLAME
FORTUNE'S MISTRESS
SHAWNEE MOON
SUNDANCER'S WOMAN
THIS FIERCE LOVING
McKENNA'S BRIDE*
RACHEL'S CHOICE*

*Published by Ballantine Books

RACHEL'S CHOICE

Judith E. French

BALLANTINE BOOKS • NEW YORK

A Ballantine Book
Published by The Ballantine Publishing Group
Copyright © 1998 by Judith E. French

http://www.randomhouse.com

Library of Congress Catalog Card Number: 98-92811

ISBN 0-345-40874-8

Manufactured in the United States of America

First Edition: October 1998

10 9 8 7 6 5 4 3 2 1

For Candace McCarthy, a dear friend and wonderful writer. Thank you for always being there for me when I needed you.

Love and war are the same thing, and stratagems and policy are as allowable in the one as in the other.
                                        —MIGUEL DE CERVANTES

Rachel's Choice

Prologue

Pea Patch Island, Delaware
April 23, 1864

"You're a dead man, Chancellor!"

A musket ball whined over Chance's head, and he dropped to his knees in the wet sand and buried his face in his best friend's chest.

"Put me down," Travis whispered hoarsely. "It's no use. I'm done for."

Chance could hear the baying of the dogs above the guards' shouting. Another few minutes and the starless night and the waist-high tangle of brush and driftwood wouldn't hide them from the bullets or the cold steel of a guard's bayonet. Travis was hurt bad; he'd taken a hit to the side and another through his thigh. Chance could hear the grate of bone against bone as he cradled him in his arms.

"Leave me!" Travis rasped.

Chance's mouth tasted of ashes; he could feel the strength draining out of Travis's body. "Can't do it, buddy. I owe you one. Remember? It's my turn to play hero."

"This is . . . different." A shuddering groan escaped Travis's throat. "No need . . . for both of us to die."

Fear twisted in Chance's gut. He couldn't see the Delaware River through the swirling fog, but he could smell the salt wind and hear the slap of waves against the beach.

He wanted to live.

Death had come for him at the Second Manassas and later in the reeking mud of a farm lane at Fredericksburg. He'd been afraid of dying before; hell, any soldier who said he wasn't scared was either a liar or a madman. But in three years of war, he'd never felt the brush of the dark angel's wings as he did at that instant.

Another musket boomed, lighting the night with a flash of fire.

"Over here!" a man shouted. "Footprints. They ran through here!"

A lantern bobbed, and Chance caught a glimpse of a barrel-chested man in a blue Union cap. The hounds sprinted closer by the second. The lead dog's bellow rang out through the clinging mist.

"Leave me, damn it!" Travis insisted. "You can still make it."

Tears streamed down Chance's face. "What do I tell Mary?"

"Tell her to name the baby after you."

"No! It's both or neither of us." Chance staggered to his feet with Travis still in his arms and dashed toward the water's edge. Travis had lost two stone of weight since they were captured at Gettysburg, but he was still almost more than Chance could carry.

"There!" a Yankee screamed.

A volley of musket fire exploded behind Chance.

Something slammed into him with the force of a sledge-hammer. There was no pain, but he suddenly found himself sprawled on the sand, losing his hold on his wounded friend.

"Travis! Travis!" Chance's voice croaked like an old man's, and he felt curiously weak as he tried to rise.

Hot on their scent, the dog pack spilled across the narrow beach. Chance could scarcely make out the guards' curses for the frenzied barking of the animals.

Chance had trouble telling up from down. Spinning stars whirled in his head, and his legs felt heavy, his muscles too weak to carry him.

"Don't let him get away! Four days' pass for any man vat blows his head off!"

That guttural Pennsylvania Dutch accent pierced Chance's stupor. *Sergeant Daniel Coblentz.*

The venom in Coblentz's words did what Chance's will couldn't. Rising on hands and knees, Chance began to crawl toward the smell of water.

Another bullet struck the sand beside him, driving needles of grit into his face and arms. And then an incoming wave washed over his hands.

"Stop him!"

"Swim, damn you!" Travis yelled. "Swim for—"

A dull thud cut off his friend's shouts, and then Chance was on his feet and plunging knee-deep into the bay. "I'll come back for you, Travis!" he swore. "I promise you— I'll come back!"

When the water reached his waist, Chance took a deep breath and dived under. The frigid tide enveloped him, blunting the force of the spinning musket ball that tore a furrow of fire along his hip.

Chance swam until his lungs screamed for air, then

surfaced long enough to gulp a breath and hear the clamor of his pursuers from a patrol boat a dozen yards away.

"Rebel bastard. Hope he freezes to death."

". . . not goin' anywhere. He left a trail of blood on the beach."

"Futterin' waste of our time. Current don't get him, the sharks will."

A searchlight skimmed the tops of the choppy waves. As the beam neared Chance's head, he let himself sink into the black water until his fingers touched the bottom before he began to swim again.

He was past hope, but if the river took him, it didn't matter anymore. He would die a free man.

Chapter 1

Rachel's Choice Plantation
Murderkill River, Delaware
May 1, 1864

Rachel Irons scattered a few handfuls of corn on the hard-packed earth beside the weathered barn and watched as the chickens pecked at the kernels. "That's the last of it," she said. "From now on, you'll have to scratch for yourselves."

Agatha, the speckled black-and-white hen with a bald spot in the center of her back, eyed Rachel with a beady stare and clucked ominously as it ruffled its remaining feathers.

Rachel couldn't help laughing at the ill-tempered bird. "I mean it, you old biddy. Find your own worms, or it's the pot for you."

Her mood sobered, and she nibbled at her lower lip. It would be the chopping block for her remaining chickens anyway if the soldiers came again. First they had taken her horses, then both oxen, her mules, and finally the pigs, the sheep, and the ducks. All she had to show for her livestock and poultry were a few promissory notes and empty pens.

She sighed and rubbed the ache in the small of her

back. It was still early; the sun hadn't burned the mist off the fields yet, but she'd been up and working for hours. She'd milked the cow, churned three pounds of butter, washed a basket of wool, and used the spade to break up a small section of garden for planting beans.

Without the horses, mules, or oxen, she couldn't plow. And if she couldn't plow, she couldn't raise corn or wheat or a decent crop of vegetables. She was getting bigger and clumsier every day. Lord knows what she would do when the babe came, and she had no way to provide for either of them or to pay her overdue taxes.

Straightening, Rachel smiled as a mockingbird lit on the roof of the well and began to imitate the cheeping of a newly hatched chick. It was hard to feel sorry for herself on this bright May morning when her daffodils were bursting with blooms and a few sprays of lilac still filled her yard with their glorious scent. She'd never been a whiner, and she wasn't about to start now. Things would work out for her; they had to.

"Bear! Lady!" she called to her dogs. "Time to check the traps."

Lady, a ginger-and-white collie, darted back and forth, wagging her tail excitedly. The younger dog, Bear, raised his massive head, unfolded his thick, shaggy legs, and yawned as Rachel fetched her sheep crook and crab basket from the shed.

Crabs and fish were a major part of her diet and also fed her dogs. Although few people would buy hard crabs, Rachel found a ready market for her spicy crab soup at Thompson's General Store, where she traded her eggs and butter.

Indian Creek branched off the Murderkill River and ran through a corner of her meadow not far from the house. Last night's rain would stir up the mud on the bottom and make for poor fishing or crabbing, but she checked her nets and traps morning and evening, seven days a week, regardless of the weather.

The damp clover felt pleasantly cool under her bare feet as she crossed the meadow to the creek. Bees buzzed and circled over her head, but she wasn't alarmed. She'd always had an affinity for bees; they rarely stung her, even when she raided the honey from the colony in the hollow walnut tree on the far corner of her farm.

Friends and relatives had often asked how she could stay alone on Rachel's Choice so far from any neighbors in wartime, but the solitude suited her. She'd been born and raised here. Rachel's Choice was hers, left to her by her mother's father, and as long as she could keep the farm, she'd never wish to leave it.

"I won't be alone when you're born, will I?" she murmured to the babe under her heart. Boy or girl, she hoped her child would love this land as she did.

The dogs had run ahead to the small tributary that opened off the Murderkill River. Now Lady's warning bark startled Rachel from her musing. Bear's deep-chested growl raised the hairs on the back of her neck. "What is it?" she called. "What's wrong?"

She hurried toward the grove of cedar trees that blocked her view of the creek bank. Her first thought was that the dogs had surprised a blacksnake. Bear hated snakes since he'd been bitten by one as a pup. If it wasn't a snake, maybe Lady had treed a raccoon, Rachel mused. She'd missed a few chickens a month ago.

She pushed aside a pine bough that blocked her view of the creek and the agitated dogs. "What are you two—" She broke off and stared at the water's edge. Bear and

Lady stood on the muddy bank, barking furiously at the spot where she'd anchored one of her crab traps the night before.

"Lady! Bear! Down!" Rachel's breath caught in her throat as she glimpsed the flash of a man's bare thigh and buttocks.

In the shallows, amid a tangle of crab trap, rope, and muddy grass, lay a naked man. The stranger's back was to her, but his blond hair and upper body were streaked with blood.

Rachel took another step toward the creek bank, preparing to plunge in and help him. But then caution overrode her instinct to go to the man. Hadn't two escaped prisoners from Fort Delaware murdered a fisherman off Broadkill Beach last month?

"Hold him!" she shouted to the dogs. "Stay!" Then, heedless of her advanced pregnancy, she turned and ran back toward the house.

"Shhh, shhh. Easy," Chance whispered hoarsely to the dogs. The incessant barking had penetrated his fog of exhaustion and forced him to open his eyes and drag himself up from unconsciousness.

Two dogs. Not a pack, but only two. Real, flesh-and-blood animals, not the devil's hounds his fevered mind had conjured up from his escape at Pea Patch Island.

Futilely Chance tugged at the snarled line that held his legs as he murmured to the black mastiff that threatened to tear him limb from limb.

The collie might give alarm with her yapping, but she wasn't vicious. Her eyes lacked a killer's gleam. It was the black one he had to worry about.

The snarling beast stood as tall as a six-month-old calf,

and his lips were curled back to reveal ivory fangs that could snap a man's leg bone like tinder.

"Good dog," he soothed.

Somewhere in the long rainy night, Chance had been certain that he'd died and gone to hell. Only hell wasn't fiery hot as the preachers claimed; it was bitter cold.

He hadn't cared much. He was past caring whether he survived or not. The pain in his arm had driven him beyond the point of wanting to live. He could feel the poison pumping through his veins with every beat of his heart. Soon there would be only blessed blackness and an end to fighting the water.

He didn't know how long it had been since he'd fled the Union prison. Days and nights had run together in his fevered brain. He hadn't eaten, and he hadn't been warm—not once. Hunger didn't tear at him, but thirst did. All this water around him and none to drink . . . The Delaware River and Bay were salty; not even his periods of dementia had made him crazy enough to drink from them.

He'd thought the river would take him; he'd almost hoped that the water would close over his head one last time. But now it seemed he wasn't meant to die by drowning. He was about to be devoured by dogs.

The collie's barking took on a hysterical note, and the hair on the black mastiff's neck stood up. "Easy," Chance repeated. "Good dog."

And then, behind him, he heard the ominous click of cold steel. "Don't move!" a woman's throaty voice commanded. "Put your hands in the air."

Chance twisted around to stare into the double barrels of a twelve-gauge shotgun. "Miss," he began. Her thumb rested on one hammer. A slender finger tightened on the trigger.

Her brown eyes widened in shock. Her already flushed cheeks burned a deeper crimson, and Chance realized that the ruins of his trousers were caught in the crab trap. Awkwardly he tried to cover his shriveled sex with his good hand.

"I . . . I said, get your hands up!"

He sat down in the water.

Her voice trembled, but the twin barrels of her shotgun held steady. "Are you deaf? Or do you want me to shoot?"

"Miss . . . ma'am . . ." Chance's head was thumping like a drum, and waves of nausea washed over him. But even in his impaired state, he could see that the lady was dark-haired, comely, and great with child. Her charms meant little at this moment. But since she was holding a gun on him and seemed confident she could hit what she aimed at, no sensible man would infuriate her any more than necessary. Therefore, prudence was in order. "As you can see, I'm—"

"Naked as a blue jay?"

"I've had . . . an accident. If you'd just call off your dogs, I can explain—"

"How you're an escaped rebel prisoner from Fort Delaware?"

"No, ma'am." In spite of his chills, he could feel the sweat running down the back of his neck. "No, ma'am, I'm not." Lies were pouring out of his mouth faster than a horse could trot, but he could see that she wasn't believing a word of it. "My boat sank. I'm a merchant from . . . from London, on my way to Philadelphia and—"

"Save your breath, Johnny Reb. Your fine Southern accent gives you away. Not Maryland. Virginia? Richmond, maybe?"

He winced at the accuracy of her barb. "No, ma'am, I told you, I'm British. My business is in London, but my family hails from the Indies."

"And I'm President Lincoln." She cocked the second hammer. "You thought if you got rid of your gray uniform, I wouldn't have the sense to know what you are?"

A wave of weakness swept over Chance, and he gritted his teeth to keep them from chattering.

She was right again. He had stripped off his coat and shirt that first night he'd gone into the water. He'd meant to steal some other clothes, but he'd never gotten the opportunity.

"Out of the creek," she ordered, "before I let you have a belly full of buckshot."

"I can't."

She took a step closer. "Don't mess with me, Reb. I'll drop you where you—"

"No! Don't shoot. I'm tangled in this line." It was getting harder and harder to summon the strength to speak. He was so damned cold, and the sun reflected off the water so that spots of light danced across his brain. "I don't mean you any harm."

"More lies?"

It was hard to keep his eyes open. "If you mean to shoot me, then do it. Just give me a drink of water first."

"Why should I?"

"A lady should—"

Her obsidian eyes narrowed. "How dare you tell me what I should do for you, you traitor?"

"If you won't give me a drink, then shoot and be damned."

"Maybe I will. I'm sure there's a bounty on your head."

"You're a hard woman to deny a man a drop of water before you send him to his Maker."

"You take me for a fool? A fisherman was murdered near here last month by escaped rebel scum. And before Christmas a woman just across the bay was ravaged by two others."

Chance rubbed his swollen eyes. It was hard to think with his head hurting so, and it was harder still to make his words come out straight.

Fine lawyer I am, he thought. My life is hanging on the verdict, and I can't match wits with a barefoot farmer's wench.

"Do I look like I'm in any condition to commit rape?"

"That's the first honest thing you've said to me."

Wearily he sagged until his chin touched the water. He was so tired. If he rested for just a few minutes, maybe he could summon the strength to break loose and fight his way past the dogs.

"Stay there," she said.

The irony made him smile. Where did she think he was going? The black humor brought a chuckle from deep in his gut. He slumped forward into the shallow water and drifted into oblivion.

Minutes or hours later—he had no way of knowing which—pain knifed through his bad arm. He gasped and tried to open his eyes.

"Get up!" the woman ordered. "I can't carry you." She struck him sharply across the face. "Get on your feet and walk!"

"Go to hell."

The palm of her hand cracked across his cheek again, and he staggered to his feet.

"That's it. You can do it. A little more," she urged, tugging at his good arm.

His left foot slipped, and she couldn't hold his weight. He sprawled face down in the mud, and his wounded arm felt as though it were on fire. He spat out a mouthful of dirt and tried to bite back a scream of agony.

The hurting became a hell of jumbled sounds and pain. Once Chance fancied he felt himself being dragged over the ground. He smelled the dogs, and a woman's newly washed hair.

Dark . . . it was dark hair, he remembered. Dark brown with a hint of chestnut where the sunlight sparkled on it.

And then he sank into a cushion of black forgetfulness where the only intrusion was the occasional bark of a dog and the blessed taste of freshwater in his parched mouth.

Chapter 2

Chance opened his eyes and looked around the semi-darkened room. He lay on a daybed in a kitchen. The only light came from an oil lamp hanging over the table and a glow from the belly of the woodstove. Near the doorway, in the shadows, he could see the outline of a woman sitting in a rocking chair.

He felt awful.

The wound in his arm throbbed, and his head was still pounding. When he tried to rise off the pillow, he was shocked at his own weakness.

Worse, he needed to relieve himself. The dull ache in his belly would not be denied, and he hadn't wet his pants since he was three years old. "Help me," he said hoarsely.

The woman rose from the chair and padded quietly toward him. "Are you thirsty?" Almond-shaped eyes watched him fiercely, and he suspected she would shoot him if he made a wrong move.

As if he could. He took a deep breath, swallowed, and reminded himself that she wasn't pointing a gun at him at the moment.

"I've need . . . need of the necessary." No gentleman should ever mention such a condition to a lady, but he

14

was past that. How much greater his shame if he were to soil her blankets?

"You've not the strength to stand. I'll bring you a chamber pot."

A rumbling growl rose from the darkness beyond the stove.

"Quiet," the woman commanded. She didn't raise her voice, but the dog lay back down.

"I don't want a pot," Chance protested. "I need to go out to your—"

"If you were well enough to walk, you'd run." She laid a palm on his forehead, and her touch was strangely gentle despite her work-worn hand. "Your fever is rising again," she said. "It's no wonder you need to pass water. You've drunk half my well dry."

Tongue lolling, the rust-and-white collie he had seen at the creek came to stand at her side. She patted the animal. "It's all right, Lady. Stay."

The woman left the room and returned minutes later carrying a covered chamber pot. "Use this. I'll empty it for you, but I'll not assist you in filling it."

Chance held back an oath as he fumbled with the china container. "Will you have the decency to leave me in private?"

She went out without replying. The collie followed her, but the ominous shadow beyond the stove remained. Chance fancied he could hear the black mastiff breathing. He knew the creature was watching him, and he knew the dog would attack at the slightest provocation.

Chance struggled to complete his task without soaking himself and the bed. His one arm was useless, his good hand as weak as an infant's. The effort left him exhausted, but at least the pressure on his bladder had eased.

The woman came back and covered the pot with a towel. Embarrassed, he turned his face to the wall as she carried it away.

Time passed. He slept fitfully. The night hours slipped away, broken only by her hand on his forehead or the taste of water on his lips. Dawn broke through the kitchen window, streaking the floor with rays of pale sunlight, and the woman was still with him.

She rose from the rocker and went to the lamp. He heard a slight puff, and the flame extinguished. "Are you awake?" she asked him.

"Yes."

"Your arm is very bad."

He bit his lower lip.

"It may mean your life."

"Where . . . where are the soldiers? Did your . . . your husband go for them?"

"No."

Chance swallowed. He would not allow himself to hope. "If you'd let me rest here, I—"

"I've never seen a wound that bad that didn't kill the patient."

He made a sound of derision. "You've seen a lot of bullet wounds?"

"No. I haven't." She went to the woodstove and used a mitt to pick up an iron lifter. Deliberately she raised one of the round lids and pushed a short length of kindling into the firebox.

"I'd rather die than lose my arm."

"You may get your wish, Reb." She eased the lid back in place and returned the handle to its resting spot on a hook beside the stove.

"I have a name. It's William Chancellor. My friends call me Chance."

She pumped water and washed her hands thoroughly with soap, then dried them on a towel. "I'm not your friend. It's my duty to shoot you or turn you over to the authorities."

"If I could just talk to your husband," he stalled.

The room was becoming lighter now, and he could see that she was tired. She wasn't as young as he'd first thought, maybe mid-twenties. Her oval face was handsome rather than pretty and was dominated by high cheekbones and huge brown, expressive eyes framed in thick, dark lashes. Her lips were well shaped, the lower slightly fuller than the top, and she possessed a nose too strong for real beauty. She was tall for a woman, and she carried herself with a proud grace despite her advanced pregnancy.

"I appreciate what you've done for me, ma'am," he managed, "but I—"

"I've done no more than I'd do for a hurt animal," she said. "Don't make more of my tending you than it is. And you can stop trying to butter me up. I'm not one of your fancy Virginia belles. I'm plain Rachel Irons, Mrs. Rachel Irons."

"Has your husband gone to war?" Each word was an effort. He could feel the sickness in his arm pulling him down into unconsciousness, but he fought it.

Common sense told him that the soldiers should have been here to arrest him by now. If they weren't here, then perhaps she didn't mean to report him. And if the soldiers didn't come, then he might still make it south to freedom.

"James will make short work of you when he returns," she said. "He has no sympathy for your kind."

"James? Your husband?" Chance knotted his good hand into a fist and concentrated on what he was saying. "Will he be back soon?"

"Soon enough." She took a cup from the table and poured hot water from a kettle into it. A strong scent of wormwood filled the kitchen. "Drink this tea," she said. "It may help with your fever, but I doubt it. My father would have had that arm off. He was a physician."

"Was?"

"He's dead. He caught cholera from a patient and died several years ago."

"But you're trained as a nurse?"

She pursed her lips. "Some women would take that as an insult, Reb."

"Chance," he corrected her.

"Most have a poor opinion of the females that follow troops into battle and make free with the bodies of strange men. But, yes, I have assisted my father. I've delivered babies and stitched up serious injuries. When I was twelve, I helped him take the legs off a woodcutter whose limbs were crushed by a fallen tree. I'm quite capable of amputating your arm."

"Woman." He struggled to keep his eyes open. "Mrs. Irons. I said I meant you no harm. But I swear, I'll come back from hell and strangle you if you cut off my arm."

"It won't be easy—not even for a ghost," she answered. "With one hand."

He could have sworn he saw the hint of a smile.

"But then, I suppose murdering a woman would come easy to your kind."

He bristled. "I've never harmed a woman."

"But if you were a murderer, you'd lie to me, wouldn't you?"

He had to get up. He had to escape from this house before the soldiers got here to take him into custody again. Instead, he lay here panting, struggling for each breath. "You can't. I won't let you."

She lifted the cup to his lips. "Drink this. We'll see what happens."

He turned his face away. "For the love of God, give me time. Just let me rest a little. I came into this world with two arms and . . . I mean to leave with all my parts."

So did my James, she thought bitterly.

Men are all alike, she wanted to say. Reb and Union. They think war's a game. They put on shiny uniforms, march to the beat of drums, and play at being soldiers. But none of them understand that war is real, and real people break.

Caught up in her own rush of hot anger, she left his side and went out into the dew of the early morning. She needed to breathe the clean air, free of the stench of blood and sickness.

"Don't be like them," she whispered to the babe beneath her heart. "If you're a boy, promise me you won't be like your father and all the rest." A single tear spilled down her cheek.

Behind her, she heard the screen door squeak, and a warm nose pushed against her hand. Slowly Rachel sank and embraced the collie. "Caught me feeling sorry for myself, didn't you, girl?" She pressed her face into Lady's soft fur. After a few seconds she stood awkwardly and wiped her eyes with the corner of her apron.

Wagging her tail, Lady stared at Rachel.

"I'm all right," she whispered, "and I guess if anybody has a right to whine, I do."

The War between the States had ruined her life.

It had made her bitter enough to wish she'd never married James Irons with his devil-may-care ways. She sighed. It had never seemed to her that she'd picked James, at least not consciously.

Since they were toddlers, she'd followed James into all sorts of mischief. He'd been forever concocting adventures, such as the time he'd turned the sheep into the Methodist camp meeting or when he'd substituted hard cider for sweet at the Sunday school picnic. And no matter what mess he got into, she'd been there, three steps behind him, trying to save him from certain disaster.

For an instant the terrified face of twelve-year-old James Irons flashed across her mind. Another boy had dared him to cross the frozen surface of Thompson's Mill Pond in late March. James had fallen in halfway across, and she'd pushed a beanpole out on the broken ice to save him from drowning. He'd never admitted that he was scared, and once he'd crawled onto the solid bank, he'd stripped off his clothes and run home stark naked and laughing.

"You had your playing at war games, James Irons," she whispered bitterly, "and just like when we were kids, you've left me to pay the piper." Only this time she couldn't forgive him. Her love for James, like her marriage, was as cold as yesterday's ashes.

She wasn't about to admit defeat. Her will was strong enough to do anything—it was her body that couldn't rise to the occasion. James and his family be damned. Providence had dropped a man into her lap, and it was up to her to use him to her advantage.

But at what cost? The man in her kitchen was her enemy. Giving him aid was more dangerous than anything she'd done in her life. Continuing to help him could cost her everything she'd worked for . . . everything she had to give her coming child.

Chancellor was badly injured, maybe even dying. He could lose that arm as easily as not. But if she could heal him . . . if she could convince him that not turning him in to the authorities would be worth his labor . . . Even a one-armed man would be a better farm worker than none at all.

Could she keep a Confederate soldier here against his will? Did she even want to try?

A crash of breaking crockery from the house tore Rachel from her reverie. "What happened?" she demanded as she threw open the kitchen door. Chancellor lay sprawled face down, bleeding on her rag rug. Shards of a shattered soup bowl littered the floor. "What have you done?" she cried as she went to his side and knelt by his head.

Chance groaned. "Not much of an escape plan, was it?"

"Has the fever addled your mind?" She took hold of his good arm and tugged. "You'll have to help me. I can't lift you back into bed by myself."

Sweat beaded on his ashen face.

In spite of her resolve not to, Rachel felt a rush of sympathy for him. He must be in terrible pain.

"You've brought this on yourself," she admonished, as much for her benefit as his. "You should have stayed on Pea Patch Island."

"Have you been there?" His fingers tightened on her wrist.

She pulled away, shaken by the haunted look in his eyes and the human warmth that had leaped between them at his touch. "You'll kill yourself."

"I'd be better dead than going back there," he said.

"Living's always better than dying."

"Maybe." His finely drawn features took on the hue of old tallow. "But Pea Patch Island isn't living."

She swallowed. "I have to do something about your arm."

"It's my arm, and my life." Then his head slumped back against the rug, and his eyes rolled back in his head.

"You're still my patient," she whispered as she pressed her fingertips against the pulse in his neck. He was very weak. If she didn't stop the blood flow from his wound, he'd bleed to death here on her kitchen floor. From what she'd seen when she'd first treated his injury, he'd been hit by an old-fashioned musket ball, rather than a bone-shattering minié ball. Nevertheless, the force of the gunshot had carried cloth and debris into his flesh. She didn't know if she could stop the bleeding, but if she succeeded, the infection could still kill him.

Taking off the arm at the shoulder would be the surest way to save his life. Shivering, she considered her options. Helping her father amputate a man's legs was far different from doing the operation herself. She knew how to administer chloroform, but if she was busy doing the surgery, she'd be unable to increase the amount of anesthesia if her patient began to wake up.

"Lord help me," she whispered. A kitchen rug was no place to perform an operation, and she was no surgeon. She quickly calculated her immediate needs: hot water, soap, clean sheets, towels, and bandages. And she'd have to gather them quickly if she wanted to have a live patient to treat.

She considered going for help but decided that was senseless. Chance would be dead before she could return.

"It's me or nothing." Rising to her feet, she rushed to assemble her surgical instruments and supplies.

Scant minutes later she pressed a chloroform cone over his mouth and nose. Chance mumbled and tried to turn his face away, but she held the sponge-filled contraption there until he sunk into a deep sleep.

"I hope you don't wake up," she murmured as she reached for her father's old scalpel. Then she turned her eyes and mind to the task at hand and forgot everything but the living flesh beneath her knife.

Chapter 3

Gunshots rang in Chance's ears. He urged his own mount forward amid the frenzied charge of horses and riders galloping up the wooded slope toward the Union line.

Minié balls flew past Chance's head, and he strained to see through the clouds of smoke.

Cannon boomed from the left, but his horse never missed a stride as he plunged up the steep incline. A riderless bay galloped past. Chance gripped the reins tightly in one hand, his cocked pistol in another. Branches whipped around his head, and he leaned low over Kentucky's neck.

The roar of muskets and the smell of powder and blood keyed his gelding to a fever pitch. Foam flew from the horse's open mouth; his muscles were taut, and his ears laid flat against his neck. Kentucky's long legs carried them over fallen logs and tangled underbrush.

Suddenly, almost under the thoroughbred's front hooves, Chance caught sight of a blue-jacketed figure lying face-down in front of them. To avoid trampling the body Chance yanked hard on the left rein. Kentucky reared and fought the bit, then pitched sideways as his left hind hoof plunged into the hollow of a rotting stump.

The gelding struggled to maintain his balance and

lost. Chance heard the crack of bone and felt Kentucky falling.

Kentucky's weight came down on Chance's right leg. The horse squealed in pain, then struggled up and stood with one hind leg drawn up and his eyes rolling in fright.

"Easy, easy, boy." Chance tried to rise and then gasped as his leg refused to hold his weight. Frantically he ran exploring fingers down his knee and calf.

Just a bad sprain, he told himself. But his horse hadn't come off as lightly.

Kentucky's hind leg dangled at an impossible angle. The animal's sides heaved, and sweat streaked his chest and neck. Huge, hurting brown eyes stared at Chance.

"Damn it," Chance swore. "Damn it to hell." His pistol lay against the trunk of a tree several yards away, and he crawled toward it. There was only one thing he could do for Kentucky now, and the thought of it sickened him worse than the agony in his own leg.

He forced his hand to hold steady as he took careful aim at the gelding's head. "A man never had a better friend," he murmured.

Gallantly the horse pricked up his ears. He nickered, wrinkling the velvet-soft nose that had nuzzled Chance a thousand times.

I can't do this, Chance thought.

Kentucky took a hobbling step toward him and whinnied plaintively.

Chance squeezed the trigger.

The earth swayed under him as the scent of rotted leaves and sweating horseflesh evaporated. In its place he smelled lye soap and the sweet, clinging odor of opium.

"Easy."

A woman's voice . . . What was a woman doing here in

the midst of a battlefield? And why were the big guns quiet?

"Chance. Open your eyes."

Slowly, with great effort, he fought his way up from the thick morass of unconsciousness. A dream . . . he'd been dreaming . . . reliving the skirmish at Gettysburg where he'd been captured by the Yankees nearly a year ago.

As Chance's mind began to clear, pain swept over him in waves. His stomach clenched, and bile rose in his throat.

"Wake up."

He felt something cool and damp press against his forehead. His arm throbbed with heat. His arm . . . Groggily he fumbled with his good hand, trying to find what hurt him so badly.

And found only space where his left arm should have been.

"No!" he screamed. His eyes snapped open and focused on the woman hovering over him.

"Easy," she murmured. "You'll—"

He seized the collar of her dress. "What have you done to me?"

"Shhh," she soothed, untangling his grip with more strength than he imagined a woman might possess. "Your arm is there. It's not gone. I've bandaged it tightly to your side to keep you from moving it."

"Where? Where?"

She guided his right hand to touch the fingers of his left. "I did what I could," she said, "but I've probably done you more harm than good. You will die if the infection spreads."

Relieved, he sank back and closed his eyes. Immediately images of Kentucky flashed across his mind. "My horse . . ."

"What horse? There's no horse here. I wish to God that there were," she replied.

He forced open his eyes and found himself in Rachel Irons's kitchen again. "Nothing," he answered. His eyelids were heavy; he wanted to close them, but he was afraid to. If he did, he knew he'd see Kentucky again . . . running, tossing his mane, and kicking up his heels.

His friend that he'd been forced to shoot . . . "I had a horse," he whispered.

"Well, I had a team of horses and they're gone. Soldiers took them." Her tone was bitter, but her touch soothed him.

He swallowed and tried to rise. "Soldiers?" It was hard to tell what was real and what was his mind playing tricks.

He closed his eyes and let the past sweep over him.

He'd lain there near Kentucky's body for a long time. The last of his platoon galloped past, and the barrages of gunfire became an occasional shot.

He propped himself up against a tree, wondering what kind of man would mourn a horse so deeply when his friends were dying at the top of that rise.

His leg continued to swell, but he was certain it wasn't broken. There was nothing to do but wait. If they'd won, some of his unit would be searching the area for their dead and wounded. If the blue-bellies had been victorious, he'd know soon enough.

Hours passed, and the day faded into darkness. With it came an unnatural quiet, broken only by the boom of artillery far away. He heard no moans from the dying, no horse's whinny, not even the call of a night bird.

Just before dawn Chance saw the first bobbing lantern in the distance. He strained to hear voices, hoping that they'd be familiar Southern accents rather than clipped Yankee speech. But his wishing was in vain.

When the two Union infantrymen leveled their rifles at him, he tossed away his pistol and surrendered.

"I'm not a coward, but neither am I a fool," he said.

"No one could call you a coward, Chance Chancellor."

Bewildered, Chance opened his eyes, looking not into the face of a Yankee sergeant but that of Rachel Irons.

"The soldiers," he murmured. "I thought I saw . . ."

"Shhh, it's the fever. You must have been dreaming." She pulled a clean sheet over him. "I've bandaged your arm again. You've been unconscious for hours." Her dark eyes were full of compassion.

"Hours?" He tried to think through the fog in his head. "Where am I?"

"In my farmhouse." She felt his forehead. "Lie still, and don't try to talk. I gave you chloroform when I excised the dead flesh and cleaned the wound; then I administered opium for the pain. It's natural that you're confused." Her tone softened. "Try and sleep as much as you can. We must give your body time to heal."

She smiled at him as her fingers closed over his. Was this the same woman who'd been so harsh toward him? He thought he remembered grabbing the front of her dress, but he wasn't sure if that had really happened or if it was another dream. And if it was real, why hadn't she been frightened? He wondered if he was dying. Strangely he couldn't summon the energy to care.

Rachel wrung out a wet cloth and laid it across his brow. "I used the last of Father's quinine to bring down your fever. Now I'm treating your wound with Indian root medicine." She smiled again. "My father wouldn't approve, but then there was a lot about me that he didn't approve of. His medical textbooks call for using nitric acid to burn out the dead tissue and for bleeding the patient." She spread her palms expressively. "Does it make sense to you that physicians should drain blood from a man who's nearly bled to death?"

"Indian roots?" His tongue felt thick, too large for his mouth. At home, in Richmond, before the war, he could have commanded the services of the finest physicians. Here he was at the mercy of an uneducated farmer's wife. And unless he was more muddled than he thought, she'd done her surgery on him while he lay on the kitchen floor. It was hardly reassuring.

"My grandmother was a Lenape Indian. People say I have her hair and eyes, but I wouldn't know. Her hair was silver gray when I knew her."

Chance licked his lips. "Water."

He heard the creak of a pitcher pump, and then she returned with a cup of water and a spoon. "Only a sip," she cautioned. "Too much will make you sick."

The few drops of water did little to quench his thirst. "More," he urged.

"Later." She laid her hand on his cheek. "You're fevered, but not burning up. When you can drink, I'll brew you willow root tea." Her hands were strong and gentle, and her touch felt better than the water. He didn't want her to take her hands away.

"More Indian medicine?"

"My grandmother was a powerful healer. People came from miles for her cures. It made my father furious, especially when her patients got better. My grandmother never charged a fee. I think that's what made Father angriest."

"Why . . . why are you doing this?" he managed to ask. "For me?"

"Sleep now," she urged him. "We'll talk when you're stronger."

Chance gave up the effort to keep his eyes open. The kitchen and the dark-haired woman faded as he drifted off into the mist of unconsciousness.

It was dark when he woke again. He was too weak to raise his head, but she lifted it and spooned water between his cracked lips. From across the room the big black dog stared at him with fierce eyes.

He didn't know anything more until sunshine shone through the window and warmed his face. Rachel smiled down at him. "Your fever's broken."

"Are . . . are you certain I still have my arm?"

"You feel it, don't you?"

"Yes, but . . . but I've heard men say . . ." His voice failed him. He wanted to tell her that it was common knowledge that many felt a missing arm after it was gone. They even had a name for it—phantom limb.

His head hurt and his thinking seemed more rational, but he couldn't put his thoughts into words. And he felt so weak. "Thank you," he whispered. His arm still ached, but either the pain was less or he'd gotten too sick to feel the difference.

"I've a bargain to offer you, Reb."

He tried to focus on her face.

"I need help to put in my crop." She touched her protruding belly, and her cheeks colored in the lantern light. "Have you ever plowed a furrow or planted corn?"

"No."

She shook her head impatiently. "I should have

guessed as much. You don't have the hands of a working-man, and your speech is too fancy. What were you before the war? A banker?"

"I'm a lawyer." He swallowed, thinking, I was a lawyer, and I will be again if I survive this war.

"I've no need of such talents. What I want is a strong back. It's impossible to hire laborers. They've all been drafted. If you'll give me your word that you'll stay until harvest, I'll not call the authorities on you. I'll hide you here until fall. After my crop is in, you can go back to General Lee or to hell for all I care."

"You want me to work for you . . . on the farm?"

"What did I just say?" She shook her head again, and one straight shining lock of dark hair came loose. "For a man who claims to make his living cheating honest folks with words, you're thick enough." She folded her arms over her chest. "I'm offering you freedom, after a fashion, and I'm risking my own neck to do it."

Chance inhaled slowly. "As a Confederate soldier, you know it's my duty to escape and return to my regiment."

"You're more dead than alive. If you did reach Virginia, you'd be of little use to your army."

"And if I did agree, what makes you think a Southern lawyer can be trusted to keep a bargain?"

"Trust?" Her brown eyes narrowed. "I'm not such a fool. Trust an escaped prisoner? Trust a man who'd go to war to keep other men in chains of slavery?"

"If you don't trust me, then why—"

"What choice do I have?"

"You want me to stay here on this farm until autumn? You give me your word that you'll not turn me over to the Union soldiers?" He drew a hand over his eyes and tried to think.

Was this woman's proposal honorable? What about Travis? He'd promised his best friend that he'd come back for him. Common sense told him that Travis had died that night on the beach, but if there was the slightest possibility Travis had survived, he had to rescue him. And he had a score to even with the Dutchman.

"Make up your mind, Reb. Yes or no."

She was right. He couldn't walk now, let alone fight his way back into Fort Delaware and kill Coblentz. And if he stayed here long enough to heal, he was only a short distance from the prison.

"Will your husband object?" he asked her. "You know you're committing treason by hiding me."

She held his gaze without flinching.

When she didn't answer, Chance knew that his earlier assumption had been correct. "Your man isn't here, is he?" he said. "Your husband's fighting in the war."

She nodded. "The war took him as well as my draft animals."

"Then you're alone here?"

She stiffened. "Alone except for my dogs and a shotgun I know how to use."

His head hurt, and it was hard to summon the energy to speak. "I told you . . . you've nothing to fear from me."

"Just a hemp necklace if I'm found out. President Lincoln takes a dim view of traitors who harbor the enemy."

He was too weary to fight a losing battle. "I'll take your offer, Rachel Irons," he answered reluctantly. "But on conditions of my own."

"You're in no position to—"

"Oh, but I am," he said. "You'll use my given name.

Reb grates on my nerves. Chance will do, or even Chancellor."

"You've nerve for a man with no options, I'll say that for you," she admitted with a chuckle.

"And you, a lone woman, to harbor a dangerous man."

"I'd sooner make a pact with the devil than the likes of you. No doubt he'd be more likely to keep his word." Her lips curved into a wry smile. "But he isn't here, is he? And he'd probably be no handier with a hoe than you."

Chapter 4

It was two days before Chance could summon the strength to crawl back up on the daybed and another day before he could sit up. Gradually his bouts with fever ended, and he felt himself begin to improve almost hourly.

Now that his mind was beginning to function again, he began to notice his surroundings.

Rachel Irons's kitchen was large and spotlessly clean with bright red-and-white-checked curtains at the window and a thick braided rug on the floor between the daybed and the cookstove. The furnishings were old-fashioned and sturdy; a large pine hutch against one wall had probably been crafted many generations ago. Rachel's dishes were plain and chipped, her silverware worn thin with use, but she kept a handful of wildflowers in the center of her table and threw open the door and windows to let in the fresh air.

It was a restful house, and although Rachel appeared to have little in material goods, she seemed naturally cheerful. When she was outside, Chance could hear her laughing and playing with her dogs. Sometimes he was certain he heard her singing.

She was not so free-spirited with him. Rachel's laughter or even smiles came few and far between when they were together. Usually she spoke to him as little as possible.

"You'll need something to wear," she said to him one day as she prepared the noon meal. Leaving the soup simmering on the back of the stove, she opened a board-and-batten door that led to a narrow, twisting staircase. "I have something upstairs that should do."

When Rachel returned, she carried men's clothing and a pair of low-heeled farmer's boots. "The shoes and trousers belonged . . . belong to my husband, James. The pants will be big on you, but I can take the waist in. The shirt was Granddad's. You're wider across the shoulders than James. I've cut the stitches and removed the sleeve. I can sew it on again later, when you mend."

"Thank you," he said. There were underthings in the pile, but she made no comment on them and neither did he.

"No need to thank me," she replied tartly. "I can't have you working in my fields in the altogether, can I?"

She helped him don the shirt, a painful procedure, then left him alone so that he could struggle into the trousers. When he slid his legs over the side of the bed and tried to stand, she came into the room and supported him as he walked to the table for the ample noonday meal.

"You've gentle hands for such a no-nonsense woman," he told her.

She averted her eyes. "Should I let you fall and undo all my nursing?"

"You've a kind heart, Rachel Irons," he replied. "I'll not let you convince me otherwise."

"My heart is none of your concern, sir. All I ask is

that you heal quickly so that you can keep your part of our bargain." She went to the stove and began to ladle delicious-smelling soup into thick crockery bowls. "I hope you're hungry."

"Always."

Chance was certain that Rachel's cooking had something to do with his recovery. He hadn't enjoyed such food for months, and he hadn't eaten so regularly since the war began.

She'd tempted his appetite with chicken broth, seasoned with onion and pepper. When he'd been able to keep that down, she'd added homemade noodles and dried carrots and mushrooms to the soup. Next she'd begun to prepare biscuits and yeast bread, both so light that he wondered that they didn't rise to the ceiling, dripping with fresh-churned butter, honey, or strawberry jam.

"I've never had such soup," he'd complimented her as he tasted the first spoonfuls.

"You can thank Agatha for that." And no amount of questioning had clarified her mysterious answer.

The chicken soup had been followed by delicately poached fish and steamed seafood that evening. Rachel's table groaned with omelets, pigeon, smoked ham, new potatoes, dried-fruit cobblers, and greens cut from the fields and woods. Her meals were simple, seasoned with herbs from the garden near the back door, and they always included fresh vegetables such as early peas, spinach, radishes, and turnips.

"I am a plain cook," Rachel explained. "You must make due with farm fare or starve."

"No man of sense could find fault with your meals," he'd replied with a smile. She didn't smile back.

Rachel Irons was the only female he'd ever known who appeared completely immune to his charms.

He'd always been a man who was fond of women. He liked the sound of their laughter and the way their skirts swayed when they walked. He enjoyed flirting with them, and he loved the taste of their lips and the soft feel of their skin. Young or old, it didn't matter; he'd always had a special relationship with females, and they seemed to feel the same way about him. A grin and a few sweet words had always earned him their trust.

This approach was definitely not working with Rachel.

"Don't poke fun at me," she said. "I know that rich people eat differently than we do."

"What makes you think I'm wealthy?" It was true, or had been true before the war, but he resented her assumption. She said "rich" in a way that made the word an insult.

"A Richmond lawyer?" She'd shrugged. "Just remember who you are and who I am, and we'll have no trouble."

Rachel did not soften toward him. She limited her conversation to his improving wound or her plans for the farm. And no matter how he tried to charm her, the only tenderness he received was when she changed his dressings.

So long as Chance remained confined to the house, he had little to do but watch Rachel as she moved through her constant chores of cooking, cleaning, washing, butter making, and keeping the woodstove and lamps supplied with fuel. She was rarely idle from dawn until long past sunset, when supper was over and she had washed and dried the dishes and put them away.

He supposed it must be tiring for a woman so far advanced in pregnancy, but she never complained. Instead, she moved gracefully from task to task. Despite her constant labor, she never looked harried or slovenly. Her night-dark hair was always confined in a neat bun at the back of her head or braided in a single plait and twisted into a circle and covered with a cap or straw bonnet. Her dresses were clean, if a bit faded with wear, and her aprons were starched and snowy white.

"Must you always watch every move I make?" she asked the following morning as they sat down to a breakfast of strong coffee, steaming porridge sprinkled with wild strawberries, and hot biscuits. "It's rude."

"Rude?" He chuckled and reached for a biscuit. "Since when has it been rude for a man to watch a pretty woman? You have a pleasing countenance, Mrs. Irons."

"Save your sweet talk for those who will believe it," she answered as she yanked the bread dish out of his reach. "Were you raised in a barn?" Rachel's hand brushed his, and she jerked back as though she had been burned.

For an instant she stared at him, and the air between them seemed to vibrate with energy. Then Rachel lowered her head. "Grace first, and then you may eat."

Without waiting for an answer, she bowed her head, whispered a few words of thanksgiving, and passed him the biscuits.

"Some people might think that it's rude never to offer a cheerful word to an ailing man," he teased as he stirred milk into his oatmeal.

"Should I go about singing and dancing with a Johnny Reb—with an uninvited guest in my house?"

"Not uninvited," he reminded her.

She frowned. "As soon as the danger of infection is

passed, you're moving out of my kitchen. There is a space in the barn where the farm help sleeps."

"In the barn?" Chance grimaced. "With animals?"

"I am a married woman. Would you have me ruin my reputation by keeping a man in my home with my husband away?"

He buttered his biscuit. If he wasn't so hungry, he would have left the table. But only a fool would walk away from such a meal. When he thought of what he'd survived on after his capture at Gettysburg . . . He forced a smile. "Come, Mrs. Irons. I've not offered any threat to your honor so far, have I?"

"No, but you'd have to get over my dogs to do so."

"Surely a lady in your condition—"

Two red spots appeared on her cheeks. "My condition is none of your affair. And a gentleman would have better manners than to mention it."

"Ah, I'm a gentleman now. Are we to spend so much time together and remain in a state of war?"

"But we are, aren't we?" Her huge, liquid eyes fixed him with a thoughtful stare. "I'm risking my life to hide you from the Union troops. Don't expect me to fawn over you as well."

The black dog, Bear, moved to her side, placing his massive body between Chance and his mistress. The older collie seemed content to watch him from her favorite spot near the cookstove.

"He doesn't think much of me." Chance glanced at the mastiff.

"No, he doesn't. You'd best keep your distance from Bear," Rachel warned. "He'll take your leg off if you cross him."

"That's reassuring." Chance's wry smile hid the turmoil in his gut. Now that he was on his feet, he wondered if he'd made a mistake in promising Rachel he'd help with her crops. He knew that she couldn't hold him here against his will, but he'd never been a man to give his word and break it. Trouble was, he'd made two vows before he'd ever set eyes on Rachel Irons. Even if Travis was beyond saving, he had to return to Fort Delaware and kill Daniel Coblentz.

It wasn't just personal, although he hated the sadistic sergeant worse than any living creature it had ever been his misfortune to know. Coblentz was a monster, a murderer, and a torturer. Someone had to end the Dutchman's reign of terror on Pea Patch Island, and Chance had drawn the short straw.

He'd always been a man of the law, but all that had changed. If it meant the loss of his soul to eternal damnation, he'd kill Coblentz with his own hands and gladly pay the price.

It was nearly two weeks from the time Rachel Irons had found him in her crab trap until he could walk as far as the garden bench. From there he could watch Rachel hoeing a spot to plant sweet corn.

Sitting outside with the sun on his face was wonderful. So long as he didn't try to stand quickly or move his arm, he felt almost human. The collie had taken to lying beside him, but the black dog still suspiciously watched every move he made.

Chance's wound ached, but he knew his shoulder would stiffen if he went too long without using it. Scar tissue would form, and that might cripple him. He might be dead inside, but he needed the use of both arms and legs. He had promises to keep.

"If you can wait a little, I'll try and help with breaking up that ground," he volunteered. "Maybe tomorrow I could—"

Rachel stopped hoeing and shook her head. "Not yet. We'll have to start plowing soon. I can't take any chances that you'll rip open that wound and be useless to me."

"You're a hard woman, Rachel Irons."

"Aye, some would say that, but I've had to be. Sit there and watch. Maybe you'll learn something about farming."

"Swinging a hoe can't be too complicated."

"No?" She shrugged. "We'll see if you say that after doing it for ten hours." She knelt awkwardly to pull a few stray weeds from the edges of her blossoming strawberries.

"What will you do when your time comes? Delivering babies is hardly my—"

"I have friends in town. I'll go there for my confinement. There will be no one here to guard you, Chancellor. Your honor must be your bond."

His honor. He nearly laughed aloud at that. Once he'd been ruled by honor, but that was before the war . . . before grapeshot and cannon fire had turned green fields into graveyards. "When will you have this babe?" he asked, averting his eyes. Without a guard it would be simple to slip away from the farm.

"Late June or mid-July." She looked up at him. "Of course, my husband, James, may be here. If he gets leave, I'll call Cora Wright to attend me, and I'll remain here on Rachel's Choice."

"James couldn't get home for spring planting?"

Chance looked around at the unplowed fields. He was no farmer, but it seemed to him that Virginia crops were sown much earlier than this.

"He would have been here if he could." She rose to her feet and began to hoe again.

"What will this husband of yours think when he finds me here?"

"I don't know." She shook her head. "We'll have to climb that fence when we come to it."

Chance rose and walked toward the brick well, intending to draw some water. He'd begun to lower the bucket when Lady began to bark. Both dogs shot off down the lane. Rachel dropped her hoe and hurried toward him.

"Quick, into the house!" she ordered. "Someone's coming." She pushed him toward the back door. "Hide. If anyone sees you, we're both lost."

Rachel followed him inside and peered out the multi-paned window beside the door. Chance leaned against the table. "Sweet hope of heaven!" she exclaimed. "It's James's father."

She looked around the room, then motioned toward the closed stairway. "Hide in there."

In seconds Chance found himself sitting on a lower step in the semidarkness with a pillow and blanket in his lap.

"Don't make a sound," Rachel warned. "My father-in-law is no friend of mine. He always carries a weapon, and he'd not hesitate to send us both to prison for high treason."

The barking grew louder, and Chance heard the rumble of carriage wheels. His heart thudded against his chest. He didn't think Rachel meant to betray him, but if she did, he was helpless to defend himself or even run.

"Father Irons." Rachel pushed open the kitchen door as her father-in-law climbed down from the buggy and tied his horse to the hitching post. "And there's Mother Irons with you. What a surprise."

Isaac scowled at her. "Can't you control these animals of yours?"

The dogs—wagging their tails and barking excitedly—continued to circle the elegant yellow-wheeled buggy.

"Your lane is in deplorable condition," James's mother declared. "I thought we'd lose a wheel in the ruts."

Isaac walked around to assist his wife. "We're concerned about you, Rachel," he said.

Ida continued her complaints. "It's ridiculous for you to live out here alone with James's precious child coming so soon." She tucked her hand through her husband's arm and lifted the hem of her skirt out of the dust.

Ida Irons was short and plump, a perfect foil to Isaac's tall, lanky frame. Rachel had always wondered where James had gotten his good looks from.

"You've missed church two weeks running," Isaac chided.

Rachel noticed that he seemed grayer than the last time she'd seen him, although he continued to carry himself as straight as ever. His formal black coat, waistcoat, and trousers were cut of heavy wool, and his starched collar and old-fashioned cravat were nearly hidden by a full white beard. It made Rachel hot just to look at him wearing so many clothes on such a warm May day.

"Missing Sunday services isn't seemly," Ida said. "Not seemly at all for one with your reputation."

Rachel clamped her lips together. Ida couldn't let a meeting pass without making some reference to Rachel's scandalous birth. It was true. Her parents had never married, and she was illegitimate. But that was old gossip, and no one but Ida Irons talked of it anymore.

Ida's close-set hazel eyes flicked over Rachel's apron front with obvious disapproval as she approached the back step. "Foolish to live way out here when you don't have to," she repeated. "But then—like your mother before you—you always did have bad judgment."

Rachel stepped back to let the older woman squeeze her fashionably wide hoops through the kitchen doorway. Ida's ample figure was stuffed into a black nankeen flounced skirt and matching Zouave-style jacket.

"I'm afraid we've come on business," Isaac explained gruffly. "Your loan payment?"

"Would you care for coffee?" Rachel asked. She'd as soon serve them sour buttermilk, but they would be her child's grandparents, and she tried not to let her anger show.

"No coffee for me," Ida said with a sniff. "My digestion is delicate."

"Nor me." Isaac's gaunt features hardened. "As I said, this is not a social call. It's been several months since we've seen any good-faith effort from you."

Rachel's stomach flip-flopped as her mother-in-law's cloyingly sweet rose perfume filled the kitchen. Overhead, near the ceiling, a paper wasp buzzed. Rachel's palms grew moist, and she wanted to sit down. She had to get rid of Ida and Isaac as soon as possible, but she couldn't give them the slightest reason to suspect that she was hiding anything.

If Chance should make a sound . . .

Rachel forced down her nausea. "I intended to come to see you the next time I took butter and eggs to the store."

"It is most inconvenient that we should have to come out here and demand what was promised," Ida fussed.

Trying to maintain her composure, Rachel went to the cupboard and took down a cracked teapot from the top shelf. "I do have some money to give you," she said as she poured the change onto the table. "I have six dollars today, and I'll have more for you after I collect for last month's crab soup at—"

"Six dollars?" Ida cried. "Six dollars is not what you owe. Your loan is shockingly late, and you'll never get a crop in this year. Every month you fall deeper and deeper into debt."

"I will get a crop," Rachel insisted. "And I intend to keep current on what James borrowed from you."

"James would expect you to pay his debts."

"And I will. I just need some time." The wasp swooped lower over Ida's bonnet, and Rachel found herself wishing it would sting her mother-in-law.

Ida shook her head. "Didn't I tell you that she'd have excuses, Mr. Irons? I think we should take the cow. Rachel doesn't need a cow."

Fury flared in Rachel's chest. "You're not taking my cow!"

"Very well." Isaac scooped the coins off the table and deposited them in an inner pocket of his coat. "Since you've decided to be difficult. I really don't want to take this matter into court, but those who borrow money should be prepared to—"

"Wait." Another moment and she'd be sick all over Ida's new kid shoes, Rachel thought. She had to get the two of them out of her house at once.

"It's for your own good," Ida said. "Debt is—"

"No, listen to me," Rachel argued. "I have something that should satisfy you. Grandfather Moore's mantel clock. It was made in London and it keeps perfect time."

"Another clock?" Ida wrinkled her long nose. "I don't know, Mr. Irons. Do we need another—"

"You could sell it," Rachel said. "If you prefer, I'll take the clock to the general store and see if Mr.—"

"No, no need. We'll accept your offer, daughter," Isaac said. "I can use the clock in my office. But it must be understood that this is only in lieu of past payments. Next month I will expect the full—"

"August," Rachel flung back at him. "The price of the clock should compensate you until then. It is a good clock, and worth twice that amount. Surely by August James's army pay should be straightened out."

"I warn you," Ida said. "I'll not stand by and see James's child raised in poverty. Mr. Irons and I are fully prepared to—"

"To what? Care for me and my child? I think not. Rachel's Choice is my home, and shall be home to James's child. I need your patience until my financial matters are straightened out, nothing more."

"Patience wears thin," Isaac said. "Mrs. Irons?"

"Yes, Isaac. It's clear that we aren't welcome in our dear son's home. If he were here, it would be—"

"Where is this clock?" Isaac demanded, interrupting his wife.

"In the parlor." Rachel hurried toward the open door. "I'll fetch it for you."

"If you change your mind about the cow, let us know," Isaac said. "I have a buyer who will pay cash."

"My cow is not leaving this farm."

"You're an obstinate young woman," Ida declared. "Disrespectful to boot."

"Am I?" Rachel asked. "Well, best you get back into your yellow-wheeled buggy and drive yourself off my farm—before I forget who you are and set my dogs on you both!"

"It may not be your farm long," Isaac warned. "If you don't meet your payments, I will foreclose."

"I'm sure you will," Rachel replied. "But for now, this is still my property. There's the door. I'm sorry you can't stay longer, but if you do, I'll say something we'll all regret."

Rachel stood outside until the buggy vanished down the lane, and then she went behind the house and was quietly sick.

"Damn them," she whispered.

James's parents hadn't believed a part-Indian bastard good enough for their only child, but James had cared for that opinion as much as he'd cared for long Sunday sermons. He'd defied them and driven Rachel to Dover in a borrowed rig and married her the day he turned of age.

Rachel's eyes stung, but she blinked back the welling tears. She would not cry, and she'd not let her prisoner know that her in-laws' visit had upset her so.

She drew water from the well, washed the sour taste from her mouth, and then splashed water on her face.

"You can come out now," she called to Chance as she entered the kitchen. "They're gone." She opened the stair passage door.

"Nice people," he said.

"My husband's parents are . . ." She looked into his clear blue eyes and searched for the right word. "Difficult."

"I can see that." Chance settled gingerly onto the lumpy mattress.

Rachel knew that he was still weak from loss of blood and his ordeal in the bay, but every day that he remained a patient was one day longer before she got her corn planted. Time was fast running out. Once, when the season was wet, she could remember her grandfather planting in mid-June, but they never harvested a full crop in the fall. The corn hadn't had time to mature, and they'd barely had enough fodder to last the winter. June would be too late for her, too late to make enough money to pay her father-in-law what she owed. And hiding Chance from the soldiers would have been a useless effort.

The wasp that had circled the room earlier lit on Chance's shoulder. He swung at it, and it stung him.

"Damn!" he shouted, knocking the insect to the floor and stomping on it. "I hate wasps."

"They must be male," Rachel replied, "since they're always looking for a fight." She took down a container of baking soda from a shelf near the stove. "Let me put something on that to take away the sting." Pouring a little into her hand, she mixed it with a dribble of water to make a paste. "It's only a wasp bite. No need to make a fuss over it."

"I'm not making a fuss," he protested.

"Hold still." She pushed back his sleeve and saw a tiny black stinger embedded in the skin. "Stop wiggling." She leaned down and drew out the remainder of the wasp and proceeded to apply the soothing paste to the swelling. "He got you good."

"They always get me good," he grumbled.

"Do they?" She couldn't keep from smiling. "It must

be a Union wasp, then. Funny, I've never been stung by a wasp or a bee. They say if a person is afraid of—"

"I'm not afraid of wasps. I just don't like them."

"Oh." She stepped back. "That should hold you."

"Thank you, again."

It was odd she should be so at ease tending a strange man, and she averted her eyes to keep him from guessing what she was thinking.

You've been too long alone, Rachel Irons, she chided herself. Shame on you, and in your condition.

"There was a mix-up with James's pay," she blurted out in an effort to direct the subject away from personal subjects. That, at least, was the truth. "James borrowed money from his father to—"

"You don't have to explain to me."

"It's no secret. Half the county knows. James wanted to buy mules . . . and other things," she went on as if he hadn't heard all that had happened between her and the Ironses here in her kitchen. "My father-in-law is demanding that the loan payments be met. That's why I have to make a crop this fall. The government is desperate for supplies. I can pay back most of what I owe if I don't lose the season. It's why I need you."

"And why you're willing to risk your life to hide me?"

She nodded. "And yours."

"Surely your father-in-law wouldn't endanger his relationship with his son by taking his farm."

"This wasn't James's farm. I inherited Rachel's Choice from my mother's father, my grandfather Moore. Of course, I did add James's name to the deed after we were married. And you don't know Isaac Irons a whit if you think he wouldn't sell us at sheriff's auction. He sent his own eighty-year-old aunt to the almshouse. Isaac didn't get to be one of the largest land owners in Kent County by being charitable."

"You value this farm highly."

"I do. And I have no intentions of failing."

"And neither do I," Chance replied. "None at all."

Chapter 5

Rachel didn't break down until later that afternoon when she was alone in the barn. She'd pinched her thumb in the stall door, a minor hurt that ordinarily would not have bothered her, but she burst into tears. Sinking down in the clean straw, she trembled from head to foot and had a good old-fashioned cry.

Everything was wrong.

She was alone with no one to trust, and her baby would be coming soon. She couldn't get her corn crop in. She was hiding an escaped prisoner in her house . . . and now she had a blood blister rising on her thumb.

After several minutes of hard sobbing, the thought that her weeping spell had begun over a mashed finger sunk in. Gradually her emotional outburst lessened and then became embarrassment.

What would Grandfather Moore think if he knew she was wailing over so small an accident? She hadn't been raised to fall into a fit of weeping over a little hurt. He and her grandmother had taught her to be stoic, to laugh over ordinary trials and tough out the big ones.

She crossed her arms on her chest and took slow, deep breaths, trying to clear her head. What was wrong with her? She was over James; she'd shed all the tears for him and their ruined marriage that she ever intended to. And surely having her baby in her arms to cuddle would be a blessing, not another burden.

She certainly wasn't crying over the pain of a pinched finger. So the only thing left was Chancellor.

"Think first, then act," her grandfather had always said. "And once you make a decision, stick with it."

Rachel wiped away her tears. She'd thought long and hard before she'd decided to help Chance. The decision hadn't been made lightly.

Harboring an escaped rebel was the most dangerous thing she'd ever done, but that didn't make it a wrong choice.

"Those who dance must pay the fiddler" had been another of her granddad's favorite truths.

She exhaled softly. If she wasn't willing to take the risk, she'd lose everything.

She'd been telling the truth when she'd warned Chance about her father-in-law. If Isaac didn't put a bullet through Chance, he'd see him hanged or sent back to the gray walls of Fort Delaware and cast into solitary confinement.

It was unwise to care so much what happened to Chancellor, she decided. She had to keep reminding herself that her very attractive prisoner was her enemy. Startling blue eyes, butter-yellow hair, and a boyish grin didn't measure the worth of a man. And neither did a warm-honey Virginia drawl and broad shoulders.

Since Chance had escaped from Pea Patch Island, he'd probably been one of the hundreds captured at Gettysburg. He might even have been the man who'd shot her James and cost him his leg. She shouldn't have pity to spare for the likes of rebels. All of her concern should be for her own situation and for the child she carried.

If her treason was discovered, James's parents wouldn't hesitate to seize her farm and her child. That was a cold, hard fact.

Bear whined and Rachel straightened her shoulders. "But they didn't catch us, did they, boy?" she said to the dog.

She seldom had company at Rachel's Choice. The farm was too far from town to encourage casual visitors. Due to the war, women were afraid to travel alone, and most men had gone off to the fighting.

She accepted the solitude of Rachel's Choice as a natural part of life, and she'd never felt lonely.

Other than the Ironses, no one had come here since Christmas, when Cora Wright's grandson had broken his arm and needed her doctoring skills. Since her father had passed away, there was only one physician in the town. And Dr. Myers would never tend to a black child.

Her father might have had a sour disposition, but he'd always given care regardless of the race of the patient. It was one of his more admirable traits, and he had few enough, truth be told. If her father were alive, he would have treated Chance to the best of his ability. And then he would have summoned the Union soldiers and demanded a reward for capturing a prisoner.

Rachel dried her eyes and walked to the corner of the barn that her grandfather had partitioned off as sleeping quarters for laborers. The room was simple: wood floor, built-in beds along one wall, a single window near the ceiling to let in light. There was a table of sorts, a homemade bent-willow chair, and pegs along the wall for coats.

She found a clean mattress hanging on the wall. It had been emptied of corn husks, but Chance could stuff it himself with salt-marsh hay. A few blankets, a wash bowl and pitcher, and some fresh sheets would make the room habitable.

It was time Chancellor was out from under her roof, for more reasons than one, she mused. He was a dangerous man, and she was becoming all too concerned with his welfare. And if they were caught—she'd pretend complete ignorance of the reb hiding in her barn.

"Wake up!" Rachel stood in the barn walkway and rapped sharply on the door of the hired men's quarters. It was daybreak, and a soft rain was falling on the tin roof.

Chance jerked upright from a sound sleep so fast that he slammed his head against the upper bunk. "Son of a bitch!" he swore.

"Mind your tongue," Rachel admonished, opening the door a crack. "It's time you started pulling your weight around here. I want you to milk the cow."

"Milk the cow," he muttered.

A milk pail clattered onto the plank floor.

"Much obliged," he said. "What time is it, for God's sake?"

"No blasphemy either. It's morning. Time for chores."

"It's still dark out," Chance protested. He forced his stiff muscles to move, swinging out of the narrow bed, taking care to keep a quilt over his nakedness. "Don't I get coffee first?"

"Milking first, then breakfast."

"I'm not a well man."

She closed the door.

"But I've never milked a cow before," he shouted after her.

"Then you can't learn any younger, can you?"

Chance fumbled for his socks in the semidarkness.

Cows. He'd never liked cows, and he'd never expected to have to extract milk from one.

His arm still hurt like hell, but he supposed that it was healing. He didn't wake with a fever in the night. Actually, his room in the barn wasn't bad. Other than the rustling of mice and an occasional cricket, the solitude had been welcome.

Being alone was one of the luxuries he'd had to give up in wartime. And a prisoner had to adjust to spending every hour—waking and sleeping—with the sounds and smells of hundreds of other men.

Nights were the worst. He'd lie on his back and shut his eyes, trying to close out the endless coughing, moaning, and cursing that threatened to smother him. Before he'd been dragged off the battlefield at Gettysburg, he'd never imagined trying to empty his bowels in a pit in the middle of an open field in plain view of anyone walking by. And he'd never dreamed how heavy stone walls would feel pressing in around him until he wondered if the cell was getting smaller or if he was losing his mind.

Officers were imprisoned inside the fort on Pea Patch Island; enlisted men were quartered outside in flimsy wooden barracks and rows of tents. It hadn't taken Chance too many months to realize that there could be no escape from inside the walls. And if only common soldiers were outside, he'd have to become one of them.

"Chancellor!" Rachel banged on the door again. "Did you crawl back into bed?"

"Coming."

* * *

The red-and-white animal was tied in a stall at the far end of the barn. As he approached her, the cow stared at him with glassy brown eyes and mooed plaintively.

He studied her from nose to tail.

She wasn't large, as cows go, but she had two lethal-looking horns and a tail caked with that stuff he didn't care to step in.

"Her name is Susan," Rachel said. "Don't walk behind her. She kicks."

Chance opened the stall door and sauntered in.

"I usually feed her before I milk," Rachel observed.

"I knew that." He set down the bucket and looked around.

"Hay is in the hayloft. I'm out of grain."

"Just give her hay?"

"Put it in the manger in front of her. The feed will keep her occupied while you do the milking."

Chance climbed the ladder awkwardly and kicked down some loose salt-grass hay. "Enough?"

"Yes."

He gathered up an armload and carried it to the cow's manger. Susan began to eat the hay.

Rachel pointed to a three-legged stool that hung on the wall. "I use that."

"All right," he agreed. He wished Rachel Irons wouldn't talk to him as though he were the village half-wit. "I told you, I've never milked a cow before, but I'm willing to learn. How hard can it be? You squeeze the tits and—"

"Teats," she corrected him. "They're called teats."

Chance gritted his teeth and concentrated on the animal in front of him. He was still half asleep and needed his morning coffee. After drinking chicory with mosquitoes floating in it, he'd come to appreciate Rachel's real coffee.

He wanted a full top-to-toe bath as well this morning. He'd been called fastidious, even a dandy by his friends, and it was true he took pride in how he looked. Until he'd been captured by the Yankees, he'd always gone against fashion and been clean shaven. A bath, a shave, and a decent haircut were long overdue.

The last thing he wanted to do on this rainy morning was yank on a cow's udder. His arm was starting to hurt again, and he'd nearly put his foot down in the patty of foul-smelling stuff in the straw.

"Do you want me to teach you how to milk her?" Rachel asked.

"Just go and do whatever you usually do before the sun comes up. Susan and I will manage without you."

She laughed. "All right, but I'm counting on that milk to make butter."

He glanced over his shoulder to make sure that she was really gone, and then looked back at the cow. The beast was staring at him again and chewing steadily. She did look fairly peaceful.

His parents hadn't kept cows. They'd purchased their milk from a free black woman who kept a dairy out of town. Maude delivered to the house. She'd come in the back door and leave eggs, butter, milk—whatever Miss Julie, the cook, needed for the kitchen. Chance was used to reaching across the dining-room table for his milk, not extracting it from the animal himself.

"Nice cow," he murmured. "Good cow." He set the stool in the straw and perched on it. He stuck the bucket under the pertinent part and inspected the creature's bag.

Her udder was pink, speckled with little black dots. It

looked clean enough, but there was an immediate choice to be made. After a minute's hesitation, he opted for the one closest to him and grabbed hold.

Susan bellowed as though he'd just sliced off her teat with a bayonet. She threw both hind legs into the air, and Chance leaped backward. He moved fast, but not fast enough to miss the stinging blow across his cheek from her dung-laden tail.

Chance's feet tangled with the bucket. He tried to catch his balance against the wall with his bad arm, but it folded under his weight. He struggled to keep from falling, but it was useless. He ended up flat on his back in the soiled straw. One leg of the stool ground into his hip, the bucket handle was still hooked over his left foot, and the cow's wicked-looking hind quarters were only inches away from his head.

"Whoa, steady, Susan. Good cow."

"What are you going down there?"

Chance looked up to see Rachel peering over the top of the stall.

"It isn't funny," he fumed. "If you value this beast, you'll get her away from me before I—"

"Before you do what?" Rachel snickered.

The cow mooed loudly, and Chance looked back just as she raised her tail.

Rachel flung the door open, slapped the animal on a bony hip, and turned her away seconds before the cow let fly with a yellow stream.

Chance got to his feet. He wasn't sure who he was less happy with, the cow or the woman. "Susan is obviously a woman's cow," he muttered between clenched teeth. "She isn't trained to allow a man to milk her."

"Nonsense. James milked her all the time. And when I

go into town, Cora Wright's grandson tends her and he's only twelve. You squeezed too hard, that's all. A cow's teats are tender. You have to handle her gently, talk to her so she isn't nervous."

"She's nervous?"

"Let me show you." Rachel retrieved the bucket and the stool and took her place beside the cow. "You do it like this," she explained. "Squeeze and pull, squeeze and pull." Two streams of milk hissed against the sides of the pail, filling the air with a comforting scent.

A black cat with a white spot on his face appeared out of nowhere and rubbed against Chance's leg and began to purr loudly.

Rachel pressed her head against the cow's belly and continued to produce a steady flow of milk. Then she rose and motioned to the stool. "Now you try."

Chance sat down, extending his hand, and Rachel positioned it on a warm teat. He applied pressure.

Not a drop came out.

"Squeeze and pull at the same time," Rachel said. "If you just pinch it shut, it doesn't work."

A crude remark rose in Chance's mind, but he kept silent. Rachel Irons might be an exasperating female, but she was a respectable woman, and he'd not insult her with crass behavior.

He tried again, remembering to tug downward as he tightened his fingers. This time milk dribbled out, not so freely as when Rachel did it, but something.

"Good," she said. "Another thirty minutes, and you'll have this licked. I'm making sausage and biscuits for breakfast. I expect at least a third of a bucket of milk this morning. Don't stop until every teat is dry, and don't let her kick over the bucket before you're done. Understand?"

"Perfectly."

"She likes it if you sing to her."

"I'm not singing to a da—to a dumb cow."

Rachel shrugged. "Suit yourself. But you can't come to the table smelling like that. I'll leave some clean clothing, a towel, and a bar of soap by the back door. Go down to the creek and have a bath before you come into my house."

"I want a razor."

"Planning on cutting your throat, Reb?"

He knew she was laughing at him, but he wouldn't give her the satisfaction of seeing that she was annoying him. "I want to shave."

"What? Give up that handsome beard of yours?"

Chance gritted his teeth. His beard was scraggly, thin in some spots, and dark in others. He looked like Zacky McCoy, who'd come down out of hills to join the Fourth Virginia Cavalry riding a raw-boned mule and carrying an old wheel-lock musket. "I need a razor."

"I'll see what I can do." She paused a few steps from the gate. "And try to stay on the stool and not under it. I'd hate to go to the trouble of patching you up again."

Susan shifted her front feet, and Chance grabbed the bucket and prepared to retreat if she became violent again. Instead she gazed at him, blinked her eyes, and belched.

"Good cow," he murmured, reaching for the far left teat. "Good Susan."

She moved slightly so that her belly lay against his cheek. Her odor was strong but not unpleasant. He could hear a multitude of rumblings from inside her body, but the milk continued to come down. Already his fingers were cramping.

Thirty minutes, Rachel had said. He couldn't imagine lasting thirty moments. It was easier for her; she had two good hands. He was doing the milking one-armed.

"Good cow," he repeated.

Talking to a cow. Travis would have loved to see this. He'd never let Chance live it down.

If Travis was still alive.

He had to be.

Travis was the brother Chance had never had, and the bond between them was closer than blood. He'd stay here until Rachel had the baby, rescue Travis if it wasn't too late, and dispose of the Dutchman. Then if he survived, he'd come back and get Rachel's crops in.

He exhaled sharply. Maybe Rachel's husband would come home from the war, and then Chance wouldn't be tied up here for months. Maybe, but he had the sinking feeling that he sometimes got when he listened to a witness lie on the stand.

Chance didn't believe Rachel's husband was coming back. Either James had left her for good, or the man was dead and buried. The question was, did Rachel know the truth? And if she did, why was she lying to him about James being alive?

Susan groaned and her skin wrinkled so that it rolled in waves over her back. "Shhh," Chance soothed. And then, almost without realizing what he was doing, he began to hum an old tune he'd often heard Miss Julie sing as she cooked.

Susan stopped wiggling, and encouraged, Chance softly continued.

> *Oh, my darlin' black-eyed Susan,*
> *Oh, my darlin' black-eyed Susan,*

> *All I want in God's creation,*
> *Is that sweet gal, and a big plantation;*
> *My darlin' black-eyed Susan,*
> *Oh, my darlin' black-eyed Susan . . .*

Then, somehow, here in this barn, with the earthy smells and the soft hiss of streams of milk hitting the bucket, Chance found a few minutes of peace . . . something precious he hadn't experienced for a long time.

Chapter 6

Miraculously Chance's fingers didn't stiffen beyond use, the cow didn't kick over the bucket, and he carried enough milk to the kitchen door to please Rachel.

"It's not what I'd have gotten," she said, "but it'll do. You'll be better with practice."

"That's a comforting thought," he grumbled.

She handed him a green plaid shirt, soft from being worn and washed many times, and a pair of gray twill trousers. Through the open door, he could smell the coffee perking on the stove, but Rachel's own scent—that of a clean and desirable woman—was stronger.

"Biscuits nearly done?" he asked, trying to keep his voice light. It wouldn't do for her to realize that he was thinking of her as a woman, rather than an employer. Not when they were alone together on this farm. He forced a boyish grin.

"The biscuits have to finish browning. You've plenty of time to wash." She glanced back and opened the door wider. "Bear," she ordered the mastiff. "Go with Chance."

The big black dog moved reluctantly past her and fixed Chance with a malevolent glare.

"Afraid I'll make a run for it?"

"No." She chuckled. "Just afraid you'll get bitten by a blacksnake, Reb. You've already been attacked by a cow."

He scowled at her. It was hard to be cross with a red-cheeked woman with flour on her nose and a dimple on one rosy cheek, but he gave it his best shot. "I asked you not to call me Reb. It was part of our bargain. If you break yours, what's to hold me to mine?"

She nodded. "You're right, I suppose. It just comes natural. It's not like I was saying something that wasn't true. You are a rebel, a traitor to your country." She regarded him intently.

"That's incorrect. I'm a Virginian, not a citizen of the United States. We seceded from the Union, remember? Officially I'm a citizen of the Confederate States of America. I could only be named a traitor if I enlisted in the Union army and then deserted to the opposing forces."

"You talk pretty," she said. "But all those words don't amount to a hill of beans."

"My name is Chance. Is that simple enough for you?" he countered.

Her cheeks flushed a darker hue. "What kind of name is that for parents to give an innocent baby?"

He stroked the stubbly beard along his jaw. "I told you before, Chance is a nickname. I was christened William Chancellor."

"Sounds more likely," she granted him. "They must have guessed you intended to read for the law." Turning away, she rattled in a drawer and produced a shaving brush and mug and a straight razor. "These were my granddad's," she said. "You're welcome to borrow them for as long as you're here."

"Thank you, ma'am." He touched an invisible hat in mock salute.

She sniffed indignantly. "You may win at words with me, but you and your kind will never win this war. And all the dying and the lives destroyed and farms burned and children left without fathers will be for nothing."

The easy camaraderie between them suddenly evaporated. "We didn't start this," he said, thinking back to the fields of fallen men and the sky so black with smoke that you couldn't see the sun. He could almost smell the stench of blood, the spilled bowels, and the charred grass and timbers.

"Didn't you? Didn't your people attack Fort Sumter, South—"

The odor of burning bread drifted through the doorway.

"Something's on fire!" he said, breaking free of his haunting memories.

"My biscuits!" She turned back to the stove and snatched open the oven door.

"Don't burn your—" he began.

"Ouch!"

A metal pan bounced off the floor, and Chance dropped the clothing and the shaving articles onto the ground. When he reached Rachel, she was standing amid scattered chunks of bread holding out a fast-reddening hand.

Chance took hold of her waist and steered her toward the sink. He saw tears in her eyes, but she bit her bottom lip and didn't cry. "Put your hand out," he ordered. He pumped cold water over her burned palm. "That should take some of the sting out of it."

She nodded. "Yes, that's better." She held her hand

under the spout again. "It's all right. See, it's not even blistering." She spread her fingers for his inspection.

"Good," he said. "I was afraid you'd really burned it badly." He handed her a clean tea towel, and as he stepped closer, so did she. Her protruding belly brushed against him, and as it did, he felt the strangest sensation.

Their gazes met, and she sucked in her breath sharply.

"Was that what I thought it was?" he asked.

"The baby kicked you. Haven't you ever felt one do that?"

"I . . ." He felt awkward talking about something so intimate, but a sense of wonder and his innate curiosity overcame his reluctance. "I didn't know they were that strong . . . before they were born, I mean."

"You should be on this side. Sometimes I think I'm carrying a mule instead of a baby." Her features softened. "Want to feel it again?"

"Could I? It wouldn't hurt it? Or you?"

Her eyes brightened with amusement. "No, it wouldn't hurt me or the babe."

Chance held out his hand tentatively, and she took it in hers and laid it high up on her apron under her full breasts. For a moment he didn't feel anything, and then there was a definite movement, followed by three strong thrusts.

Chance swallowed, dropped his hand, and moved away. "It's a wonder you get any sleep nights with that going on," he observed. He'd never taken much notice of pregnant women before, and he had to admit that he'd gone out of his way to avoid contact with that part of a woman's world. But he didn't think of Rachel as fat or cumbersome as he had those other females.

Instead, oddly enough, Rachel's advanced condition made him feel protective and something more . . . something that was uncomfortable to admit to himself.

She was almost a mother, and she was another man's wife. Only a cad of the worst sort would imagine . . . Chance turned away, afraid that the growing tension in his loins might show.

Think of the baby inside her, he told himself.

He took a deep breath and then another. Yes, he had to think of Rachel's delicate condition, not her full, ripe breasts or the delicious feminine glow about her.

Having the baby pushing against him seemed a miracle of sorts. For the first time he thought of the child to come not as part of Rachel but as his or her own person. And he hoped mightily that he was wrong, that Rachel's man wasn't dead or a runaway, and this little one would have a papa coming home from the war. He wanted Rachel and the baby to have a strong man to put food on the table and to cut firewood to keep the house warm in winter. He didn't want to think of Rachel Irons as a widow or her infant as an orphan. Neither of them deserved that. They should be cherished and cared for.

He looked back at her, hoping that she had missed what could have been an awkward moment between them.

Rachel's cheeks flushed crimson. "You'd . . . you'd best see to your bath," she said stiffly, gesturing toward the door. "I'll salvage what I can here and start the sausage cooking."

"If you're sure that you're all right?"

She nodded. "It was a stupid thing to do. Burning the biscuits, I mean," she said in a rush. "I'm fine. My hands are tough," she assured him as she gathered the fallen biscuits off the floor. The broken pieces went into a pail; the best of the bread she brushed off and put on a plate on the table.

He picked up the bucket of milk. "Where do you want this?"

"Set it in the sink. I have to strain it through a cheesecloth before . . . before I put it down the well to keep it from souring." Rachel had gathered a mantle of dignity around herself and was suddenly his jailer-employer again.

"We wouldn't want the dogs to get the milk after all the work I had to—"

Rachel's eyes widened. "They'd never touch the milk. What kind of dogs do you have in Virginia that you can't trust them to stay away from—"

"Ill-trained ones, I suppose."

She folded her arms. "Go on with you," she said. "And don't forget to shave. I'll admit, I'm curious to see what's hiding under that thicket on your chin."

"Are you insulting my beard?"

"You probably should shampoo your hair with turpentine. I didn't notice any nits when I nursed you, but you may have crawlies."

"I don't have lice!"

She pursed her lips thoughtfully. "I suppose you'd know if you had an infestation, but I'll have no vermin in my house."

"I assure you, ma'am," he replied with icy formality, "I'd be the first to know. The lice are so big on Pea Patch Island that the prisoners toss them into the soup to add meat."

He felt his bowels twist as he remembered the thin

gruel of potato skins and the wormy bread that the Union army considered decent rations. "The truth is, the boys up there are surviving on rats and rotten bacon."

Rachel's brown eyes dilated with compassion. "I'm sorry," she said. "We've heard stories about the deaths, but we assumed that disease—"

"Hundreds," he said flatly. "Thousands. No one knows for certain. There is no medical care, no decent shelters for the sick, no clean water. The island reeks of the dead. The Yanks stack the corpses like firewood and row them across to the Jersey shore to bury in mass graves."

She paled. "It's why they call it war, isn't it? Men die."

"They die," he repeated. "When they're starved and left in the rain without proper shelter or their wounds are allowed to fester. They die when they drink water that horses have—"

"Enough," she cried. "You've made your point." She nibbled at her lower lip. "I . . . I'm sorry if I seemed uncaring. I'm not so hard-hearted to wish anyone to suffer so." Her eyes flashed as she delivered a parting shot. "Even if you Confederates do as much or worse to our men at Andersonville."

"It seems there is enough callousness for both sides."

She blanched. "It does trouble me to think that any here in Delaware could be so cruel to any human being, rebs or not."

Cruelty isn't strong enough, he thought. Depravity and madness, perhaps. "I assure you that if I had any blue-backs, they've all drowned in the salt waters of the bay."

She raised a dark eyebrow questioningly.

"Lice. The Yanks call them gray-backs, and we return the favor. Pea Patch is alive with bugs, mosquitoes, greenhead flies, lice—"

"No more, please," she protested.

"I rest my case."

Rachel folded her arms over her stomach. "You are the darndest man for words I've ever laid eyes on. You could talk the comb off a banty rooster."

Chance turned and headed toward the door. He could almost swear his head was itching, but he refused to scratch. A man had to keep some dignity about him, even if he had to suffer for it.

Rachel sank into a chair. Her back was aching, and she felt all hollow inside. What was it about Chance Chancellor that made her tongue as thick as a butter paddle?

"I've been too long alone," she whispered to the orange tabby curled on a window seat.

What was she thinking to allow herself to be so free and easy with this stranger who had invaded her home?

She rose and took her broom from the corner and began to briskly sweep up biscuit crumbs. Work had always filled her days as thoughts of her coming child eased the uncertainty of her future.

She had to admit to herself that if Chance had been anyone but a rebel soldier, she might have welcomed his friendship. But only a foolish woman would forget why he was here and what he represented.

In Richmond, before the war, a gentleman such as Chancellor would have considered himself far above her in class and situation. He was educated, probably wealthy, and no doubt had a wife and children at home.

Still, she hadn't mistaken that look in his eye when she'd let him touch her belly. Even a country wench with eight years of formal schooling knew when lightning passed between her and a man.

Pole-axed, her grandmother had called it. There was a Lenape word for the sudden attraction between a male and female. It translated roughly as *struck down,* but Rachel couldn't quite remember it. The meaning was plain enough.

She tried to ignore the warm flush of pleasure that radiated through her as she remembered that slow appraisal Chance had given her.

He was a very attractive man, and no doubt he was accustomed to having the ladies at his beck and call. But she wasn't fool enough to think that he cared about her for her own sake. He'd been a long time without feminine companionship, she imagined. But if he thought she was ripe for a quick roll in the hay, he would be greatly surprised.

Men were men, and she'd often thought that the good Lord had made them with more brawn than brain. She could not fault Chance for lusting after her in his heart. So long as he kept his hands to himself and remembered that he was here on her forbearance, they'd have no problem . . . so long as she could control her own wayward thoughts.

She'd thought that she'd given up on the foolishness between men and women when James had destroyed the love they'd shared. "Damn you!" she murmured.

If James hadn't gone to war . . . if he hadn't come home an angry stranger . . .

She flung the broom back into the corner.

It must be the pregnancy that was making her so fanciful. Women told her that they'd done all sorts of strange things before the birth of their children—craved unusual foods, taken odd notions. She would not allow herself to fall victim to an escaped rebel prisoner because her reason had been squeezed out by tight apron strings.

Chance Chancellor could put his wide shoulders and his big hands to a plow. She'd see how sweet he talked after a long day of planting or hoeing weeds. And once she had a babe at her breast, she'd be too full of thoughts for her new son or daughter to stare at a man with calf eyes.

But how were they to plow without an animal to pull the plow? And if they couldn't work up the ground, there would be no way to put in a crop. She didn't have a dollar to her name, and a decent mule would cost fifty at least. Then, if by some miracle someone would sell her a beast on credit, the soldiers might come and take that as well.

Still wrestling with the problem, Rachel set the table and put the sausages on to fry. She beat several eggs with milk and salt and pepper, and slid them into a pan.

The door opened and Bear ambled inside. Rachel glanced toward the entrance and gasped in astonishment. Chance Chancellor was far younger, clean shaven, than she had guessed—and far more handsome. He filled her kitchen doorway with a lazy grace.

"I guess that means you approve." He grinned at her and ran a hand over his damp chin.

I do, she thought. Oh, I do.

She forced herself to speak sternly. "So long as you come clean to my table, you may shave or not to suit yourself."

"You should have gone for the law, madam," he teased. "You'd make an imposing judge. The defendants would tremble in their boots when you entered the courtroom."

"Don't mistake my kindness for sympathy," she said testily. "If you overstep your bounds, I'll not hesitate to shoot you as I would any mad dog."

His shoulders stiffened. "If I've offended you, my apologies."

"Sit," she ordered.

"Yes, ma'am."

She brought the food, and they ate in silence. Rather, Chance ate, and she toyed with her eggs and sausage.

It was hard for her to keep her eyes off him, but she'd not give him the satisfaction of knowing that he'd perturbed her.

"This is the Sabbath," she said when he was finished. "If I hurry, I can take the rowboat upstream and walk to late services at our church. Turn the cow out into the pasture and clean out her stall."

"On Sunday?"

"You've had your days of rest," she replied. "I'll take your healing wound into consideration, but chores must be done on a farm, and I can't do everything myself."

"How do I get the cow to go where I want her to go?"

"I'll show you how—this time. From now on, you must tend Susan yourself. I'll expect you to bring her in for milking before supper."

He followed her outside. They crossed the hard-packed farmyard in silence. Rachel had her hand on the wooden door latch when Lady began to bark.

"Somebody's coming!" Rachel said. Her heart began to race. It was impossible that she could have more visitors so soon! Had Isaac guessed that Chance was there? Had someone seen him?

"Quick, get inside!" she cried to Chance. "Hide in the loft, and don't come out until I call you, no matter what!"

Chapter 7

Rachel gathered her skirts and hurried across the farmyard as Bear added his deep booming bark to Lady's frantic outcry. By the time Rachel reached the big linden tree near the well, she could see a horse-drawn wagon coming up the lane.

Squawking chickens scattered as the dogs charged off to greet the visitors. A gray cat fluffed her tail into a bottle brush, and she and all five kittens dived to safety under the poultry coop.

"Miss Rachel!" a boy's cracking adolescent voice called. "Miss Rachel!" A round-faced black youth riding bareback astride a lanky chestnut mule broke from the throng and trotted toward her. "Miss Rachel! We come to put in your corn!"

"Solomon!" She hurried toward him. "Are you serious?"

The boy laughed. "Yes, Miss Rachel. We've all come to help you!"

Behind Cora Wright's grandson came the Walker twins on a spotted pony, and a farm wagon full of dark-skinned men and women. "Howdy, Miss . . ." The twin holding the pony's reins began. His brother slid down off the animal's rump and shyly finished the greeting: ". . . Rachel, ma'am."

"Hello," Rachel replied. She could never tell the nine-year-old brothers apart. David and Goliath were identical twins, as black as coal dust with huge, beautiful eyes and soft, lilting voices that could charm the birds from the trees. "I'm glad to see you both."

A two-wheeled cart pulled by a team of dun oxen followed the wagon, and behind that, coming around the bend, Rachel could see another pair of oxen, several men on horseback, and a crowd of people on foot.

"Preacher's brought the whole church to help you out, Miss Rachel," Solomon declared.

Cora's oldest son, Pharaoh, drew the team of horses to a halt. Immediately, a bevy of squealing children in various shades and sizes spilled over the sides of the wagon and began chasing each other around the yard.

"Mary, see to that baby," a woman called. "Step to it, girl!"

Mary, no more than eight herself, crawled under the wagon to retrieve a laughing toddler. As the little girl backed out, a chubby boy—minus a bottom front tooth—tugged at one of her many beribboned pigtails.

"Ouch!" Mary gave her tormentor a shove that sent him head over heels across the grass.

"You young'ns mind your manners," Cora shouted. "Stay out of Miss Rachel's garden. If I see one flower broken, you'll answer to me."

Rachel, still too full of emotion to speak a sensible word, twisted the hem of her apron and stared at Cora. "I never expected you to . . ."

"Of course you didn't," Cora replied in a matter-of-fact tone. "But here we are."

Pharaoh climbed down from the wagon seat and lifted his mother to the ground as carefully as if she'd been made of spun glass. Rachel caught sight of Pharaoh's wife, Emma, and their oldest daughter, Pauline, among the milling women unloading picnic baskets from the cart.

"We've come to put in your crop," Cora Wright said with a twinkle in her eyes. A small woman without an extra ounce of flesh, Cora was neatly dressed in a plain gray muslin skirt and bodice with a starched white apron. Her blue-black hair, streaked with white, was drawn tightly into a coiled braid at the back of her head and partially covered by an old-fashioned mobcap.

"But this is the Sabbath," Rachel managed.

Cora hugged her warmly, and Rachel caught a faint scent of lavender and herbs. Cora Wright was immaculate in her person but always wore a gris-gris, a tiny leather charm bag containing an assortment of magical ingredients, around her neck to ward off ghosts, witches, and evil spirits.

"Preacher moved the church here this morning," Emma said, coming up beside her mother-in-law. Emma dwarfed Cora; the younger woman was nearly six feet tall and broad of shoulder.

Rachel had heard that Emma had once been a house slave on a great plantation on Virginia's Eastern Shore. Local rumor had it that Cora and Pharaoh had smuggled Emma north to Delaware when she was fifteen. Rachel didn't know if that was true, but she did know that Emma possessed an education far beyond her own.

Most folks in Kent County believed that Cora Wright and her son Pharaoh were ringleaders in the Underground Railroad, a secret group that assisted runaway slaves. But no charges had ever been brought against the family because Cora Wright was too well respected. In her role of midwife, she'd delivered the children of two sheriffs, several judges, and more farmers than Rachel could count. Cora Wright might be a poor black woman, but she was an important part of the community, and even pro-slavers knew when to mind their own business.

Four husky parishioners struggled to lift a plow from the back of another wagon, and Pharaoh went to take charge. "Easy with that," he warned. "No sense taking it down here. Roll it on out to the field, then pull it off." He lowered his voice and glanced back at his mother. "Blockheads."

"I don't know how to thank you," Rachel managed.

"There's no need to make a fuss." Cora patted Rachel's arm. "Haven't you and your grandparents gone out of your way enough times when we were needing? I don't know what's wrong with those white folks that they can't find time to help out a lone woman in need. Someone should show them the meaning of Christian charity."

"Where do you want us to start plowing, Miss Rachel?" Pharaoh asked.

He was so tall that Rachel often wondered how a tiny woman like Cora had given birth to him. Pharaoh's muscular arms and brawny shoulders proclaimed his blacksmith's craft. His voice was deep and slow; his movements were steady. Only someone who had known Pharaoh all his life as Rachel had could guess that beneath his gentle exterior lurked the fierce spirit of an African lion.

Six years earlier, two slave catchers had come north to Delaware in search of runaways, and they'd been found dead in the marsh chained to a tree by their own iron shackles.

Her husband, James, and Pharaoh had been friends since they were boys, and James had told her that he believed Pharaoh was responsible for the murders. James said that the black man had admitted as much to him.

Rachel drew in a ragged breath and tried not to look at the barn. If Pharaoh discovered Chance hiding there, she wouldn't have to worry about being arrested. Pharaoh would drive a pitchfork through Chance's heart and throw his body in the swamp. Pharaoh Wright hated slavers, and he considered every Confederate soldier his sworn enemy. The only thing that had kept him out of the army was that he refused to be bound by any authority other than his mother.

"Miss Rachel?" Pharaoh interrupted her thoughts. "Where do you want us to start?"

"Oh." She tried to hide her nervousness. "In the west field," she stammered. "I had corn there last year and—"

"You plow up the garden plot first," Cora ordered. "The ladies mean to put Miss Rachel's garden to rights before dinner. You put one man to plowing and those boys to working up the soil. Emma can mark the rows. Have you got string, Miss Rachel? Lord knows if these addle-brained girls have brought—"

"I've got string," Rachel assured her. "I've some seed but—"

"We brought plenty of seed," Cora replied. "Sweet corn, butter beans, string beans, beets, onion sets, collards, carrots, squash. It's late for cabbage, but—"

"I've cabbage and greens already in," Rachel supplied.

"Addie's got some nice tomato plants," Cora said. "We'll set them in the shade by the well until we're ready. They sun-scorch easy, you know. Can't be too careful with them roots." She patted Rachel's hand again. "Don't you worry about a thing. We brought enough food to feed Grant's army. We'll spread blankets under the trees and set out our—"

"You're welcome in my house, Cora Wright, you and all your friends. You know that. When did I ever ask you to eat outside?" Rachel said. "We can—"

"No need to say another word, child. You can't help the color of your skin. This world being what it is, and people—even my people—being what they are. Lord knows, some of these girls can't know a scrap of nothing without telling it to the whole world. We'll spread our dinner cloths outside for a real Sunday eating-on-the-ground. You just sit down with us and none will be the wiser. I'm not too proud to eat on the ground, and any what is should look to their own salvation." She gave a small sniff and glanced around. "Where is Preacher George? That man will be late to his own funeral."

"He's coming, Mother Wright," Emma said. "He's bringing two families from down the Neck. And those Freeman boys, Jack and Gideon. They're bringing the second plow and another pair of oxen."

A smiling mulatto woman, trailed by three bright-eyed little boys, joined the group around Rachel. "Mornin', Miz Rachel," she said. "You lookin' pert. When that little'n comin'?"

"Good morning, Janetta," Rachel said. "I can't thank you all enough for giving up your Sunday to come and help me this way. I never expected—"

Janetta grinned wider, exposing a gold front tooth. "The Lord provides, Miss Rachel. When Miss Cora got up in front of the congregation last Sunday and told us how you was tryin' to farm this place all alone and your little'n a-comin', well, there weren't a dry eye in that church, I can tell you."

She shifted a fussing light-skinned infant from her hip to the crook of her arm and covered herself modestly with a bright shawl as she began to nurse the babe.

"Don't tell me you and Joe have had a new arrival," Rachel teased. "I saw you at Easter and you were as slim as—"

"Lord, save us! No!" Janetta protested. "This ain't my chile. With my Joe away guardin' them rebs? You know better than that, Miss Rachel. This is Mrs. Thomas's boy, Jacob Lemuel. Mr. Lemuel Thomas got my Joe a good job in the kitchen at Fort Delaware." She laughed again. "My babe? With skin like clabbered milk? You know I wet-nursed young Mrs. Thomas's last two young'ns. She don't want to chance ruinin' her figure with young'ns pullin' on her teats."

Rachel nodded. "He did look light for one of your boys, Janetta. I didn't think you'd be steppin' out on Joe."

Janetta squirmed with delight. "And me a deaconess of the church? Bless my soul, Miss Rachel. Don't you be sayin' such around Milford. My Joe would be home from Pea Patch in two shakes of a dog's tail."

"You and you, come with me!" Pharaoh commanded as he stripped off his Sunday-go-to-meeting coat and white shirt. "And you, Zeus, you start plowing the garden patch."

Other men began to shed their church clothes. Muscular arms and shoulders in every shade from ebony to toffee gleamed in the sunlight. Teenage girls giggled and whispered to each other as they spread out blankets under the trees and placed wicker and split-oak food baskets in the deep shade. Rachel caught whiffs of fried chicken and sweet potatoes and fresh-baked apple pies.

"I'll never be able to repay you all," she murmured to Cora.

The older woman chuckled. "Just keep doing what you've been doing all your life," she answered. "Treat us with respect."

"How could I do any less?" Rachel hugged her warmly.

"Preacher's coming," Emma called. She pointed to an approaching wagon driven by a stout man dressed all in black and wearing a wide-brimmed felt hat.

"Praise God!" Janetta shouted. "Brother George!"

"Amen!" chimed an older man with snow-white hair.

Preacher George reined in his team and stood up. "Are you ready to work?" he demanded. "Are you ready to do His work?"

"Yessuh!" cried a young boy.

"We are!" boomed Pharaoh.

Affirmation rolled from every throat. "Yes!"

"We ready!"

"Then, let's do it!" Preacher George declared. "For the Lord and Mr. Lincoln!"

As the men and boys turned toward the fields, Rachel glanced at the barn and offered a silent prayer of her own for these good friends and for Chance—that he would have the good sense to stay where he was. Then Cora called her name, and she hurried to direct the boys in where to start planting the tomatoes in her kitchen garden.

*　*　*

Chance burrowed under the mound of salt-marsh hay and tried to ignore the scurry of tiny feet as mice fled that corner of the loft. Below, in the open walkway, Chance could hear the murmur of voices and a woman's husky laughter.

"They'll miss us."

"No, they won't," a deeper male voice answered.

Chance rubbed the itch on the side of his nose and hoped he wouldn't get the urge to sneeze. He'd been hiding here for hours. The sunshine coming through the louvered barn window had lessened in intensity, but the loft was still close and overwarm.

He'd feared at first that a troop of soldiers had come to arrest him. He didn't like the helpless feeling of being trapped with nowhere to run. When he'd heard children's voices—black voices—he'd been relieved but puzzled. Why had so many people come to Rachel's isolated farm if they weren't searching for him? What did they want?

Finally, when he could stand the suspense no longer, he'd crept to a crack in the horizontal boards and peered out. Seeing teams of horses and oxen working Rachel's fields had stunned him and deepened the mystery.

Chance had remained hidden throughout the day despite his thirst and the keen hunger he felt when the smells of food drifted up to tempt him. He tried to remember if the door to his room was closed below. If anyone saw the made-up bed or his spare shirt, they'd know Rachel had a man here. But he couldn't worry about that. Going down the ladder to check would put them both in more danger.

Several times children had entered the barn. Once a boy had climbed to the loft. Chance had been afraid that the child and his companions would discover him, but a woman had called the lad outside.

The hours had passed slowly. Chance had never considered himself a patient man, but he'd had a lot of practice since his capture at Gettysburg.

He wondered what had become of his friends in the Powhatan Guards since he'd last seen them charging up that wooded slope. He didn't think many had been taken prisoner. Travis had given him the names of three men who'd died, but counting himself and Travis, he knew of only seven who'd been captured in the skirmish.

Of those seven, only Dave Pointer and Travis had been alive when he'd fled Pea Patch Island. William Adams died of his wounds before they'd reached Fort Delaware. Red Bailey had coughed out his life in the next cell inside the prison, and Charley Pritchett had expired after they'd taken off his leg at the hip.

Young Jeremy Stewart . . .

Chance closed his eyes, trying to erase the memories of Jeremy's blackened and contorted face. The boy had run away from Greenview Military Academy and lied about his age to join the Fourth Virginia after his father was killed at the Battle of Kelly's Ford. His mother's only child, Jeremy was the best rider Chance had ever seen, but still too young to shave . . . and too damned young to die by his own hand.

Icy hatred rose from the pit of Chance's gut and pressed against his chest like a dead weight. He'd witnessed a lot of bad things since he'd signed on with the Powhatan Guards in the spring of '62, but nothing had torn at him like Jeremy's senseless death.

He hadn't been there in time to save Jeremy that night,

but the one thing he could do for the boy was to kill Sergeant Coblentz.

Chance had never considered himself a vengeful man, or one that could cold-bloodedly plan another's murder. But putting Coblentz in his grave would be no different than shooting a rat. At least he hoped it wouldn't.

"Pharaoh . . . You stop that."

Chance tensed. The couple had moved nearer to the ladder.

"Sweet molasses."

The woman's sensual laughter rolled up through the floorboards of the loft. "We can't," she protested.

"We can," her lover coaxed. "Up there. In the loft. No one will know."

Hair prickled at the back of Chance's neck.

"If Preacher finds out . . ."

Chance heard a deeper chuckle.

"I won't tell him."

The ladder creaked.

"No, Pharaoh. Everybody's out there working. We should be . . . Mmmmm, darling, don't."

"You like it, don't you, Emma girl. And you like this . . . and this."

Chance swallowed the rising lump in his throat. They were coming up, and his odds of remaining undiscovered had just plummeted. It was too late to run.

"I need you," the man pleaded. "Feel this big thing I got for you?"

Emma whispered something that Chance couldn't make out, and then he heard the tread of bare feet on the wooden planks.

"Pharaoh . . ." She groaned.

Clothing rustled and something small and hard that

might have been a button hit the floor and rolled off into the hay.

Sweat broke out on Chance's forehead as the embrace became more heated and the exchanged words turned to breathy moans and meaningful tussling in the hay.

Emma's eager whimpers made Chance's own loins tighten. How long had it been since he'd lain with a woman?

I can't think about that, he told himself.

But it was impossible. The musty odor of sex filled the air; he could feel the tension skimming the surface of his skin. His mouth was dry, not from fear but from an emotion just as primal.

Listening to the two was torture, but he couldn't risk the movement it would require to cover his ears. . . . And he couldn't stop picturing a woman in his mind, a woman with lighter skin than he supposed this Emma possessed, and dark, fathomless liquid eyes.

Rachel's image rose behind his clenched eyelids. He could taste her mouth on his . . . feel her ripe breast swollen by childbearing cupped in his hand. He could imagine stroking her naked belly and drawing a sweet nipple between his lips and suckling until she whimpered with pleasure.

"Yes . . . yes!" Emma panted.

"Do you want it? Do you want all of it?"

"Yes . . ." she answered. "Now! Now!"

Chance jammed his thumb between his teeth and gave up all attempts to control his own response to the erotic lovemaking going on not three yards from where he lay. His throbbing sex pressed tightly against his trousers; his fingers knotted into fists.

"Deeper! All of it—I want all of you!"

Another minute and Chance would shame himself by staining the clothing Rachel had lent him. Desperately he tried again to think of burning houses, dead dogs, anything but the obvious.

Another lost cause, he swore silently. First secession, and now this.

War was hell.

Chapter 8

"Why are you swimming now?" Rachel called to Chance through the soft twilight. "And why in your trousers?" When the last of Preacher George's congregation had departed, Rachel had gone to the barn in search of Chance and found him missing. Lady and Bear had tracked him to the creek, and she'd followed.

He was bare to the waist, and the corded muscles of his arms and shoulders gleamed wet in the last of the fading light. His butter-yellow hair framed a square-jawed face with well-defined cheekbones and a classically straight nose.

He's a devilishly handsome man, Rachel thought, in spite of his healing wounds and the fact that he was still too thin. Chance was far too good-looking for any woman to trust—let alone one in her position. She pursed her lips firmly and tried to ignore the giddy butterfly-wing flutters in her chest.

"Thank God you stayed in the barn," she continued, struggling to keep her tone from revealing her reaction. "I was terrified that you'd come out of hiding. Pharaoh would have killed you if he'd found—"

He grinned lazily. "I'm not as easily killed as you seem to think. Or as stupid."

"Well, actually." She took a deep breath. "Actually, I told Cora Wright that you were stupid."

Chance stared at her. "Said I was what?"

"Stupid."

"Woman, what the hell are you talking about?"

She sat down on the bank and crossed her arms over her chest. "I had to think of something. Having you here was way too dangerous. So I told Cora that I was hiring a new farmhand. Cora is the black woman who—"

"You told her about me?"

"There's no need to shout. If you stop interrupting me, I'll explain. I couldn't take the risk that Cora would send Pharaoh or one of her grandchildren over to see how I was doing. So I told her that my cousin Jane from New Castle was sending a man to help with the work."

He waded toward her. Water dripped from his hair and trickled down over his muscular shoulders. "I'm supposed to be a stupid hired hand?"

She winced at the granite in his voice. He wasn't accepting her idea as easily as she'd supposed he would. "Not stupid exactly. I knew that if you opened your mouth, your Virginia accent would give you away. And if you were seen, people would ask questions as to why you weren't in one army or another. So I said you were dumb."

His features hardened. "An idiot."

"No, not that. Slow. And mute."

"Mute? I can't talk and I can't enlist. What can I do?"

"Simple tasks. Milk the cow. Hoe the garden."

"You expect me to play the part of an afflicted—"

"It's not like we have a lot of other plans. You can't work in the cornfield if you're hiding in the hayloft."

His disapproving expression changed to one of amusement. "I don't think much of this," he admitted. "But it's more than I've come up with."

She clapped her hands together. "I am brilliant."

He grimaced. "Devilishly inspired."

"Thank you." She laughed. "Naturally, I'll need to cut your hair."

"Cut my hair? The hell you will. I—"

"No one who looked at you would believe that you're not . . ." She struggled to find the right words. "You look too . . . too . . ."

"Roguishly handsome?" He arched an eyebrow.

She giggled. "Healthy," she corrected. "You look too healthy."

"Hmmph," he grumbled. "I suppose all mute men in this state have bad haircuts."

"Not all of them, Chance. Just this one." She chuckled. "Be serious. I'm trying to save your neck. We need to find you some worn clothing or cut a few holes in what you're wearing. And you'll have to practice your walk."

"My walk? What's wrong with my walk?" He moved closer to the shore, and the water level of the creek dropped to his hips.

"It would be more realistic if you shuffle a little," Rachel said. "Just when someone's around. So long as you don't talk, and you hang your head and—"

"Bark like a dog?" he suggested.

"Abner isn't crazy. He's just slow."

"Abner."

"Potts. Abner Potts." She couldn't resist a smile. "But Abner's very obedient. Once you teach him how to do something, he can keep doing it."

"Oh, he can, can he?"

She squirmed under his gaze and rushed to ease the

tension between them. "Yes ... yes. And did you see what Cora Wright and her friends did for me?" she blurted out. "They planted my crop and the garden. And they've loaned me a horse. We'll be able to cultivate the fields, and I can ride him to town—so long as the soldiers don't confiscate him."

He nodded, half turned, and dived under the water.

She took a deep breath and rubbed the small of her back. All day she'd been troubled by an ache, but she'd been on her feet since dawn. It would never have done to sit and be waited on, not when some of the colored folk were so conscious of her white status.

"Chance?" He hadn't come up, and she felt a momentary unease. Then his head broke water, and he took several powerful strokes with his good arm. "Oh, I thought for a moment that I was going to have to come in and pull you out," she said.

"That will be the day."

"I'm sure you swim as well as you do everything else," she replied, feeling suddenly weary.

She sank onto the soft grass and let the scent of newly turned soil fill her head. For weeks—months even—she'd worried that she'd not be able to put in a crop this year. Now that awful weight was lifted from her shoulders, and she was weak with relief.

"Are you coming out of there?" she demanded of Chance. "I won't have to cook tonight. Cora left enough food to feed an army." When he seemed to ignore her, she lost her patience and signaled to Bear. "Fetch!" she ordered her faithful giant. "Bring him in, boy."

Bear ambled down the bank and splashed into the water. Lady, who hated getting her feet wet, contented herself with racing up and down the bank and wagging her tail.

"I'm coming," Chance answered. "No need to set the hounds on me." He grinned as he splashed toward her. "Don't get all prickly with me. I'm slow, remember."

"But obedient."

"Yes, ma'am." He squeezed the water out of his hair. "It was hotter than Hades in that loft."

"Don't blaspheme," she admonished. "I'll thank you to remember your manners, Abner Potts. I'm a Methodist, and I don't approve of rough talk."

Chance laughed, and the deep, merry sound sent shivers down her spine.

"You hide under the hay all day, and you'll come down saying worse," he replied. "And saying *Hades* is not blaspheming. It's another word for hell."

"I know what it means. I may have only finished the eighth grade of a one-room country school, but I'm not stupid."

"I never thought you were."

Little sparks of excitement danced along the surface of her skin. That soft Richmond drawl of his was enough to make a saint doubt salvation, and Rachel knew she'd never been a saint.

"So long as you're already wet, fetch in my crab trap," she hedged. "I didn't check it today."

He stood knee-deep in the water, looking at her. "Isn't it a little late in the day for crabbing? Unless you're planning on steaming crabs tonight . . ."

He was right, of course. The thought of cooking crabs and shelling them to make soup when she was already exhausted was too much.

"It's too warm for crabs to keep, alive or cooked," he said. "But if you want—"

"On second thought, we'll leave them until tomorrow," she agreed.

"Yes, ma'am." He nodded and touched an imaginary hat with two fingers.

He was poking fun at her. Even when he wasn't, Chancellor's fine manners were sometimes disturbing. She felt her cheeks grow warm. "You can check the traps first thing in the morning, before you milk the cow," she said a little sharply.

"Whatever you say, ma'am." He strode up the sandy bank and stopped a little ways from her. "Your friends," he began, "they were all colored, weren't they?"

She nodded. "Free men and women of color, yes."

"I heard Lincoln freed the slaves."

"No, not these people. Well, you're right, President Lincoln did free the slaves. But Pharaoh, Cora, Preacher George, and the others—they were free before the war, some for generations. It surprises you, doesn't it, that colored folk would do for me what no one else would?"

"No." He wrung the water out of his pant legs and reached for the shirt he'd left hanging on a tree limb. "No, it doesn't. I've known a lot of decent blacks, most of them, actually."

She shrugged in disbelief. "I wouldn't expect one of your kind to understand."

"My kind?" He stepped nearer, his shirt draped carelessly over his muscular forearm. The light was fading fast; it was already too dark for her to see the startling blue of his eyes, but she could feel the force of them burning into her skin.

"A man who can condone owning another human

being—the kind of man I've always hated." She drew in a ragged breath as shivers raised gooseflesh on her arms. She raised her chin, trying to brazen out the moment. "A man who'd go to war against his country to defend the despicable institution of slavery."

"You think that's why I enlisted?"

He was so close that she could smell the creek water in his hair, feel his breath on her face. She swallowed, trying to maintain her bravado. "What other reason could there be?"

"Have you ever asked me if I owned slaves? Or if I enlisted to defend slavery? Personally, I abhor the practice that one human should own another. My mother was born in England. Her family considered slavery to be barbaric. Mother refused my father's offer of marriage until he freed all his slaves and signed a legal contract with her that he would never buy another human."

"But you're fighting to defend the institution."

"I'm not. I never was. Slavery's a dying evil. It's immoral and it's impractical."

"Impractical?"

"Yes. Few Americans possess the wealth to own slaves, and fewer still have the stomach for it. If this war hadn't ignited, Congress would have eventually outlawed slavery as England has."

"You've never owned a slave?"

"Never," he replied.

"Why then? Why are you fighting?"

"Loyalty to my fellow Virginians, defending home and hearth against the *War of Northern Aggression.*"

"Pretty words," she mocked. "Can you look me in the eye and tell me that you believe them?" She shook her head. "You're as bad as all the rest. You wanted to wear shiny buttons and follow the drum."

"Maybe . . . maybe you're right."

Tightness in her chest made it hard to speak. The air around them seemed charged with the same invisible energy that she'd felt before a lightning strike. "I've no wish to argue with you. And if I wronged you by believing you worse than you are, I'm sorry. It's only natural that I'd believe a Confederate . . ." She swallowed. "If you're not a slaver, I'm glad."

"Neither me nor my parents."

"That's that, then," she murmured. He kept staring at her, making it difficult to think clearly. "The cow's been milked, and the horse is stabled," she managed. "If you'll come to the house, Mr. Chancellor, I'll give you something to eat. I want to change that bandage and see if . . ."

"It's Mr. Chancellor now, is it?" He stood there as if he expected something more of her.

She was conscious of the chirp of crickets from the grass along the creek and the faint yellow blink of a lightning bug in the gathering dusk. The air felt soft on her cheeks, and the clover under her bare feet smelled as sweet as any store-bought perfume.

"Rachel . . ."

Chance was taller than James; she had to look up to meet his gaze. And woman's instinct told her that she should run—that she was risking more than her farm and her physical safety. Instead, she moistened her lips and took a step toward him.

His shirt fell soundlessly from his lean fingers and drifted to the grass. "Rachel," he repeated huskily. "We shouldn't . . ." She could hear the unspoken longing in his voice.

"No, we can't," she agreed. If things were different, if it wasn't for James and the war . . .

Chance reached out and touched her cheek. "You're shivering, Rachel. Don't be afraid of me. I'd not hurt you for all the world."

But you will, she protested silently. Each time he said her name, something loosened deep inside her. She felt too weak to stand, helpless to do anything but lean ever so slowly into the circle of his arms.

His lips brushed the line of her lower lip, softly, so softly that tears welled up in her eyes.

"This is crazy," he said. "I must be out of my head."

"Yes," she agreed.

"But I've never done anything more right in my life," he continued, and the rich timbre of his voice made her tremble even more.

She couldn't summon the strength to say anything more, but she made no effort to escape. Instead, she tilted her head to meet his warm lips and sighed as his mouth fitted perfectly to hers. His breath was sweet and clean; he tasted faintly of mint.

For long seconds he kissed her with exquisite tenderness, and she reveled in the joy of being held and cherished by a man. Sighing with contentment, lulled by the spirals of tingling sensation that ran through her veins, Rachel slipped her arms around his neck and pressed herself against the wide expanse of his bare chest. Then the simmering heat of their caress flared into a forest fire.

And lightning struck.

Not lightning from the sky, but the pent-up longing in her heart that Rachel had denied for so long. Heat flashed through her, and she parted her lips, desperately wanting more.

Chance didn't fail her.

His tongue touched hers, retreated, and met her seeking one again. He groaned deep in his throat, and desire stripped her of caution. Her head fell back, and he kissed her throat and the soft hollow below her ear.

"Rachel, Rachel," he whispered.

He kissed her eyelids and the corners of her mouth then and skimmed the surface of her upper lip with his tongue. And when their mouths molded to each other's again, it was with greater passion.

She wove her fingers into his hair and felt the swelling proof of his need by his ragged breathing and the force of his touch. Still she did not care.

"It's been so long," he murmured. "So long since I've held a woman . . ."

She could not get enough of his kisses or his touch. And when she twisted in his arms and felt him wince as she leaned her weight against his bad shoulder, it was Rachel who pulled him to the grass.

"I've never met anyone like you," he said as they parted long enough to draw breath. "Never."

"Shhh," she murmured. "Don't talk, don't say anything." She didn't want to hear his lies, didn't want to think where this was leading. She only wanted him to go on kissing her.

"I can't . . ." she started to say, and then broke off. "I'm too far along with the baby to . . ."

"It's all right," he answered hoarsely. "I just want to touch you. Will you let me touch you, Rachel?" He cupped the swell of her breast, and her breath caught in her throat.

It was fully dark now, the night made even darker by

the thick canopy of oak leaves overhead. She could no longer see Chance's face or the color of his hair.

And his kisses were no longer enough. . . .

She wanted to feel his hands on her breasts, stroking her, caressing, easing the heavy ache that made her nipples hard and sensitive against the fabric of her worn linen shift.

He kissed her again with exquisite tenderness and slowly, tantalizingly, began to undo the buttons at the nape of her neck. "Rachel, Rachel," he whispered.

She knew she had to stop this madness, but his scalding kiss made her giddy with wanting him, and she let their lovemaking go further.

Chance unfastened her buttons, one by one, until she wanted to scream at him to hurry. Between kisses he pushed her dress off one shoulder. Finally there was nothing between his hand and her naked breast but a thin layer of linen.

"So soft," he murmured huskily. "So soft."

And to her surprise he lowered his head and brushed her nipple with his lips.

"Oh," she cried.

His breath was warm against her flesh. He teased the nub of her breast with his callused thumb until her nipple tightened and throbbed, then used his hot tongue to caress it.

She tugged at her shift and heard the cloth rip, but she didn't care. All that mattered was the feel of his mouth on her breast, and the sweet ribbons of bright pleasure that shimmered inside her.

She lay back in the thick clover and let him take freedoms that should have belonged only to a husband. And

Chance proved that he was no stranger to the ways of a woman, teaching her things that James never had.

"Darling Rachel," Chance whispered. He drew first one nipple and then the other between his lips and suckled until she felt yearning curl in the apex of her thighs.

He's different from most men, she thought. *He's not selfish. He cares about pleasing me as well as himself.* Somehow that added to her own excitement.

She traced the line of his collarbone and caressed the curve of his shoulder, then trailed her fingertips across his muscular chest.

How long they kissed and fondled each other, Rachel could not have said. But when Chance slid an exploring hand beneath her skirts, a warning went off in her head and she forced herself to pull away. "No more," she said. "Please, no more."

"I'll not force you," he rasped. "There are other ways to—"

"No." Emotionally shaken, she rose unsteadily to her feet. "I know what you must think of me, and you have every right to name me slattern."

"Rachel . . ."

She steeled herself against the need in his voice. "I don't ask you to believe me, but I've never done that with anyone but James."

He stood up abruptly, unable to hide his disappointment or to quell the pain in his loins. "This is a dangerous game you play."

"I will not risk my child for the sake of slap and tickle. I told you I couldn't . . . or I tried to tell you. If you thought—"

"I thought nothing," he answered. "I accuse you of nothing. I'd hoped . . ."

She pulled up her shift and gathered it together over her breasts. "I made a mistake," she said. "This will never happen again. Do you understand?"

"If you say so."

He was hurt and she couldn't blame him. She had allowed him to think that she'd give him what he wanted. What they both wanted, she corrected herself. She swallowed. "I'm sorry, Chance. I've been so lonely, and—" She turned away from him. "If you are a gentleman, you'll not mention this again." Swiftly she began to walk down the path toward the house.

She reached the back door and threw it open. Lady nosed through ahead of her. How could she have been so stupid?

But she knew how. She had only to think of Chance's lips on her breast to go all soft and woozy inside. "Bear!" As soon as the big dog's tail was safely inside, Rachel slammed the inner door and shot the bolt.

She didn't even pretend that she was locking Chance out. She knew better. She was locking herself in.

"If it wasn't for the baby . . ." she whispered.

Would she really have let Chance make love to her? It was a question she didn't want to answer.

She jerked closed the curtains and went to the cookstove. A reservoir on the side of the stove held warm water, and she dipped some out into a basin. She wanted to throw herself into her bed and pull the covers over her head, but she couldn't until she'd bathed away the day's grime.

What must Chance think of her?

"What does that matter?" she grumbled aloud.

He was a Johnny Reb. By rights, she should hate him. If she were a decent woman, she'd hate him.

But she couldn't.

Carrying this babe had surely sapped her brain that she could do such a thing, she thought as she fought back tears. She needed Chance Chancellor for the strength of his back, nothing more. Women often lost their good sense in the last months of their pregnancy. Once she was safely delivered, she'd remember who she was and what Chancellor was, she promised herself.

As sure as the sun would come up tomorrow, she'd pretend this never happened. And if she couldn't, he'd have to go, and the farm be damned.

"This farm and Rachel Irons be damned!" Chance kicked at a dirt clod and swore the foulest French oath he could summon up from his winter in Paris.

The woman was impossible. She treated him as though he were a leper, then allowed him . . . He exhaled slowly and his mouth went dry as he thought of what liberties she'd permitted . . . and those he'd come close to tasting.

She was as dangerous as a jury of Southern Baptists.

Why? Why had she done it? And why had she let him go so far only to throw cold water on his lovemaking?

Men had a name for women who promised everything and then withheld the prize, but in honesty he couldn't taint Rachel with such a term. She'd been genuinely drawn to him as he was to her. Sensual, passionate . . . infuriating.

What a lucky man James Irons was. Or an unlucky one. If he was alive, then his wife had betrayed him in the worst possible way. And if he wasn't . . .

If James Irons was dead, then he—Chance—was in even more jeopardy. Rachel drew him in ways that were more than physical.

She claimed to be a married woman, the wife of a Yankee soldier—maybe even one who'd tried to kill him at Gettysburg. She was a barefoot country girl without family influence or wealth. If he'd brought her home to Chancellor Hall before the war, she would have been shunned by Richmond society and his business associates as well. And after the war ... Win, lose, or draw, she'd be unwelcome in his world and as out of place as a tobacco cutter in a judge's chambers.

Rachel Irons, with her Indian blood, was a poor choice for a rich Catholic lawyer whose ancestors had helped to settle Jamestown. He'd have had to look high and low to find a worse match.

He'd become so involved with Rachel and her problems that he'd put her needs ahead of Travis's. The thought that his best friend might have survived the flying bullets and the dogs on the beach of Pea Patch Island only to die waiting for him was more than Chance wanted to face.

He kicked another furrow of plowed ground. Travis couldn't wait until Rachel's crop was harvested in the autumn. He'd promised Rachel that he would help, but what of the oath he'd made to Travis? What did a man do when one oath canceled out another? Or when a beautiful, courageous woman had risked her own freedom to save his life?

And how could he live with himself if he didn't rejoin his company—if he hid out here, safe from the war, while his comrades were facing musket balls and shot?

He had no choice. He was a soldier, and he had a duty to complete his mission at all cost. He'd stay a few days more, a week or two at most, until his shoulder was better, and then he'd steal Rachel's skiff and sail back to the prison to rescue Travis. Hell, once he killed Coblentz, he'd likely never come out of Fort Delaware alive himself.

Even if he did love Rachel—which he sure as hell didn't—he had no future to offer her. Getting away from her was the best thing he could do to insure her safety and that of her baby.

He needn't worry about Rachel; she'd been none the worse for helping him. And she had friends. Hadn't they come and planted her crops for her? She could ask them to help work her fields, or she could let her father-in-law take her land. What did it matter to him? Delaware wasn't part of the Confederacy, and she wasn't his concern.

Rachel would be disappointed to lose her free labor, but that was his own fault for being so gullible. Any soldier would do the same thing.

Wouldn't he?

Chapter 9

Chance tossed and turned on his mattress. Sleep would not come no matter how hard he tried. Travis's face hovered behind Chance's closed eyelids, and his friend's last words echoed in Chance's head.

"It's my turn to play hero," Travis had said. "Leave me."

And he had. He'd swum away from the accursed swamp that was Pea Patch Island and saved his own skin. What would he tell Mary? How could he face Travis's wife and tell her that Chance was cowardly enough to abandon her husband?

Oh, Mary, Mary ... Once, Chance had thought she would be his wife and the mother of his future children. Freckle-faced Mary, with her laughing green eyes and quick wit, was just the sort of woman his mother had expected him to wed.

Mary's great-grandfather had been a war hero, and her father owned prime real estate in Richmond as well as hundreds of acres of rich farmland. Chance and Travis had known Mary since they all were babes in arms. She was pretty, Catholic, and independently wealthy.

Yes, Mary was the perfect woman for him. But he'd dallied a bit too long with the scarlet ladies, and he'd put off formalizing a relationship he'd taken for granted. And when Travis confided that he intended to ask Mary for her hand, Chance had bitten back his disappointment, gotten drunk, and wished them both well. And he'd stood up as Travis's best man.

Over the years his infatuation with Mary had softened to friendship, but that wouldn't make his task any easier. She always had been able to see through his excuses.

Exasperated, Chance rose and lit the kerosene lantern and dressed. His shoulder was still stiff and painful, but the flesh around the wound showed no signs of mortification. There was no reason for him to remain here for a few more days. That was putting off the inevitable. A day could make all the difference in whether Travis lived or died. He could take food from the kitchen and leave tonight. Rachel's farm was in as good shape as it was likely to be, and he was no farmhand.

He would need provisions, but there was food aplenty in buckets in the well where Rachel had hung the perishables to keep them cool. He'd take enough to last him for a day. There was no need to leave her a note; she'd likely have the soldiers on his trail soon enough when she found that he was gone. And she should consider herself lucky he was taking her boat instead of the horse.

Since Rachel took the dogs into the house with her at night, he didn't think the animals would hear him in the yard. After what had nearly happened between them, he wanted to avoid a confrontation with Rachel. If that made him a coward, so be it. He'd be doing her a favor to get out of her life as quickly as possible.

Chance yanked on the boots she'd provided, opened the door leading into the barn, and stopped short.

Rachel stood just outside in bare feet and a lacy white nightgown. Masses of dark hair hung loose around her shoulders, and her cheeks were ghostly pale. "Chance!" she cried, wide-eyed and frightened. "Help me!"

Then he saw the wet spots staining the hem of her garment. "What is it?" he demanded. "What happened?"

"I—" She gasped and doubled over, clasping her hands to her swollen abdomen. "My water's broken," she said. "It's the baby—come too soon."

Chance's skin prickled. "Rachel?"

He set the lantern on the floor and managed to catch her as she crumbled. Pain knifed through his injured shoulder as he swept her into his arms.

"Help me," she said between clenched teeth.

"I'll fetch a doctor," he offered as he carried her in to his bed.

"No!" She gripped his forearm so tightly that her nails dug into his flesh. "No!"

The spasm eased and she sucked in a jagged breath. She fell back against the pillow and licked her bottom lip where she'd bitten it. A thin trickle of blood ran down her chin, and he wiped it away with his finger.

"Rachel, I can't do this," he said in a rush. "I don't know anything about delivering babies. Hell, I've never even seen a newborn."

She closed her eyes, and he noticed again how thick and dark her lashes were against her cheeks. As black as a crow's wing, he thought.

His shoulder wound throbbed, but he would have welcomed the hurting and more if he could have taken her pain. His voice grew husky with concern. "I'll go for help."

"No, you can't. They'll arrest you if you do."

"It doesn't matter. You need—"

"No time," she answered. "The baby's coming. You can't . . . can't leave me alone."

Raw fear skittered down his spine. "I'm not the person to do this."

"You're all I've got." She fixed him with a pleading stare. "If you leave me, the baby will come and I won't be able to—" Another contraction seized her, and she covered her mouth with her hand to keep from crying out.

Chance waited helplessly for what seemed an eternity until the spasm passed. And when it finally did, he asked her, "What shall I do?"

She took several deep, slow breaths. "Go to the house—"

"Shall I carry you there?"

Rachel shook her head. "No. Don't move me. I don't want to hurt the baby. Go inside and fetch clean sheets and towels. You'll need hot water. In the reservoir in the stove. Roll up your sleeves and wash with lye soap. Wash harder than you've ever done before, then pour liniment over your hands. There's some on the tack-room shelf."

"Yes. I know where it is." His knees felt weak.

"Go into the parlor," she said. "There's a black bag beside the stove. It's . . ." Her eyes glazed with pain and she gritted her teeth. "Go! Damn it!"

Chance ran.

She's going to die, he thought. Mother of God, I'm going to foul this up, and she's going to die in front of my eyes.

It was like looking into a black abyss. One minute he was out the door and on his way back to rescue Travis, and the next, nothing mattered but saving the woman that lay in agony in the barn.

Nothing.

Rachel Irons had suddenly and irrevocably become his concern. He had to help her, but he didn't have the slightest inkling how. And he knew if he failed, his life would lose something precious.

When he came back with what she had asked for, he found Rachel on her feet, leaning against the wall. "What are you doing out of bed?" he demanded, reaching for her arm.

"Are your hands clean?" she asked. "Don't touch the floor, or you have to wash all over again."

"What are you talking about?"

"Cora Wright told me. Her mothers don't die of childbed fever like so many other women do. She says everything must be clean—sheets, her hands, the patient. I don't know why it works, but it does. And she makes her mothers get up and walk within twenty-four hours. She claims it drains away the bad spirits."

"You're not an ignorant woman, Rachel. How can you talk such nonsense when you're having a baby? Bad spirits? Listen to yourself."

She walked unsteadily back to the bunk and sat down. Chance saw that the bottom half of her nightgown was soaked in fluid. She was breathing in short, regular pants.

"My grandmother was . . . was Lenape. Indian. I told you that. She said that Cora was right, that—agggh." She pressed her abdomen and a shudder ran through her body.

Chance slipped his hand into hers, and Rachel squeezed until he thought his bones would break.

When she could speak again, she whispered hoarsely, "When the baby starts to come out, you'll see the head. Take it in your hands, but don't pull. Just support and guide it. It will be slippery. Don't drop it when it slides out."

"Jesus," he whispered.

"As soon as it's here," she continued painfully, "clean out the mouth so that it can breathe. There's silk thread in my bag. Knot the cord in two places, close to the baby's navel. Then cut between the knots. There are scissors in the bag. Pour alcohol over them first. In the blue bottle, marked 'Dr. Jay's Laxative Bitters,' is corn whiskey. Use that."

"Laxative Bitters," he repeated dumbly. Once, in the Battle of Williamsburg, he and Travis had dismounted to save Joseph Sutherland, another man in their company who'd had his horse shot from under him. Sutherland's right leg was shattered, and Travis had tied a leather strap around Sutherland's thigh to stem the loss of blood until they could get him to a physician. Chance hadn't felt as helpless then as he did now.

"Keep the baby warm," she insisted. "I think it's early. It may be very small. Don't let it take a chill."

"Can't I go for this Cora Wright?" he insisted. "I can take the horse and bring her back—"

"No," Rachel repeated. "I told you. It's coming too fast. If I pass out, I can't help the baby. He—she could suffocate. You have to be sure it can breathe. I can't lose James's baby."

"Why the hell isn't James here to do this for you?" Chance demanded. "He should be doing this, not me."

"Because he's dead. That's why! You killed him! He's dead and buried in Barratt's Chapel."

"Me?" He stared down at her as if she'd lost her mind. "How could I kill him? I didn't even know him."

"You were at Gettysburg, weren't you?" she accused. "James was shot at—oh, oh, my . . ."

Her face turned a deep red as the labor contractions intensified. They were coming closer together, and each one seemed stronger. Even Chance knew that meant birth was imminent.

His stomach churned. He'd never considered himself to have much of a yellow streak, but right now he felt like running.

"I didn't kill your husband." He dipped the corner of a towel in the basin of water and wiped the perspiration from her face. "I didn't kill anybody at Gettysburg. Not unless you count my horse."

This time when the pain passed, she sat up and clutched his good arm. "I've got to walk," she insisted. "Help me walk."

"You stay right where you are." Having babies must make women crazy, he thought. Crazier than they already were.

"I need to walk!"

"You told me not to touch you."

She thumped him with her fist. "Will you help me or not? If not, get out of my way."

"All right, all right. But don't blame me if your babe falls on the floor." He supported her as she got to her feet and began to circle the small room.

"I thought women were supposed to be sweet and motherly when they were giving birth," he said. "You're as testy as a judge with hemorrhoids." Sweet Mary. Had he actually said that to a lady? He must be as demented as she was to forget his manners and speak so. "Forgive me, Rachel," he said. "I shouldn't have—"

"What? Lied to me about murdering my husband?" She leaned against him and caught her breath.

"I told you, I didn't fire my pistol that day. It's true we charged a Union position, but I never got close enough to—"

"Why should I believe a traitorous rebel dog? Worse than a hound dog—a Virginia lawyer."

"And who told me that her husband was alive? Alive and coming home? That wasn't exactly the truth, was it, lady?"

"You Southern son of a snake! No gentleman would remind a woman of innocent fabrications made in desperation to protect herself."

"This Southern son of a snake lawyer is all that's keeping you from—"

"What? You're threatening me? You're going to leave me to die?"

"I didn't say that, Rachel," he soothed. "You're simply the—" He broke off, unable to say anything that would soften what he wanted to say. "I'm sorry your husband is dead."

"I'm sure."

"I am," he answered. "You're a good woman. You deserve more than you've had."

"You don't know what I've had. You don't know anything about me."

"I know you've got a good heart—good enough to nurse me back to health when you could have turned me in for a reward."

"I didn't do it to be good," she replied. "I did it to save my farm."

"I don't think so."

"I did. Why should I care if another traitor dies?"

"You're talking nonsense, Rachel. This war is at fault. It—"

"Your doing, not ours. You fired on Fort Sumter."

"Not me," he replied. "It must have been another Chance Chancellor. I was delivering the closing arguments on Earl Mosby's charge of horse stealing before the honorable judge Byron Jeffries. My bullets wouldn't have carried that far from Richmond or my client would be doing twenty years."

He could see her preparing a blistering counterattack when another contraction racked her body and she doubled over. This time a stifled moan escaped her clenched teeth.

His anger vanished. "Shall I take you back to bed?"

Rachel shook her head. "No. No. It will pass."

He cradled her against his chest and buried his face in her soft, sweet-smelling hair. "Scream if you want to," he whispered. "You don't have to be brave."

"Shut up."

They walked for what seemed like hours while sweat soaked her body. Her breathing became a quick hard panting when the contractions took hold, then eased in the short space between.

"Talk to me," he urged.

"What do I say?"

"Anything. Tell me about your childhood . . . your family."

She shuddered. "I think I'd better lie down."

He half carried her to the bed and held her hand while she gritted her teeth against the pain. "I wish I could do this for you," he rasped. She was as courageous as any soldier under fire, but his own sense of dread increased with each contraction.

"I was a love child," she whispered. "Did I tell you that? My father never married my mother."

Chance laid a damp cloth on her forehead. "Yes, I'm listening, Rachel. Go on."

"No one ever told me why. Maybe it was because he was an educated doctor and she had Indian blood. Some people said . . . said he had a wife in Philadelphia. I don't know."

"Your mother never said?"

Rachel shook her head. "She died . . . when I was born. I never . . . never knew her. Him, I knew later. My grandparents raised me. They didn't like him, but they didn't stop me from seeing him when I was older. They never forgave him."

"He must have loved your mother."

"Maybe . . . He never said. He wasn't good with people . . . my father. But he cared about his work, and he was a good physician."

Chance stroked her hair away from her face. "Keep talking," he said.

"My grandparents loved me. My father never did, but he taught me. I was grateful for that. I—" She broke off, and her eyes widened. "Oh! It's coming! Now! Chance!" She struck his bad shoulder with her fist. "Do something!"

Pain arced through his body. He bit back a groan and crouched at the end of the narrow cot. Rachel's fingers knotted into tight balls as she drew up her knees.

There was a gush of bloody fluid, and something dark appeared between her legs. Chance stared as the object bulged slightly and then receded. "Is that the baby's head?"

"Yes, damn it!" she yelled. "Get it out!" The contraction passed, and Rachel took another deep breath.

"You can do this," he said. "It's all right. You can do it," he soothed.

This time, when the baby crowned, Chance forced himself to place his hands on either side of the wet head. Rachel groaned, pushing with all her might, and the baby's head slid out into his cupped palms. Another moment and more effort on Rachel's part, and the infant slipped completely out.

"I've got it!" Chance cried. "It's a boy."

"A boy?"

Moisture clouded Chance's vision. The baby had a mop of thick, black hair and nails on his fingers and toes. He was so tiny. Chance hadn't expected a newborn to be so small and so perfect. Well, almost perfect . . . His head was a little pointy and his color pasty white.

Rachel leaned forward and reached out for the baby. "A boy? Let me see him."

Chance didn't answer. Methodically he followed Rachel's earlier instructions, balancing the slippery infant in one hand while he cleaned out the mouth and tied and cut the thick cord with shaking hands.

The baby still wasn't moving, and his eyes were closed. He looked like he was asleep, and Chance didn't need Rachel to tell him that something was wrong.

"Why isn't he crying?"

"He's small, Rachel," he answered. Awfully small.

"Chance?"

He turned the infant over his arm and smacked it on the back. "Come on," he said. "Wake up, boy. It's time to wake up."

"Give him to me," Rachel insisted.

Her voice was weak. She was nearly as white as the pillowcase under her head.

He tried to think what to do. How could a baby be born perfect but not breathing? "Come on, little boy," he urged thickly. "You can do it."

Damn his eyes for watering! He could hardly see. He didn't know why they were clouding up.

"Give me my son."

Chance wrapped the infant in a towel and laid him on the floor. The blankets under Rachel were stained with bloody fluid, and now more was running out between her legs. "I'm worried about your bleeding," he said. "You—"

"Never mind me," she protested. "It's the afterbirth coming. It's natural."

He rolled up a blanket and put it under her legs. "Here," he said. "Can you put these towels—"

"Yes, yes," she said. "The baby! Is he breathing?" Her voice had taken on an edge of hysteria.

Chance shook his head.

"No! Please don't let him die. Please . . ."

He picked up the child and shifted him to the crook of his arm. The infant was so small, so fragile that he was afraid he'd break the tiny bones if he used too much force. He patted the babe's back, but there was no sound, no response. He might have been holding a rag doll.

Icy numbness swept over him in waves. *Stillborn.* Rachel's babe was stillborn. She'd lost her husband, and now her child was dead as well.

"Chance!"

One word, one word that pleaded her case more than an hour-long summation. Rachel trusted him; she be-

lieved he had the power to save her baby. He couldn't let
her down.

Seizing the tiny ankles, he lifted the still infant in the
air as the towel fell away. With two fingers he tapped the
blood-stained buttocks and was rewarded with a small
choking gasp.

"Give him to me."

"That's it," Chance said to the child. "That's it. You
can do it. Breathe. Breathe." He smacked the baby's bottom again and listened.

Nothing.

It was too small to live, he thought with a sinking
heart. No bigger than a pup.

And then he did something he hadn't done in a long
time. He closed his eyes and prayed. *Dear God, let him
be all right. Let this little one live.*

Rachel was weeping now. "Give me my baby," she repeated. "Please, please, give him to me."

Chance grabbed the towel off the floor, swaddled the
limp baby against his chest, and ran out of the room.

Chapter 10

"No! Don't take him! Bring him back!"

Rachel's scream echoed in Chance's ears as he raced out of the barn clutching her lifeless baby. Branches tore at his face, and he hunched protectively over the small body as he left the path and dashed through the grove of cedars to the edge of the creek. Both dogs were hard on his heels.

Half sliding down the sandy bank, Chance nearly lost his footing, then vaulted the last distance into the shallows. He dropped to his knees and plunged the infant under the water.

When he lifted the child up, the baby tensed and kicked once, then went limp again. "Please," Chance said. "Please God, give me this, if you never give me another thing."

And then he placed his mouth over the minute nose and mouth and blew, gently filling the infant's lungs with air.

"What are you doing?" Rachel shouted.

He glanced up to see her standing unsteadily on the bank. Without answering her, he gave the baby two more breaths and dipped him again.

This time Chance felt the child's body convulse as

soon as the cold water closed over him. Limp muscle surged to life as Chance yanked the choking infant out. The babe's face darkened, he opened his tiny mouth, and he let out a man-size shriek.

"Yes, yes!" Chance cried. "That's it! Yell!" He nestled the now squirming babe in the crook of his arms again, scooped up a few drops of water, and made the sign of the cross over the infant's forehead. "In the name of the Father, Son, and Holy Ghost," he whispered, "I christen thee—" He looked back at Rachel, speechless now in the moonlight. "James David Irons," he finished quickly.

Chance could barely hold on to the wet, shivering infant as he waded back to shore. Wailing furiously, the babe arched his back and thrashed his arms and legs with surprising strength. Small fists thudded against Chance's chest, and a down-covered head wobbled precariously.

Rachel sank onto the ground and held out her arms. "Give him to me," she begged.

Chance paused only long enough to wrap the protesting infant in the dry towel before handing him over to his mother. And as she clasped the child to her and covered his face with kisses, Chance turned away and wiped furiously at his eyes.

Within seconds the babe's angry screeches became soft gulps and whimpers. When Chance looked back, he understood why the infant had calmed so quickly. Rachel had drawn aside her nightgown and put him to her breast.

She raised her head and smiled at Chance. "You saved him for me," she murmured. "If it wasn't for you . . ." She left the rest unspoken, and Chance felt the constriction in his throat grow even tighter.

"How did you know to do that?" she asked.

He shook his head. Bands of iron compressed his

chest, and he found it hard to breathe, let alone talk. The sight of her there, holding her living son, filled him with such emotion that he didn't know how to deal with it.

"We'd . . . we'd best get the two of you back to the house," he said gruffly.

"I saw you," she insisted. "You blew the breath of life into him."

Chance shrugged. "I didn't know. I just . . ." He exhaled softly. "Hell, I saw my father's groom do that with a hound pup. The runt of the litter was born dead. Jethro dipped it in a bucket of cold water and then blew in the pup's mouth. It worked for a hound, so . . ."

"A hound?" She laughed, and the sound lifted the heaviness from his heart. "Hound or jackass, I don't care. Look at him," she said. "Look at how strong he is. You said he was tiny. He's not tiny. He must be close to seven pounds."

"He sure as hell looked tiny to me. And you said it was too early for him to be born—that you weren't due until July."

"I thought so. I guess I made a mistake. I must have gotten pregnant earlier than I'd thought. He can't be more than two weeks early, that's certain. Look at his chubby legs." She kissed the baby's fingertips.

Chance kicked at the dirt with a soggy boot. "You saw what else I did, too?"

"I did."

He didn't know how a woman who'd suffered so much—who'd just given birth—could rally so, but he wasn't going to doubt a miracle when it was handed to him.

"James *David* Irons?" she demanded. "What was all that about?"

"I christened him," Chance admitted.

"*You* christened him? *My* son? My Methodist son. You're a Catholic, aren't you?"

"Guilty."

"And I suppose you think you've made my son one, too?"

"I didn't know if he'd live, Rachel. I didn't think. I just . . ."

"You were concerned for my son's soul."

"Yes. It seemed important." He corrected himself. "It is important."

"I never took you for a religious man."

He knelt beside her. "I never thought I was. It's been years since I went to confession or heard mass." He cleared his throat. "If I've offended you . . ."

She laid a hand on his forearm. "You haven't," she said softly. And then she laughed again. "I suppose I'm lucky you didn't name him Robert E. Lee Irons."

"David was my grandfather's name. He was a good person, Rachel."

"Even if he was a Virginian?"

"You would have liked him, Rachel. He was an honorable man who never turned the needy from his door, regardless of the color of their skin."

"Maybe I would have liked him," she replied.

Chance stroked the back of the baby's head with two fingers. His hair was silky, as soft as duck down, and the small, squeaking noises the infant uttered filled Chance with an overwhelming protective feeling. He wanted to gather both mother and child into his arms and hold them.

He never wanted to let them go.

He inhaled deeply of the warm night, savoring the rich

scent of fresh-turned earth, the sight of the moonlight glinting like silver off the waters of the creek, and the far-off hoo-hoo of a great horned owl. He wanted to hold on to this moment, to lock it away so that he could summon it up in the midst of cannon fire and the sound of dying men and horses.

"I think I can walk if you'll let me lean on you," Rachel said.

"What about him?"

"I've got him," she answered.

"I could carry you," Chance offered. "I think . . ."

"I ran here, I can damn well walk back."

"But . . ." He knew he should take command of the situation, but he felt shaken, unwilling to argue with her. "You were bleeding so badly—"

"That's natural," she said. "The afterbirth. I'm all right now. Really."

"I'm a poor midwife," he admitted.

"I think you're a fine one," she said. "And wee David thinks so, too."

"You call him David?"

Her mood grew tender. "You gave him life, Chance. I think calling him by your grandfather's name is a small price to pay for such a gift."

Two weeks later Chance hunched forward, attempting to hold the heavy cultivator upright and guide the horse between the rows of vegetables at the same time. If he reined the horse too far from the beans, he'd miss most of the weeds, and if the metal blades cut too close, he'd destroy the plants.

"Whoa, whoa there, Blackie," he called to the horse. This experience gave him an entirely new perspective on farming, and greater respect for those who spent a life-time tilling the soil. There was much more to growing vegetables than he'd thought.

Rachel's instructions had seemed simple. The horse was trained to pull, and the ground had been worked only two weeks before. So why did he have blisters on each hand, a pain in his back, and dirt in his mouth?

"Straighten up!" Rachel called. "You're cutting too deep in the center!"

"Too deep, too shallow," Chance muttered under his breath. What did she want out of him? He was no field-hand. He was trained for the law, for pity's sake.

Blackie reached the end of the row and cut across the end of the onions, digging out the last three feet and burying the sets in a heap of dirt.

"Chance!" Rachel cried.

"Whoa!" He reined in the horse and surveyed the damage. His last row wasn't bad, if you didn't count the beans crushed by Blackie's hooves. He might need to make a second run or finish up with a hoe. But the onions would definitely have to be replanted, if he could salvage them.

The horse swung his head around and gave Chance a sly look. Then he snatched a sprig of corn and began to chew steadily.

"Devil beast!" Chance shouted.

They'd been at this business for most of the morning; rather, he had been at it. Rachel and the baby sat in the shade of an oak tree and supervised.

Not that he'd expect her to do the actual labor. Davy kept her busy day and night. Chance hadn't realized how often a baby needed to eat, or that he wouldn't be born knowing the difference between day and night.

Davy spent most of his daylight hours asleep or nursing, and his nights crying. Colic was Rachel's opinion, and Chance had to agree, since he didn't have any other suggestions.

But other than being overly red and a little wrinkled, Chance had to admit little Davy was coming along far better than he'd expected. His head had even assumed a nice round shape, and once he'd dried off, all that peach fuzz on top had become a thatch of black hair.

Chance had never taken much notice of infants before, but this one was different. Davy seemed to have a personality all his own. A man could read the intelligence in those big eyes, eyes that had started out a deep blue and darkened every day. And he had a way of holding on to Chance's finger that made Chance feel like he'd drawn a royal flush in a high-stakes poker game.

Being there to help bring Davy into the world had been a miracle. Seeing that little boy turn from white and lifeless to pink and crying lustily had been the most profound moment of Chance's life, and he felt privileged to have witnessed it. He also felt strangely tied to the babe, as though every new trick Davy learned was something to rejoice and take pride in.

Chance was in trouble and he knew it. He'd been ready to leave the night that Davy was born. In spite of the strong feelings he'd come to have for Rachel, his duty had called him. But now . . . now everything was different.

Before the baby came, Rachel was a married woman. Now he knew for certain that she was free. If he hadn't given his word to Travis or if he hadn't drawn the short straw so that he was committed to killing Coblentz . . .

Chance paused to wipe the sweat out of his eyes.

There was no *maybe* for the two of them, and he was lying to himself if he tried to think otherwise. He'd sworn to uphold the Confederacy, and the war was far from over. If he survived Pea Patch and what he had to do there, he still had to go back to killing men he didn't hate.

He gritted his teeth. His world was the law, politics, and for now, a war that couldn't be won by either side, a war that he wasn't certain he'd survive.

He'd gone into the Fourth Virginia with his eyes open. Let other men whoop and yell about the superiority of Southern marksmanship and courage. He'd never kidded himself that it was money and factories that won wars. Lincoln's armies would succeed despite the ineptitude of some of his generals. And when it was over and America had torn out her own gut, most people would forget why the hostilities had begun. All the economic reasons for secession would vanish but one— the existence of slavery.

Men and women had to give themselves high-sounding reasons for committing the most foolish of acts, and nothing Americans had ever done was as stupid as making war against their own brothers. This political struggle had begun over the price of cotton and the need for New England mills to have it. Throw in a dubious election of a pro-Yankee president, add a few hotheads on both sides, and a lot of teachers, farmers, and lawyers like him found themselves hip-deep in Armageddon.

"I'm no good for Rachel or the boy," he murmured too low for even Blackie to hear. "I'm burned out and burned up." He was better suited to laying waste to farms like this one than he was to raising crops.

He leaned into the wooden handles of the cultivator and clicked to the horse. "Walk on," he said.

The iron teeth turned the surface of the earth as the animal plodded on, and Chance tried to keep his eyes and mind on the task at hand and away from the hopelessness of loving Rachel Irons.

"Rein him tighter!" Rachel called. Her hands itched to put little Davy in a safe spot and take the reins herself. Cultivating was easier than plowing, and she'd done her share. But it was too soon after Davy's birth for her to attempt heavy work, and she'd never shame Chance by showing him what a novice he was.

Whatever hatred and fear she held toward Chance Chancellor had vanished the night he'd delivered her of a healthy son. Southern rebel or devil's brother-in-law, it didn't matter to her. Chance had shown once and for all what kind of man he was, and she'd never forget it.

She'd had no illusions when she'd come to him in the barn. Most men would have run and left her. And Davy would have died without him. Chance had been terrified, but he hadn't deserted her, and when Davy was limp and dying, Chance had found a way to breathe life into him.

She and Chance were bound forever through Davy, and if she had her way, they'd be bound in other ways.

What had happened before she'd gone into labor—when she'd nearly allowed Chance to make love to her—that had been real. "I wonder if you know how much I want you, Chance Chancellor?" she murmured as she draped a blanket over her shoulder and tucked a nipple between Davy's small pink lips. "He doesn't know, does he?" she whispered to the baby. "No, he doesn't, but he will. You lost one daddy, but we're not letting this one get away."

Davy's mouth closed hard on her nipple, and she winced. She was still tender, but other women had told her that this soreness would pass. Her body would adjust to Davy's demands, giving him the exact amount of milk he needed.

She raised her gaze from her small son and studied the man working her garden. He'd improved greatly since she'd caught him in her crab trap; the matted yellow beard was gone, and his finely hewn face had filled out. Even his eyes seemed bluer, less haunted.

He'd rolled his shirtsleeves up above his elbows, but he was sweating so much that the thin linen clung to his arms and shoulders like a second skin. Corded muscles flexed taut from the breadth of his broad shoulders to his long, sinewy thighs.

Horseman's legs, Rachel decided. He was more at home on a horse's back than behind a plow. No infantry-man or artillery soldier—she'd wager Chance Chancellor was a cavalryman and an officer.

But Johnny Reb or not, he was a prize figure of a man. And that sweet way of talking he had was enough to send shivers down a decent widow's spine.

"Some folks would say that we're harboring a traitor, Davy," she whispered to the baby. "But that's not so, is it? As long as we keep him here on Rachel's Choice, he's not shooting at any Union men, is he?"

She chuckled and kissed dark wispy curls on the crown of Davy's head. The baby gave a squeak and sucked even harder. "Patience, love," she said as she switched him from one breast to the other. "It's not easy doing our patriotic duty, is it?"

"Finished!" Chance shouted as he lifted the cultivator teeth and guided the horse around the end of the last row. "We're done!"

"Not by a long sight," Rachel whispered to the baby.

"Not yet, we're not." She waved and threw Chance her sweetest smile. "Wonderful!" she cried. "And now that you've got the hang of it, you can start on the cornfield right after dinner."

Chapter 11

Nearly three weeks later, early one sunny morning, Rachel took Chance to the creek to show him how to put out her crab traps. Since Davy's birth she'd been unable to set her snares, and she was afraid that if she didn't prepare her crab soup and take it to the crossroads for sale, someone else would steal away her business.

Rachel had brought the baby, intending to take him in the rowboat with her, but Chance had protested so strongly that she'd ended up hanging Davy's sling from a tree limb, Indian fashion.

"Taking an infant in a boat. I never heard of such nonsense," Chance grumbled as Rachel dug an oar into the water and turned the bow of the small, flat-bottomed rowboat left and parallel to the creek bank. The boat was crafted of white cedar, light as cork, and weathered to the color of poplar bark.

"This is hardly Delaware Bay," Rachel replied wryly. "We're only a few yards from shore. If the boat sank, I could wade to shore with Davy."

"Maybe," he conceded. "But a tiny baby like that. If you slipped—if his head went underwater—he could easily drown. And you're only five weeks from childbed. You should not be rowing a boat. I could—"

She cut him off with a wave. "You know as much of boats as I know of Latin. I come of hardy stock, Mister Chancellor. Having babies is natural. If I lay abed, who would care for my farm?"

"A lady would never—"

"But I'm no lady, am I?" She laughed at his disapproving expression. "Drop the trap here," she ordered. "I'll not let you spoil this beautiful day with your griping." In truth, she did move a little more slowly than normal, but she was more than capable of maneuvering this little dory.

The flowing water was clear enough to see the sandy bottom. Between the shadow of the boat and a clump of cattails, Rachel caught sight of a sunfish darting silently past to hide in the cool depths.

She'd loved this creek since she was a small child. The natural beauty and ever-changing sounds of the water filled her with an inner peace.

She felt closer to God here than she ever had amid the hymn-singing in her church, and today was particularly soothing. Sunlight sparkled through the canopy of trees, tinting the surface of the water a hundred shades of blue-green, and the air was filled with birdsong and the soft rustle of tree boughs creaking in the wind.

Being here with Chance felt so right. For a little while, she promised herself, she'd forget who he was and the impossibility of loving him. Instead, she'd just enjoy this sweet time and this precious sense of well-being.

On shore Davy's sling swayed slightly, and she could hear him cooing contentedly. Bear lay beside Lady under the tree. The black mastiff's eyes were closed, but Rachel knew that neither animal nor human would get near the baby without a fight. She wasn't sure if the two dogs knew that Davy was a child, not a puppy, but regardless, they'd adopted him as their own. Lady would bare her teeth and Bear's hackles would raise if Chance came too close to Davy without Rachel being in the immediate vicinity.

"Is this where you want this to go?" Chance asked as he balanced a wood-framed wire crab trap on the side of the boat.

She nodded.

Obediently Chance lowered the first of three weighted traps that she'd baited with fish heads into the water.

"Fish isn't the best bait," she explained. "Chicken necks are better, but my hens are all using theirs at the moment."

Chance's face creased in a boyish grin, and Rachel felt a sudden rush of affection for him. He'd caught his slightly curly yellow hair back at the nape of his neck with a leather thong, but it still gleamed like ripe wheat in the bright sunshine.

A pity I had to cut it so irregularly, Rachel thought. She imagined that Chance was as vain as a woman about his looks. For an instant she allowed herself to wonder what he'd looked like in his military uniform.

All spit and polish and sweet Southern charm, she suspected. No doubt he'd set many a poor girl's heart fluttering with that heart-tugging smile that started at the corners of his lips and spread to a dancing twinkle in those startlingly vivid blue eyes.

Rachel waited until the current carried the boat about ten feet away from the first trap, then lowered the tip of her oar to turn the vessel. "Put the next one here," she said.

"This close?"

"I've been catching crabs here since you were in short pants. I guess I know where the good spots are."

She trailed one hand over the side of the boat as he dropped the second trap. She'd bathed this morning in her room, but the creek water felt warm and inviting. She wondered if it was long enough after Davy's birth to safely swim. "One more," she said. "We'll put that last trap in the center of the course, near that cedar stake."

"There's no float for this trap," he replied.

"You don't need one. We'll tie it to the stake."

"You did this by yourself every day—before I came, I mean?"

She looked at him in surprise. Did he think she was as helpless as a Richmond belle? "I didn't move the traps every day, but yes—I did tend them. I told you, I make crab soup and sell it at the store between Frederica and Milford, not far from Barrett's Chapel."

He looked at her again, and this time his blue eyes clouded with compassion. "That's where . . . where Davy's father is buried, isn't it?"

She nodded. "James is there in the Irons family plot."

"He died at Gettysburg?"

Rachel exhaled softly. She didn't want to talk about James. It was too pleasant a morning to dredge up those memories. The good times and the early joy of her marriage were all mixed up with what happened after the war came, but she felt she owed Chance an answer. "Gettysburg killed him, but he didn't die there."

A great blue-gray heron glided over the creek as Chance secured the final trap to the pole and settled on the wooden seat, facing her. Rachel kept her gaze on the graceful bird. She knew that Chance was waiting for her to say more, but the words lodged in her throat like dry gravel.

Hesitantly she moistened her dry lips.

She'd loved James so much for so long, and then he'd changed . . . or she had. It went against her grain to say bad things about the dead, but it was suddenly important to her that Chance know how things had been between her and James before he died.

Slowly the constriction in Rachel's chest eased, and she began to explain.

"I didn't see much of James after he enlisted." She curled her hands tighter around the weathered handles of the oars. The worn cedar had long before lost even a trace of paint, but the nicks and cracks were old, familiar friends.

Water trickled through a seam in the bottom of the boat, wetting her bare feet, and absently she made a mental note to tar the bottom soon.

"Lots of good men had to go to war, Rachel," Chance said quietly.

She nodded, trying not to admit how much she appreciated his attempt to defend her dead husband—his enemy. "But . . ." Rachel inhaled slowly, hoping the tears wouldn't come to shame her. "James took to war as if he'd been born to it."

"Men react in different ways," Chance said. "It's hard for a woman to understand—"

"No." She shook her head. "You asked me, now be still and listen. James did love war. God help him, I think he even liked the killing."

Chance didn't answer, but his jawline hardened.

"Once James marched off," Rachel continued, "I never saw much of him again. A week here, a few days there, in three long years. We'd been married two years before he joined up, but after that—until he was wounded at Gettysburg—I don't believe we spent above three weeks' time in each other's company."

"It must have been lonely for you," Chance said.

"Sometimes." She closed her eyes for just an instant, trying to remember what it had been like when James had gone away and she was left to cope with the long hard days and longer nights in an empty house. How many times had she awakened in the night and lain in her bed weeping for the missing of him?

But that had passed with time. And over the months, her longing for James had become a sinking feeling that he had ceased to love her.

"What hurt most was that I suspected that James didn't always take leave when he was given it. The farm . . . and me . . . We weren't exciting enough for him."

Chance cleared his throat. "Getting leave can be difficult."

Rachel shook her head. "I've a cousin that served in James's regiment. Tom came home on leave, but not my James. Like I said, I think he took to the excitement of war."

"Until Gettysburg."

"He was wounded bad there. As soon as we received word, his father and I took the wagon to a hospital east of there and brought him home more dead than alive. James caught a minié ball on his right shin, and the doctors took his leg off at the knee. They made a sloppy job of it, and it pained him a lot. He had to drink to kill the hurt, or maybe by then he just had to drink."

"He died of infection from the amputation?"

"It never healed properly. I suppose the injury might

have brought about his death in time, if it hadn't been for the weakness in his chest and his thirst for rotgut whiskey. He seemed to get better for a few months." Her voice dropped to a whisper. "He died hard, Chance. He lasted into autumn; then his sickness returned. He went to skin and bone, and he coughed out his life in my arms."

She passed a hand over her eyes and gazed at an oak leaf floating by on the surface of the water. But not before he left me Davy, she thought. She'd never tell Chance that her son was conceived on a night that James had come home drunk and fighting mean. Or that he'd forced her to have sex with him when he stank of another woman's cheap perfume . . .

"Davy is James's legitimate child," she said aloud. "James was well enough for that between his bouts of fever. If you were thinking—"

"I wasn't thinking he wasn't," Chance answered gruffly. "Why would you—"

"I won't have you think me cheap or Davy a bastard." She let go of the left oar and raised her palm to silence him. "Let me say this. What I did—what we did—here on the creek bank the night Davy was born . . ." She took a breath and tried to make the words come out right. "There's not been another man in my life since James and I took our wedding vows. I came to him a virgin, and I never cheated on him while he was away at war—never wanted to."

"He's dead, Rachel. You're a widow. What you do now—"

"What I do now is between me and my God," she said, hoping that he couldn't hear her heart hammering inside her chest. "I'm no whore, Chance Chancellor, but I want you to know that I'm not sorry for what we did."

"I don't want you to be sorry. I want you to—"

Davy's wail cut through Chance's answer. Instantly Rachel twisted around to see what was wrong. At the same time, she spun the bow of the boat and leaned hard into the oars to push the small craft toward the bank.

A mockingbird flew up from the branch above the baby's head, and Davy's tiny fists flailed angrily. Neither dog had stirred from their spot on the grass.

"What's wrong, Davy?" Rachel called as the bird began to scold loudly from the safety of the treetop. "Did the mockingbird scare you?"

"No wonder he's frightened," Chance said. "A tree is a damned odd place for a baby, if you ask me."

Rachel scoffed. "You don't want me to take him in the rowboat or leave him on shore. Just what should I do with him?"

"Stay with him. Mothers shouldn't—"

"What mothers, Chance? Mothers who have slaves or nursemaids to care for their children? I'm a farmer's wife. I . . ." She broke off, realizing that she wasn't a farmer's wife anymore.

"I didn't mean—"

"What you know about babies I could heap in a nutshell," she said. "How many times must I tell you? I'm a plain woman. I'm not wealthy enough to have servants. I'll tend my boy as I tend my farm. Don't worry on his account. I'll let no harm come to him. And so long as you keep your share of the bargain and help me get in this year's crop, you won't owe me or Davy anything."

Chance's shoulders stiffened. "I meant no insult. I could have put out the traps by myself. I've not done it before, but I can learn." The bow of the boat touched shore and Chance climbed out.

He strode to the tree and lifted Davy down despite Bear's warning growl. "Shh, shh, baby boy. It's all right," he soothed as he shifted baby and sling onto his good shoulder and began to pat the infant's back gently. When Davy continued to flail his arms and legs and scream, Chance parted his shirt so that the baby could snuggle against his bare chest.

Davy's shrieks became sobs and then hiccups.

Rachel's pique dissolved in an instant. Not one male in a hundred had such an easy way with infants, she thought. James never would; he'd been terrified of small children.

Chance jiggled the baby and looked back at her. "Am I doing this right?"

"Davy seems to think so." She averted her eyes and climbed carefully from the boat. Her breasts were full and tight, and whenever her son cried, they ached. She was beginning to leak milk onto the bodice of her blouse. "Give me the baby," she said as she reached for him.

"He's fine," Chance replied. "I've just got him settled."

Rachel looked down at her chest. "I need him," she said. She hoped that if Chance noticed her blouse, he'd think the dark spots nothing but water. "He's hungry."

Frowning, he handed her the child.

Rachel cuddled Davy against her. God, but he smells sweet, she thought, sweeter than salvation. A sensible woman should be satisfied with such a little miracle as Davy and ask for nothing else of life.

She kissed the crown of his fuzzy head, and he uttered a contented sound that made her go all soft inside.

"Doubtless you can find more for me to do in the garden," Chance said.

She glanced up at him. "The garden could probably use another turn. Unless you wanted to hoe the corn."

"I've cultivated your damned cornfield until I've got blisters on my calluses. There's nothing left to—"

"Weeds grow, Chance."

"You're awfully bossy today."

"I gave you your choice, the garden or the corn."

"Some choice." He grinned at her. "You love this, don't you? You don't mind the long hours in the fields or the waiting to see if it will rain."

"No, I don't mind the work." She turned her back and tucked Davy under her oversize blouse so that he could nurse. "I do worry when the rain doesn't fall."

Davy tugged vigorously at her nipple, and she smiled down at him. "Not so fast," she cautioned. "You'll choke yourself."

"Can't blame him," Chance murmured.

"Mind your tongue, sir," she warned. It was strange how a woman could feel so needed when a babe suckled at her breast. The sensation was nothing like what she experienced when a man did the same thing. Both were wonderful and miraculous, but nothing alike.

"My mother never did that."

"What?"

"Nursed her children."

"Oh." She knew that well-to-do women gave their babies to hired girls to suckle, but she'd never been able to understand the practice.

"Mother is very proud of her figure," Chance explained. "She would have feared to spoil it."

"My grandmother fed me on goat's milk until I was

old enough to eat solid food. I can remember being very small and sitting on my grandfather's lap, drinking milk from a coffee cup. He never talked much, but he didn't have to. I always felt safe in my granddad's lap." She switched Davy from one breast to the other. "There you go, you greedy little piggy," she whispered.

"Your father didn't object to your grandparents keeping you?"

She laughed. "I didn't lay eyes on Father until my eighth birthday. He and my grandfather couldn't stand one another. I think Father was afraid of Granddad."

"You had a strange childhood."

"Not for me. It was the way things were." She patted Davy's round little bottom and snuggled him against her. "Later, when I did come to know my father, I was fascinated by what he did. Grandmother taught me a lot of what I know about healing, but I wanted more. If Father hadn't been a doctor, I doubt I would ever have spent any time with him."

Davy lost interest in the breast, and Rachel shifted him to her shoulder and burped him. "What of your own father, Chance? Did you love him?" She turned back to face Chance.

"Love my father? Of course."

"You spent a lot of time with him? Did he take you fishing? Did he teach you to swim?"

Chance laughed. "My father was a very busy man, an important lawyer. He often traveled to Washington and Philadelphia to consult on other—"

"But what about you?" she demanded. "Did he teach you to ride a horse?"

"He paid for the finest instruction and an imported

Welsh pony. When I outgrew the pony, he bought me a thoroughbred—"

"Granddad taught me to ride on a workhorse," Rachel said. "Bareback."

"Barefoot as well, I suppose."

"How did you guess? You're a snob," she teased. "I'll wager I had as much fun riding the cows and the pigs as you did—"

"My fancy horses," he finished for her. "I think you're the one who's the snob, Rachel Irons. And I believe I know just the right medicine for that."

"Oh you do, do you?"

Chance took a step toward her. "Yes, ma'am."

A warning twinge raised the hairs on the nape of Rachel's neck. "Chance . . . What are you—"

But she'd waited too long. His arms went around her and the baby, and his mouth came down on hers. This time she didn't struggle for more than a second.

She assumed he'd meant the kiss to be a teasing one, but in the heartbeat's space between the meeting of their lips and the heat that leaped between them, all that changed.

Rachel tumbled headlong into his caress as her knees turned to butter and her insides dissolved in a flurry of bird wings. He wasn't kissing her so much as devouring her, and she had no defense against him.

She was vaguely aware of Chance's fingers tugging at the ribbons of her bonnet while his other hand molded to the small of her back. She was trembling so that she was afraid she'd drop Davy.

Her wide-brimmed straw hat slid off her head. He pulled out her hairpins one after another until the heavy mass of her unbound tresses tumbled loosely around her shoulders. And then his mouth left her throbbing one and kissed a fiery trail down her throat.

Rachel sucked in a ragged breath, and Davy began to scream at the top of his lungs. Chance released her so fast that she nearly lost her balance and fell.

"I'm sorry," he managed. "The baby. I shouldn't—"

"He's all right. He's fine." Rachel took another breath and shook her head. It was hard to think, impossible to reason.

"He's frightened."

Davy's howls reached fever pitch, and she rocked him in her arms. "It's all right," she repeated. The baby sniffed several times and began to hiccup loudly once more. Real tears were streaking his face.

"Is he hurt? I didn't—"

"Tears," she said in astonishment. "His first tears."

Davy's gaze met hers, and the pout became a beaming smile that started at the corners of his precious mouth and spread to every curve of his chubby little face.

"He's smiling," Chance said. "Look at that. Isn't he too young to smile?"

Ignoring his question, she risked a glance into his face and saw to her satisfaction that Chance was as shaken as she was by the intensity of their heated kisses. His cheeks were flushed, and his blue eyes still smoldered with an inner fire that made her go all warm and shivery inside.

He wants me, she thought . . . as much as I want him.

She ached to have him touch her breasts, to have him kiss and lick them as he had on the night Davy was born. She could feel the growing need inside her, a yearning that made her skin feel too tight and her hands itch to touch his hair and skim her fingers over his lips and tangle in his yellow hair.

Just thinking about him made her damp and slick between her thighs. This was something she'd never known before, even though she'd been a wife for five years.

She had loved James, but he'd never sent sensations ripping through her body like this. James's lazy lovemaking had been warm and comfortable, an easy coming together that left her feeling satisfied and sleepy.

Not like this . . .

Nothing had prepared her for this wild urge to forget that it was midmorning and that she had a babe to tend . . . forget everything but pulling up her skirts and lying here with Chance in the thick green grass.

She wanted to know the feel of him inside her and arch to the thrust of his swollen shaft as he poured his hot seed into her womb.

Rachel swallowed, wondering if Chance could read her mind . . . almost hoping that he could.

"Rachel?"

"I think we all need cooling off," she said, then turned and splashed waist-deep into the creek with Davy clasped tightly in her arms.

Chapter 12

"Woman, you are impossible," Chance declared after he'd followed her into the water.

"Because I think we're doing something we'll both regret?" She sank backward in the water until she was wet from the nape of her neck to the soles of her bare feet.

"Give me that baby," he said. "There's no need to drown him because you've taken leave of your senses."

She let go of Davy and watched from the corner of her eye as Chance carried him back to shore. The water felt good, but that wasn't why she'd plunged in. She'd taken the only escape route available before she'd done the unthinkable.

Heaven help her, she wanted him with a fire that would not be banked down or smothered under the ashes of her responsibilities.

If she allowed Chance to make love to her, it would be she who faced an illegitimate pregnancy, not he. He'd be gone, leaving her to face the shame. Not that she was totally ignorant of ways to prevent conceiving an unwanted child, but the aids in her father's medical chest had been known to fail.

She should never have let things progress so far

between them. He was here to bring in her crop—nothing more. And if he didn't like it, that was his concern.

Rachel was still on edge hours later when she bid Chance good night and locked her kitchen door. More perturbed at her own foolishness than his, she climbed the stairs and flung herself facedown on her bed.

Davy was fed and sleeping; the two dogs sprawled on the floor at the foot of the steps. They slept, but she couldn't. She lay awake listening to the wind rattling the loose shutter on the back of the house.

The day, which had begun with such promise, had given way to scattered rain and impending thunderstorms. Branches growing from the big yellow poplar scraped against one chimney, and patters of rain beat an uneven tattoo against the windowpanes.

Restlessly Rachel pounded her pillow into shape and then tossed it to the far corner of the old-fashioned high bed. "I probably wouldn't have become pregnant," she muttered. The women in her family found it difficult to conceive. Both she and her mother were only children, and she hadn't taken any precautions before Davy was born, years into her marriage with James.

She wondered if she'd avoided certain unhappiness by rejecting Chance's offer, or insured it. He'd made no promises. And if he had, what did she really know of him besides what he had told her?

There were depths of sorrow in Chance Chancellor that his laughing manner could not hide. He might not hide his pain in a bottle as James had done, but Chance was weighed down by a troubled soul.

Far off, beyond the Murderkill, lightning illuminated the sky, and a rolling cascade of thunder rumbled ominously. Rachel raised her head and glanced toward the cherrywood cradle where Davy slept soundly.

"Why can't I be content with what I have?" she whispered more to herself than to her little son.

The only answer was the gathering force of the wind-driven rain and the slow, measured tick of her china wedding clock on the mantel.

Rising from the bed, Rachel went to her dressing table and began to remove her hairpins, one by one. The shadowed face looking back at her from her mirror seemed too full, too vulnerable to be her own reflection, but the eyes were hers and they could not hide the truth.

She wanted Chance.

Slowly, stunned, she sank into a chair and let the implications of this decision sink in.

Not for a few moments of pleasure, not even for a secret affair of passion; she wanted him as she had once wanted James . . . with wedding vows and gold rings and promises of growing old together. Forever.

She did. And she was willing to risk everything to have him.

The thunderstorm rolled over the farm and faded in the east. Davy woke, and Rachel fed him again and rocked him back to sleep before blowing out the candle, donning a clean linen nightgown, and climbing between the sheets herself. As she drifted off to sleep, she heard the first echoes of a second storm approaching.

Sometime later she was awakened by a loud banging on the kitchen door and Bear's deep-throated bark interspersed with Lady's incessant one.

Rachel scrambled out of bed, still half-asleep, and made her way to the landing of the front staircase without lighting a candle. Outside, wind and rain beat against the house, and a dull boom of thunder added to the reverberating discord. She'd been yanked from a dream of the kiss she'd shared with Chance. Her pulse raced as she hurried downstairs to let him in.

Had he changed his mind? Decided that he couldn't bear another moment apart? Or had lightning struck the barn? she wondered as she crossed the sitting room to the kitchen.

"What is it, Chance?" she called out. "Quiet! Quiet!" she ordered the dogs. A brilliant flash momentarily blinded her as she yanked the bolt and swung open the back door.

A tall, bulky figure filled the doorway. Lady charged past Rachel and out into the yard.

"Chance, I—"

The collie's bark deepened to a threatening growl.

Bear's angry snarl raised the hair on the back of Rachel's neck. Sensing that something was wrong, she tried to close the door.

A man's yell was followed by a heavy thud. Lady yipped once and then squealed in pain.

A heavy weight slammed the door back, catching Rachel and flinging her against the wall as Bear lunged at the intruder.

A split second later, a pistol blast rattled the kitchen windows. Bear's roar twisted to an agonized yelp before he slumped to the floor and his whining ceased.

Head ringing, Rachel gasped for breath.

"Get up, woman! Ye ain't hurt."

The stranger's slurred words were so heavily accented that Rachel had difficulty understanding him.

"Ya kilt her, Cleve," declared another man. "Ya promised me ya wouldn't do that this time." His was a youth's voice, awkward and unlettered, but just as chilling.

Rachel crouched motionless as the pain in her head receded to a dull ache. Two of them, she thought. Two rebs had forced their way into her house. She didn't need to see them; she could smell their unwashed bodies, the oily hair, and rotting wool uniforms. And above all that she caught a scent of putrid flesh and raw whiskey.

"Ye alone here, woman?" Cleve demanded.

"Yes." She thought she heard Lady whine outside the door, but the fury of wind and rain made it impossible to tell. Bear lay motionless. "You killed my dog, you bastard."

"Shut yer trap or you'll be next," the boy threatened. "That beast bit me clean to the bone."

"You sure there ain't nobody else here?"

That was the one called Cleve, the bigger man, the one giving the orders. "Just me," she said.

A wail from upstairs proved her a liar. And the fear welling inside Rachel turned to icy hatred. They might have gotten Bear, but she'd see them in hell before they'd harm her son.

"No one's here but me and my baby," she covered quickly.

"Lie to us, Yankee woman, and we'll kill ya certain," Cleve threatened.

The boy laughed. "Kill you certain," he repeated. "Maybe kill you certain anyway."

"Shut up, Harley."

"Ya heard him. Cleve'll shoot you like he shot that damned devil dog of yourn."

Another flash of lightning showed a man's outline near the stove. She heard the scrape of an iron stove plate and then saw a faint glow of coals. The scent of a cheap cigar drifted toward her.

"Ye got a lamp, Yankee woman?"

"I do." Her head hurt so badly that it was hard to think.

"Light it," he ordered.

Rachel pushed her way up the wall and moved cautiously toward the table. Davy's frantic cries stiffened her resolve. No matter what happened to her, Davy mattered most—Davy and Chance. She couldn't let herself fall to pieces.

"Be quick about it," Harley said.

Rachel's searching fingers found the edge of the tablecloth. Forcing her hands to remain steady, she located the oil lamp and her blue glass bottle of matches. In seconds a yellow light flared, illuminating the kitchen.

The hulking brute by the stove leaned on a rifle and leered at her with hooded eyes. His tattered shirt hung open to the waist; his trousers ended in rags that left both scabbed knees exposed. The crown of his head was bald, but tangled gray locks straggled down over his shoulders from a monk's fringe above his ears. His nose had been broken more than once; it ran crookedly down his face to end in a ragged red scar and shattered, green-furred teeth.

"Well, well, Harley, lookee here. We found us a pretty one, ain't we?"

"Looks like," his scarecrow companion agreed.

Rachel spared him a glance, taking in his knife-blade face, pasty skin, and thickly bandaged hand. Seventeen, she thought, not a day older. And not likely to see eighteen if the hand wasn't tended to. He was the source of the foul stench of putrefaction. By the looks of the stained cloth wrapped around his fist, he had a raging infection.

In his good hand the boy held an old rusty pistol, barrel pointing in her direction. But she refused to allow terror to make her stupid. Armed or not, this overgrown child with the wounded wing could be dealt with. It was Cleve who worried her.

She looked back at the older man with the rifle. "What do you want? Food? Money? I've plenty of the first and none of the second. There's a horse in the barn. You're welcome to it." She tried to smile at him. "You're greatly mistaken if you think I'm a Yankee sympathizer. My brother's serving in the Confederate navy."

"Yeah?" Harley's mouth sagged open.

"Shut up, you fool," Cleve said. "She's lyin' to save her own skin."

Rachel wouldn't allow herself to guess where the two had stolen the guns or to wonder if the red stain down the front of Harley's shirt was Chance's blood.

Where was Chance? Had they gone to the barn first and murdered him? If they hadn't, had he heard the gunshot and known she was in trouble? Or had he simply believed the boom to be thunder?

Her knees felt as though they'd buckle under her; each breath was an effort, but she wouldn't let them see how terrified she was. "Are you hungry?" she asked.

"Cool one, ain't ye, Yankee woman." Cleve slid aside the metal lid and spat tobacco juice into the stove. "Mayhap me and Harley kin warm ye up a little."

"My husband and his brothers are due back before morning," she lied. "You'd best make tracks before they get here. My brother-in-law is a sheriff's deputy."

"Comin' in afore mornin'," Cleve taunted her. "Ye take us fer fools, woman? Ain't no men here." He glanced around the kitchen. "No men's boots, no pipe or razor strap. Just you and the young'n, I 'spect."

He took a step toward her, and Harley chuckled.

Rachel wanted to run, but Cleve stood between her and the door, and Davy lay helpless upstairs in his cradle. "I can tend that hand for you," she offered. "It looks festered."

"You got whiskey?" Harley asked.

"No whiskey, but I can drain the poison and wash—"

"Maybe she wants to give ye a bath, Harley?" Cleve suggested.

"M'leg hurts worse than the hand," the boy said. "Damn dog near chewed my leg to ribbons."

Davy's cry tore at Rachel's insides. "I need to go to my baby," she said.

"What you got up there?" Cleve asked. "A rifle? Shotgun?"

"Maybe one of them li'l old sissy pistols," Harley supplied.

"Go up and fetch yer young'n down, Yankee woman," Cleve said. "Harley, here, can trail along to see that ye don't get into nothin' ye shouldn't."

"No." Rachel shook her head. She didn't want Davy near them. He was safer where he was. "You leave my baby be. I won't give you any trouble."

"Course ye won't," the big man agreed. He took a step toward her. "Get up there and git that brat."

Rachel lit a second lantern and walked back through the parlor and up the front stairs. The narrow kitchen passageway would have been quicker, but she hoped the intruders wouldn't realize that the small door led to the second floor as well.

She'd thought of grabbing Davy and climbing out a

window, or digging her granddad's old pistol out of the chest. But with Harley hot on her heels, she could do nothing.

Davy was screaming at the top of his lungs. Feeding him would calm his anger, but she didn't want to bare her breasts in front of these animals. When she reached her bedroom, she carefully set the lamp on a table. Snatching up a dressing gown from the chair, she flung it around her shoulders as she went to her son.

"Please," she said to Harley. "Don't hurt my baby."

"What's he to me? I seen many a grown man cut down. A squalling Yankee brat don't matter to me."

"I told you, we're not Yankees. We're Southern sympathizers here," she lied. "Lots of folks in lower Delaware are." She gathered Davy into her arms, pulling the folds of the dressing gown around them both and cradling him against her breast. Where was Chance? she agonized. She refused to believe that he was dead.

Davy's cries subsided as he found her nipple. Rachel held him against her and motioned with her chin toward a dresser on the far wall. "There's jewelry in that box," she said to Harley. "Take what you want."

"Don't try no tricks wi' me."

"A gold locket," she murmured, "and a man's pocket watch."

He seized the leather box and dumped the contents on the bed. Her mother's locket and chain tangled with an old copper brooch and her grandfather's silver watch. Harley scooped up everything in his hat. "Gosh dern, look at this!" he exclaimed. "I ain't never had me no watch."

"What's takin' so long up there?" Cleve shouted.

"We're coming," Rachel answered. And then to Harley

she whispered, "Put the watch in your pocket. Otherwise, he'll just take it from you."

Harley loomed over her, and she shuddered from his stench. "You got money hid somewhere?" he demanded.

"Do I look like I've got money?"

He grabbed a handful of her hair and twisted it until tears welled up in her eyes. "We got waysa makin' you tell." He groped at her with dirty fingers.

"Let go of me," she cried, twisting away. "You'll lose that hand if it's not looked after. At least let me wash it and put on a fresh bandage."

His grip loosened and she backed away. "You don't want to die, do you?" she asked. "You need medical attention."

"Harley!" Cleve bellowed from downstairs.

The boy shoved her toward the steps. "Ya gonna fix us some bacon and eggs," he said. "Ya got eggs?"

"Yes," she replied, glaring at him. "Mind your manners." Inside she was shaking with fear, but she knew that any sign of weakness would be her downfall.

"I want bacon and eggs, and some white gravy and biscuits," Harley replied. "We ain't et decent in months. Then you kin tend that dog bite and this here hand. After that . . ." He laughed suggestively. "After ya kin find some other way to be nice to us. I ain't never had me no Yankee woman."

"I told you, I'm not a Yankee." She blew out the lamp, then hurried to the hall landing, keeping her distance from Harley.

Davy squirmed in Rachel's arms as she descended the stairs. She was so terrified that she felt numb inside. The thought of rape by these two sickened her. Even worse was her growing suspicion that they meant to kill her and

Davy before they left. Oh, Chance, where are you? she screamed silently.

"Ye swivin' her up there?" Cleve asked Harley as they came back into the kitchen.

"You promised me first go at her," the younger soldier said.

"I ain't done wrong by ye yet, have I, boy?" Cleve asked. "We may want to hole up here a few days. If we do, they'll be plenty of lovin' for both of us, won't there, gal?"

Rachel didn't answer. Averting her eyes, she circled around him to tuck Davy into the wood box behind the stove. The baby fussed momentarily and then popped a fat thumb into his mouth. She whispered a silent prayer and pulled the lid of the container over him.

"Your friend says you're hungry," Rachel said as she straightened. "I've got roast pork hanging in the well," she lied. "If you want me—"

"Bacon and lots of it," Cleve said. He pointed to a smoked haunch hanging from a rafter.

"Eggs," Harley chimed in. "And biscuits. Don't forget the biscuits." He spilled the jewelry onto the table, and Rachel noticed that her grandfather's watch was missing.

Good, she thought. If she could pit the two against each other, she might find a way to save Davy.

Bear's massive body lay sprawled by the door. A pool of blood soaked into the rug near his head. Rachel couldn't resist kneeling beside him and stroking his thick fur. To her surprise, she felt a slight movement beneath her hand.

"Bear," she whispered. The dog's eyes were closed, but he was warm to the touch. She skimmed her fingers over his neck and head, quickly locating the furrow where the bullet had grazed his skull.

"Git away from thet dog," Cleve said.

"You didn't have to kill him," she protested.

Harley chuckled and pointed the pistol at Bear. "Pow!" he taunted.

Rachel drew a slow, deep breath. Bear was alive. How long he'd lain without moving, she didn't know, but she had to think of something fast. If they guessed that he wasn't dead, they'd only shoot him again.

Turning away from Cleve, Rachel walked to the pump and began to wash her hands. As she did, she glanced at the rain-streaked window. And for just an instant, in the flash of lightning, she caught sight of Chance's face.

He put a finger over his lips and vanished so swiftly that she wondered if she had really seen him or if it was her imagination.

"What was that?" Harley said, coming to the pump. "I thought I saw . . ."

"What?" Cleve demanded.

"Lightning," Rachel said. "I think it struck a tree in the yard."

Harley elbowed her out of the way and stared through the windowpanes. Thunder rumbled overhead, and gusts of wind battered the house.

Suddenly Rachel heard the sound of shattering glass from the parlor. Clive and Harley lunged across the room, and Rachel dashed to the table and blew out the lamp.

Chapter 13

The kitchen was plunged into total darkness. Rachel ducked behind the stove, snatched Davy from the wood box, and fled out the back door into the pouring rain.

Her only thought was to get the baby to safety. If she took the boat, she could escape up the creek, or she could run into the woods and through the marsh to Cora Wright's farm. But doing either of these things meant leaving Chance alone to face two armed men.

She stopped running just outside the barn door. *Chance.* She couldn't abandon him any more than she could have deserted little Davy.

It took only seconds to dart around the side of the barn to the empty sheep shed. Even in the pitch dark Rachel could find the gate and feel her way to the manger. She laid a screaming Davy inside and heaped dry hay around him to keep him warm. "God keep you," she whispered before dashing back to the house.

The door was open, as she'd left it, and the house was still. From the formal parlor, on the other side of the front staircase, came another crash of glass and breaking furniture. She thought she heard Bear whimper as she crossed the room and ran up the kitchen steps.

The spare room above opened into a hall; from there

she could reach her bedchamber. Rachel didn't need a light; she'd been raised in this house and knew every inch of it. Beside the fireplace, in a narrow cupboard, stood a double-barrel shotgun. Grabbing the heavy weapon, she crept down the front stairs.

She nearly reached the bottom when a pistol went off. Cleve swore, and a bottle rolled across the floor.

"Damn you, Harley, ya got me!"

She froze, trembling from head to foot. She wanted to call out to Chance—to know if he was alive or dead, but she knew that if she spoke, she'd give away her position. She clenched her teeth to keep them from chattering and waited in total darkness.

Finally, when several minutes passed, she could stand the suspense no longer. "Put your hands up!" she cried. "I've got a shotgun, and I'll use it!"

"Get down!" Chance yelled from only an arm's length away. He flung himself over her, knocking her back against the steps and pinning the heavy shotgun between them as Cleve's rifle spat fire and lead.

The ball tore through the banister and smashed a hole in the parlor wall. Splinters of wood sprayed Rachel's arm.

"Are you hurt?" Chance demanded.

"No . . . I don't think so," she replied breathlessly. His weight pinned her against the steps, and his nearness was nearly as unnerving as being shot at.

"Give me the gun." It was impossible to ignore the authority in his voice.

Without arguing, Rachel released the weapon. As he rose, she twisted under him and scrambled up the steps.

"Don't move a muscle," Chance shouted from below. "Breathe and I'll blow you to hell."

Rachel shivered. She'd lived side by side with this man for weeks and had never heard this deadly tone.

"Drop your guns and kick them away."

"Yer bluffin'," Cleve answered.

One barrel blasted. Window glass and wood shattered.

Rachel dived onto the floor of her bedroom and lay there with her heart racing.

"Still think I'm bluffing?" Chance asked. "This is a double, and I'm saving the last shell for the first one of you who—"

"I got my hands up!" Harley shouted.

"Same here," Cleve mumbled.

"Rachel, bring a lamp!"

"All right," she answered. She found the table and matchbox, but her hands were shaking so hard that she dropped it and matches scattered across the rug. She got down on her hands and knees to retrieve them.

On the second try she struck a spark and ignited the oil-soaked wick. Seconds later she descended the steps with the oil lamp in hand.

Rain-laden wind blew through the smashed window into the parlor. Harley and Cleve stood with raised hands in the far corner of the room. Cleve's trouser leg was soaked with blood, and both men's faces showed evidence of a fight. Chance held them at bay with her shotgun. One eye and his lower lip were swollen, and the knuckles on his right hand were bleeding, but he didn't seem to have suffered any serious injuries.

Rachel lifted the lamp and surveyed the damage. A table was overturned, two chairs and a whale-oil lamp were smashed, and bottles were broken. A marble mortar and pestle lay on the floor, and brass scales were flattened. A leather box of dental instruments had been overturned in the confusion and lay trampled underfoot.

"No need to cause such a fuss, Cap'n," Cleve said. "We didn't hurt the woman."

"We're on the same side," Harley reminded Chance.

Chance glanced at Rachel. "Set that lamp down, pick up their weapons, and fetch some strong rope."

She nodded, still too shaken to speak.

"How come a fine Southern boy like you ain't fightin' fer the *cause*?" Cleve demanded as Rachel snatched up his rifle from the floor.

"Get down," Chance said. "Slow and easy. Hands behind your head."

Harley, face bleached to the color of a dead flounder, was blubbering and begging for mercy. Trying not to feel pity for him, Rachel retrieved his pistol and returned to Chance's side.

Chance examined the handgun and tucked it into his belt. His countenance was grim, his movements controlled. Tingles of apprehension skittered down Rachel's spine. She could taste sulfur in the air; at any second, she expected him to squeeze the trigger again.

"What you gonna do wi' us?" Harley dropped to his knees. "Ya can't shoot us. We're willing to share, fair 'n' square. We're yer own kind."

"Shut up, Harley," Cleve muttered as he stretched out on the glass-covered rug.

"The rope," Chance reminded Rachel.

She found a length behind the wood box and cut it in two. Chance handed her the shotgun. "If either of them makes a move, shoot the other one," he ordered. "I'll take care of the first."

Neither intruder risked Rachel's aim. Chance fastened

the prisoners' hands behind their backs and hobbled their legs. Finally he linked the two men together, neck to neck, leaving just enough rope for them to walk.

"Will you be all right here?" Chance asked her, exchanging Cleve's rifle for the shotgun. "Lock yourself in the house and don't be afraid to use this if you have to. I'm going to take them far enough away so that they won't be a danger to you."

"I've got to get Davy," she said. "I put him in the sheepfold." Her knees were weak, and she was terrified, but she couldn't leave her son outside.

"Yer lettin' us go, Cap'n?" Harley whined.

"Get the baby," Chance said. "I'll wait until you get back. I can't be certain if there are any more like these two running loose tonight."

As Rachel hurried through the kitchen, she stopped to light a second lamp and then a lantern. Apprehensively she paused to check Bear again and found his eyes partially open and his breathing stronger. "Good boy," she murmured. "Good dog."

The mastiff tried to raise his head.

"You'll be fine," she promised. Bear's pitiful whine made her throat tighten. "I'll make you better."

If Bear had survived, then perhaps Lady might be alive as well, Rachel reasoned. She stepped out the back door. The rainfall had slackened to a light mist, and the occasional flash of lightning shimmered far off on the horizon.

"Lady! Here, Lady!" she called. But there was no familiar answering bark. "Lady!"

Then her heart plummeted as she caught sight of the still form lying in the shadows of the house. "Oh, Lady!" she cried.

Oblivious to the mud, she knelt beside the collie and threw her arms around her. "You were faithful to the end, weren't you, old girl," she whispered. Tears slid down Rachel's cheeks, and for a minute or two she weakened and wept uncontrollably.

Her eyes were still red and swollen when she returned to the kitchen with Davy. The baby was sound asleep and seemed none the worse for his adventure. She kissed the crown of his head and laid him on the daybed. She was propping a pillow beside him to prevent him from falling off when Chance came in.

She looked at him. "What will you do with them?"

He frowned and shifted the shotgun from one arm to the other. "What do you suggest?"

Shoot them, she wanted to cry. Shoot them as you would any vermin. But she bit back her ire and went to the stove reservoir for warm water. "My Lady's dead," she murmured. "They killed her."

"I know. I stumbled over her in the yard. I'm sorry."

"And they shot Bear." She found a cloth and some soap to wash Bear's wound and set the bowl down on the dry sink. "The bullet made a nasty gash along his skull," she explained as she turned to face Chance. "He lost a lot of blood, but I think he'll be all right."

"You thought they could protect you, didn't you?" he declared hotly. "You've no business out here alone. Do you know what would have happened to you if I hadn't been here?"

She recoiled. "This is my home," she answered. "Where else would I go?"

"In town, where it's safe. Damn it, woman. Don't you realize that there's a war going on?"

"You've no right to talk to me like that! I'm grateful

for your help, but I saved your neck, and don't you forget it."

He laid the shotgun across the table and seized her shoulders. "Rachel, I—"

Suddenly her righteous anger turned to something else. She flung her arms around his neck and kissed him. His hard mouth softened under her assault, and he enfolded her in a crushing embrace.

"Rachel," he whispered.

The intensity of his searing kiss stripped away the last of her defenses. She parted her lips and welcomed the thrust of his hot tongue and the feel of his hands on her body.

"Chance, Chance," she murmured. For a few brief seconds the world faded, leaving her alone with him, caught in the maelstrom of a kiss that seemed to go on and on.

And then he gently pushed her away. "This isn't the time."

She drew in a ragged breath. "I don't want you to go away," she whispered. "I want you to stay with me."

"I don't want to go, but I must," he answered huskily. "I have to get these two away from the farm."

"I don't mean that," she replied. "I mean I want you to *stay* here on Rachel's Choice. Don't you want me?"

His face flushed with emotion. "You know I do." He caught a loose lock of her hair and rubbed it between his fingertips. "It's all wrong for us."

"Because you're a rich lawyer and I'm the grand-daughter of an Indian?"

"Damn it, Rachel," he flung back. "We're past all that, you and me. I'm a soldier. I have to go back to the war, and you . . ." He swallowed. "There's no place in your life for a Confederate—"

"You promised me!" she said. "You gave your word to me that you'd get my crop in."

He nodded. "I did, and I mean to keep my promise. But when fall comes, I'll leave. It wouldn't be fair to you if I made promises I can't keep."

"The war won't last forever."

"Rachel, listen to me." He cupped her chin in his hand. "Darlin' Rachel, the war widowed you once. I'll not let you wait and hope for me to return. You deserve better than what I could give. I'm a cavalry officer. In a charge I'm out in front, leading my men. If I were a betting man, I'd make no wager on my staying alive to see the end of this conflict."

She was trembling from head to foot. "I'll not ask you to give up your cursed war, Chance Chancellor. I ask only that you love me for a little while. Until you have to go. Can't we accept our fortune and enjoy what time we have?"

"Do you know what you're saying, Rachel?"

"No ties, Chance. We'll live for here and now, and we'll let the future take care of itself."

"And if I leave you with an unwanted baby?"

"Never unwanted if it's your child." She hadn't known that she felt that way until the words came tumbling out, but it was true. If she did quicken with Chance's child, she would always have a small part of him, and she would love it as fiercely as she loved wee Davy.

"You're serious," he said, stepping back and gazing into her face. "You're willing for me . . . for us . . ." He trailed off as she began to weep again. "Don't cry." He pulled her into his arms again. "It tears my heart out when you cry."

"Can't you pretend to want me?" she whispered, pressing her face into his chest.

"I don't have to pretend," he grated. "It's not that you're not good enough for me, Rachel. It's me, it's what I've done . . . what I have to do."

"For a little while," she begged.

He swallowed. "So long as you know it's only—"

"Until harvest," she finished.

He kissed her again, and she clung to him as though she were drowning.

Davy's fussing cry tore her away.

Chance straightened and picked up the shotgun. "I'll take them away now. Stay inside until I return. It may not be until morning."

"If you turn them in to the authorities, they'll tell on you," she said. "You'll be arrested as well."

He nodded. "Where are the extra shells for this gun?"

"Upstairs, in my bedroom. I'll get them for you."

"Tell me where. I'll find the shells."

"You can't let them go," she said. "I think they've committed murder. They're bad men, Chance, awful men."

"I'll make sure that they won't come back to harm you or Davy." He put her grandfather's watch into her hand. "I think this is yours."

She nodded. "Yes, it is. But what are you going to do with them?"

"Don't ask me that," he replied in a low voice that made her shiver.

"But . . ."

"Not now or ever."

Rachel cleaned and tended the wound on Bear's head, then left the house to bring hammer and nails and sail-cloth from the barn to cover the window. She swept up the glass and stacked the broken chairs for repair, then returned to the kitchen to wait.

Sometime in the hours between midnight and dawn, Davy woke. Rachel fed him and sang him back to sleep. Bear lapped a little water from his bowl and crawled to Rachel's feet. The head wound was still seeping blood, but the dog's eyes seemed clearer, and she was certain that time would heal his injury.

Wide awake, Rachel continued to rock, still holding the baby in her arms. Davy's soft, steady breathing and the feel of his warm little body against her breast eased her heart.

Shortly before daylight Chance returned. Bear's whine alerted Rachel, and she put Davy on the daybed and picked up the rifle.

"It's me," Chance called.

She let him in and bolted the door.

"I put Lady in the barn," Chance said. "If you'll stir up some coffee, I'll bury her."

She nodded. "Near the creek. Where the sun will keep her old bones warm."

His hair was wet, his clothing relatively dry. "I took a swim," he explained.

She wanted to ask about the two rebs, but she didn't dare. "Would you like breakfast?" she asked. She was suddenly shy. Only a few hours before, she'd agreed to be his woman—to sleep with him without the benefit of marriage—but she was so weary that she couldn't think straight. And now that there was nothing holding them apart, this seemed the wrong time.

"Just coffee," he replied. "You go back to bed. You look worse than I feel." He flashed a slow grin at her, and suddenly the room seemed to brighten.

"I'll take the baby upstairs with me," she said.

"No, leave him. He'll be awake soon. I'll look after him while you catch a few hours of sleep. We'll have time enough together."

Not enough, she thought. Not when I want you with me until hell freezes over.

He wrapped his arms around her and kissed the top of her head. "Sleep," he ordered. "Tomorrow is another day. We'll start over tomorrow."

"Yes," she agreed. "We will." She stepped out of the circle of his arms but held tightly to his hand. "There's something you have to know about my marriage to James."

"He is dead, isn't he? That was the truth?"

"Yes." She took a deep breath. "James died last fall, before the first snowfall."

"Then there's nothing you need to tell me."

"But I do," she murmured. "Since we were kids, James and I were a matched team. We went together like raspberries and briers, bread and honey. No other boy ever gave me a serious look after James blacked Will Satterfield's eye for bidding on my picnic basket at the fair. I married him for love, but our marriage ended a long time before Gettysburg."

"War is worse on some men than others," Chance said.

"You don't understand," she insisted. "The stranger who came home from Pennsylvania wasn't my James. He wore James's face, but he was different inside."

"Lots of men—"

"Listen to me," she pleaded. "I don't care about other men. This was *my* husband who had changed. My world is Rachel's Choice, and it was always James's, too. But after he joined up, he stopped caring about the farm and about me. His mind burned with cheap whiskey, card gambling, and painted whores. We argued constantly, and he hit me hard enough to loosen a tooth. For weeks James stayed drunk and mean. I wouldn't have let him stay here, not if he wasn't so sick. And I never would have made a child with him if he hadn't forced me into his bed."

"Rachel . . ." Chance's eyes widened in compassion.

"I just wanted you to know," she whispered. "I don't hate James. I tell myself that he was sick in the head. But I despise the war that ruined him."

Chance nodded. "I know you do."

She released his hand. "I had to tell you," she said softly. "It's important to me that you understand that what I feel for you is real—not a substitute for what I had with James."

She didn't wait for an answer. Instead she walked quickly through the parlor and up the front stairs. She'd told Chance what she'd kept locked in her heart, and saying it lifted a heavy weight off her shoulders.

"Tomorrow is a start," she whispered. "A start for us and for Davy." And no matter what happened, she knew she'd never regret giving her love to Chance Chancellor. For him it might be three months, but for her it would be forever.

Chapter 14

Rachel awoke to the smell of something burning and the sound of Davy's shrieks. She leaped out of bed to run downstairs, still in her nightdress. Tentacles of smoke seeped into the sitting room, making her eyes water.

"Where's the baby?" Rachel cried as she burst into the kitchen.

"Davy's outside." Chance coughed and gestured to the woodstove. "The smoke's coming from the stove."

Thick black clouds billowed out of the oven and filled the room; Rachel could barely make out the kitchen table. "Are you trying to burn my house down?"

Choking, Chance flung open the window over the dry sink. "It's nothing," he managed. "It will clear out in no time."

Rachel held her breath to avoid the worst of the smoke and dashed out into the yard to look for the baby. To her relief, she caught sight of him immediately.

Davy, tiny arms and legs flailing, lay in a wicker laundry basket. Bear crouched close beside him in the shade of the brick well. The mastiff whined a greeting to Rachel and thumped his tail against the hard-packed earth.

"At least one of you had the sense to get Davy out of

there," she said, scooping up her little son and shushing his angry cries. "There, there," she crooned. "You're all right."

Bear nuzzled her ankle. "And you're going to be all right, too," she murmured to the dog. A nasty gash scarred one side of his head, and his hair was matted with dried blood, but he wriggled joyfully when she petted him.

Last night's terror seemed far off in the bright morning sunshine. "We won't think of those rebel bastards, will we?" she whispered. She couldn't help wondering what Chance had done with them, but he'd warned her not to ask, and she was content to leave things that way.

She shifted Davy to her shoulder and scratched Bear under the chin. "At least I've got you." Losing Lady was like losing a dear friend, and she knew that the big black dog would miss the old collie as deeply as she would. The two animals had been inseparable.

Sadness welled up inside her. The collie had been gray around the muzzle, but she had a few good years ahead of her. "I won't cry," Rachel murmured. "I won't." But she couldn't stop the lump from forming in her throat.

The squeak of the back door made her look up. She stared at Chance's soot-blackened face and then began to snicker. "Merciful heavens, look at you," she declared. "What happened?"

"Making breakfast."

She stood up and bounced Davy on one arm. His wails had subsided to hiccups and an occasional sob of indignation. "Let me guess," Rachel said solemnly. "You tried to make biscuits and burned them."

"Corn bread." Chance grimaced. "And it didn't burn— at least, it didn't burn in the pan."

"How do you figure that?"

"The batter overflowed. I couldn't take the pan out because the bread wasn't brown, but what was on the bottom of the oven kept smoking."

"How full did you make the pan?"

He threw her such a dirty look that she burst into peals of laughter.

"What's so funny? It could happen to anyone."

She snickered. "First you dive through my parlor window, then you shoot out another, and now you blacken my house with smoke."

"I saved your derriere, Mrs. Irons, and don't you forget it."

She nodded. "That you did. Let me take Davy upstairs and tuck him into his cradle, and I'll help you clean up the mess."

"Deal."

"And this time I'll make the breakfast, if you don't mind."

Twenty minutes later, after caring for Davy, she rejoined Chance in the kitchen. Most of the smoke was gone, but black smudges stained the ceiling and walls, and remained on his face.

"You look like Quantrill," she teased. "He couldn't do this much damage on his worst raid." Dirty bowls and utensils littered the table. Eggshells, cornmeal, and coffee grounds spilled over onto the rug. The stove glowed red, and a pan of burnt eggs sat on the reservoir lid. A second cast-iron frying pan contained what must have been bacon; that, too, was blackened to a crisp.

"A mess," Chance said, handing her a cup of coffee. "I hope it's not too strong."

Rachel took a sip and puckered up her mouth. "Needs milk and sugar," she gasped. When he looked hurt, she added, "But I like my coffee strong." And then she couldn't resist teasing him. "Of course, this would melt horseshoes."

"Fine, insult my efforts."

She turned the stovepipe damper to reduce the fire and began to gather the dirty dishes. Then she noticed a handful of violets in a teacup in the center of the table and glanced at Chance questioningly.

"For you," he admitted. "The trouble started when I went to pick the damn flowers. Bacon and eggs with corn bread didn't look so hard to do."

"Thank you." A scratchy feeling in her eyes made her tear up. "It's been a long time since anyone's brought me flowers." She rubbed her cheek absently, and Chance chuckled.

"You've got flour on your face," he said. "No, higher," he said as she tried to brush it off. "Let me do it."

He moved closer and she tilted her head up. He's going to kiss me, she thought. Her lips tingled, and she closed her eyes in anticipation.

Instead, Chance scooped up some of the spilled flour off the table and tossed it into her face.

"Why, you!" She sneezed once and again, and lunged for him. "You sneaky devil!" she cried.

Chance dodged around the table. "Make fun of my coffee, will you?" he taunted her.

Rachel circled the table, and he threw another handful of flour mixed with coffee grounds. His aim was off, and she escaped without a speck on her, but her blood was up. "I'll get you, you dirty reb!" she threatened teasingly.

"Now, Rachel," he soothed. "You can take a joke."

"Oh, yes," she promised him. "I can—but can you?" Her gaze lit on the basket of eggs on the edge of the dry sink.

"Oh, no! Not that!" he protested.

"If there's one thing a country girl learns," she said, "it's how to throw rocks at rats."

"I surrender!"

"No quarter!" The first egg hit him square in the chest, the second on his good shoulder, and the third, dead on in the center of the forehead.

He stood stock-still, egg white and yolk running down his face and over his clothing.

"Now we're even," she cried triumphantly.

"Says who?"

She squealed as he leaped onto the daybed and heaved a pillow at her. She ran around the rocking chair and scrambled to the far side of the table. As she did, her hand trailed through a soft plate of butter.

"That's cheating!" Chance shouted.

"All's fair in war!" The lump of butter struck Chance's chin and dribbled down his neck. Laughing, Rachel dashed out the back door and hid behind the well.

"Woman!" He brandished the honey pot. "I've got something for you."

"No!" She ran toward the barn, scattering hens. "I give up. You win!"

"It's too late."

Barefoot, clad only in the thin linen of her nightgown, she fled into the barn and up the ladder to the hayloft. Chance came right behind her, and as he tried to climb after her, she showered him with an armful of hay.

When he kept coming, she darted to the loft window,

threw it open, and let herself down the outside of the barn on a thick rope hanging from the rafters.

"Rachel!" He slid down the rope, still clutching the honey. She was halfway to the creek when he caught her around the waist, and both went rolling in the deep clover.

They ended up with Rachel flat on her back and Chance astride her middle. "No! No!" she protested, but she was laughing so hard that she could hardly get the words out.

"All right, you Yankee wench, this is where you get yours," he said in an exaggerated drawl. "Plead for mercy."

"Never!"

He pinned her wrists over her head with one hand and dipped two fingers of his free hand into the honey. She squirmed under him, and the sensation sent shock waves of heat through his loins.

"Mother of God," he whispered. Slowly he drew a dripping fingertip over her top lip, then bent to taste the sweetness.

She giggled. "You're all hay and yuck."

"Am I?" He grabbed the pot and dumped the honey on her throat, trailing gooey threads over the rise of her breasts. Then he released her hands and kissed her again.

Her laughter became a satisfied sigh as she circled his neck with her arms. "Oh, Chance, you are one of a kind," she said.

Their gazes met, and his eyes filled with uncertainty.

Her insides clenched. What would he think if I told him that I love him? she wondered. Instinctively she knew that it was too soon to tell him how she really felt.

He drew back and looked deeply into her eyes.

"There's only here and now, Rachel. I can't give you tomorrow."

"Then I'll take now," she whispered.

"You're certain?"

"I am." She caressed the taut muscles of his shoulders, savoring the small tremors of pleasure that spilled down her spine. Heady with anticipation, she moistened her lips with the tip of her tongue and felt his breathing quicken.

He rose and pulled her up after him, then gathered her into his arms. How strong he is, she thought as she wound her arms tightly around his neck. For a brief moment she stared into his luminous eyes and wondered if she would ever regret this moment. Then her senses reeled as Chance slanted his mouth, and she leaned close to meet his searing kiss.

She wrapped her legs around his waist as he half slid, half stumbled down the creek bank and waded into the water. Heat flooded her body as he thrust his tongue deep into her mouth, and she moaned softly.

"You don't need this," he murmured, tugging at her nightgown. The thin linen caught around her hips, and he ripped it from hem to neckline, leaving her completely unclad in the hot morning sun.

"No more than you need this," she replied as she began to unbutton his shirt. The warm water lapped delightfully over her buttocks to her waist, covering her but hiding nothing.

"A woman after my own heart."

Chance slid one hand down her back, running his lean fingers along the hollow of her spine and tracing the curve of one hip.

She closed her eyes and leaned back until her unbound

hair trailed in the water. Around her the creek surged with the sounds and smells of pulsing life: the high-pitched *kee-kee-kee* of an osprey, the chatter of a squirrel, and the *wer-ump wer-ump* of bullfrogs. The air hung heavy with the rich scents of crushed mint, damp earth, and the bite of brackish water.

"Rachel," Chance murmured. "Sweet, sweet Rachel."

She felt him twist beneath her as he pulled off his trousers and tossed them back onto the bank. In seconds she felt the heat of Chance's naked skin against hers.

Sighing, she ran her fingers through his hair and burst into laughter as she encountered the sticky residue of matted hay and drying egg.

"Save us!" she cried as her eyes widened. "You're badly in need of a bath, sir."

"And whose fault is that?" he asked, bending his head to kiss her again.

Still laughing, she twisted out of his embrace and dived into deeper water. He plunged in after her, and she scooped up a handful of sand from the bottom and circled him. When they broke the surface, she came up behind and scrubbed his back and shoulders until he cried out in protest.

"Enough! You'll . . ."

She bobbed under again, and this time he was gone when she broke water. "Chance? Where are you?" She waited, treading water, as the seconds passed, anxiously watching for some movement around her.

Then, without warning, she felt strong hands seize her around the waist and thrust her up into the air. "No!" she cried.

"Yes!" Laughing, he claimed her mouth with his,

then lowered his head to draw an aching nipple between his lips.

Desire surged through her. She dug her fingers into his shoulders and arched her back as sweet sensations spiraled down to the pit of her belly and made her shudder with need.

He raised his head and gazed into her eyes. "Are you certain?" he whispered.

Rachel couldn't speak. Instead, she took his hand and put it between her legs. Chance groaned, and she felt his shaft thicken and throb against her bare thigh.

Incessant hunger made her bold and she clung to him, sighing as his fingers delved into the sensitive folds below her triangle of dark curls.

No other man but her husband had ever touched her so, had ever made her tremble with wanting him. She had not believed that such smoldering heat burned within this golden man.

"Love me," she begged him.

Chance pressed his lips into her hair and whispered sweet words as his fingers worked magic. Tension built within her, and she squirmed closer and closer, breath coming in quick, ragged gasps, until she could feel the strong, rapid beat of his heart.

Yet she wanted more.

Her body tensed, muscles straining, pulse racing. "Now!" she cried. "I want you—now."

Chance caught her waist and held her, and she felt the first hot nudge of his sex against hers. She opened to him as a flower welcomes the summer rain, and he filled her with his ardent power.

She climaxed on his first thrust.

He laughed as a cry of wonder broke from her lips,

then drove deep. For an instant they were one. He kissed her again and brought her to a fever pitch with powerful, slow strokes.

This time they reached the summit together, and she felt him shudder and heard his groan of release as they toppled over and tumbled into empty space.

Later he made tender love to her once more in the shallows, shaded by an ancient beech tree. Afterward, she lay content in his arms and listened to the whisper of the creek and the indignant chirping of a Carolina wren.

"There's not another woman like you, Rachel Irons," Chance said softly.

She smiled and kept her eyes closed. She was anxious to see if Davy was awake, but she was reluctant to break the spell of this special time.

Chance wound a lock of her hair around his finger. "This is what life should be," he murmured. "Warm sun, a beautiful woman in my arms, and not the boom of a single cannon."

"I don't want to think about the war," she whispered. "I don't want to think at all."

"Nor I, darlin'." He lifted her hand and kissed the pulse at her wrist.

She chuckled softly as he planted feather-light kisses along her forearm up to her elbow.

"I think I'm sitting on a crab," he teased.

"I hope not."

She sighed and looked up at him. Golden sprinkles of stubble covered his chin and cheeks. She touched him lightly, wanting to fix every inch of him forever in her mind, so that she would never lose these precious memories.

"I should have shaved this morning."

"No. Remember? You're a hired hand. You're supposed to look scruffy. It's much too dangerous for you to remain here looking fit for military service."

"I'm putting you and Davy at risk."

"You are, but . . . Oh, Chance." She twisted out of his arms and knelt in front of him. "I couldn't bear it if something happened to you."

"Shhh, don't talk like that. I'm a soldier. Don't pin your hopes on me."

"You don't have to go back to the war. You could stay here with me. It won't last forever—you said so yourself."

His mood sobered. "Before I met you, Rachel, I made a promise to a friend. I have to keep that promise." His eyes clouded and she thought she saw the hint of a tear. "His name is Travis, and he's the best friend I ever had. I left him on the beach . . . that night that I escaped from Pea Patch Island."

Numbness spread through her body, and she suddenly felt chilled. "You're going back for him, aren't you?"

"I am."

"What makes you think he's alive?" She stood up and tried to cover herself with her hands as she looked for the ruins of her nightgown. "He's probably dead. You know that."

Chance nodded, and his features grew taut with concern. "I've told myself that, but I can't be sure. Travis and I have always had this bond. It's not something I can put into words, but we've been together since we were children. We've gotten in and out of scrapes that neither of us should have lived through. I have this feeling that I'd know if he were dead. I can't live with myself if I don't go and make certain."

"They'll kill you." She found his shirt and draped it around her. "Lots of men have gotten out of Fort Delaware, but no one has—"

"Been fool enough to go back," he finished.

A lump rose in her throat. She hadn't guessed that the thought of losing him would hurt so much. "If it wasn't for this Travis, could you care about me, Chance?" Her eyes narrowed, and she straightened to her full height. "I want the truth from you. No more lies between us."

"I wish it were that simple."

She shook her head. "No excuses. You never tried to make more of this than it is. I'm not the kind of woman a fancy lawyer—"

"Damn it, Rachel, it's not that and you know it." He leaped to his feet, and his features hardened. "I took an oath to uphold the Confederacy. So long as the war lasts, I have to fight."

"No, you don't."

"You'd rather I was a deserter?"

"Yes," she shouted. "Hell, yes. I'd rather have you desert a hundred times than end up fodder for some Union cannon."

"You're a woman," he answered gruffly. "You've no notion of what honor means to a man."

"You stupid bastard." Angry tears welled up in her eyes. "And you've no notion what you're throwing away," she cried. "It's a lost cause. You know it, and I know it."

"Maybe," he said. "But whatever comes, I've got to—"

She didn't wait to hear the rest. She turned and ran toward the house.

"Rachel! Rachel, wait!" he called.

Halfway to the barn, she stopped and faced him. He came toward her barefoot and pulling up his wet trousers with sections of yellow hair falling over his forehead.

"We said this would be only for here and now," he reminded her. "You agreed."

Her chest felt tight; she wanted to lash out at him for his stupidity. "This isn't a game of checkers," she said. "It's my life. Can I help what I feel for you?"

"And I care about you—and about Davy. But I can't hide here for the rest of the war."

"Go, then! Go and to hell with you! I don't need you, Chance Chancellor. I don't need you at all!"

Chapter 15

"Rachel!" Chance called. "Wait."

She stalked away, brown eyes spitting fire and her back as straight as an infantryman's. His wet shirt clung sensually to her full hips and ended halfway down her thighs, exposing long, shapely legs and slim ankles. Her thick, dark hair hung nearly to her waist, and drops of water caught in the strands reflected rays of sunshine like stars in a night sky.

She was one hell of a woman.

"Rachel!"

She vanished around the corner of the barn and he hurried after her, treading carefully to avoid stubble under his bare soles. When he reached the house, she was already upstairs. He heard Davy fussing just before a bedroom door slammed.

Chance shrugged and looked around the kitchen. Bear raised his head and uttered a low growl. "My sentiments exactly," Chance said.

She'd told him to go. If she didn't want him here, then he was free to leave . . . free to return to Pea Patch and settle old scores.

All he had to do was turn his back on the woman he'd come to think of as his own.

"Son of a bitch," he muttered as he located the broom and began to sweep up the mess. Why in hell couldn't she understand? What kind of man would he be if he allowed himself to hide out the war in safety while his friends died?

He stooped to retrieve the butter dish from the floor. Bear had licked it clean. "At least you're good for something," he said to the dog.

It was hard to stay mad at Rachel when memories of their idyll at the creek still made him hard. He knew that if he shut his eyes and concentrated, he could taste Rachel's mouth and feel the silken texture of her skin.

Damn, he didn't have to try. The clean woman-scent of her lingered in his nostrils. Just thinking about her lush, rose-tipped breasts was enough to drive him crazy.

She was impossible. Irrational. Yet, he wanted nothing more than to take her in his arms and make love to her again.

It shouldn't have been that way. He liked women, always had, but once he'd had one, some of the mystery and excitement was lost.

Not this time.

What he felt for Rachel was more than physical. It was dangerous—she was dangerous. He had the awful sinking feeling that he was about to experience something he'd thought would never happen. He suffered from all the symptoms of falling in love.

And he was long past that human failing.

"Absolutely not," he said.

The massive black dog blinked and lolled a tongue the size of a man's hand.

"Forget it." Chance briskly wiped down the table and returned the flour box and salt crock to the cupboard. He was scrubbing the corn-bread pan when he heard foot-steps behind him.

"I can do that," Rachel said. "The cow hasn't been milked this morning."

"Yes, she has." He pumped cold water over the pan.

"Oh."

He glanced at her. She wore a purplish gingham dress and white apron, and her glorious mane of hair was neatly braided and pinned up on her head. She held the baby in her arms, and her hips swayed slightly as she walked.

It's a trap, Chance thought. *Holy Mother of God, I was safer charging a Union line at Manassas than I am in this kitchen.*

Davy was wide awake and cooing contentedly. Chance wiped his hands on a striped towel and reached for him. Putting the baby between them was the only thing that would keep him from claiming that saucy mouth of hers here and now. "How about if I hold him and you finish this?" He motioned to the dirty spoons and bowls heaped in the sink.

"All right." Her features were smooth and expression-less, but she couldn't hide the light in her eyes when she looked at him.

She handed him Davy, and Chance carried the squirm-ing infant over to the rocking chair. She'd put the little boy in a long dress, and it was like trying to hold a goat in a bag. "Why does he need all these clothes in this heat?" Chance asked her. He untied the baby's bonnet and slipped it off so that he could kiss the crown of his head when Rachel wasn't looking.

"Since when did you become an expert on child raising?"

"Rearing. Child rearing," he corrected. "You raise cabbages, not babies."

"Damn few cabbages you've ever raised," Rachel snapped as she began scrubbing a bowl hard enough to take the pattern off.

"No need to get testy on me. I said I'd stay long enough to get your crop in and I will." Chance bounced Davy on his knee. The baby flashed him a drippy smile. "Hey, he smiled at me."

"He doesn't know any better."

"Rachel, use sense. You can't expect me to—"

"I don't expect anything of you but farmwork. This morning was—"

"I won't hear that kind of talk. We both wanted it."

She put the clean bowl aside and reached for a wooden spoon. "You're right. We've nothing in common out of bed. Nothing."

"That's not true, and you know it."

She shook the spoon at him. "As if you or your rich lawyer friends would have noticed me if we'd passed each other on the streets of Richmond before the war."

"I'd have noticed you anywhere," he replied mildly as he wiped the baby's chin with a napkin. "And nothing that happened before Sumter means anything now. It's a different world, and none of us will ever be the same, not even you."

Davy began to fuss, and Chance shifted him to his shoulder and patted his back until the baby gave a loud burp.

"Be easy with him," she said. "He's not a sack of corn."

"Is he crying? If he didn't like it, he'd be screaming, wouldn't he?" Chance replied.

Davy began to gurgle happily.

"There, what did I tell you?" Chance said. "You don't know anything about my life, my family, my friends. You judge them out of ignorance."

"So now I'm ignorant?"

He scoffed. "There's no class war between us, Rachel. You're as fine a lady as it's ever been my honor to meet."

"Exactly the kind of woman you'd bring home to your mother."

"Hardly. You're the wrong religion to suit Mother, and your blood isn't blue enough." He shrugged. "Is that what you wanted me to say?"

She flushed. "I suppose so."

"You wouldn't like Mother very much, Rachel, and I suppose the feeling would be mutual. In all honesty, I'd have to admit that Mother is somewhat of a snob."

She sank into a chair. "There's no need to talk of your mother. I didn't—"

"She's probably much what you'd expect and more. My mother is a beautiful woman, but very cool in nature, even to her children. Appearances are of the utmost importance, not whether an action is right or wrong, but how it looks to the people who matter."

"But you said that she was against slavery. That doesn't sound like a cold person to me."

"Slavery was one of Mother's charities. She was always kind to her black servants and her dogs. Mother was very fond of dogs, more so than she was of her children."

"But surely she loved you. You're her son."

"In her way. Aunt Milly was my nursemaid when I was small. She was born in the islands, and her skin was the color of coffee and cream. She used to sing to me in

Spanish, and she was never too busy to listen to Travis and me when we came home from school. We adored Aunt Milly, but when I was ten, my little sister made the mistake of calling her Mama. My mother discharged her that day. She had my father put her on a boat headed south to the Caribbean. I never saw her again."

"You must have missed her terribly," Rachel answered softly. "But I don't understand. What does that have to do with us?"

"You think that I don't want to stay here because of who you are and who you think I am. But that's not what's important. I'm just a man, Rachel, a man who might have been happier if he'd grown up here on the banks of Indian Creek with grandparents who loved him than born a Chancellor. You're richer than you know. You've always been. You'll be fine here. You and Davy will live through this war, and you'll go on to have a good life."

Rachel laid her hand on his arm. "But not with you?"

"It's not our differences that keep us apart, it's what I have—"

"The noble soldier," she said. "The battle to keep people like your Aunt Milly in chains."

"Haven't we gone over this same argument before? The fight between the North and South isn't about slavery. It's over the price of cotton. Slavery would have withered under its own weight. Another generation and we would have seen the end of it without a bloodbath that will haunt America for a hundred years to come."

Rachel shook her head. "I can't win against you and your fancy lawyer's arguments. Like I said, Chance, we're too different to understand each other. Farmers have better sense than to breed plow horses with blooded stock."

"You compare yourself with a mare?" he teased. "It's not our differences that keep us apart, Rach; it's this damned war. Another time, another place . . ."

He broke off before he said something that would tie him even more to this place, and this woman. Why did a man find what he'd spent a lifetime searching for and then be unable to reach out and seize it?

God, but he liked the feel of this child in his arms. Davy was soft and warm, and he smelled like a fluffy baby chick. James will never know what he's missed in this boy, he thought.

Chance tried not to let the notion that he could make Davy his own son settle in his mind. It was hard refusing the life that Rachel held out with both hands. But he had other obligations that came before his own happiness.

He had to kill a man, he reminded himself. Even if Travis was already dead, he had to put Daniel Coblentz in his grave.

"You like the killing?" she demanded.

Rachel's sudden change of tactics startled him and made him wonder if she could read his mind.

"You like putting a bullet through a man?" She twisted around to glare at him, oblivious to her dishcloth dripping soapy water onto the floor.

Damn woman's intuition. His mother had been the same way. She'd had the uncanny knack of knowing what mischief he was going to get into before he did. He wondered what she would think of Rachel Irons, and he had a suspicion that despite their differences, they would have gotten along just fine.

"I hate the killing," he replied. "I never much cared for shooting anything, not even game."

Rachel dropped the cloth into the wash pan and came toward him. "I'd shoot you again if I thought it would keep you here."

"That's a comforting thought." He rose and laid Davy on the daybed. Then he pulled her against him as she sobbed softly. "Didn't you just tell me to leave?" he whispered into her hair.

"I didn't mean it," she answered raggedly. "You know I didn't mean it."

"Oh, Rachel, Rachel. What's to become of us?" He hugged her even tighter.

If he could have Rachel and Davy for a little while, he'd accept that blessing as a gift from the Almighty. With luck, he could store up enough happiness to last him for the rest of his life.

"Oh, Chance, haven't I given enough to this war?" she pleaded, clinging to him. "I loved James since I was four years old, and he never lived to see his son's face. If you go, I know I'll lose you as well."

He couldn't answer. His own gut feeling was that he couldn't murder a sergeant and come off Pea Patch alive. And even if he did survive the island, the war might stretch on for years. So he just held her, and after a few minutes she straightened and stepped away.

"I'm sorry to make such a fool of myself," she said.

He brushed a tear from her cheek. "It was special for you—when we made love—wasn't it?"

Her eyes widened and a faint blush tinted her high cheekbones. "Yes," she answered. "It was." Then she averted her eyes. "The best."

He grinned. "Me, too."

"Reb's honor?" A sparkle of mischief danced in her eyes.

"Absolutely."

She swallowed, and her voice took on a rich, whiskey timbre. "You never told me what unit you served with."

He tried to ignore the knotting in his gut. "Fourth Virginia, Powhatan Guards."

She exhaled slowly. "I thought from the first you must be cavalry. You have a horseman's hands."

"Is that good or bad?"

"Since you're not a farmer, they'll have to do." She glanced around the kitchen. "Thank you for cleaning this. I was dreading it."

"You did your share to make it that way," he said.

"I did, didn't I?"

She smiled at him, and he felt a flush of warmth under his skin. The knots in his belly tightened to an aching. He yearned to lay her back against the kitchen table and find out how easily those little pearl buttons at her throat came undone.

"I don't want you to go, Chance," she continued. "Not now, not in the fall."

"But you understand why I have to." When he'd suckled at her breasts in the creek, he'd tasted her sweet mother's milk. Now he wanted to taste it again.

"I understand why you think you have to."

"You're a rare woman, Rachel, but you're as stubborn and illogical as every other woman." His heart was racing. Surely she could see how much he wanted her. She'd have to be blind to miss the bulge in his trousers.

"There'd be fewer wars if *illogical* women had their way."

"You may be right," he agreed. "But I still think you'd

make a hell of a lawyer." He opened his arms, and she came into them. And for the better part of an hour, neither thought of war, or danger, or tomorrow.

"Miss Rachel! Miss Rachel!" Pharaoh's shout dragged Rachel from Chance's arms. They lay entwined on the daybed with Davy tucked between them. As she struggled to rise, the baby started to cry.

Bear barked and pushed open the kitchen door with his head.

"Get upstairs," Rachel said urgently. "Hide and don't come out, no matter what happens. That's Pharaoh. He'll kill you if he finds you here."

Putting a pillow between the baby and the edge of the bed so that he wouldn't fall off, she struggled to close the front of her dress and pull down her rumpled skirts. She shoved the wooden kitchen door nearly shut and peered out, hoping her disarray wouldn't show. "Pharaoh! I'll be right out."

"You all right, Miss Rachel?"

"I'm fine. Just a minute," she called as she tried to pin up her hair.

The big black man slid down from a stocky gray horse and strode toward the house. Cradled in one arm, Pharaoh held a .50 caliber Hawken rifle, and thrust through his belt was a wicked-looking corn knife.

Bear had left off barking and was wagging his tail, but Pharaoh didn't stop to rub the dog's head as he normally did.

Rachel's stomach knotted, and she smiled to cover her discomposure. "Good morning."

"What happened to Bear?" Pharaoh asked as she stepped out the door. "That a baby I hear crying?"

"Yes, my baby."

"Mother was worried about you. She was down in Lewes looking after her sick aunty, or she would have been over here to see how you were. Garden looks good."

Two more men rode up behind Pharaoh's horse. Rachel recognized Jack and Gideon Freeman; both carried firearms. "I'm good," she answered Pharaoh. "Tell Cora that I had a boy. I call him Davy." She greeted the Freemans by name, and they nodded in reply.

Pharaoh looked around suspiciously. "You certain you've had no trouble?"

"I haven't," she lied. "But somebody clubbed my collie to death and shot Bear."

"When?" Pharaoh's ebony eyes gleamed fiercely. Sweat ran down his face and glistened on his bare shoulders and forearms.

"I'm not sure. They ran off after a rabbit before dinner last night. Bear was at the back door this morning, and we found Lady in the meadow."

"Who's *we*?" Rachel knew that Chance wouldn't last two minutes against these three. She had to keep them from seeing the broken windows and get them away from Rachel's Choice. "Abner and me. You know, Abner's the hired man my cousin sent down from New Castle."

"Where is he?" Pharaoh demanded.

"Fishing by the creek, I think. He's not real smart, and he can't speak a word. Is something wrong? Are the soldiers coming again?"

"Gideon said they took his wife's pigs yesterday, but we didn't see any troops on the road. The county's up in arms over another prisoner escape. They say fifteen rebs overpowered a patrol boat and got away from Fort

Delaware three nights ago. Two women were murdered near Taylor's Bridge."

"You think it could have been them that killed Lady?"

"See any tracks around the body?"

Rachel shook her head. "No, but all that rain could have washed them away."

"And you didn't hear nothin'?"

"No. Not until Bear came whining to the house."

"We'll look for signs just the same. Mind if we have some water?"

"Help yourself," she offered. "And I could find you something to eat, if you'd like."

Pharaoh motioned to the other two men. They dismounted and one lowered the bucket into the well. "Just water for us and the horses," he said.

Rachel noticed that there was a fresh bloodstain on his pants leg. "And none of the rebs has been caught?" she asked.

"Didn't say that, Miss Rachel."

Gideon carried a gourd of water to Pharaoh. He drank half and poured the rest over his close-cropped hair. "Obliged, Miss Rachel," Gideon said.

"I'm obliged to you for helping get my crops in." The more she looked at Pharaoh's corn knife, the more certain she was that the blade was smeared with blood. She gazed directly into the black man's eyes. "Did you find them?"

Pharaoh smiled. "Whatever give you that idea, Miss Rachel?" he asked in the false ingratiating tone she'd heard him use around white strangers. "We sees 'em, we fetches the sheriff, we does. What us negra boys gonna do wit' reb soldiers?"

Rachel nodded. "And how many didn't you see?" She

wondered if Chance had released the men who'd invaded her house, and Pharaoh had found them.

The Freeman brothers exchanged nervous looks.

"One, for sure, we didn't see," Pharaoh answered softly. "And two more never saw us." He tapped the barrel of his rifle.

"Should I be afraid?" she asked. "Do you think any of them are hiding around here?"

"We'll give your farm a good look-see," Pharaoh assured her. "I want to talk to that man of yours. He can hear, can't he?"

"Oh, yes, he hears fine," Rachel said, "but he's not real bright. Try not to scare him."

"I'll tell my mother your babe is here. She may want to ride over."

"Tell her that I'll be glad to see her anytime. And I hope Aunty Eunice is feeling better."

"She's passable for ninety-one," Pharaoh replied.

Rachel and Pharaoh made small talk while the horses were watered. She didn't go back into the house until the three rode out of the yard. Then she sat in the rocker and nursed Davy, waiting a good third of an hour before she called to Chance.

"I think they're gone," she said from the foot of the stairs. "You can come down."

"Mean-looking neighbors you have," he said as he descended the steps. "Is the custom here for them to carry rifles?"

"Blacks, you mean?"

He shrugged.

"Pharaoh makes his own customs." She fixed him with a suspicious gaze. "You looked out the window?"

"How else could I be sure you were safe?"

"Pharaoh wouldn't hurt me. He's been a good friend. You're the one who has to worry about him. They said they were hunting some runaway rebs. I think they killed three of them."

Chance's mouth hardened.

"Maybe they caught up with the two who were here."

"No, they didn't find them."

"So this was three more prisoners?"

Chance shrugged. "Appears so. If your friends were telling the truth."

"I've never known Pharaoh to lie to me."

"I'm sorry to hear it, then."

"After what those rebs did here?" Her temper flared. "They deserved killing."

"Those two were vermin, but most Southerners are no better and no worse than the people around here. Not one man in ten would raise a hand to a defenseless woman."

"One in ten." She scowled at him. "I don't think much of those odds."

"You haven't seen what Union soldiers have done in the South. You've been spared the most of it, living here. But Southern women and children have suffered. If I had my way, anyone who lifted a hand to a civilian would be hung."

"At least we're agreed on something," she said. "Let me put Davy upstairs, and then I want to cut your hair. Pharaoh may come back. And if he does, he'll expect to see Abner. If not him, his mother or more Union troops. It's time you started playing your part, Chance."

"You want me to act up a storm?"

She nodded. "Yes, I do. Either that or risk hanging. Take your choice."

"The way you put it, you give a man few options, woman."

She smiled at him. "I'd say I've given you far more than you deserve."

Chapter 16

Rachel watched from the garden as Chance lifted a sagging board in the pound fence and drove a nail through it into the post. Not even the loose tattered clothing and ragged haircut could still the butterfly wings in her stomach or calm her rapid pulse whenever she looked at him.

He turned toward her and grinned boyishly. Chance had let his beard grow to a sparse stubble and topped his absurd appearance with a moldy straw hat that he'd let the cow chew on. Now he swept the hat off his head and bowed in an exaggerated flourish.

She giggled and stuck out her tongue at him.

"Is that any way to treat your hired hand?" he demanded in a mock offended tone.

"Quiet." Teasing, she raised a finger to her lips. "You can't talk. Not a word."

She hoped that others wouldn't see through his disguise as easily as she did. It was a dangerous game of masquerade they played, but Chance couldn't work her fields if he remained in hiding.

Was it possible that shrewd Cora Wright would fail to recognize the intelligence in Chance's eyes? Would patrolling Union troops be fooled and not notice the patrician lines of Chance's face or his military-school polish?

Each day Rachel watched and listened for the sound of horses or the squeak of carriage wheels on the farmland. And every night she thanked God that they had escaped discovery once more.

After the rain the weather turned baking hot and dry. Together she and Chance cultivated the corn and hoed and weeded the garden. He waded chest-deep in the creek to net fish for salting, and used the rowboat to pull her crab traps while she churned butter and began to put up vegetables for the winter.

The angry words the two had exchanged the day Pharaoh and the Freeman brothers had come had been quickly lost in the sheets of Rachel's tall four-poster bed. It was impossible for her to remain angry with Chance when desire sizzled and crackled between them like summer lightning.

Between searing kisses, he'd repeated his promise to stay until fall, and she had vowed to keep their differences from ruining this precious time together.

Strangely, now that they were intimate, Rachel had come to accept that these weeks together were all that they would ever have. Chance would go back to the war and die in some senseless battle or survive and return to his life of wealth and privilege. Either way, she knew that she would never see him again.

Her place was here on Rachel's Choice with little Davy, and the sweet passion she shared with Chance now was a once-in-a-lifetime gift . . . one she feared would end all too soon.

Be happy with what you have, she told herself. Save

the tears for later; there will be years and years for weeping over what can never be.

The day before, when a week had passed without
Pharaoh's return, Rachel had hitched the horse and driv-
en to the crossroads to sell her crab soup and eggs. She
took Davy with her and left Chance behind on the farm
with strict orders to hide if anyone came.

At the store she'd checked her mail for James's death
benefits but found nothing except a terse reminder of her
overdue taxes.

"I don't understand," she'd told Chance that morning
at breakfast. "James was due military back pay when he
died. And now I'm supposed to get a widow's pension."

"It's good to know that Lincoln's government is as
slow in paying as ours," Chance replied wryly as he
cleared both plates from the table.

"It's no joke," she'd said. "I need the money. James's
father will expect a payment in August, and I've nowhere
to raise it. I must find something to pay my taxes and to
satisfy the Ironses, or I'll have no home for Davy."

Chance slid into the chair across from her and pushed
his coffee cup closer so that she could refill it. "Can't you
sell some of your land?"

Rachel shook her head. "James signed a note, giving
his father a lien against the property."

Jiggling Davy on his lap, Chance had carefully cut
himself a slice of rhubarb pie. "You'd love some of this,
wouldn't you?" he murmured to the baby.

"Don't you dare give Davy pie. He's much too little to
eat solid food."

"Poor little man. You don't know what you're missing," Chance murmured as he dipped the tip of his finger
in the pie and touched it to the infant's rosebud mouth.

Davy smacked his lips and waved his chubby arms excitedly.

"See," Chance said. "He loves it."

"You're impossible." She held out her arms. "Give him to me." She carried Davy to the rocker and sat down, draping herself in a shawl so that she could nurse him without exposing her breast. "Did the nasty old reb give my darlin' yucky old rhubarb pie?" she murmured.

Chance rose and came to stand beside her. "Don't," he said quietly. "I like to watch."

She felt her cheeks grow warm, but she made no protest as he removed the shawl. Instead, she turned her attention to Davy and tried to ignore Chance's gaze.

"How much do you need?" he asked, suddenly serious.

"Altogether?" Rachel tightened her fingers around the hem of Davy's linen gown. "Including last year's taxes and this year's, three hundred eighty-seven dollars and sixty cents."

"That's all?"

She stiffened in surprise, and her nipple slipped from the baby's mouth. Davy squealed angrily, and she cradled him against her, guiding his head until he found her milk again. Then Rachel glared at Chance. "I can see you've never tried to live off the land. That may not be a huge amount to a rich lawyer, but it's enough to see Davy and me lose everything we've got."

He rubbed unconsciously at the scar on his shoulder. "Surely your friends . . ."

"My friends are as poor as I am."

"Your father left you nothing when he died?"

She swallowed, uncertain as to how she could explain her father to Chance. "He left me his instruments and personal belongings. His money went to a nephew. Father forgave me for my dark skin, but not for ignoring his wishes. He didn't want me to marry. He wanted me to continue my education and become a teacher. When I wed James, Father swore I'd live to regret it."

"A hard man."

"No," she murmured, "just stubborn."

"He should have provided for you," Chance insisted. "Most of our family money is tied up in property in Richmond and Atlanta. Not the best investments at the moment. But I do have funds on deposit with a London bank. I can give you enough to pay off your note. Hell, I can give you twice that. I—"

"I don't want your money!"

"Don't be stupid. I mean to make a will, leaving what's left to you and Davy. I can draw up the document myself, but we'll need witnesses to make it stand up in a court of law."

"No, you won't," she said. "I didn't tell you about the debts so that I could beg money off you."

"Funny, I didn't hear you beg. I made you the offer."

"And I told you that I won't take your money," she snapped back at him. "There's a name for women who take money for what I've given you freely."

"And I'd better not hear it from your lips," he warned her. "It's not like that with us, Rach."

"I hope not!"

Two hours' weeding in the garden cooled her temper, and now she wondered if she'd been hasty. But accepting Chance's offer would make her feel cheap, as if she were no better than the camp whores that James had boasted of having. It's my problem, she thought. Mine, not his, and I'll find a way to work through it.

She bent over a plant and pulled off a potato bug, mashing it under her bare heel.

"I'll finish this row," Chance said, coming up behind her and putting his arms around her. "It's too hot out here for you."

She turned, and her straw hat slipped back off her head. "A fine farmer you'd make," she teased as she slipped her arms around his neck and began to knead the corded muscles at the top of his spine. "This is a fair day."

He bent and kissed her mouth.

"Chance, I'm hot and sweaty," she murmured. Yet, she pressed herself against him, molding the curves of her body to his and savoring the giddy feeling of euphoria that wafted through her.

She wanted him to go on holding her. She wanted the three of them to capture this day and hold it forever. Here in her farmyard there were no battles, no scent of blood, and no bitter politics that divided neighbors and made waste of rich fields and lovely cities.

"It's too pretty a day to work," she said between kisses. "If you'll finish this row and the next, I'll make us a basket dinner, and we can eat it down by the creek."

He looked down at her with a twinkle in his blue eyes. "Hmmm," he teased. "I don't know. That's a difficult decision. It's hard to find something more enjoyable than hoeing vegetables."

She stood on tiptoe and whispered a bold invitation in his ear, and his arms tightened around her.

"That might convince me," he answered solemnly.

"It might?" She stepped away from him. "That's my final offer, sir. Take it or leave it."

He chuckled. "I'd have to be a bigger fool than I am to leave it, wouldn't I?"

Later they lay on a blanket beneath the trees on the banks of Indian Creek and shared hard-boiled eggs and a wedge of sharp cheddar. Rachel stretched out on her back and stared up at the green canopy of leaves overhead while Chance carefully sliced the cheese and fed it to her, bite by bite.

"Ummm, excellent." He finished off the last crumb and reached for a dill pickle. "Did you make these?" he asked.

"No, mine from last year are all gone. I bought those from the store."

She rolled over onto her stomach, leaned on one elbow, and looked over at Davy. The baby was still asleep, napping soundly in a split-oak laundry basket on the far side of the blanket. Bear sprawled beside the baby, his eyes on the food, hoping for a handout.

It was much cooler beside the creek, and the trill of flowing water added to the sensual pleasure of the lazy afternoon. "You've told me nothing about your family," Rachel said. "Are you certain you're not hiding a wife and six children?"

Chance grinned. "No, Rachel. No wife, no children. None but Davy." He glanced at the dozing infant. "The amount of trouble he put me to, I should at least be able to claim him as my godson."

"I suppose you are his godfather," she agreed as a rush of warmth engulfed her at his words. "But he's a Methodist, not a Catholic."

"He can't be a Methodist. You haven't had him christened in the church."

"You have more arguments—"

"Than a Richmond lawyer?" he finished, and they laughed together.

"You were saying," she prompted. "Your family?"

"No awful secrets," he replied. "No mad aunts hidden in the attic of the family mansion. One father, deceased, one mother, currently residing in London with my stepfather, and—"

"London?"

"Yes. She went to visit my older sister, Annabelle, and found a husband within six months. Annabelle made off with a peer of the realm, Sir George Randall, and Mother captured the heart of Lord Whitfield. My stepfather was a banker before his older brother choked on a chicken bone. Now he's Earl of Whitfield."

Chance spread his hands. "Had enough?" Rachel shook her head. "All right," he continued, "but you did ask for it. Our baby sister, Katherine, is twelve, lives with Mother, and is as fiery a rebel as you'll find south of the Mason-Dixon line. Then I have several uncles and aunts, one surviving grandmother—also in England—and scores of cousins."

"All rebels, I suppose?"

Chance grimaced. "I'm afraid so, all but the English lot, and they lean to the Confederacy as well. Tradition, family bloodlines, and cheap cotton. Yes, they're definitely not fans of your Mr. Lincoln."

"President Lincoln," Rachel corrected.

"That's one way of looking at it," he conceded. "But there was a great deal of hanky-panky in the vote counting. Some observers believe the election was stolen."

"You Virginians need to find an excuse for your treason."

"We're treacherous," he said. "You need to keep your eyes on us every moment." His own eyes twinkled merrily as he trailed a hand lightly over her ankle and up her calf.

Rachel shivered. Chance had only to touch her, and her thoughts turned lecherous. She closed her eyes and tried to lie still as his fingertips caressed her bare knee.

"Even an innocent, unsuspecting Yankee maiden sleeping by the creek?" she murmured. "And then?"

She squealed as Chance uttered a mock growl and pounced on her. For a moment they wrestled playfully on the blanket, and then he kissed her and began to pull the pins from her hair, one by one.

"Chance!" she protested.

"I like your hair," he whispered. "And I like your upper lip." He leaned close, traced the outline of her mouth with the tip of his finger, and then kissed it. "And I'm wild about your throat."

She sighed with pleasure as he unfurled a ribbon of soft, moist kisses along her neck. "And . . ."

"And what?" she asked.

"And you wear entirely too many clothes." He lifted a heavy section of her hair and kissed the hollow behind her ear and she laughed.

"That tickles."

"I've something for you that tickles more than that."

She stroked his jaw and ran her fingers over his muscular shoulders. She could feel the heat of him pressing against her thighs, burning through the layers of clothing that kept them from touching skin to skin.

"Let's go swimming," he whispered in her ear.

"I'm quite happy where I am."

"Swimming is good exercise."

"You just want to get my clothes off." The air, which had seemed so cool and refreshing, was suddenly warm. Moisture formed in the crease between her breasts, and it was hard to breathe.

"Smart woman." He rolled off her and took her hand. "Come on," he urged, tugging her along.

"Chance Chancellor, you are insatiable," she teased. But so was she. She couldn't get enough of him. And every moment that they were apart, thoughts of Chance filled her head. Just hearing his voice made her go all soft inside.

"I warn you. You're my prisoner," he threatened. "Come peaceably, or I'll be forced to—"

Bear's bark cut him off. Rachel jerked free of his hand and heard the pounding of hooves from the direction of the farmyard. Davy began to wail.

"Into the water," she cried. "Pretend you're pulling the crab traps." She scooped up his ragged hat and tossed it to him, then began to pin up her disheveled hair.

Cora Wright's grandson Solomon galloped toward them on a sleek black horse. "Miss Rachel! Miss Rachel! Soldiers coming!"

"Did they come to your grandmother's place?" Rachel asked as she picked up the crying baby.

"Just before nooning, but Granny dreamed it last night. She had Pharaoh hide her stock in the swamp. She says hide your horse and cow. They're taking everything with four legs for the army." He pulled off his straw hat and wiped away the sweat.

Rachel handed Solomon a jar of honey water, and he drank every drop. "How far away are they?"

"I don't know," the boy answered. "I heard shooting at Miller's farm, so I cut through the woods. Mr. Miller has two sons fighting for Lee, so Pharaoh says." He stared at Chance. "That your hired man?"

"Yes. He's strong, but as dumb as an onion."

"Soldiers might take him. They took Gideon Freeman."

"They won't want Abner. He can't talk at all, just makes noises." She tapped her head. "I think he's a few bricks short of a load."

"I got to go, Miss Rachel. They'd take me for sure, if they see me."

"Where are you riding to next?"

"The swamp. Pharaoh's camped out there. He says he can stay there until judgment day if he has to."

"Can you take Susan?" Rachel pointed to her cow grazing in the far corner of the meadow. "She's got a halter on. You can cross Indian Creek at the bend and follow that path through the marsh. Once you're in the cattails, no one will see you. " She snatched up a loaf of bread. "Take this. You won't be able to bake in the swamp."

"Thanks, Miss Rachel." He tucked the bread into a saddlebag. "And Granny says for you to take care. These soldiers may not be Johnny Rebs, but it's still not safe for a woman alone."

"Tell her to look after herself. And tell her that I'm not alone. I have Abner."

Solomon kicked the black horse into a run and jumped the pasture fence. He rode toward Susan, caught her, and looped a rope through her halter. Then he pulled down two rails of the fence to lead her out of the field.

Rachel watched anxiously until they entered the woods; then she turned to Chance. "We have to hide the horse," she said. "You heard?"

He nodded.

"Go and get Blackie. You'll have to take him into the woods. I—"

He splashed through the shallows and climbed the bank. "Like hell, I will. I'm not leaving you and Davy to face the Yankees by yourselves." He reached for the baby. "It might be best for the three of us to hide and let them have the horse."

"Are you out of your mind? Blackie isn't even my horse! And, to my way of thinking, we're in more danger with you than without you."

"Give me Davy."

"No. You get Blackie."

Chance shook his head. "Not unless you take him somewhere safe." His face darkened with anger. "Hell, woman, this is no time for you to be obstinate. You could take Davy in the boat and row—"

"And let them steal everything in the house? Not on your life," she replied hotly.

"Rachel . . ." He put a hand on her shoulder. She whirled and began to run toward the farmhouse.

"Be rational!" he shouted after her.

She hesitated for an instant and glanced back at him. "If I was rational, I'd never have risked my neck to save yours, would I? Now, do something about my horse!"

Chapter 17

A half hour later Rachel stepped out into the yard wearing a clean black skirt, a matching high-necked blouse, and a snowy white apron. She'd pinned her hair up severely and topped her widow's attire with a black straw bonnet and a pewter cross fastened at her collar.

A half-dozen mounted soldiers in Union blue milled in her yard, stirring up dust. Behind them, in the lane, came a heavy wagon with two civilians on the seat. One Rachel recognized as the county sheriff, John Voshell; the other man, gray-haired and dressed in working clothes, was a stranger.

Rachel shielded her eyes from the bright afternoon sun, smiled, and addressed a sergeant who seemed to be in charge. "Good morning, Lieutenant. Won't you step down and take some refreshment on this hot day?"

"Sergeant, ma'am," he corrected her in a clipped Yankee twang. "Sergeant Henry Pyle. Collecting livestock for our brave boys." He consulted a small pad of paper. "Your neighbors tell me you have a good cow."

Rachel sighed. "Had a cow. I leased one from Judge Ridgely in Dover, but somehow . . ." She spread her hands in a helpless gesture. "The judge sent his hired man to collect the Jersey last night. It's quite distressing, I can assure you. I'd planned on—"

Sergeant Pyle drew a line across his pad with a stubby pencil. "You wouldn't try to deceive us, would you, ma'am?"

"Me?" She tried to look surprised. "Not at all. I was hoping you'd come by. There's the matter of payment for the livestock that was appropriated earlier this year. I was promised—"

"Not my affair, Mrs.—"

"Irons," she supplied. "My dear husband James, God rest his soul, died in defense of his country. I should hope that I would not withhold anything which would help defeat the Southern rebels." She waved at the sheriff. "There's Sheriff Voshell. He can vouch for me. Sheriff! Will you tell this gentleman that my loyalty to the cause is unwavering?"

The sergeant glanced at the sheriff. "Do you know this woman?"

Sheriff Voshell nodded. "Afternoon, Miz Irons."

"Sheriff." She smiled at him. "I hope you haven't come about my taxes. I know I'm late, but—"

"Not today, Miz Irons. This is an unofficial visit on my part, a courtesy to the military. I haven't wanted to press you about the back taxes, due to your loss, but I can't continue to ignore your delinquency."

"I know, and I'm grateful for your kindness, sir. But I'm expecting James's death benefits from the government any day. I'll pay in full as soon as they come in."

The sheriff nodded. "It better be soon, ma'am."

"It will be, I promise you," Rachel replied.

Pyle broke in. "So she's a genuine war widow?"

"Yep, but I'd search her barn for the cow just the

same." The sheriff doffed his hat. "No offense, ma'am. Just doin' my job."

Rachel smiled at him. "And none taken, I'm sure."

"Who's here?" Pyle asked her.

"Just me, my son, and Abner Potts, my hired hand. Please don't frighten Abner. He can't speak, and he's . . ." She tapped her head with her index finger.

"Never heard of this Potts," Sheriff Voshell said.

"My cousin sent him down from New Castle," Rachel explained. "He's a godsend, I can tell you. Before Abner came, I didn't know how I'd manage, what with the new baby."

Four of the soldiers dismounted. One went into the chicken house, another headed for the pigpen. The others entered the barn.

Please, God, don't let Chance or Blackie be in there, Rachel prayed silently. Goose bumps rose on her arms, and she forced herself to remain composed.

Upstairs Bear kept barking at the window, and Rachel could hear Davy crying. She was glad of the noise. With luck, the racket would cover the sound of the chickens she'd hidden in the crawl space under the kitchen floor. Enough was enough, she'd decided. President Lincoln would get no more of her poultry or her livestock.

"Nothing in there," a young soldier called from the doorway of the chicken house. "Corn, chicken poop, and feathers, but no chickens."

"Ma'am?" The sergeant scowled. "Have you hidden your birds? Private Billings has found evidence of poultry."

"No, indeed," she protested. "What a question. You're welcome to search my house."

"Then where be your chickens?"

"Taken, sir, by a weasel. Two fat hens I had. What was left to me after the last time your people came by to rob me. And that devil's minion sucked every drop of blood from my birds. If I didn't know better, I'd think the creature had been sent out by the army to plague me."

"Those are hard words," Pyle replied. "There's a war on. Men have to eat."

"Indeed!" she flung back at him. "And so do widows and children. I've yet to see a penny of what was promised to me from the government. My babe and I are living on greens and fish." She shook a finger at him. "My husband, God rest his soul, is owed death benefits, and I haven't seen his back pay—let alone my widow's pension."

"So what you're sayin' is that varmints et your poultry?" the sergeant asked.

"One chicken, Molly by name, I fed to the reverend, last Sunday. I roasted it with wild onion and stuffed it—"

"Never mind." He vigorously crossed out something else on his paper. "No chickens."

"Sarge!" A red-haired soldier came out of the barn. "Found a horse in here."

Rachel's heart sunk. She started toward the man, but Sergeant Pyle waved her back. "Stay where you are, ma'am."

"My hired—" She broke off as Chance, leading Blackie, ambled out with a foolish grin on his face. It was all she could do to keep from bursting into laughter.

Chance limped heavily on his left side; Blackie limped on the right. Somehow the sturdy little horse had lost most of the hair on his mane and tail, had bald spots on his knees and sides, and was caked with manure and straw. Poor Blackie's nose was running, and disgusting yellow matter lodged in the corners of his bloodshot eyes.

"You call that a horse?" the soldier who'd checked her pigpen taunted the redhead. He swung up into the saddle and moved his mount a distance away from Blackie and Chance as if they were contagious.

"What's wrong with that animal?" Sergeant Pyle demanded of Rachel.

"Nothing's wrong with him," she replied. "He's a wonderful horse. My grandmother drove him to church every Sunday for years."

"Check his teeth," the sheriff advised.

Red approached Blackie, then stepped back in disgust as a trickle of foam dripped from the little horse's lips. Blackie began to cough, and the private shook his head. "Not me, Sarge. Let Wilson touch him."

Chance stood wide-eyed beside Blackie and stared at the soldiers. His mouth hung open, revealing blackened stumps of teeth, and he shuffled aimlessly from one foot to the other like a child who needed to use the necessary.

Something looked odd about him, other than his performance, Rachel mused. Was one shoulder higher than the other? Sweet Jerusha! Chance had a hump between his shoulder blades. She moaned and buried her face in her apron to keep from snickering.

"You! What's your name?" the sergeant demanded brusquely.

Chance grinned wider and let his tongue dangle out of his mouth. Lawyer, hell, Rachel thought. He should make his career on the stage.

"Abner? Are you Abner Potts?"

Rachel choked as Chance nodded excitedly. Pointing to his mouth, he jabbered a string of nonsense.

"Speak up," the red-haired private said, giving Chance a shove.

Chance turned toward the man.

Don't lose your temper, Rachel cried inwardly. Please, Chance, don't ruin your performance now. We'll all be hung!

To her relief, Chance squealed with delight, snatched a metal button off the man's shirt, and tilted it so that sunlight reflected off the shiny surface.

The soldier tried to recover his button, but Chance cradled it against him and limped across the yard to hide behind Rachel.

The sergeant shook his head. "Anything else in that barn?" he asked.

"Nothing but this sorry pair," Red said. "And I don't know which one is more worthless."

"Pardon, sir." Rachel tried to ignore Chance's tugging at the back of her skirt. "Abner's naught but a poor afflicted creature—one of God's own angels. I'll gladly pay for the button. Abner is—"

"I can see what he is, lady," Sergeant Pyle said. "Mount up." He swore at one of his men who rode too close to Blackie. "Keep your horse away from that animal. Can't you see it's sick?" He glanced back at Rachel. "I'd advise you to shoot that horse," he said. "And your hired man as well." He waved to the sheriff. "Let's move on. We're wasting daylight here."

"But my money!" Rachel protested. "What's due me. How do I collect—"

"File with the proper authorities, ma'am." Sergeant Pyle dug in his pocket and drew out a silver dollar. "Here, take this," he said, as he tossed it to her. "You need it more than I do."

"God bless you, sir," she called after him. "And you, Sheriff Voshell. God bless you both!" She smiled at their retreating backs. "And keep you far away from me," she finished softly.

Then Chance began to chuckle.

"Damn your hide," she said when she was certain that it was safe. "What have you done to poor Blackie?"

"What were you thinking?" she demanded later, when they'd dumped buckets of water over Blackie and washed the honey out of his eyes. "I said I had a mute working for me, not a . . ." She gasped in exasperation. "I could picture myself staring out of the bars at Fort Delaware."

"It worked, didn't it?" He lifted Blackie's foot and deftly pried a stone out of the frog. "Sorry, old boy," he murmured to the horse. "But you're better off pulling a plow here than an ammunition wagon." Chance glanced at Rachel. "War is worse on the animals than on the men."

"And how did you get him to cough and run from the nose and mouth?"

Chance grinned. "Pepper. Black pepper in his grain."

"Monster," she accused. "And where did you learn to playact like that?"

" 'All the world's a stage,' " he quoted. "And a court-room all the more." He chuckled. "I've always enjoyed the theater."

"I'd love to see a real play some day," she confided. Now that the troops were gone and her poultry and animals were safe, it was hard not to laugh at Chance's efforts.

"And I'd love to take you to see one." He pulled off

his shirt, and his hump slid to the ground, a tangle of rope and strips of torn cloth.

"What would you have done if someone touched that thing on your back?" she asked.

He winked at her. "They'd have had to catch me first."

"Well," she replied. "One thing is certain. If you survive the war and you can't go back to the lawyering trade, you can always buy a gypsy wagon and go on the road selling snake oil."

"We could do it together," he teased. "The world-famous Doctor Cyrus Calcutta and his lovely assistant, Princess Bubbling Water. We'll dress you in buckskin and beads. You can learn a war dance, and I'll—"

"Take the audience for every cent they've got," she supplied. "Not much different than what you did before the war."

"Ah, madam, you wound me," he cried dramatically as he clutched his fists to his chest. "That I, a man of letters who has sworn to uphold the laws of the land, should suffer such—"

"But you haven't, have you?" Suddenly serious, she gazed at him and wondered if she'd fallen easy prey to his gilded words. "You've not upheld the laws of our country."

"No," he admitted. "Not to your way of thinking. But I'm a Virginian, honey. What would you have done if Delaware had joined the secession? Could you have turned against your friends and neighbors? Fought against your cousins?"

She shook her head. "I guess not." She covered her face with her hands. "Why does life have to be so damned complicated? I wish that we could tramp the roads with a medicine show. I wish . . ." She trailed off, realizing how foolish she sounded.

Her throat tightened and she looked away from him. There wouldn't be any after the war for them, she reminded herself. And all her wishing wouldn't make it any different.

That night, after the mantle clock struck twelve, Rachel and Chance lay awake in her bed. Exhausted from making love, neither could sleep. Instead, Rachel rested her head on his sweat-dampened chest and listened to the steady throb of his heart while he caressed her unbound hair.

A light breeze stirred the curtains and lifted some of the still heat from the bedchamber. Outside, lightning bugs flashed on and off, and mosquitoes droned beyond the cheesecloth barrier Rachel had fastened over the open windows.

Chance's lean hand cupped one of her breasts, and their bare legs intertwined. Tonight their lovemaking had been quick and fierce. Thinking of his tumescence filling her was enough to send tremors down her spine. But for all the passion of their coming together, she wondered if this time of holding and whispering in the darkness wasn't sweeter still.

She loved Chance's smell, and she loved the feel of his powerful horseman's thighs and taut buttocks. She liked to tease his nipples until they puckered into tight knots, and she thrilled to his callused fingers stroking her body.

"I do love you," she whispered languidly. "No, shhh." She put her hand over his mouth. "Don't say anything. Don't spoil tonight. You don't have to love me back, Chance. Just let me—"

He pushed her hand away. "Don't. You're tearing me apart, Rachel. I do . . . Hell, woman, I can't stand this. I can't do it."

She stiffened in his arms. "Can't do what?"

"Can't stay here, hiding behind your skirts while Travis may be—"

Rachel twisted to her knees and seized his shoulders. She felt him wince as she tightened her fingers on his healing wound. "Travis is dead!" she said. "You can't kill yourself for a dead man. I won't let you."

"You can't stop me."

"What about me and Davy? What's going to happen to us if you throw your life away?"

"I'll go to Philadelphia and leave instructions with my English bank. I'm making a will, and everything I've got goes to you."

"Like hell!"

Davy started to whimper and she went to him and set the cradle to rocking. "I told you that I'm not taking your money. If you do survive the war, you'll marry someone of your own kind and—"

"You are my kind, Rachel." He rose from the far side of the bed and began to pace the floor. "I care about you and Davy, more than you'll ever know."

"But you don't love us?"

"Don't ask what I can't give. I care about you, more than I've ever cared about any woman and child. Does that satisfy you?"

"No, it doesn't." She sank down on the floor beside Davy and laid her head against the side of the cradle. "You must care about him deeply," she said, "your friend, Travis."

"You'd have to fight in a war to know what real friendship can mean. Soldiers depend on their comrades. You can shut your eyes and catch a little sleep, knowing he's there to watch your back, or you can charge a defended hill and be certain that if your horse is shot out from under you, he'll ride through cannon fire to pick you up." He crouched and put his arms around her. "I can't live with myself if I abandon him, Rachel. Can you understand that?"

"Why now? Why tonight? It's been weeks since—"

"I don't know." He pulled her against him and crushed her to his chest. "Maybe it was the sight of those blue uniforms. All I know is that I can't call myself a man if I go on hiding."

"What if you knew for sure?" She raised her head and touched his cheek. "What if I went to Fort Delaware and found out if he is dead or alive?"

"I won't let you do that. This is my—"

"I don't want to hear that. It's my concern and Davy's. How do you expect to get inside the prison? Women go there all the time to sell things, carry letters, to visit the Union soldiers. I can do it, Chance. I can."

"And how will you know Travis if you see him? You can't very well ask for him, can you?"

"I'll think of something."

"You'd take Davy there? You don't know what it's like. Yellow fever, typhoid, measles, pneumonia, even lockjaw. You can't take a baby into that. I won't trade Davy's life for Travis's."

"No," she answered softly. "No, I won't take Davy. I will leave him with Cora. She keeps goats as well as cows. He'll have milk, and he couldn't have better care."

"You're nursing him."

"I'll manage." She gave him a little shove. "If we find out that he's dead, will this be an end of it? Will you come back to the farm with me?"

"Until harvest," he agreed. "Only until then. After that, I've got to try and find the Fourth Virginia, wherever they are. I have to see this war through, Rachel."

"So you keep telling me." She lifted Davy from his cradle and sat down on the side of the bed to feed him. "I can take jams and jellies to sell," she murmured. "And pies. Blackberries and blueberries are ripening. I'll take you with me to point out Travis."

"And if I won't be a part of this?"

"You will." She slipped her hand under Davy's head and rubbed his soft curls. "First we'll go to Philadelphia to this bank of yours, and I'll let you loan me enough to pay off James's father and settle my tax bill. That way, if anything goes wrong, the farm is safe for Davy."

"You expect me to travel to Philadelphia with a hump on my back, playing the part of your mute servant?"

"No." She looked at him. Moonlight played over his face and chest. "I'll dress you in James's uniform and wrap your face with bandages. Once we're clear of Kent County, none will know that James Irons is dead and buried. We'll travel up the bay by sloop."

"You've a sloop? Where?"

"Hidden behind Cora Wright's house."

"You never told me you had a sailboat."

"You never asked."

She fixed him with a level gaze. "I love you, Chance. That doesn't mean I trust you completely."

"Maybe with good reason," he answered.

"How comforting."

He kissed her with infinite tenderness. "You're the best thing that's ever happened to me, Rachel Irons, and don't you ever forget it . . . no matter what."

Chapter 18

At midmorning the following day, Cora Wright stood on the creek bank and watched as a stranger rowed Rachel and Davy to her landing.

"I told you they were coming, Granny!" Mary Lou cried as she jumped from one foot to the other. "I see the baby."

"Hush, child," Cora scolded softly. "Don't shout like a fieldhand. Mind what I've taught you."

"Yes'm," the six-year-old replied.

"Good morning!" Rachel called. "I've brought little Davy for your blessing."

Cora leaned on her walking stick and studied the white man in Rachel's rowboat. Pharaoh had told her that Rachel had a new hired man that wasn't quite right, but Cora liked to see people and judge them herself. Youngsters, even her boy Pharaoh, were apt to jump to conclusions. A woman who'd lived as long as she had knew better.

"Watch your step with that baby," Cora warned Rachel. "He's young to be taken visiting."

Rachel laughed and hurried up the slight rise. "I wanted to be sure you were all right," she said as she gave her a warm hug. "Were the soldiers here yesterday?"

"Here and gone," Cora replied, taking the baby and cradling him against her breast. "They found nothing worth stealing but a smoked ham, and it was sour in the middle if you ask me. Likely it will give some of them the backyard trots."

"Is the livestock safe?"

"Safe as in God's pocket. Pharaoh has them in that high spot in the marsh. Quickmud all around it. If you don't know the right path in, that black swamp water will suck you down without a trace. Emma's there with him. She's a good wife, and a good daughter-in-law. My family was blessed when she came into it."

"From what I hear, Pharaoh's been hunting more than rabbits," Rachel said.

Cora smiled with her eyes. "Where'd you hear such gossip? You know better than to pay attention to loose talk. Pharaoh's been busy with his forge." Her son's hatred of slavers was a dangerous subject, even with a friend like Rachel. It was wiser to steer the conversation away from Emma and Pharaoh. "I want to hear all about your delivery."

"He came too soon for us to send for you," Rachel said. "Luckily, my cousin and her neighbor were down from New Castle. The neighbor, Mrs. Harquest, has nine children; two she brought into this world all by herself. She knew what to do for me and the baby."

"Fortunate you weren't alone." Cora peered into wee Davy's face, inhaling the babe's sweet, healthy scent and judging his muscle tone as he squirmed in her arms. "This is one fine boy," she said. "He's a keeper, certain. You did good, Rachel."

Strange how a woman could bring so many little ones into the world and still treasure each like a new penny,

Cora thought. White, brown, red, or black, she loved them all. Something about Rachel's story didn't feel right, but she'd never known the girl to lie. Maybe the cousin's visit was just luck.

Rachel laughed. "I hoped you'd approve of Davy. I wasn't intending to trade him for a speckled pig."

They laughed together at that, almost as if they weren't separated by skin color and custom. Rachel and her family were decent white folks, certain. She'd known Rachel Irons since she was born, and she'd never been disappointed in her yet.

"I appreciate you sending your grandson to warn us yesterday."

"I'll send your cow home with young Solomon when I'm sure it's safe," Cora said.

Together they walked through the vegetable garden, across the hard-packed yard, and into the house. Bright-eyed children giggled and trailed after them like bevies of quail chicks.

Cora turned and said, "Back to your chores, all of you. Moses, you haven't finished hoeing the corn, have you? And you, Abraham. Did you check your fishnets this morning?"

Boys and girls alike scattered, and she smiled. Young ones were the heart of families, and she had always believed that family was the strongest force under heaven—stronger than armies, stronger even than death. So long as families clung together, she had hope for the future.

"These aren't all your grandbabies, are they, Cora?" Rachel asked. "I thought I knew all of yours."

"Hmmp." Cora waved Rachel to the rocker in front of the fireplace. "I believe I've given up counting myself.

Some of them are Emma and Pharaoh's. Abraham is Preacher's boy; those girl twins in the yard are Gideon's. His wife, Jesse, she's working at Johnson's store. Her girls are old enough to watch their little brother, but I told them it's not safe to leave young ones home alone with all these soldiers tramping the roads."

Rachel sighed. "I agree. But I'm afraid I've come to add to your burden. I wanted to ask a favor."

"Ask away, girl. It's been troubling my heart that I wasn't with you when this little man-child came into the world. If there's anything—"

"Could you keep Davy? It would just be for a few days, maybe four or five. I have to go upriver to Philadelphia. I don't want to take Davy to the city in summer. He might catch something bad. I need a bank loan to pay off James's father, and—"

"What about your breast milk? You could dry up or take the milk fever without him nursing."

Rachel bit her lower lip. "I'll try to get back in three days. I can't think of any other way. I have to have the money."

"And these penny-pinching little banks won't loan to a woman, will they?" Cora declared. "Well, what needs done must be done. Try squeezing out some of the milk, gentle now. Maybe you'll be all right." She motioned to her great-niece Daisy, who was rolling biscuit dough. "Daisy, you think we could manage this little white baby for a few days?"

"Yes'm, Aunt Cora, I believe it would be no trouble at all. What's one more chile to look after?"

Cora smiled at Rachel. "There you have it. Daisy's my right hand, after Pharaoh's Emma. If Daisy says we can do right by your Davy, I suppose we can."

"I appreciate it, Cora," Rachel said. "I wouldn't leave him with anyone else. My father-in-law—"

Cora made a rude noise. "Him! No need to explain. But you take care. It's dangerous for a woman traveling alone in these times."

"Don't worry about me. I'll take Abner. He's mute and none too smart, but his back is strong."

Cora rose and went to the open hearth where a kettle hung over the coals. "You'll take tea," she said. "And you'll stay for dinner. I've got a nice haunch of venison and some fresh cabbage and potatoes."

"I brought you some jars of honey," Rachel replied. "I nearly forgot. They're in the boat. I'm sure the children have a sweet tooth."

Cora laughed. "Don't they always. Never knew a child who didn't." Something didn't ring right with Rachel's story. It wasn't like Rachel to leave her new babe, even for a day. And that Abner, showing up out of the blue like he did, was a lucky thing for Rachel's Choice. Maybe too lucky. She'd have to ponder on it.

"I'll just go and fetch the honey," Rachel offered.

"Don't think of it," Cora said. "I'll send one of these boys. They've got more energy than a yearling bull. Now, you just sit there, hold that pretty baby, and tell me all the news."

Three days later, Chance and Rachel guided her small sloop, *Windfeather*, north up the Delaware River past Pea Patch Island. Despite an overcast sky, the single sail billowed and snapped in a brisk breeze. Whitecaps foamed the biting salt air and soaked the two of them to the skin as the boat skimmed over the water's surface.

Above them the gray stone walls of Fort Delaware

bristled with heavy guns. Off *Windfeather*'s port side, patrol boats circled the island. Gulls wheeled and shrieked as they dared the sharks to snatch bits of garbage from the river.

Rachel shivered as she watched the dark fins slice the water. "Why are there so many sharks here?" she asked.

"They know that scraps from the kitchen will be dumped into the water over there." He pointed to the right side of the prison. "There's a canal that runs up to the kitchen areas. Blood, bones, offal from butchered animals. The men say that the Yanks feed the sharks to keep them close to the prison. I know of two men who were eaten by them while I was there. At least I think it was two. What washed up on the beach wasn't enough to tell."

"That's horrible," she said. "Inhuman."

"You'd be surprised what men will do to each other in time of war. Do you have any idea what will happen to us if they catch me in this blue uniform?" Chance answered hoarsely.

The sight of Pea Patch Island sickened him and made him doubt his sanity in allowing Rachel to accompany him on such a mission. Not even the whipping wind could mask the stench of the prison. Refuse bobbed in the water, and once he caught sight of something that could have been a man's leg.

A larger vessel, riding low in the waves, edged away from the shadows of the fortress. Shrouded in canvas, stacks of cargo lined the deck. A soldier on the bow waved, and Chance waved back. "Smile," he urged Rachel.

He looked back at the approaching boat. "Fall over and drown, you son of a bitch," Chance hissed.

Rachel maneuvered the *Windfeather* clear of the military vessel's path. "Do you know that man?" she asked Chance.

"No."

"Then, why—"

"That's the Finn's Point ferry," he said. "They're carrying the dead to bury on the other side of the river in New Jersey."

"So many?"

Chance swore under his breath. "It's summer. Heat's worse than cold for spreading disease. Pea Patch is a swamp at low tide. At high tide the prisoners say it's part of the river. Likely another typhoid outbreak has stacked up the dead like cordwood." He set his jaw and stared straight ahead, not bothering to answer as Union soldiers shouted greetings from the deck.

The *Windfeather* sailed on, slowly passing the town of Wilmington and finally reaching Philadelphia at dusk. "We'll have to sleep on the boat," Rachel said. "I've no money for an inn. It's probably safer for us anyway."

They anchored in a cove and made a meal of cold sweet potatoes, hard-boiled eggs, and bread. As night cloaked the riverbank, brilliant stars winked on, one by one, and a clouded moon rose over the trees on the far side of the river. Swarms of mosquitoes buzzed around Rachel and Chance's heads until they retreated to the tiny cabin and sealed the hatch.

The interior of the sloop was pitch dark, but Chance had no trouble locating the narrow bunk that ran along the starboard side. He sat down and swatted at the whine of a mosquito.

"A nice welcome to the City of Brotherly Love," Rachel said as she cuddled up beside him.

"My sentiments," he agreed. "It's hot enough to bake biscuits in here, but at least we're not being eaten alive." He smacked another mosquito between his hands.

"We came for money, not a pleasure trip," she reminded him. "Wait, I've got something."

She fumbled in the dark and returned with a small metal container, which she pressed into his palm. "Rub this on your bites. It should help reduce the itching."

"What is it?" He raised the can to his nose.

"Goose grease, vinegar, and rue."

"Great, now I'll smell like a dead goose." He anointed two bites on his neck and another on his forehead, then gave the ointment back to her and kissed the crown of her head. "You smell good. What is that in your hair? Apples?"

"Apple blossom."

"I like it," he said. She raised her head and he kissed her mouth tenderly.

"Oh, Chance," she whispered. "Please don't get killed on me."

His chest tightened. "Aren't you frightened for yourself at all, woman?"

"Terrified."

He hugged her against him. "I could have used you in my company. You've more nerve than most, and more common sense than the lot." He tilted her chin and kissed the tip of her nose. "Get some rest, honey," he ordered. "I'll keep watch." The words sounded good, but how much protection he could offer her was anybody's guess.

Rachel's taste lingered on his lips.

If things went wrong and she and Davy had to pay the price . . . Running from the guards on the beach at Pea Patch Island had been bad, but nothing like this.

He wiped the sweat off his forehead and shifted his back against the rough planking. Outside, the night was quiet with no sounds but the gentle lapping of waves against the hull. His gut twisted with uneasiness. Protect her? Hell, the pistol they'd brought with them would be useless if soldiers attempted to arrest them for treason. He didn't mind risking his own life, but he'd not gamble with Rachel's more than he had already.

"Tell me about lawyering," she murmured sleepily, cutting into his black reverie.

"Most is tedious work," he replied.

"But not all."

"Go to sleep." He wanted to be alone with his demons. And most of all he didn't want to answer questions about tomorrow, about what would happen when he went into the prison.

She persisted. "How did you come to choose law as a way of making a living?"

He thought a moment and then chuckled softly. "I suppose I liked the challenge," he admitted, "and I had a respect for the law."

She caught his hand and gently massaged his fingers, kissing the pad of each in turn. "Tell me about some of your cases."

"Only if you stop that." Odd how such a thing could make a man's loins tighten. "You may be sorry you asked. Once I represented an accused hog thief who . . ." He gasped as her hand brushed his groin. "Rachel!"

"Don't you like it?" she teased.

"I like it fine, but . . ."

"But . . ." She laughed softly and began to stroke the length of his swelling cock.

"You're insatiable, woman."

He lost his place in the unbelievable tale of his encounter with the Reverend Jacob Thomas and pulled her into his lap. "You want to play?"

"Do you know a good game?"

He crushed her mouth and slipped searching fingers under her skirt. "I'd love to play."

Their lovemaking was slow and passionate. And later, when he'd brought her to climax twice and satisfied his own raw hunger, he held her and finished his story. After that, despite her protests, he followed with another about a rascal cleric who talked a parishioner out of a prize heifer.

Eventually, Rachel drifted off with her head in his lap, but Chance found no such peace. Blending flesh and soul with her was a touch of paradise, but seeing Fort Delaware had brought back memories that refused to fade.

He'd seen so many men die in their own vomit, helped carry too many gray-clad bodies onto the Jersey death ship. Some had slipped away quietly in their sleep; others had died hard. But worst of all had been young Jeremy Stewart.

Travis and he had stolen boards to build the boy a coffin, and they swaddled him in his threadbare blanket. They'd threatened to strangle any man—Union or Confederate—who robbed it from him. But Chance could still see Jeremy's blackened face, and his fingers ached to tighten around Coblentz's throat.

God rot his bowels! The Dutchman deserved to die. He'd been tried and condemned by a jury of good men. Every breath he drew was one too many. Killing him would be justice, not an act of murder.

But he couldn't explain it to Rachel ... couldn't

justify what he meant to do. Some things were better left unspoken, no matter how the silence wore at a man's soul.

Carefully he rose and went up on the deck again. A breeze off the water helped with the mosquitoes, but being bitten was better than being trapped in that cabin with his regrets.

He set himself to finishing his disguise, wrapping his leg with splints and bandages, and then slipping a lead fishing weight in his shoe to insure that he limped when he walked. Rachel had wrapped a bandage around his head before they'd left the farm. Now he covered one eye and most of his face and neck, leaving only small holes to breathe. Again he would have to pretend to be mute. No amount of thespian skill could cover his Virginia accent, and one slip would mean disaster for their plan.

He didn't doubt that the two of them could reach the banking house, but if Benjamin Gordon was no longer with the Philadelphia branch or if the English solicitor refused to give them the money, they'd be in deep trouble.

That thought made him laugh. When hadn't he been in trouble since his horse had taken that spill in the forest at Gettysburg? Hell, since he'd joined the Confederate army. Any Virginian who could face down Rachel Irons and her dogs should be able to manage an aging English banker, shouldn't he?

The next morning they walked a short distance to Chestnut Street and Chance's imposing London Bank. After some urgent discussion, Rachel was able to convince a clerk that Mr. Gordon would be willing to see Mr. Irons without an appointment.

The stout, bespectacled clerk led Chance away, leaving Rachel to cool her heels in the imposing marble lobby for more than two hours. She waited nervously while elegantly dressed patrons, police, and soldiers passed by. And each time Rachel caught sight of a uniform, she was certain the bank employees had discovered Chance's identity and the soldiers had come to drag the two of them to jail.

Finally, when she was about to demand to be taken to Chance, he appeared with the exceedingly proper Mr. Gordon. The tall Englishman was whip-thin with a florid complexion and a neatly trimmed white beard and mustache. In contrast, his head was covered with an ill-fitting jet-black wig, so ridiculous in appearance that Rachel nearly dissolved into laughter.

Chance took her arm and escorted her out through a side door, where Mr. Gordon hailed a passing carriage for hire. The three rode through the streets of Philadelphia to an inn where the solicitor had rooms.

There Mr. Gordon ordered a late breakfast for her and Chance. When they had eaten, Gordon handed Rachel a parcel and a sheaf of papers. "There is your five hundred dollars. A copy of Mr. Chancellor's will is enclosed as well."

"His will?" she asked, confused. "I told him—"

"Nevertheless . . ." Gordon stroked his beard and stared fiercely at her. "Mr. Chancellor has named you and your minor child, James David Irons, as his sole beneficiaries— subject, naturally, to any later will. Our bank will act as guardians for the minor child until he reaches the age of twenty and one. Since Mr. Chancellor has also set up a stipend for the boy, you—as his mother—may petition the bank for moneys to clothe, feed, and educate him."

"All I wanted was a loan," she protested. "I didn't ask for five hundred dollars, and I never agreed to—"

"I believe the less said, the better," Gordon replied. "You should consider yourself quite fortunate, Mrs. Irons. Considering the circumstances—"

"What circumstances?"

She turned to Chance, but he simply grinned and spread his hands.

"The driver will take you wherever you want to go," Gordon said, "but if I'm asked, I dropped you a few blocks from the bank, and I never laid eyes on either of you again."

"As you wish," Chance said.

"I'm doing this for the family," Gordon said. "But I don't approve."

Chance nodded. "So you've already told me."

"Your country's differences are none of my business," Gordon continued. "The bank's position is strictly neutral."

The solicitor left the inn by one door; she and Chance hurried out by another. On the way back to the sloop, Chance insisted the carriage driver make several stops; once at a shop that sold secondhand clothing, and again at a grocery, where he purchased a basket of fresh bread and several dozen eggs. Finally he halted the vehicle along the street to buy a child's wagon from a peddler.

"You'll need something to carry your wares in," Chance had explained to her. "I won't be able to help you, seeing as how I'm so badly injured."

When they reached the comparative safety of the *Windfeather*, she waited for Chance to explain his actions. Instead, he pressed the Quaker clothing into her arms and steered her toward the hatch.

"I'm not taking five hundred dollars from you," she said. "I won't be bullied into it. And I didn't ask you to—"

"Just put on the dress," he ordered. "You can pay me back the five hundred. We don't have time for this now."

"A Quaker? Why do I have to be a Quaker?" Rachel demanded. She frowned as she inspected the plain gray dress and severe black bonnet.

"Hurry," Chance insisted. "If you hurry, we can catch the outgoing tide at noon."

"But I don't know any Quakers. I don't know how they're supposed to speak."

"If you have fresh bread, the Yankees won't care what you say."

"What's all this about a stipend for Davy?"

"I want to provide for him, for both of you when I'm not there to do it."

"I can care for my own child. I don't need your charity," she insisted.

"Please, Rachel."

Chance was bandaged so completely that only one blue eye showed, but even that was hard to stare down. "Damn you, Chance Chancellor," she muttered. She guessed that he was as nervous as she was about their coming attempt to get in and out of the prison. If they had the sense of a horseshoe crab, they'd sail right past Pea Patch Island and back to Rachel's Choice.

Against her better judgment, she shut the hatch and changed into the Quaker dress. It was large around the waist and high on her ankles, and it smelled musty and none too clean.

"This is your revenge on me for Abner's clothing," she called up to him as she tugged at the offending material.

"This looks abominable," she complained. "Am I supposed to 'thee' and 'thou' the soldiers as I peddle my bread and jams?"

"Hurry up," Chance shouted. "I need you to help with the sail."

She pulled the bonnet over her hair and stuffed a round loaf of raisin bread up under her skirt and tied it over her stomach. "We'll see how you like that, Mr. Chancellor," she said. "If I have to be a Quaker, I'll be a pregnant one."

Chance's eyes narrowed when she came on deck. "What do you think you're doing?" he demanded. "This isn't a game. We could both end up with our necks stretched."

"You think I don't know that?" she snapped. "Who's got the most to lose here?"

"You do," he admitted after a moment. "I'll understand, Rachel, if you want to call off the whole thing."

"Would you?" She touched his hand. "It's what I'd like to do. But you wouldn't be satisfied, would you? You'd go on thinking about Travis, wondering if he's alive."

He nodded.

Rachel went forward to pull the anchor. "Let's do it, then," she said.

Chance turned the tiller, and the *Windfeather* drifted into the channel. The outgoing tide carried them past a tall clipper ship headed upriver and a barge loaded with salt hay anchored along the muddy shore.

Rachel took Chance's place at the tiller, and he raised the sail. The bright noonday sun reflected off the water, causing her to squint as she watched a great blue heron flap up out of the reeds and glide soundlessly across the river.

"We won't have to go into the fort proper," Chance said. "The common soldiers are housed in wooden sheds on the island. Only officers and civilian traitors are kept inside the stone walls."

"That's comforting," Rachel replied as she moved to sit beside him. "Is that where you were kept?"

His gaze met hers, and for an instant she thought he wasn't going to answer, but then he nodded. "I was a captain in the Fourth Virginia Cavalry. Am a captain," he corrected himself. "I spent five months in an officers' cell, two of them in solitary confinement for trying to escape." His features hardened. "Some of the guards were sadistic and the food was worse than I'd feed to pigs, but we were dry and we had bunks to sleep on."

"I don't understand. If officers were kept in the main prison, how did you get out?"

"Stories began to filter in about the conditions on the island for the enlisted men. And after two attempts to break out, I realized that the only way off Pea Patch was from the wooden barracks in the common quarters." A faint hint of a smile played over his taut lips. "I convinced them that I was a private, masquerading as an officer. My punishment was five lashes and exile to the common section of the island."

"Is that where you found your friend?" she asked.

"Travis had used common sense. He'd gotten rid of his insignia before he was captured. He knew that our boys needed leaders to keep them alive once they got to prison. Travis was my first lieutenant, and a better one I never hope to see."

She lay her head against him. "If you joined the enlisted men to help them, why did you escape?"

"Two of ours, Will and Charley, died of their wounds; Red Bailey was carried off by consumption; and the baby, Jeremy Stewart, hanged himself. Dave Pointer was the only one left of the Fourth Virginians, besides Travis and me. Dave was supposed to go with us that night, but he never showed up at the meeting place."

"So they may both be dead?"

"Probably." He squeezed her arm. "You don't have to do this," he said. "I can put you ashore here and take the goods to sell myself."

She scoffed. "And end up shot the moment you open your mouth?"

"Other Virginians have joined the Union forces."

"And shown up at a federal prison selling bread and jam?" She made a sound of disgust. "You can't do it alone, and you know it."

"Maybe not."

In spite of the heat, she shivered. This was crazy, she thought. She should be home with Davy. What if she never saw her baby again? What good would Chance's money do Davy if he were an orphan?

She bit her lower lip and stared out at the black water. Until now she'd done nothing but hide an escaped rebel, something that might be explained away as the act of a foolish woman. This was different. She was assisting a Confederate soldier to spy on a Union prison, and the courts would show her no mercy if they were caught.

"I guess the trick is not to be caught," she whispered into the wind.

"That's the idea."

"God help us." But would He? she wondered. What

they were doing was wrong, even if they were doing it for the right reason. She was risking everything for the love of Chance, and he for love of his friend. Surely that had to count for something with the Almighty.

Resolutely she pushed her apprehension aside, tightened her hands on the gunnel, and fixed her gaze on the river ahead.

Chapter 19

Rachel's heart pounded as she towed her high-sided wagon full of ham, bread, and pies down the crowded Fort Delaware wharf. Around her, oxen, horses, merchants, foot soldiers, civilian officials, servants, and sweating laborers jostled for position on the narrow roadway. Cursing teamsters cracked bullwhips, wagon wheels creaked, and horses shied beneath the broiling August sun.

Dogs barked, a load of barrels shifted and slid into the marsh beside the plank-lined track, and a blue-uniformed messenger on horseback nearly collided with Rachel's wagon. She dodged the bay's steel-shod hooves, shouted angrily at the rider, and returned his rude gesture with an equally insulting one.

"Remember that you're a Quaker," Chance admonished.

She glanced over her shoulder at him limping along with the aid of a crutch and bit back an oath. What had he gotten her into? The humid air reeked with the stench of gunpowder, tarred ropes, manure, and human waste, and it was impossible to take a step without sinking ankle-deep in animal droppings. Greenhead flies, no-see-ums, and mosquitoes bit her exposed flesh and buzzed around her head. The coarse wool of her dress chafed her skin and itched unmercifully.

"Couldn't you have made me a dockside slattern?" she hissed at Chance. "At least I could have worn less clothing."

"Do you think I'm comfortable bound up like an accursed mummy?" he whispered. "Besides, it's your job to look pious," he answered. "Thou should not lose thy Christian charity, sister."

"I'll give *thee* a taste of charity, if we ever get out of here alive," she promised. She wondered why Chance had bothered with such an elaborate deception. Amid the milling crowds and the confusion, she was certain she could have ridden an elephant past the high, granite walls of Fort Delaware without anyone noticing.

As they reached the main entrance to the fortress, the wooden thoroughfare gave way to dusty lanes leading in different directions. One path led across a bridge and through a guarded gate to the forbidding, gray-walled enclosure. A second lane circled the murky green waters of the moat and ran around the stone prison. The third road cut across the potholed field to a log palisade rising out of weeds. On the far side of this barrier lay the wooden barracks that housed the common prisoners.

Rachel realized she was on the wrong side of the road to reach the enlisted men's prison. She waited as a produce wagon, a cart of flour, and a platoon of youthful recruits spilled past her. Then, losing patience, she rested her dirty shoe on the rail of the wagon, hiked up her petticoats, and adjusted her garter.

The driver of an ale wagon taking the center lane gaped fish-mouthed at Rachel's exposed leg. His lead mule turned to the right, and the rest of the team followed, carrying the vehicle directly into the bridge approach. The right front wheel tangled with the left wheel of a colonel's gig, dumping the officer, a bulldog, and an elegantly gowned woman into the green-scummed moat.

A sutler, directly behind the gig, reined in short and guided his team left to avoid hitting the overturned carriage.

In seconds orderly chaos became bedlam as soldiers dived into the water to rescue the officer and his lady. The bulldog climbed up the bank and rushed at the infantrymen, vehicles overturned, and draft animals became tangled in harnesses.

With the way open, Rachel hurriedly pulled her wagon across the road in front of the riot and walked toward the high wooden fence. Chance hobbled after her, sputtering with indignation.

"You're not a farmer," Chance fumed. "You're a damned gypsy. Have you lost your mind?"

"Keep quiet," she answered tersely. "Remember, your wounds keep you from talking."

At the gate she had to answer the same questions that she'd been asked when she'd docked her sloop at the landing. "Come to sell my goods to the brave soldiers," she said meekly.

"Why here in the common barracks and not up at the castle?" a red-faced corporal demanded.

Rachel adjusted her bonnet. "A falsehood was spread about my pies," she lied smoothly. "Someone accused me of using green apples and giving a captain a belly-ache. There was nothing wrong with my pie, I can tell thee. 'Twas only his own greed, that he could eat the whole in one sitting." She tried to look pitiful. "He's barred me from the main fort, he has, and me with four small children to support. 'Twas most un-Christian of him."

"Which captain might that be, ma'am?"

She shrugged. "Does thou think I ask the name of every customer? A big man he was, with full jowls and little neck."

The soldier grinned, exposing a rotting front tooth. "Pass on, Quaker lady, but if you don't sell all your wares, remember Johnny O'Brady on your way out."

"Thank you, brother," she said.

The sentry raised his weapon and stepped in front of Chance. "What's your business here?"

"He can't talk," Rachel said, tapping her own throat. "He's my husband, or what's left of him. Poor James, I can't leave him at home. Last time I did, he wandered off into the hog pen and I found him eating slops."

"My sympathies, ma'am." The corporal motioned to a red-haired private, and the private opened the gate just wide enough for them to pass through.

Rachel stopped a few feet inside the walls and stared. Chance had told her that the island was little more than a swamp, but she hadn't expected this soggy hell.

Not a proper road or speck of grass remained. Instead, churned ruts of stinking black ooze led from the guard station to wooden barracks more suited to curing lumber than sheltering enemy soldiers. Pools of stagnant water sprinkled the landscape, and through a line of scrubby trees she could glimpse the Delaware River.

Rachel had steeled herself for the inhumanity of prison life, but she hadn't imagined it would be like this. Ragged men, stripped to the waist, bathed and washed clothes in the filthy sinkholes. Others sat in the mud, smearing their arms and faces until they looked like caricatures of the teams of black laborers digging ditches in the hot sun. And others . . . Sweet Lord in heaven! Some men were relieving themselves in full view.

There were hundreds of prisoners, maybe thousands, swarming over the island like flies. Scarecrows in the remnants of Confederate uniforms crept toward them, calling out with hollow voices.

"Ma'am, have you any food to spare?"

"Please, missus, I haven't heard from my family in two years. I'm Dan White from Federalsburg. Could you send a letter for me?"

"Have you bread for a fellow Christian, sister? Anything at all."

"Mercy, lady . . ."

An old man stretched out a bony hand. "There's been a mistake. I don't belong here," he whispered hoarsely. "I'm the king of Spain. You've got to help me."

Chance swung his crutch in a threatening arc. "Keep back," he warned. "You'll get nothing here but broken bones."

Shaken, Rachel turned and stared at him. "Surely I can part with—"

"Nothing," he said. "Give them one bite, and you'll never get inside the barrack enclosure with a crumb." He grabbed her arm, and his fingers dug in. "Be careful, Rachel. Ask for the commanding officer. He won't see you, but it will take time. Sell your goods as slowly as you can. Stall, ask to see the chaplain—the hospital. Give me an hour. I'll meet you back here."

She stiffened. "You're leaving me?"

He leaned close to her ear. "I have to, darling. No one would talk to me if you were along. I need to find someone who might know about Travis."

Panic seized her and her knees went weak. "No!" she

cried. "You can't leave me." She clutched at his shirt, but he pried loose her fingers.

"There are guards inside. No one will molest you if you use common sense and stay in the common areas."

"Please don't go," she begged him.

"I'll stay with you until you reach the entrance. You're tough; you'll be fine."

"I may be tough, but you're a son of a bitch," she muttered as she hurried toward the barracks, dragging the wagon after her.

A group of chanting blacks carrying shovels and led by a Union sergeant crossed directly in front of her. One man, near the end of the line, stopped singing, turned his head, and studied her.

Pharaoh! It was Cora's Pharaoh!

Rachel almost called out to him but caught herself in time. Cora's son gazed past her at Chance, and for a moment she read suspicion on Pharaoh's sweating blue-black face. Then he picked up the spiritual on the chorus and strode on without ever acknowledging her presence.

"Chance," she whispered when the work party was out of earshot. "Did you see . . ." But Chance was gone, slipped off into the crowd of prisoners. And she was alone, facing yet another guard station and more questions.

"Vat is yer name and business, voman?" a burly Union soldier shouted. Sweat stained the armpits of his soiled shirt, and the stench nearly made her gag.

She took a deep breath and replied, "Good day to thee, brother. I'm Charity Goodfellow, and I've come to see thy commanding officer on an important matter."

"Sech as?" The sergeant's right eye was bloodshot and

swollen as if he'd been fighting, and an inflamed boil on his neck exuded yellow pus. The giant scratched at the carbuncle with dirty, broken nails, and she noticed that two fingers on one hand were missing the last joint.

"A private matter." By his accent she judged the man to be Pennsylvania Dutch, and by his smell he couldn't have bathed since his sixth birthday.

"Says you." He spat a cud of tobacco on the ground beside her, spraying the hem of her skirt.

She flinched back, and he grinned.

"What is thy name?" she demanded.

Ignoring her question, he scratched his whisker-stubbled chin. "Show me vat you got in dat vagon."

Rachel pulled back the canvas, exposing her food-stuffs, and the man dug a handful of crust and blackberries out of the center of one of her pies.

"Swine!" she accused.

He laughed again and grabbed for another pastry.

"One is enough for you." Rachel seized the ruined pie and thrust it at him. "You may as well eat the whole thing, since thee put thy dirty hands in it. Now let me pass."

The Dutchman watched her with piggy eyes as he stuffed a quarter section of the pie into his mouth and slowly chewed it. "You a fancy voman?" he mumbled. "Maybe a rebel come to break out our prisoners?"

"I am first cousin to thy good chaplain," she answered hotly. "And if you do not let me pass, I shall see that you greatly regret it."

"What's going on here?" A lieutenant with thinning hair appeared in the open doorway. "Is there a problem?"

"Yes, there is." Rachel flashed her sweetest smile. The officer was short and gaunt; the obnoxious sergeant dwarfed him. "I've come to sell my bread and pies. I was given permission to enter, but this man"—she waved at the Dutchman—"he's eating my goods without paying."

The lieutenant scowled at the sergeant. "Have you nothing better to do, Sergeant Coblentz? Come with me, ma'am. It's hardly fit for a lady in here, but . . ."

"Why thank you, brother," she replied. "My breads are as fine as thou may taste anywhere. And I've jams for sale as well as sweets." Picking up the wagon handle, she followed the officer inside, leaving Coblentz to finish off the remainder of her blackberry pie.

Lieutenant Cochran had escorted her through the outer barracks and into a center compound that contained rows of equally decrepit housing.

No breeze could blow inside the courtyard, and the broiling sun seared her skin and turned her dress to a damp, suffocating wrapping. Wooden planks between buildings were covered in mud and slime, and it was impossible to walk without sliding off and wetting her shoes. It was all Rachel could do to keep from being sick at the foul odors that seeped up from the ground and drifted from the barracks.

The lieutenant sent an orderly to find the captain, but before the officer could arrive, word of mouth had carried the message that fresh bread and baked goods were available. Cochran bought two of her pies, a jar of jam, and a loaf for himself. But she barely had his money in her pocket before two more officers showed up and asked her prices.

"The same as usual," she said, not having any idea what a pie was worth.

Apparently they were worth hard silver. Her entire stock vanished in less than five minutes.

After everything had been sold, Rachel asked Lieutenant Cochran if she could pray for the poor unfortunates in the hospital. That gained her a little time, but she was forced to face the horrible sights and smells of the infirmary. Men with half their faces blown away lay side by side on the reeking straw pallets with those suffering from dysentery and measles. Along one wall flies crawled over the stacks of the dead awaiting transportation to the funeral boat. And after viewing the misery and hearing the cries of the patients, she wondered how the doctors could tell the sick from the expired.

Finally, when she could stand no more, she told Cochran that she must return to the landing if she was to catch her boat. He guided her back to the entrance, and this time, when she passed through the heavy wooden doorway, the Dutchman wasn't there.

She looked for Pharaoh, but he, too, was gone. Two blacks were shoveling mud out of a drainage ditch, but neither of them was Cora's son.

Rachel had dreaded passing through the open ground, but few of the prisoners paid her any mind as she walked back to the spot where Chance had promised to meet her.

If she'd been frightened coming in, she was terrified now. The thought of being trapped here was enough to make her palms sweat and her mouth go dry. If Chance had been taken . . .

But she couldn't let herself think of that. Instead, she pictured Davy's laughing face and imagined the three of them sharing a dip in the cool waters of Indian Creek.

What would she do if Chance wasn't at the fence?

How long should she wait before deciding that he wasn't coming?

She shivered despite the temperature. She loved Chance fiercely, more than she'd ever thought any woman could love a man. And she didn't know if she could stand losing him.

But to her relief, as she approached the guard station, she saw him leaning on his crutch in the shadows. Her heart skipped a beat, and it was all she could do not to run to him and throw her arms around his neck.

"James," she called. "Thou has wandered off again. I was afraid for thy safety."

He hung his head.

"Come now," she said. "We must go home." The coins she'd received for the sale of her wares hung heavily in her pocket as they signaled for the sentries to let them out of the compound.

Chance shuffled after her, keeping close behind as she hurried out into the open space and took the road to the wharf. The thoroughfare was still crowded, but now most of the wagons were going in the opposite direction.

Rachel wanted to ask him if he'd found out anything about Travis, but was afraid to give him away. Both remained in character until they reached the sloop and pulled anchor.

As they slid away from the dock, Rachel took the tiller. Chance moved woodenly to raise the sail. The water between the fort and the small town of Delaware City was crowded with boats, and the outgoing tide ran swiftly. Guiding the *Windfeather* safely among the larger vessels was difficult.

Once they reached the channel, Rachel's heartbeat slowed to near normal. "It was awful in there—terrible," she said. "Heaven help those poor men." She shuddered. "You couldn't pay me to go back in there. Thank God you escaped. It's a death house."

Chance moved to the bow of the boat and gazed out at the Jersey tree line on the far side of the river.

"He's dead, isn't he?" Rachel asked. "I'm so sorry, Chance."

He didn't answer.

She lashed the tiller and went to him. "You tried," she murmured. "There's nothing more you could have done for Travis."

Chance coughed, a deep racking hack that shook his whole body.

"Where did you get that?" she asked, laying her hand on his shoulder. "I'll make you a chest plaster when we get home."

Chance's shoulders sagged. Another coughing spasm seized him, and he began to choke.

Rachel patted him hard on the back. "You can't blame yourself," she said.

"Oh, but I can."

Rachel snatched her hand away as though she'd been burned. "What in—"

He turned his head, and she gasped. The single eye staring out of Chance's bandaged face was brown.

Chapter 20

"Who are you?" Rachel cried. "You're not Chance!"

"No, ma'am," he replied. "I'm Lieutenant Travis Bowman. Did Chance mention my name to—"

"I know who you are!" Rachel backed away from him. Suddenly her chest felt constricted, and black spots drifted past her line of vision.

I'm going to faint, she thought as she slid down the gunnel to sit on the deck. She put her head down and fought the sickness that churned in her belly.

"Don't take on so, ma'am," Travis said. "I assure you, you're in no danger from me. Chance said—"

She glared at him. "That son of a bitch said this would be all right with me? He told you that I'd volunteered to commit treason?"

"No, he . . ." Another fit of coughing prevented Travis from finishing.

"You're ill, aren't you?" Anger replaced her nausea, and she got to her feet.

Travis sucked in a rasping breath. "I took a bullet through the lung, ma'am. I was wounded when Chance and I tried to escape last spring."

Rachel shook her head. "That's more than an injured lung. You sound consumptive to me."

"And you're afraid of catching it." His cultured speech was that of a gentleman. "That's understandable, ma'am. If you'll just put me ashore, preferably on the Delaware side of the river, I'll trouble you no more."

Rachel gritted her teeth. If she opened her mouth, she'd shame a dockside strumpet with her language.

"Chance took my place," Travis explained, "but he intends to make another escape attempt tonight, before he's recognized." More coughing racked the lieutenant's body. "He wants you to return to your farm and wait for him," he said. "He expects to be there in three days, perhaps four."

Rachel returned to the tiller, but she couldn't tear her gaze away from Travis. Had she been blind that she didn't realize that someone other than Chance was wearing James's uniform?

James's pants seemed to fit this man better, so perhaps Travis was an inch or so shorter than Chance. He was definitely narrower across the shoulders, and his hands were smaller.

She moistened her numb lips and tried to comprehend how she'd been so completely deceived by the ruse.

A patrol boat crossed in front of the *Windfeather*, so close that she could have hit the soldier at the helm with a rock. Quickly Rachel glanced over her shoulder at the island fortress. Rows of gun ports lined the granite walls, artillery powerful enough to blow a warship out of the water, let alone her tiny sloop.

The reality of the situation shook her to the core. Travis was aboard the *Windfeather*, and Chance was a prisoner on Pea Patch Island. If she was caught, no amount of excuses would satisfy the authorities. For her own safety, she had no time to argue with Travis. She needed to get as far from here as possible.

But how could she possibly run and leave the man she loved trapped in this living horror? If a few hours inside had sickened her, what must it have been like for Chance when he was locked up for so many months? And how had he found the raw courage to go in again?

"If you'd rather not put in on the beach," Travis said, breaking into her reverie, "perhaps you could steer the sloop into shallow—"

"Shut up!" she snapped. "Shut up, sit there, and try to look like an injured Union soldier." She forced back her nausea, and smiled and waved to the guards on a second patrol boat. "Nice day," she called.

"Where you headed?" a soldier shouted.

"Duck Creek," she lied. "I sold all my pies at the fort." The sergeant motioned for her to pass by.

Rachel's mind raced as she tried to think what to do with Travis that would keep them both out of prison. He was clearly too sick to turn loose. He'd be captured again in a matter of hours. That or die in the first ditch he came to.

Sweet hope of heaven! What had possessed Chance to go back into that place and allow those gates to close behind him? But that was a stupid question—he'd done it for Travis. He'd known that Travis couldn't survive long in his condition and that his friend hadn't the strength to swim the river.

"He'll die in there," she said with awful certainty. "And if he doesn't, I'll kill him myself."

It was long after dark when Rachel arrived at Cora Wright's cabin. "I'm sorry," she said when the midwife opened the door. "I couldn't go the night without Davy."

Rachel had left Travis Bowman in the marsh back where the creek angled off the main river, and come the rest of the way to Cora's alone. If she was lucky, she'd thought wryly, Travis would wander off, fall into a sink-hole in the marsh, and drown.

"Come in," Cora said. "We're still awake."

Rachel stepped under a ring of deer antlers into the circle of pale yellow lamplight. Immediately she was engulfed in the comforting scents of herbs and spices that filled Cora's tidy cabin.

A slab of smoked bacon, strings of beans, and circles of dried squash hung from the overhead beams among a score of hand-woven African-style baskets and mysterious leather pouches. The spotless wooden floor was strewn with colorful rag rugs, and the plastered walls gleamed white.

On the hearth a kettle of soup simmered merrily over a tiny bed of coals. Daisy rose from the rocking chair beside the fire with Davy in her arms. "He's sleepin', Miss Rachel," the girl said shyly. "He sure did miss you."

Rachel gathered Davy into her arms and tried to blink back the moisture that gathered in the corners of her eyes. "And I missed you," she whispered into the curls at the nape of his neck.

Davy uttered a contented sigh and snuggled close. His rosebud mouth puckered into a pout, and he made tiny sucking noises.

Immediately milk began to dribble from her swollen breasts and soak through her bodice, but she was too happy to care. "Darling, darling," she murmured.

"Let Miss Rachel sit there, girl," Cora ordered. "You just hold him, just rock and hold him."

How good Davy felt, how warm and sweet-smelling.

For several minutes Rachel blocked Travis and Chance from her mind and thought only of her baby.

"You finished your business up in Philadelphia?" Cora asked as she pushed open the door that led from the main room to her bedchamber. "You can go on to bed, Daisy. The little ones will be up early, and you'll need your rest."

Daisy murmured softly and left the room.

"She's a good girl," Cora said, "but what I have to say to you doesn't need witnesses." The midwife settled into the chair by the table, pulled a basket of knitting into her lap, and looked at Rachel expectantly. "Now, what have you been up to?"

Rachel felt herself flush. "What do you mean?"

"None of that. We've been friends far too long for you to lie to me. Not much goes on in these parts that I don't know about. Who is that man you have living on Rachel's Choice, and why did you go to Philadelphia with him?"

Rachel swallowed. "Does Pharaoh know?"

Cora made a sound of derision. "He's suspicious, but he don't know all I know. My grandchildren gather huckleberries in your woods. They saw that blond-haired man of yours working the cornfield. The man they saw seemed too fit to be your cousin's hired hand come to help out." She took an unfinished sweater from the basket and began to knit. "It's dangerous, what you're doing, Rachel. Best you tell me everything."

"I can't," Rachel whispered. "You won't understand." She shivered. "Even I don't understand."

"Your mother-in-law asked about the baby, if it was born yet. She said you'd run her off your place."

"They want to take my farm."

"Your cousin came with another woman who delivered your baby, and his own grandparents don't know he's alive. Have you been telling me the truth about Davy's birth? And if not, why would you lie to me?"

Rachel drew a long, slow breath. "I did lie, but I had a good reason. Swear you won't tell anyone?"

"A fool could see you're carrying the weight of the world on your shoulders, girl. And no one's ever called me slow-witted. Out with it."

"Can I trust you?"

"You left your son with me, didn't you?"

Rachel hugged Davy tighter. "His name is Chance," she murmured softly, "and I caught him in my crab trap. . . ."

For nearly an hour Cora listened without saying anything. And finally, when Rachel had run out of words and there was no sound but the scraping of a tree branch against the cedar shake roof, Cora answered.

"You believe he's a good man?"

"I do. I know he's a Southerner and—"

"That's not what I asked you, girl." Cora rose, rubbed her spine, and stirred the snapper soup. "I want to know if you think he'll do right by you."

"He gave me the money to pay Isaac, and he made a will, leaving money for Davy if he should die. I never asked him for—"

"A man like that," Cora cut in, "a gentleman lawyer, he could be using you, Rachel. Rich men think they can buy anything in this world."

"No, not Chance. He cares for Davy, and he could have run away once his shoulder healed. He stayed to take care of us. And now he's gone back in there for love of his friend."

Cora chuckled. "Pulled one over on you, didn't they? Fooled you something fierce." She went to the cupboard and took down two cracked pottery bowls. "Take a little soup with me?"

Rachel nodded. "Yes, thank you. I haven't eaten since breakfast."

"You need to eat, girl. You'll lose your milk if you don't eat."

Davy stirred in Rachel's arms and began to fuss. Rachel undid her bodice and nursed him. She no longer wore the gray Quaker clothing. That dress she'd rolled into a ball and hidden under a loose board in the lower deck of the *Windfeather*.

"So you've traded one prisoner for another," Cora said. "And what do you mean to do with this one?"

"Take him home, I suppose."

Cora frowned. "Keep this man away from Davy. Lung fever spreads. Davy could catch it."

"You can't imagine what it's like . . . that place," Rachel said. "You hear stories, but to actually see and smell it . . . to hear the groans of the sick and dying."

"My people have groaned and died. How many had pity on them?" Cora asked. "When Emma was stripped to the waist and beaten like a dog, who wept for her? And who cared when her firstborn child wasted away from hunger because she didn't have enough milk to feed both her babe and her master's?"

"Evil is evil, Cora. I guess I'm not very good at hating, not even hating the enemy. I didn't want to fall in love with Chance Chancellor. I fought it with every ounce of my strength, but I lost. And if he dies on Pea Patch Island, it will break my heart."

"Sounds to me as though you didn't use much judgment in picking a man," Cora admonished. "A reb, and a fancy, rich Virginia lawyer, at that."

"This war can't last forever," Rachel replied. "He won't always be a reb."

"But you'll always be what you are. A woman with too much loving in her for her own good. Your own father done you wrong, girl. And your James as well. Don't let this one take advantage of you."

"It's late to give me that advice," Rachel said. "I know you don't agree with what I've done—with what I'm doing right now in hiding Chance's friend. But I'm counting on you to keep my secrets."

"I know half the secrets in this county," Cora answered, "borned some, buried others. I suppose a few more won't bend my back into the ground."

Chance flattened himself against the wall and waited until Coblentz blew out the lantern and crawled into his cot. Mosquitoes feasted on every inch of Chance's exposed skin, but still he steeled himself to wait motionless until the sergeant's drunken mumbling became a steady whistling snore.

Still Chance did not move. He'd known that coming back into the prison would be hard, but he'd not expected his bowels to cramp and his skin to feel too tight for his body.

Finding Travis had been easy; changing places with him had taken only a few moments in the hospital supply room. He'd never intended to attempt to rescue Travis with Rachel along. He hadn't wanted to endanger her life. But once he saw Travis's sunken eyes and heard his rattling cough, he'd realized that his buddy was close to death. Convincing Travis to switch was the hardest part, but in the end Travis's yearning to see his wife and baby daughter before he died was enough to do the trick.

"I'll get out," he'd promised Travis. "I've done it with my arm half shot off. I can do it again."

Luckily no one had missed Travis at nightly roll call. Either someone had answered for him, or the corporal had been too lazy to take count at all. But in the morning, when breakfast rations were doled out, Travis would be found absent, and the camp would be up in arms.

All he had to do was murder Sergeant Daniel Coblentz and escape before sunrise.

Coblentz deserved death more than any man Chance had ever known. If truth be told, Coblentz wasn't a man; he was an animal who preyed on the defenseless. And if it cost him his own life in the attempt, Chance had to deliver justice.

For young Jeremy Stewart . . . for Jeremy and all the other men that Coblentz had ravaged on Pea Patch and maybe other places before.

Chance had never been one to judge a man's private life. So long as no one else was hurt, what was it to him if a man preferred his own kind to a woman? Or if he preferred a sheep for that matter, so long as the sheep didn't mind.

It was common knowledge that Sergeant Coblentz offered extra rations and favors to those prisoners that would go into his room and submit to his perversions. Not that anyone ever received the food or blankets the next morning, but that was the lie Coblentz told.

Other guards might enjoy seeing a prisoner whipped or thrown into the hole, a board-covered pit where the temperature was said to rise high enough in the noonday sun to fry bacon. And other Yankee soldiers stole and cheated the prisoners out of their blankets and meat rations, and were quick to shoot a man if he wandered too close to the river's edge. But Coblentz had ordered Jeremy spread-eagled on the guardroom floor and had used him like a woman in front of a dozen witnesses.

And Jeremy, still more boy than man, had hanged himself, rather than live with the shame.

Chance had always believed in the law, and taking a man's life—even Coblentz's—was an act outside the law. Fort Delaware stripped the honor from many of the soldiers imprisoned there. Now it had taken his, but he'd hoped he wasn't acting out of blind revenge.

Jeremy's friends had summoned a makeshift judge and jury from the ranks of prisoners. Robert Aston, a Methodist deacon, had stood on one leg, holding himself upright with a bloodstained crutch, to plead Coblentz's case. The cleric had ignored his fever and the pain of his crudely amputated limb to argue for hours, begging the jury to spare the sergeant's life and leave his sentence to God. But the twelve men had found Coblentz guilty of unnatural crimes and demanded his death.

And when they'd drawn straws to see who would execute the sergeant, Chance had pulled the short one.

He'd thought long and hard about what means he should use to kill Coblentz. It would have been more fitting if Coblentz had been awake to know what was coming, but that meant taking a terrible risk. And if Chance wanted to kill the sergeant and still make his getaway without alarming the other guards, he couldn't put a bullet in his head. That left a knife or his bare hands. And Chance didn't want to dirty his hands by tightening them around Coblentz's filthy neck.

And so he waited, knife in hand, for the right moment to cut the sergeant's throat.

Rachel guided the *Windfeather* back to the clump of reeds where she'd bid Travis to wait for her. The sloop gently nosed against the muddy bank, and Rachel listened for a few moments to the night sounds of the marsh.

In the distance an owl hooted; closer, some small creature rustled through the grass. There were no stars visible, but Rachel didn't need light to show her the way. She'd sailed this creek since she was a small child, and she knew every crook and shallow.

Finally, when she was convinced that no other boats were near, she called out to him.

"I was beginning to wonder if I'd been permanently abandoned," he replied. "I know I asked you to put me ashore, ma'am, but this mosquito sandbar wasn't quite what I had in mind."

"Come aboard," she said. "Damned if I know what I'm going to do with you, but I fancy that Chance would be mightily annoyed if I lost you before he got back."

"Yes, ma'am, I believe he might be."

She helped Travis to climb over the side and was shocked at how weak he was. "I'm hiding you," she said reluctantly, "but if anyone finds you, you have to say you got to my farm on your own."

When she reached Rachel's Choice, she made him wait on the sloop until she carried Davy and Chance's money up to the house and lit the lamps. Bear licked her hands, barked, and scampered around her like a pup.

"Good boy," she said to him. "Good dog. Did you think I wasn't coming home?"

Later, when Davy was safely tucked into his cradle with the money bag under his mattress, she left the big black dog to guard him while she put Travis in the hired men's room in the barn. She brought him freshwater from the well and a medicated syrup to ease his hacking cough.

"Are you hungry?" she asked.

"No, ma'am, just tired."

"In the morning I'll fix you a decent breakfast and see what I can find to help clear the congestion in your chest."

As she left his room, she heaped hay in front of the door to keep out any curious visitors and went to her own bed. But even though she was weary unto death, sleep wouldn't come; she was too worried about Chance.

"In the morning I'll ride Blackie into town and pay off Isaac," she whispered aloud, but she knew that she wouldn't. She would wait here until Chance came home.

Three days he had told Travis, maybe four. Not so long, not if she filled her days with farmwork. There was so much that needed doing. He'd be here before she knew it, she told herself.

"You will, won't you?" she whispered into the dark room. "You must come home . . . for Davy's sake and mine."

Chapter 21

The next four days were the longest Rachel had ever known. She cared for Davy, tended Travis, and hoed her garden. Solomon hadn't returned her cow yet, so there was no milking to do. But she did have beans and tomatoes to pick, fish to salt, and cucumbers to wash and put down in brine to pickle.

She worked from first light until she blew out her lamp long after sunset, but her mind was not on the chores her hands performed. She could think of nothing but Chance and the dangers that faced him between Fort Delaware and Rachel's Choice.

She could imagine him shot trying to escape, being devoured by sharks in the bay, or cramping up, slipping under the surface of the river, and drowning. If he died in the water, his body would wash up on some deserted beach, and she would never know what happened to him.

Once she woke screaming in the middle of the night after dreaming that she'd found Chance on a sandbar, his handsome face eaten away by crabs.

Not even Davy's morning smiles and joyful cooing could dispel Rachel's fears or her awful premonition that something dreadful had happened to Chance.

"Please, God," she prayed. "I'm not askin' you to give him to me. Just let him live."

On the evening of the fourth day, Rachel walked the creek bank with Davy in a sling on her back and Bear trailing after her. And when she found no trace of Chance, she pulled anchor on the sloop and sailed out to the river and down to the bay. She saw three deer grazing in the marsh, an osprey swooping over the river with a fish in his talons, and a huge snapping turtle, but no other human.

"Where are you, Chancellor?" she cried in despair. But the only answering call was the shrill hunting cry of a nighthawk.

The next morning, after she'd dried and dressed the baby, she put him in a safe spot and began to bake blueberry muffins, pumpkin cookies, and raisin scones. She used every dusting of sugar and white flour in her cupboard, and then she mixed corn bread, sweetening it with wild honey.

A few peaches were ripe on the tree near the barn. She picked those and packed them into a basket with hard-boiled eggs and fresh-scrubbed carrots from her garden.

"I'm going back to the fort," she told Travis when she brought him his evening meal of eggs, crab soup, corn bread, and honey. "Something's happened to him. I know it has."

The lieutenant lay propped up against the wall on Chance's narrow bed, the bed where Davy had been born. Travis's face was ashen, his features drawn. She didn't believe that he was much older than Chance, but it was hard to tell because illness had drained him of youth and vitality.

"If he dies, it will be my fault," Travis answered in his

cultured Virginia drawl. "I was wrong to let him trade places with me." He swallowed, and his Adam's apple bulged out on his thin neck. "You see, ma'am, I have a little girl I've never seen. I knew my wife, my Mary, was with child, but I didn't know if . . ." He inhaled a shallow breath, and Rachel heard the ominous rattle in his chest. "Another prisoner, a man named Mitt Welsh, told me that he'd seen Mary in church when he was home on leave. He said that Mary had a baby girl in her arms. He didn't know the baby's name." Travis swallowed again, and his brown eyes clouded. "I just wanted to hold her once . . . my baby daughter. I just wanted to see her and my Mary before—" A spasm of coughing took away his breath.

"If Chance is dead, it's his own doing, not yours," Rachel said. "I've seen Pea Patch." She smoothed the folds of her apron. "No man deserves to be penned up in there. I wouldn't treat my hogs so—if the army had left me any hogs."

"You shouldn't go," he replied weakly. "That's no place for a woman."

"No, it isn't," she agreed, "but I'll not rest until I know what's happened to him. There's eggs in the henhouse, beans and tomatoes in the garden, and bacon and ham in the smokehouse. You'll have to manage for yourself while I'm gone. Be careful and try to stay out of sight. If you hear my dog bark, that will mean someone's coming."

"I'm sorry to put you at risk, ma'am. I should have stayed where I was, but I wanted so badly to see that baby girl of mine."

"You will," Rachel replied, but she didn't believe it. In all likelihood she'd have a grave to dig for Travis Bowman on Rachel's Choice. "I mean to dress as a Quaker again," she explained. "If it got me inside once, it should work this time."

She knew she'd have to ask Cora to watch Davy again, but she was dreading explaining where she was going. Cora might refuse to help.

Pharaoh was home again. Rachel had seen him crossing her meadow on horseback with a pack of hunting dogs. If Cora confided in her son, Pharaoh would try to stop her from going. He might even come to the farm and murder Travis.

She should be putting Davy first, but she couldn't. So long as there was the slightest hope that she could get Chance out of Fort Delaware, she had to try. "I should think of my child, but I love Chance."

Travis smiled, and for an instant she saw the ghost of a dashing cavalry officer. "I know," he replied. "He's a hard man not to love." And then he touched her hand. "There's a decent Yankee guard in there. His name is Cochran, a lieutenant. If you get into trouble, ask for him. He won't help you free Chance. Cochran's too honorable for that, but he will protect you if he can."

"Then he couldn't be bribed?"

Travis ran his fingers through his light brown hair. "Not Cochran." His lips tightened into a thin line. "There's a Dutchman, Sergeant Coblentz, who could. Daniel Coblentz would sell his own mother for two bits, but he won't be of much use to you."

"Why not?"

Travis shrugged. "Because he's the man Chance stayed inside the prison to kill."

"You're sure you know what you're doing?" Cora Wright asked Rachel at the door of her cabin. She held

Rachel's baby in her arms. "You think this Richmond lawyer is worth risking losing your babe and your land for?"

"I'm in love with him, Cora."

Cora frowned and tried to find the words to convince her that what she was doing would only bring her grief. "He won't marry you, child. No matter what he promises you, he'll go back to his own life and his own kind."

Rachel shook her head. "That doesn't matter. What matters is that I've got to save him, if I can."

"And if you can't? What happens to your Davy?"

A single tear trickled down the white girl's face. "There's money, Cora, lots of money for Davy's keep. I've written a will leaving the farm to him if I don't come back. I hope you'll look after him for me."

Cora sighed. "Love. What has it ever caused a woman but trouble? You're mad as a hatter, girl."

Rachel nodded. "I know, but if I don't try, I'll spend the rest of my life regretting it."

"Go on, then. I can see there's no stopping you. I'll tend to your boy as long as I can. But if you go to prison, that father-in-law of yours will hear of it, and he'll come for little Davy."

"I knew I could trust you, Cora."

"You've been a friend to me and mine for a long time. You may be white on the outside, Rachel Irons, but inside, your blood is the same color as ours. I won't help you for your reb's sake, but I'll do it for you. Go with God, child."

Rachel brushed her baby's cheek with one finger, then turned and ran toward the landing.

"Don't say I didn't warn you," Cora called. This was bad business and no good could come of it. Rachel was a loving woman and the best neighbor anyone could ask for, but even Rachel—smart as she was—would have trouble getting into a Union prison and freeing her man.

Still cradling Davy in her arms, Cora walked across the hard-packed earth to her son's forge. "Pharaoh," she called.

The ping of a hammer striking iron told her that he was still shaping the shoes for Nathaniel's mare. A blast of hot air hit her as she rounded the corner. Pharaoh saw her coming and paused, stopping the swing of his heavy hammer in midair.

"Mother?"

She smiled at him. He was a good boy who'd grown into a good man. It had been her lucky day to find him, abandoned by the side of the road, still wet from his birthing. He'd been the first of the children she'd taken to raise, and none would ever take his place.

Pharaoh, she'd named him, after an old Egyptian king. He hadn't looked much like royalty when she'd pulled him squalling from that mud hole, but she reckoned he'd grown into the name. His high cheekbones, wide, strong nose, and full lips made him a handsome man, and his dark African eyes and broad shoulders gave him an aura of power.

But best of all, her son was wise, and not too full of his own ginger to listen to his mother. She never doubted that Pharaoh would do what she asked of him, no matter what he thought privately.

"Pharaoh," she said as she approached him. "I've a chore that needs doing."

He laid down the hammer and wiped the sweat from his brow. "What now, Mother?"

"I know you just came back, but I want you to take another trip up to Pea Patch Island."

His eyes narrowed. "What scheme have you hatched up?"

"Come to the house, son. I'll explain it all."

Pharaoh's lips thinned to a hard line.

"As a favor to Mother, dear."

"I was afraid you'd say that," he replied, and then he grinned at her.

The first person Rachel saw as she nosed the bow of her sloop against the dock at Fort Delaware was Pharaoh. She immediately thought that he'd come to prevent her from rescuing Chance.

"Mornin', Missy," he called. "Sho glad I ketched up wit you. Yore grandaddy wants you back to de house, right now."

"My grandfather?" She was totally confused. Why was Pharaoh talking like an uneducated fieldhand? And, since she'd heard him working in the forge at Cora's, how had he gotten here to Pea Patch Island ahead of her?

Pharaoh leaped onto her boat. "No, Missy. Don't tie up here," he said with an exaggerated shake of his head.

"How did you get here?"

"Nearly run two horses to death to do it," he answered softly. Then he raised his voice again. "You gots to get back to Delaware City. Now." He smiled foolishly at her, but the expression in his eyes was fierce.

A Union officer walked down the dock toward Rachel's boat. "Anything wrong here, ma'am? Is this negra bothering you?"

Rachel's mouth went dry. "Not at all," she replied.

"He works for my grandfather. An emergency at home."
She smiled at the captain. "A good day to thee."

Pharaoh pushed off from the piling. "You take the
tiller or I will, Miss Rachel."

Heart pounding and hands numb, she turned the boat
back toward the port town of Delaware City.

"You been hiding a reb on your farm all this summer,"
Pharaoh said when they were far enough from the landing to keep from being heard. "All the time I was hunting
snakes, you had a rattler in your house."

"Your mother told." She hadn't believed that Cora
Wright would betray her, and the thought made her sick
to her stomach. "He's not like you think."

"A slaver."

"No, not a slaveholder. Chance's family doesn't believe in owning slaves."

"So he told you." Pharaoh's grim features might have
been cut of swamp oak.

"Please," she said. "You don't know him like I do.
He's a good man, Pharaoh."

"Fighting to keep other humans under the whip."

"No. That's not true. He told me that he joined
the Confederate army because he couldn't go against
his neighbors and friends, not because he believed in
slavery."

"And that's supposed to make a difference to me?"

A dark form glided under the boat, and Rachel stared
down into the brown water. "I think that was a shark."
She shuddered. "I hate sharks."

"They're good eating, if you know how to cook them.
My Emma fries up—"

"Why are you here, Pharaoh? Why don't you just
mind your own affairs?"

He knotted the line and scowled at her. "I am minding my business. I'm doing a favor for my mother."

"What did she tell you to do?"

"Find you and keep you from doing something stupid."

"Are you going to have me arrested?"

He shrugged. "Me? Have a white woman—a Quaker woman—arrested on my say-so?"

Rachel flushed and looked down at her plain gray dress. "His name is Chance. He means the world to me."

"Family."

"What?" Puzzled, she looked up into his face again.

"Family means everything to my mother. She wants me to help you get this reb free and see that he does the right thing by you."

"I don't understand. You mean you haven't come to stop me? You want to help me get Chance free?"

"And see that he marries you."

"Marriage? Who said anything about marriage? He never asked me to marry him."

"Figured as much."

"Don't judge him before you've met him."

"I already have."

"I can get inside the prison," she said. "I've done it before."

"You will wait for me at Delaware City. I'll go back and find out if your reb is still in there or if he's been hung for escaping."

Rachel's fingers tightened on the tiller as she guided the small sloop around a larger vessel bound for the prison with a load of flour. "How can you find him? You don't know what he looks like. You don't even know his last name."

"Mama said you told her it was Chancellor," Pharaoh replied. "And you can give me his description."

"I still don't understand what you can do."

He scoffed. "Lots of black folks work inside those walls. We have our own telegraph system. White people don't take notice of us, or if they do, it's as a servant. Fetch-and-carry boy. That's me. Invisible. And a man who isn't seen can go anywhere. I'm a darn sight more valuable to your reb than a Quaker lady who can't take a step without fifty soldiers' eyes on her."

Rachel nibbled unconsciously at her lower lip. "What will you do if you find him?"

"Try and get him loose."

"Why? Why would you help us if you hate him so much?"

"Not doing it for you or him, Miss Rachel. Doing it for my mother. It's her notion. And whatever my mother wants, she gets, if it's in my power to give it to her."

"And I'm just supposed to wait until you come back?"

"That's right."

"And if you don't succeed?"

Pharaoh smiled, but the expression in his eyes remained cold. "Then I guess you'll have to try your plan after all. That, or go home empty-handed."

"You won't betray us to the soldiers?"

"If I meant to, would I tell you?"

Chapter 22

The sun's heat burned through the metal door of the punishment box and sucked the last vestiges of fluid from Chance's body. Consciousness came and went. He'd lost all track of time; he didn't know if he'd been in this broiling pit in the ground for hours or days.

Once it had rained. Water seeped in around the edges and dripped in through the lock. He'd savored every drop of moisture, eagerly lapping the muddy liquid from his hands and arms.

He couldn't remember if the Union officer had sentenced him to hang or be shot, but he remembered the feel of the lash ripping through his shirt when they'd whipped him. And he could see Coblentz's grinning face in the last seconds before they'd thrown him into this hole.

I should have killed him when I had the opportunity, Chance thought. Should have . . . should have . . . should have . . .

He laughed, and the sound of his voice echoed horribly in the small space. There was no room to stand or sit. He lay on his lacerated back in an oversize coffin and fought to keep his sanity.

It was easiest to let go, to stop thinking rationally and

let the blackness envelop him. There was no pain without reason, and no terror when he drifted on the brink of nothingness.

He'd never known a man to come out of the pit alive. Among the prisoners it was said that those who went down into that grave lasted two days at most.

Strangely, the hate he'd felt toward the Dutchman had seeped away into the damp earth beneath him. He'd been discovered as he left Coblentz's room, after he'd already made the decision not to kill him. He simply didn't have the grit to murder a sleeping man, not even slime like Daniel Coblentz.

But I should have, he thought. Then, at least, I'd be dying for something. This was a waste and a hard way to leave this world.

If he survived the pit, it would only be to appear at his own execution. And a wiser man would let the heat and the despair take him.

His back felt as though it were on fire. Infection must have set in—perhaps even gangrene. Did a man know when he was dying, or could he lie already dead and be none the wiser? Maybe he was a ghost and didn't have the sense to realize it.

Could a ghost have such vivid memories of a flesh-and-blood woman? Would a specter hold the scent of a freshly bathed baby boy? He didn't believe that was possible.

It was Rachel who kept him alive; so long as he drew one breath after another, he might see her again . . . hold her in his arms.

I should have stayed with you on Rachel's Choice, he thought. I should have forgotten the war and been content to plow your rich fields and hear the sound of your laughter in the twilight.

Rachel's lack of ostentation, her simple way of life, even her Indian blood, which would be so shocking to his Richmond friends and neighbors, were insignificant compared to the love he felt for her.

She'd given herself to him in the shallows of Indian Creek. He'd swum naked beside her, and they'd splashed each other with sparkling handfuls of water. He wished he could submerge himself in that glorious current now; he would trade a year of his life to drink his fill of that clean liquid.

Chance laughed again. Who was he to trade years of his life for anything? He had only hours or minutes left. Or nothing . . .

"Rachel . . . Rachel, I need you," he murmured weakly. And then the space closed in around him, and he lapsed into a tortured dreamworld of parched earth and grave-yards beneath a molten-red sun.

Rachel anchored her sloop on the outskirts of Delaware City and looked at Pharaoh. "Do you want to take the boat back to the island?" she asked.

"A good way to lose *Windfeather* is to loan her to me," he'd said. "Whites are suspicious of a black man who owns something this valuable."

"We're not all so cruel," she argued. "Surely if you ex-plained that—"

"Tell me that when you've lived with skin the color of coal."

Rachel took a step backward under the force of his bit-ter gaze. "White men are giving their blood to free your people from bondage," she said. "We're not all evil."

"No." His eyes lost their malevolent glow. "No, you're not. At least I tell myself that." His expression softened. "Wait here for me," he said.

"How long?"

"Until I come for you."

He dived overboard and swam to the reedy shoreline, and a short while later he'd caught a ride to the island on a barge. Hoping against hope that Pharaoh could be trusted, Rachel watched him until she could no longer make out his rough-hewn features among a group of other laborers.

The hours passed slowly. The sun became a huge crimson globe seeping rays of orange and gold across the western horizon. Dusk fell, and Rachel was alone with the quiet noises of the river. She could see lights from the town and Fort Delaware, but the sounds of human activity were strangely muted.

By noon the following day, Pharaoh had not returned. In desperation she pulled anchor and raised her sail to catch the wind.

An hour later, carrying Chance's five hundred dollars and pulling her wagon of pies and bread, she entered the gate to the common prisoners' section of the island.

She knew she should have been prepared for the heart-rending scene between the guards' station and the barracks, but the sight and smells of sick and dying prisoners were overwhelming. Despite her sympathy, she did not stop walking, and those ragged men who flocked around her to beg a bit of food or ask for favors made no attempt to stop her.

A corporal admitted her to the barracks. Knees weak from fear, she followed him through an empty dirt-floored building into the open space where she'd sold her baked goods before. Only one prisoner was there, a small, thin-faced boy sweeping the hard-packed earth, but she could hear the coughs and groans of many others through the thin walls that separated the courtyard from the hospital.

Union soldiers crowded around Rachel, quickly buying all she had in her wagon. She scanned the doorways and an open porch on the far side of the compound, but she didn't see the Dutchman or the lieutenant she'd met earlier.

Unsure of what to do, she started to walk through the passageway that led to the chaplain's office. She'd gone only a short distance when her path was blocked by a red-haired private.

"No admittance into the inner prison, ma'am," he said. "We've had some attempted prison breaks, and regulations are being enforced."

"But . . ." Her heart pounded as she searched frantically for some excuse to remain. If they put her out, how would she find Chance? "I need to see the chaplain on an important religious matter," she said.

"He's not here, ma'am. Gone to Jersey to read over the dead. You'll have to leave."

She waved her heavy, leather-bound Bible under his nose. "But I must—"

He pointed back the way she'd come. "You'll have to leave at once, or you'll be held for questioning. By rights, pie sellers should remain outside the walls. Whoever admitted you—"

"You got a problem vit this voman?"

Rachel turned to look into the face of Daniel Coblentz. "Actually, Sergeant," she stammered, "if I could talk to thee in private, perhaps . . ."

"No problem, Sarge," the redhead said. "She was just leavin'."

"About your business, Zuckerman." Coblentz pushed open a door and motioned Rachel inside. "So," he said with an unpleasant smile. "You come back to see Coblentz, after all."

"I want information about a relative of mine," she murmured. "I was told that you . . ." She drew in a deep breath. "I'm willing to pay."

He laughed. "Of course you are. In vat vay did you think to pay Coblentz? Vith money or . . ."

"Money," she said quickly. "I need to know about a prisoner—if he's here."

"So, little Quaker, you are not so pure after all, are you? You are a rebel spy, maybe?" He took a step toward her and she fought to keep from gagging at the stench from his broken, discolored teeth and unwashed body.

"I am no spy. For pity's sake, I only wish to know the welfare of my cousin William's son."

"How much?" He stared pointedly at the bodice of her gown.

"What?"

"How much will you pay to know if he's dead or alive?"

"Twenty dollars."

Coblentz sneered. "I thought you vas serious."

"Fifty?"

"More like it." The sergeant ran dirty fingers down her left forearm. "Vat's his name, missy?"

"Chancellor."

Surprise and recognition registered in Coblentz's eyes. "Chance Chancellor?"

Hope surged through her as she nodded. "Yes. That's him. Is he here?"

"Let me see the color of your money."

"You think I'm stupid, to carry so great a sum on me?" she lied. "But this much I have." She emptied her pocket of the assorted bills and coins she'd received from her baked goods and offered it to him.

"He's here," Coblentz answered, snatching the money from her hand and counting it. "You're short."

"I have more on my—" She broke off and corrected herself. "My companion, Brother Paul, has more money. I will not cheat you."

"By damn, you von't. No one cheats Daniel Coblentz of what's his." He touched her cheek, and she flinched. "But you ain't after vord of dis Chancellor are you? You vant more. You vant maybe he should escape from Pea Patch Island."

"That would be illegal," she stammered, backing away until she pressed against the closed door. "Thou cannot think that I would attempt to bribe a Union officer."

"Good thing," he said. "It's a hangin' offense, bribing a United States soldier. But . . ." He put one hand on either side of her and leaned close. "You kin have him for a thousand dollars."

"I don't understand," she answered, shoving her Bible into his face and twisting free. "What are you saying?"

Coblentz wiped his mouth and nose. "Heavy-handed vith that good book, ain't ya, voman?"

She circled a table piled with clean, folded bandages and tin bedpans. The room was small and dingy, lit by a single window. Chairs were stacked against one wall, and blankets filled one corner. There was little room to avoid intimate contact with the sergeant. "I am a decent widow, friend," she said. "It is not seemly that I permit you to put your hands on me."

"You did come to help Chancellor escape," the Dutchman accused. "You ain't no more Quaker than I am. You're a damned secesh rebel." He swept a stack of bandages off the table. "Let me see the color of your money, voman. One thousand dollars, and you can have him."

Hair stood up on the back of her neck. "I don't have a thousand."

"How much vill you give? No dickerin'. Take it or leave it. How much is a gray-back murderer vorth to you? He tried to kill me, you know, your Chancellor. They sentenced him to hang by the neck until he vas dead." He chuckled. "You ever see a man dance on the end of a rope? He loses control of his bladder and—"

"Enough! I have five hundred dollars. It's yours if you can get him off this island in one piece," she dared.

"Oh, I can do that all right, missy. Hand over the money."

"You get it when Chancellor's free."

Coblentz laughed. "It's like that, is it? You think Sergeant Coblentz is crook? You think he take your money and not let Chancellor go?"

"Something like that." Rachel met his stare with one as steady. "I'm no fool, Sergeant. Five hundred dollars is a lot of money, more than you'd make in six months. And if you try to double-cross me, you'll have to kill me to shut me up. My family has a friend on President Lincoln's staff."

"I keep bargains. Unsatisfied customers are bad for business."

"How? How will you do it?" she demanded.

"There's only one way off this island for a prisoner,

the death ship to Jersey. Your man vouldn't be the first reb smuggled out of Fort Delavare in a coffin."

She swallowed, willing her knees to hold her up a little longer, praying the sergeant wouldn't realize how terrified she was. "When?"

"There's a boat leaving here at dusk." He held out his hand. "All of it. And don't try to cheat me. If you can't pay, there are plenty others who vill."

"Stay where you are," Rachel warned him. She turned her back and lifted her skirt to pull loose the pouch of money. "You can count it, if you want. There's five hundred there, in new fifty-dollar bills." She faced Coblentz again and tossed the packet to him. "Where do I get Chancellor?"

"Finn's Point." The sergeant thumbed through the currency. "Good. You are an honest voman." He grinned at her, exposing his green, mossy teeth. "See the chaplain."

She frowned. "The chaplain? I don't understand."

"Simple." Coblentz licked his bottom lip. "Ask for the body. He'll give it to you."

"The body?" she repeated.

"Yah." The Dutchman grinned wider. "No trouble. He hands corpses over to their families all the time."

Disbelief spilled through her body. "But Chancellor's alive. You said he was alive!"

Coblentz unbuttoned the front of his shirt, and Rachel caught a glimpse of black curling chest hair as the sergeant shoved the money inside. "I never said he vas alive," the Dutchman corrected. "I said he vas here, and I promised you I could get him off the island." He laughed as he grabbed for her arm. "You came too late, missy. Chancellor's already dead."

"No!"

His hand closed on her wrist. "Yah. He's dead, and now you vill give me a little something more. Something to pay me for taking such a risk." He pawed crudely at the front of her gown.

"You son of a bitch!" Rachel cried. Seizing a bedpan, she slammed it against the side of Coblentz's head. He groaned and slumped sideways, and she hit him again.

He went down like a sack of wet sand.

Rachel ripped open the front of his shirt, grabbed her pouch of money, and fled out the door. She dashed back into the courtyard, took hold of her wagon handle, and hurried back toward the door to the outer compound.

The same corporal was on duty as she passed through his guard post. "Sold it all, I see," he said to her.

"Thanks be to God," she murmured.

She was too numb to cry. Chance was dead, and she'd just assaulted a sergeant after attempting to bribe him to release a rebel soldier. If she didn't get away from Fort Delaware soon, she'd end up staring through the bars of a cell.

Somehow she made it through the prisoners' area and out the gate. She left her wagon beside the walls and walked as fast as she could toward the docks. She was nearly there when she heard a commotion behind her.

"Stop!" a man's voice yelled. "Stop that voman!"

Rachel ducked in front of a mule team and scrambled onto a cart between two half-grown boys. A mounted officer trotted past her, headed back toward the fortress. Between the line of wagons, she saw Coblentz and two soldiers running after her.

She slid down from the back of the cart and dodged between a coal wagon and a flatbed carrying straw. Two black women were driving a flock of geese down the dock. Ignoring the angry shouts, she ran through the squawking birds, climbed down a ladder, and jumped off a wooden plank into a dory. The boat tipped under her weight, but she caught her balance and used the oars to row along the bank to the spot where she'd tied up her sloop.

Once she reached the *Windfeather*, she pulled the anchor and let the racing current carry her out into the river.

"Stop her!" Coblentz shouted. "There! Shoot her! Shoot the thief!"

The soldier beside him raised his rifle. Rachel heard a crack and saw a puff of smoke. A small hole appeared in the sail beside her head, but she didn't stop to worry over it. She scrambled back to the stern and took the rudder, steering the sloop around a larger vessel and turning south with the outgoing tide.

When she looked back, she saw that Coblentz and one of his companions had caught the line to the dory and were climbing in. Coblentz crawled up to the bow and took the rifle while the other soldier manned the oars.

The Dutchman stood up and fired at her again.

Rachel ducked her head and prayed for wind. The sloop turned slightly, and the sail puffed out.

A patrol boat rounded the tip of the island. Coblentz waved the rifle and pointed toward Rachel's sloop. The tide caught the dory, and it bounced along over the surface of the whitecaps, gaining on the *Windfeather*.

Rachel looked back over her shoulder at the rowboat as the Dutchman crouched and shook his fist at her. The rising wind carried the word "whore" over the waves to her. She couldn't hear all they were saying, but Coblentz and the other soldier were plainly arguing. The private kept pointing to the water and then back to shore while Coblentz reloaded his weapon.

The guards in the patrol boat turned toward the dory, but they were fighting wind and current, and the sea was whipping the waves into a three-foot chop.

Rachel's sloop leaped ahead as her sail filled. She held to the center of the channel between the mainland and Pea Patch Island, coming dangerously close to the patrol boat. As she passed the heavily armed vessel, a guard motioned to the fins cutting the water near his boat.

She nodded. "I see them!"

Behind her, the Dutchman stood up and lifted his rifle just as the dory plunged into a trough. Coblentz flew out of the small boat like an arrow from a bow. He hit the water with a splash, went under, and surfaced waving his arms and yelling.

The private laughed and guided the rowboat into a circle before pulling in his oars. He stretched out his hand to the cursing sergeant, but before he could reach him, the Dutchman rose and suddenly sank. When he came up, he screamed once and then vanished.

"Sharks!" the private shouted. "Sharks!"

The patrol boat cut between Rachel and the dory, and without looking back, she turned her sloop toward the widest part of the river.

Devil take him, she thought with a shudder. Coblentz was the worst sort of human scum, and she hoped Lucifer would make him a warm welcome in the bowels of hell.

Chapter 23

Rachel spent the night on the sloop, hidden in the thick reeds of the Jersey shoreline. She hardly slept at all. Instead, she spent her hours agonizing over the loss of Chance and swatting mosquitoes.

At first light she splashed water on her swollen eyes and dressed in her own clothing. She weighted down the Quaker dress with lead fishing sinkers and buried it in the mud. Then she sailed her boat along the river until she came to the first village, anchored there, and asked directions to Finn's Point.

She caught a ride with a Nanticoke Indian woman carrying butter and eggs to sell in the next town, and the matron was more than willing to share her breakfast of bread, hard-boiled eggs, and buttermilk. Rachel had no appetite, but she ate anyway. She knew she would need her strength to carry Chance's body home to Rachel's Choice.

The day was cloudy and overcast, threatening rain. Across the river, from the west, came rumbles of distant thunder. For once Rachel paid no heed to the weather; her sorrow was so great that she could hardly summon the energy to walk the last half mile from the main road to Finn's Point burial ground.

She asked directions from a boy surrounded by a flock of black-faced sheep. He didn't speak, merely pointed through the stand of white pines toward the river.

Dry-eyed, Rachel made her way through the fresh mounds toward the burial party. To her left a gang of black men sang an old spiritual as they dug a deep pit in the marshy earth. A white corporal on horseback was obviously overseeing the operation.

I'll not let them put Chance's body in a mass grave, she thought, not if I have to shoot someone to stop it. As she neared the blue-coated soldiers, she saw that most wore neckerchiefs over their faces to mask the smell of corpses.

Another couple was there ahead of her; an old woman wept and prayed over a canvas-wrapped bundle. Rachel saw the gray-haired man exchange heated words with an officer. Finally the soldier threw up his hands and walked away. Immediately the woman took one end of the wrapped body, and her companion took the other end. They lifted the heavy burden and carried it back toward the main road.

"Sir!" Rachel called. "Wait, sir, if you please."

A pasty-faced captain wearing a chaplain's insignia turned toward her. "If you've come to claim a body, you must have the proper forms," he said. "Otherwise, don't bother me."

"Reverend, please," she replied. "If you'd just listen to what I have to say."

The ominous sound of thunder reverberated across the river, and dark clouds boiled overhead.

The soldier on horseback rode over to them, dismounted, and handed his bay gelding's reins to a black boy. "Shall I escort the lady off the property, Captain?" the corporal asked.

The chaplain ran a hand through thinning sandy-colored hair and shook his head. "No need for that, Chambers." He glanced back at Rachel. "Ma'am, I just told you. You must make an application through proper channels."

Rachel stared past him as he rattled on, delivering a speech she guessed he must have made dozens of times before. Spatters of rain struck her face, and the wind picked up.

A group of soldiers stood idly near the dock. Beyond them a procession of sweating black men carried canvas-wrapped bodies from the boat. One brawny African, midway down the line, caught Rachel's immediate attention because he looked so much like Pharaoh.

". . . like to help in any way I can," the chaplain concluded, "but my hands are tied."

"I have money," Rachel supplied hastily. Needles of rain borne on the salt breeze dampened her dress and hair. "I'd be glad to pay you—a donation perhaps to your church. But I . . ." A shaft of lightning illuminated the forbidding clouds, and a loud clap of thunder rang in her ears. "I want to . . ." Rachel trailed off as a team of corpse bearers—including the man she was now certain was Pharaoh—veered off to the left, away from the path.

"Where 'o you think you're going?" a soldier with a lit pipe in his hand called after them.

The chaplain looked to see what the problem was. "You there!" he shouted. "Halt! Stop those two men!"

Pharaoh and his accomplice, a short, muscular, light-skinned black, began to run, bearing their grim burden between them. Sheets of rain hindered Rachel's visibility as the storm bore down on them.

"Stop them!" the chaplain cried, fumbling in his holster for a pistol.

As he drew it, Rachel screamed and threw her arms around his neck. "What's happening?" she cried.

"Get away from me, woman!" The captain shoved her roughly aside. She stumbled against the corporal, then regained her balance. "Oh! Oh!" she wailed. "Help me, please. My ankle, I think it's broken."

One of the soldiers by the edge of the dock fired a rifle. The other black men carrying bodies dropped them and scattered. Some ran back to the boat; others fled into the river.

"Hold that woman! She may be part of this," the chaplain ordered, but the rainfall was so heavy that his voice didn't carry to his troops.

Rachel continued to scream loudly.

The corporal grabbed for her arm, but his foot slipped on the wet grass. She dodged his grasp and dived under his horse's neck.

Shouts came from the black crew digging the mass grave. "Shootin'!"

"Somebody firin' at us!"

"Get down!"

The workers dropped their shovels and swarmed out of the hole. Still yelling, they ran en masse through the pelting rain, toward the Union soldiers. As three of them dashed past Rachel, the black boy holding the corporal's gelding pushed the reins into Rachel's hands.

"Take the horse, lady!" the youth hissed. "Run before they clap you in irons."

Rachel thrust one foot into the stirrup and slapped the

animal's neck with the leathers. The bay leaped forward while she struggled to get her other leg over the wet saddle amid the tangle of her skirts and petticoats.

"Don't let her get away!" the chaplain shouted.

Breathless, Rachel clung to the horse's mane and lashed the gelding's rump with the dangling ends of the reins. The bay leaped over a low hedge and then an open grave, but Rachel kept her grip and gradually worked her way upright on the animal's back. She found the other stirrup with her toe as she yanked her mount's head to guide him back onto the level path.

The horse's hooves threw clods of mud into the air as they tore down the road at full canter. Behind her, Rachel heard the crack of rifles, but she leaned low over the gelding's neck and urged him faster. As she galloped through the grove of pines, Pharaoh suddenly appeared in the lane dead ahead of her.

She yanked the bay up so hard that he reared, nearly pitching her off. "Pharaoh! What are you—"

"No time!" he shouted. "We can't outrun them carrying him. You'll have to take him on the horse."

She struggled to hold the bucking animal. "What? Take who?" She could hardly understand him above the sound of the downpour.

Pharaoh crashed back into the trees and returned seconds later with his teammate. Between them, they supported Chance.

He looked more dead than alive; Chance's eyes were swollen slits, his ashen skin tightly drawn over the bones on his face.

"Sweet Jesus!" Rachel threw her weight forward, bringing the bay down, and forced him to a shuddering stop. "Chance . . . I can't believe you're alive!" she cried.

"You'll have to take him up behind you," Pharaoh said. "Tom and I can't get away if we have him to worry about."

"No!" Chance staggered forward and grabbed the bay's cheek strap. "Put me in the saddle," he rasped. "I'm too weak to hold on behind her, but put my feet in the stirrups and I'll ride to hell and back."

Rachel didn't argue. She kicked her right foot loose and flung herself off the horse. Pharaoh and his comrade lifted Chance onto the animal's back; then Pharaoh boosted her up behind him.

"Soldiers comin'!" Tom warned.

"Go!" Rachel yelled.

"Take my sloop," Rachel said. "It's anchored in Rose Harbor. Pick us up at Hangman's Cove in two days."

Pharaoh slapped the bay's rump and took off running. Chance dug his heels into the gelding's sides and whipped him into a gallop. Rachel shut her eyes, pressed her face into Chance's bloodied shirt, and locked her arms around his waist. Branches tore at her hair and sleeves, but she didn't feel the pain.

Somehow Chance was alive, warm and breathing. That was all that mattered. And not even the bullets whistling past their heads could dim her unrestrained joy.

"You're alive," she whispered. "You're alive."

She wouldn't attempt to make sense of it now, but if they survived this wild ride and the hail of gunfire, she vowed she'd strangle him with her bare hands.

When they reached the main road, Rachel told Chance to turn the horse east along the river and then left at the first woods road they reached. To her surprise he didn't do as she asked. Instead, he rode past the narrow opening in the trees, then reined the horse to a walk and backed him thirty feet before entering the pine forest. He guided the animal on a zigzag course, crossing a stream and finally meeting up with the rough track a quarter of a mile from the place where it intersected with the wide thoroughfare.

"No sense in making it easy for them to track us," he said painfully.

Chance had been telling the truth when he'd told Pharaoh he was too weak to hold on. As it was, he could barely keep himself upright in the saddle. Although he refused to hand over the reins, it was Rachel who bore his weight as they threaded deeper and deeper into the pine barrens, long a refuge for those who avoided authority.

And rain continued to fall; the path narrowed to a bushy, sodden deer trail. Without the sun Rachel soon lost her sense of direction. She could only hope that the trail led away from the Delaware River and into the forest rather than doubling back to civilization.

When Chance slumped forward, only barely conscious, Rachel slid off the horse's rump, took the reins, and led the gelding. Her shoes were soon as soaked as her dress, but she kept going, lifting one mud-encrusted foot after another. Blackberry vines scratched her legs and arms and tore at her clothing. And when the thunderstorms passed, sometime in midafternoon, the woods became a stifling hot maze of downed trees and swampy sinkholes too deep to wade.

Just before dusk, when she was too tired to walk another hundred yards, Rachel saw a movement in the brush ahead. She stopped short as a hound began to bay.

"I smell smoke," Chance said.

She jumped and snapped her head around to stare at him. He hadn't spoken in over an hour, and she'd thought him unconscious. "What do I do?" she asked him.

"Wait," he managed. "We're . . . we're too done in to run."

She leaned against a pine sapling and caught her breath. The dog continued to bark, and after a while an olive-skinned boy appeared through the trees, a musket cradled in his thin arms.

"Whatcha want?" he called.

"Please," Rachel answered. "Do you have water? A place we could rest? My . . . my husband," she lied. "My husband's ill."

"You lost?" the boy demanded.

"No," Rachel replied. "Not if this is south Jersey."

The boy laughed. "Come on. Gran has a batch of fry bread on the stove. I reckon you're hungry and mosquito bit."

"Definitely an understatement," Chance murmured.

The youth led the way to a two-room cabin in a small clearing with a well beside the front door. A white-haired woman came out to greet them and instructed the boy to unsaddle the horse.

"Give him water, Vernon. Tie him in the lean-to." She stared at Rachel and Chance through faded eyes. "Come in," she said. "Come in and set and keep your troubles to yourself. I can see you're running from somebody or somethin', and the less I know about it, the better."

The old woman who introduced herself as Granny Pritchett helped Rachel get Chance off the horse and into a low bed near the fireplace. Their hostess frowned and muttered under her breath when she saw the extent of his injuries, but she asked no questions. Instead, she put a kettle of water on the hearth to heat and offered Rachel a pot of ointment to rub into Chance's back.

"I'd wash them cuts with lye soap and salt water," Granny Pritchett advised. "He'll not thank ye for it, but it might save his life."

That night, when the old woman and her grandson had retired to the other room, Rachel sat beside Chance's bed and demanded answers.

"Why?" she asked. "Why were you stupid enough to trade places with Travis? You knew what that prison was like."

Chance closed his eyes and didn't answer. He lay face-down, on his belly. His back was too inflamed to bear the weight of his body, even against a soft feather-tick mattress.

"I thought you were dead," she said. "That sergeant, the Dutchman, took my money to let you go. And then he said you were already dead."

"I was."

"What are you talking about? You couldn't have been dead or you wouldn't be alive now. How did Pharaoh get you aboard that ship with the bodies?"

"You sent him, didn't you." Chance's voice was dry and cracked, hardly more than a croak. "I wondered about that."

"His mother sent him. Cora. She told him to help me get you free. But I—"

"I wanted to kill Coblentz. I'd given my word . . ." He cleared his throat. "It's a long story, Rachel. Someday I'll tell you why I wanted him dead, but—"

"He is."

"He is *what*?"

"Dead." She shuddered, remembering Coblentz's screams

as the sharks attacked. "He took my money, the money you loaned me to pay off the farm."

"You gave him your farm money?"

"I took it back once I found out he meant to cheat me." She squeezed Chance's forearm and stroked his stubbled cheek with trembling fingers as if to convince herself that he was flesh and blood and not the stuff of dreams.

Finding him alive when she thought she'd lost him forever made her all bubbly inside. She wanted to laugh and cry at the same time. And she still wanted to pound him for giving her such a fright.

"Are you certain?" Chance asked. "Coblentz is dead?"

She nodded. "As dead as you can get. I hit him over the head with a bedpan and ran. When he came to, he chased me. I reached the sloop and cast off, but he followed in a dory. He was shooting at me, and he stood up to take better aim."

"He shot at you?"

She scoffed. "I've got a hole in my sail to prove it. Anyway, he fell into the water and . . ." She swallowed. "The sharks ate him."

"Near the prison?"

"Yes." She ran her fingers through his clean damp hair and leaned forward to caress his temple, but he pulled her down to kiss her full on the mouth. "Oh, Chance," she murmured thickly. "I thought I'd lost you."

She bathed him with her own hands and rubbed medicine into his wounds. His clothes, they burned. Granny promised to find him something to wear in the morning. For now, his nakedness was covered by a worn linen sheet.

"How's Davy?" he whispered. "Is he all right?"

"Yes, he's with Cora. She'll take good care of him."

"I miss seeing that little smiling face first thing in the morning. He's some boy, our Davy."

His words made Rachel go all warm inside. "Our Davy," he'd said. She wished that it could be true, that he would stay with her and be Davy's father . . . and her husband.

"Climb into bed with me," he whispered.

"You're feverish," she answered. "I don't want to hurt you."

Chance grimaced. "You've been thumping against my back all afternoon. A little more of you won't make me feel any worse, and you might make me feel a lot better."

She clasped his right hand and bent to kiss his finger-tips, one by one. "You're much too ill for *thumping*," she murmured.

"I'm cold. I need warming."

"You're a devil, Chance Chancellor." But she undid the buttons on her bodice and slipped off her skirt, petti-coat, stockings, and camisole. She eased into the narrow bed beside him, wearing only her corset and drawers.

"Ouch." He groaned. "Your bones are jabbing me."

"That's not my bones," she whispered. "It's my stays."

"I don't care what it is. Take it off."

Despite the delicious thrill that skittered down her spine, Rachel felt herself blush. "What if Granny Pritch-ett comes out? Or the boy? What will they think of me?"

He chuckled. "You told them that you were my wife, remember? Where else would a wife be, but by her sick husband's side?"

"I shouldn't be doing this," she grumbled. "You're much too ill for hanky-panky."

"Who said anything about hanky-panky? I just want you beside me, Rachel, sweet. You kept me alive, you know. They threw me into the pit. It's a grave for the living. When the sun heats the metal lid, a man knows what hell feels like."

Her throat constricted, and she made no protest as he fumbled with the ties at the back of her corset. "How did you get away?" she whispered.

"Pharaoh and Tom pulled me out of the hole. At least, I think it was them. They carried me to the infirmary. You have to be able to stand up to hang. I'm not sure how they managed it, but I think they switched me with a dead man. Nothing's too clear in my head, but I heard the surgeon tell someone that Chancellor was dead."

Rachel's stays loosened, and she freed her aching breasts. She hadn't nursed Davy in days; she'd thought that her milk would dry up, but so far it hadn't. "I'll leak milk all over you," she whispered.

"I've bled all over you," he answered. "It seems a fair trade."

She snuggled close to him, taking comfort from his long, lean leg and hip and the weight of his arm across her back. His velvety Virginia accent seeped through her weary body and drained away her aches and pains.

"Is Travis safe?"

"Home on *Rachel's Choice*," she whispered. "I told you, didn't I? He's bad sick, Chance. I don't know how long he'll live, but when I left him, he was safe."

"I didn't want to endanger you," Chance said hoarsely. "But I couldn't leave him there. I counted on the ruse working long enough for you to get him on board the *Windfeather*."

"It did that," she admitted. "But it's lucky that you weren't where I could get my hands on you. I think I would have killed you myself."

"I'm sorry."

"No, you're not, you lyin' bastard." She punched his arm lightly. "You'd do it again. Admit it."

"I would."

"Damn right, you would."

He chuckled. "For a devout Methodist, you use a lot of profanity."

"If I do, it's your fault," she retorted. "I never did until you washed up in my crab trap."

He kissed her bare shoulder, and she sighed contentedly. "You smell good," he murmured.

"Not as good as I would if I'd had the bath instead of you," she teased.

Her eyelids felt heavy, but she fought sleep. In the morning she'd have to figure a way to get home. With Chance in such bad shape, they'd never make the meeting with Pharaoh. They must cross the bay and reach the farm without being caught by the Union soldiers.

But that wasn't what bothered her most. Worse was the thought that she'd found Chance only to lose him again.

"Be careful what you pray for," her grandmother had warned.

Rachel had made a bargain with God, and she'd not complain when Chance rode out of her life. But that wouldn't make it any easier to accept.

Chapter 24

Three days later Granny Pritchett's grandson, Vernon, led Rachel and Chance to Hangman's Cove shortly after nightfall. All three wore patched and threadbare clothing, and Rachel had stained Chance's hair and skin with a dye made of walnut hulls to disguise him.

Vernon promised to turn the stolen horse loose in a farmer's field far from Finn's Point, but Rachel refused to surrender the animal until it had carried Chance out of the pines and back to the river. He was improving, but the ordeal had taken its toll on him, and the lacerations on his back were far from healed.

Chance didn't expect Pharaoh to be at the meeting place, but it was impossible to know who to trust, and the Delaware River was heavily patrolled. If Rachel tried to buy passage home from the wrong fisherman, she and Chance would end up dead or in irons.

Rachel tried to hide her disappointment when she found the cove dark. "No lights," she whispered to Chance. "No sign of any boats at all."

"I told you that it was a waste of time to come here," he answered softly. "We're days late. If he and Tom did escape the soldiers and reach your sloop, they're a long way from here."

"Pharaoh wouldn't desert me," she insisted.

"I have to go back," Vernon put in. "I can leave you the horse if you want, but Gran expects me—"

"No." Chance dismounted. "You take the gelding and get out of here while the getting is good. You've done enough for us. Go home to your grandmother."

Rachel had offered Granny Pritchett money for her help, but the old woman had shook her head. "You've Lenape blood in you," she said. "I see it in your eyes. Our people look out for one another."

Now Rachel slipped the boy a twenty-dollar gold piece. "Buy something for yourself," she said.

"No. Can't. Gran said I weren't to take no money off ye."

"Please," Rachel coaxed. "If you don't want it for yourself, buy something your grandmother needs."

"All right," he agreed. "I reckon I might find her a cookstove for this much money. Her back gets to aching, standing over that open fireplace."

"Now what?" Chance asked when the horse's hoof-beats faded away in the distance. "I wouldn't recommend swimming the bay. I've done it, and it leaves a lot to be desired."

"We'll wait," she said.

"Wait for the Union troops to capture us?"

"No." She sat down on the beach. "You don't understand. I told Pharaoh to meet me here. If he went home without us, Cora would send him back. If we wait long enough, he'll come."

"You're a trusting woman, Rachel," he said as he settled down beside her.

"I am," she replied. "Isn't that what got me into this

trouble in the first place? It's not enough that I'm a Confederate spy; now I'm a horse thief as well."

He chuckled, and they snuggled together under the single blanket Granny Pritchett had given them and watched the stars twinkle on, one by one.

In time a pale, shimmering moon rose over the water. The radiant moonlight danced across the surface of the bay, painting the marsh grass and lapping waves with liquid silver. And as Rachel listened, she was certain she could hear a haunting melody played by the salt breeze as it threaded through the swaying reeds and wound around the spreading beach-plum bushes.

"This must be an enchanted spot," she whispered to Chance. "It makes me feel . . ." She searched for the words to describe the swelling emotion inside and then sighed in defeat. "Happy," she finished lamely.

"I've been in worse places," Chance replied. He cupped her breast gently and leaned close to kiss her. "Much worse."

The caress was her undoing. She met his desire with equal passion, tangling her fingers in his hair and pulling him down to cover her with his hard muscular body. Both knew the need for caution, but the sand was soft, and the yellow moonlight as intoxicating as any wine.

"I love you," he said as he pressed his lips against the hollow of her throat. "You'll never know how much I love you."

"And I love you." She moaned softly, unable to stop her trembling any more than she could hold back the waves of heat that spilled through her body. "Forever and ever, Chance, just you."

Neither could wait. He came into her with hard, deep thrusts, and she cried aloud as the world tilted and ex-

ploded in one great burst of release . . . bringing an endless shower of falling stars and sweet, sweet joy.

Afterward he held her, and they laughed and whispered like carefree lovers, sleeping only fitfully before
awakening at dawn to listen to a flock of wild geese calling plaintively overhead.

"Autumn's coming," Chance said as the cries of the
waterfowl drifted over the water. "Soon it will be time to
harvest your corn."

"Not yet," she whispered. "Not for a while." It was too
soon; she wasn't ready to part with him yet. But woman's
instinct told her that when he did go, he'd leave something of himself behind. She was certain that they'd
made a child together on this warm sand, a babe that she
could hold close in her arms and cherish when Chance
was only a memory.

"I've got to go back to the war," he reminded her.
"You know that."

"Yes. I know that, but I don't want to think about it. I
only want to think about us—you, and me, and Davy—at
home, milking, tending the garden, having dinner together."

"Milking's not my favorite subject," he said.

"You," she admonished. "You know what I mean.
I like the quiet times together. That's what I want to
remember."

"Oh," he teased. "So nothing that happened on this
beach is worth remembering?"

She laughed. "Chance Chancellor, must you be
so . . . so—"

He silenced her with a tender kiss.

She pulled away. "Wait. Did you hear something? A

splash?" She peered into the gray mist that hung over the bay. "Out there."

"No, I didn't. It was probably a fish jumping."

"A big fish, more like an anchor." She rose and hurried down to the waterline. The tide was out, and she ran barefoot over broken clamshells and bits of driftwood.

Her heartbeat quickened. It was an anchor being dropped that she'd heard; it had to be. Lifting her skirts, she waded out.

"Rachel, come back here," Chance called from the beach.

But she didn't stop until the waves broke over her knees. And minutes later, when the sun's first rays pierced the mist, she caught sight of her sloop anchored a hundred yards off shore.

Pharaoh had come back for them, just as she'd known all along that he would.

Halfway across the bay, while a stiff breeze drove the *Windfeather* toward the Delaware shore, Pharaoh crossed the deck to where Chance was sitting. He seized him by the front of his shirt, lifted him off the deck, and slammed a massive fist into his jaw. "That's for being a damned rebel," Pharaoh declared.

Stunned, Chance stumbled back against the mast.

"What are you doing?" Rachel cried. Frightened, she let go of the tiller and ran toward the blacksmith. Surely Pharaoh didn't mean to betray them now. "You can't—"

"Stay out of this, Miss Rachel," he warned. "This is between Richmond and me. And now that I got that bad feeling toward him out of my system, we can talk, man to man."

Pharaoh yanked Chance up onto his feet, and Chance

threw up his left arm to defend himself from another blow. The black man chuckled, let go of him, and stepped away.

Heart in her throat, Rachel tried to wedge herself between the two. This couldn't be happening. They were only hours from home and safety, and there wasn't a Union patrol boat in sight.

"Stay clear, Rachel," Chance said. "I can take care of myself." He knotted his fists and took a boxer's stance.

Pharaoh grinned, flexing muscles along his huge arms and burly shoulders. He wore only cut-off trousers, and his bare skin gleamed ebony-blue in the bright sunlight.

"You look like you can take care of yourself, reb," Pharaoh scoffed.

Chance rubbed his chin gingerly; his jaw was rapidly swelling, but his dazed expression was quickly hardening to anger.

"I needed to get that hit out of my system," Pharaoh explained. "You know how I feel about Southerners, Virginians in particular. He's lucky I just hit him. Usually I do a lot worse."

"You're not going to hit him anymore, then?" she said.

"Nope. I mean to throw him into the bay," Pharaoh answered matter-of-factly. "Unless he agrees to do the right thing by you."

"What the hell are you talking about?" Chance asked.

"You'll marry Miss Rachel today. Either that, or you'll have a long swim to land."

Rachel's face flamed as she laid a hand on Pharaoh's shoulder. "This is none of your affair. I know you mean well, but I'll have no part of a shotgun wedding."

Pharaoh jabbed his broad finger at her. "It's not for

you to say, Miss Rachel," he said. "The reb's got no choice. Either he saves your reputation or—"

"Shut up, both of you," Chance snapped. "I'm capable of speaking for myself."

"We don't need your fancy words, lawyer," Pharaoh said. "You will marry her or—"

Chance's pale eyes glinted steel. "I like to do my own proposing, if you don't mind."

"Chance," Rachel interjected. "You don't—"

"I said *quiet*!"

Rachel opened her mouth to reply, then thought better of it.

"I meant to speak of this later, but I do have honorable intentions toward the lady. Rachel, will you consent to become my wife?"

It was her turn to be stunned. "Since when?" she murmured. "When did you decide that you wanted to marry me?"

The hint of a smile showed on his lips. "Do I have to give you the precise hour and day?"

She leaned back against the gunnel, unsure as to whether she should laugh or cry. "Yes," she stammered.

"Objection, your honor," Chance countered. "That information is immaterial."

Rachel rested her hands on her hips and glared at him. "I think not. Objection overruled."

"Sidebar, your honor. Counsel is attempting to badger the witness."

"Quit this foolish talk," Pharaoh boomed. "Are you or aren't you going to accept his offer, Miss Rachel? Because if you ain't, I mean to toss him overboard."

"No," she said. "I'm not going to marry him, and

you're sure as hell not going to pitch him over the side of my boat. Not unless you mean to throw me over as well."

"What do you mean you won't marry me?" Chance shouted.

"Miss Rachel, think what you're saying."

"I know what I'm saying." She looked into Chance's eyes. "I love you, but I won't marry you. Not when you're going away to fight again. It's stupid. I've been widowed once by this war, and I don't mean to go through the same thing again." Not even if I'm pregnant, she thought fervently. Not even if I have to face the world with a nameless child in my arms.

His face paled. "You won't marry me?"

"Ask me again, when the war's over. If your offer's still good, I may take you up on it then. Not before."

"Well, I'll be double damned," Pharaoh said. "You just tell my mother I tried to do what she wanted. Damn." He spread his palms in a gesture of bewilderment. "White or black, women are just the same. There's no logic to them." Shaking his head, he retreated to the stern and took hold of the tiller, righting the sloop's direction to put them on course for home.

"You're sure about this," Chance said softly to Rachel.

"As sure as I've ever been about anything."

He tried to pull her into his arms, but she wouldn't let him. Instead, she turned away and stared out at the bay, listening to the sound of the waves against the boat and the cry of a hunting osprey overhead. That way she could convince herself that her tears were caused by the sting of the salt wind, and not from the ache in the depths of her soul.

Cora met them by the dock, her wrinkled brow creased even more with concern. "Your father-in-law's been here with the sheriff," she called before Rachel could reach her. "They took your baby."

Pharaoh embraced his mother. "You and Emma and the children weren't hurt?"

Cora scoffed. "Of course not. We're fine. But Davy's with his grandparents. That worthless octoroon Patsy Cummings was here yesterday wanting me to concoct her a love potion. You know I never mess with that kind of thing. Anyway, she saw Davy and asked who he was. I wouldn't have told her, but one of the children said that he was yours."

"And Patsy went back to Ida with the tale," Rachel finished. She felt ill. She knew her mother-in-law wouldn't hurt Davy, but getting him back would be hell.

"That Patsy does laundry for half the white folks in town. She told Miss Ida, you can take that for gospel."

Chance tied up the boat and came to stand beside Rachel. "When did they take the boy?" he asked.

"Not an hour ago. You didn't miss them by much," Cora answered.

Emma ran down the path from Cora's cabin and flung herself into her husband's arms. A flock of children followed her; they surrounded the two, chattering and tugging on Pharaoh's arms. He raised his voice above the din to address his mother.

"I told him he had to marry her, Mama, but she won't have him."

Cora turned a withering gaze on Chance. "Is that so, Virginian? You think you're too good for our Rachel?"

"You have it all wrong," Rachel put in. "He asked. I refused him. I don't want another soldier husband."

"You'll live to regret the day," Cora predicted. "It's been my observation that once a woman's set on a man like you are him, they'd best marry. Else they risk burning in hell."

"I'll worry about my salvation or lack of it later," Rachel said. "Right now I have to get Davy away from Ida and Isaac."

"I'm coming with you," Chance said.

"You can't," she replied. "You'll be hung. Cora said the sheriff was with them. You've got to stay hidden."

"You can pass me off as Abner."

"No." Reluctantly she shook her head. "You don't know my father-in-law. He'd suspect the Lord Jesus if he showed up on my farm. He'll tell the sheriff to arrest you first and ask questions later."

"Damn it, woman," Chance argued. "Must you always have things your way? How much respect would you have for me if I stayed here and let you deal with them yourself?"

"More than I'd have for you if you played the fool and got yourself hung senselessly," she flung back. "Can't you see, Chance? This isn't about honor or pride. This is real. And this is something I can do a hell of a lot easier by myself. If you come, we'll both end up dead or in twin cells on Pea Patch Island."

He glowered at her. "You expect me to—"

"Stay here with Cora." Then suddenly she remembered Travis and she went cold inside. "Travis," she murmured. "He's in my barn. The sheriff will—"

"He won't find him," Cora assured her.

"Why not? Is he dead?" Rachel demanded. "He was sick when I left but—"

"Not dead," the old woman said. "On his way home. My grandboy brought word this morning that folks was headed toward your farm. I sent the girls over to fetch him."

"Then Travis is here?" Chance said.

"No, not here. It's not safe." Cora pursed her lips. "It's bad business, all this hiding of rebels, girl. If I didn't know you better than I do, I'd suspect you were one of them." She sighed. "But I know you're not. I figure that you had your reasons."

"So if he isn't dead and he isn't here . . ." Chance left the rest unsaid.

"Mama told you," Pharaoh grated. "If she says she sent him home, then she did."

Cora smiled. "The Underground Railroad, reb. We sent your Travis home the same way we've been bringing slaves north for years. Only we sent him the opposite way." She chuckled. "He'll be safe enough, if his lungs don't kill him before he gets there. He ought to be halfway to Salisbury by now."

Rachel took a deep breath. "That's that, then. Travis is taken care of. And if I don't get home quick, Ida will be halfway to Milford with my Davy." She turned and grasped Chance's arm. "If you love me, if you want to spend the rest of your life with me, then you'll be man enough to wait here. You'll let me see to paying my father-in-law what I owe and getting my son back."

"You've still got the money?" he asked her.

She nodded and patted the front of her dress. "Safe as it was in your bank. Enough to settle the loan, pay my taxes, and buy this winter's necessities." She glanced at Cora. "Is Blackie here? I can get to Rachel's Choice faster on horseback."

"The boys have him with our livestock in the swamp, but Pharaoh's gray is tied out back," Cora answered.

"I'll throw a saddle on him," Pharaoh offered. "Deacon's spirited, but you're a good rider. If you keep a tight rein, I think you can handle him."

Chance kissed her. "Be careful, darling."

"I'll try." She hurried after Pharaoh, then stopped and looked back at Cora. "Keep Chance from trying to be a hero," she said. "He hasn't kept his part of the bargain yet. He promised to get my fall crop in, and if I have any say in the matter, he's not going anywhere until my corn's harvested."

Chapter 25

The gray horse's mane and tail streamed like banners in the wind as he galloped down the woods trail. Rachel rode hard through the forest as far as the fallen tree at the entrance of the swamp road. Leaping over the rotten log, she made the hard turn and took the Taylor's Neck short-cut down a path so narrow that brush and branches scraped her arms and legs from both sides of the track.

When they reached low ground, Rachel had to use all her strength to rein the spirited hunter to a trot so that he wouldn't lose his footing in the mud, but once they crested the ridge at the edge of her meadow, she kicked him into a run once more.

The audacity of James's parents amazed and infuriated her. She had fully expected Isaac to bring in the authorities when her payment was late, but she'd never thought that they would dare to take Davy. And unless she fell off this horse and broke her neck between Cora's cabin and Rachel's Choice, Rachel swore that it would be a decision that her in-laws would come to regret.

Rachel was breathless; her hair was undone and tangled with leaves, and her mouth tasted of horse and mud. Her pulse was pounding, not with concern for her own safety but out of fear that she couldn't get Davy back from James's parents.

A covey of quail burst up almost under the gelding's feet and he shied, nearly throwing her, but she got him under control again and let him have his head. And when the horse thundered toward the cornfield fence, she never hesitated.

"Jump!" she cried. Deacon tried to turn left at the last moment, but she held firm and kicked him in the sides with her heels.

The gray flew over the four-rail fence as though he had wings, missing the top bar by a foot. His hooves touched the earth, and he lunged ahead, tearing through the field, trampling corn stalks and ripening ears of grain. The gate at the far end of the field stood open, and they dashed through it and galloped on toward the farmhouse.

Rachel heard Bear's deep, rumbling bark before the barn loomed up through the trees, and she guessed that Isaac was still on Rachel's Choice. She only hoped that James's mother hadn't already taken Davy back to their home in town.

Foam flew from Deacon's mouth, and his nostrils flared. The gray horse's heaving sides were streaked with sweat, and he was breathing heavily as they rounded the sheepfold and pounded into the yard, nearly running Isaac down.

Sheriff Voshell, mounted on a wall-eyed roan stallion, shouted a warning. Isaac, who'd been aiming his pistol at Rachel's dog, leaped back and scrambled to shelter behind the brick well.

"Put that gun down!" Rachel shouted. Deacon squealed and danced sideways, scattering chickens and spooking

Voshell's mount. The roan wheeled around and lashed out with a hind hoof at Rachel's horse.

Deacon sidestepped the kick and delivered a sound thump of his own before Rachel got him under control and turned her attention back to James's father.

"Leave my dog alone!" she ordered as Isaac raised his pistol again.

"The mastiff's dangerous. He needs to be destroyed!" Isaac said. "He attacked my wife."

The sheriff, red-faced and breathing heavily, dismounted and walked toward Isaac without taking his gaze off Rachel's horse. "Calm down, Mr. Irons. No need for that, now. I'm sure Miss Rachel can control her dog."

Rachel glanced back at Bear. He crouched, hackles raised and teeth bared, in front of Isaac's buggy. And from the back of the two-wheeled carriage came the shriek of a hungry baby.

"First you steal my son, now you try and shoot my dog!" Rachel reined the gray horse in between the men and Bear. "I'll have you charged with kidnapping," she threatened her father-in-law. "How dare you come and take him from Cora Wright without my permission?"

Bear whined excitedly and thumped his tail as Rachel moved closer. Then he bared his teeth and snarled as Isaac circled Rachel and moved toward the buggy.

"Shoot that creature!" Ida urged through the open kitchen window. "Shoot the dog and get my grandson before he's eaten alive."

"Shut up, Ida," Isaac shouted. Then he glared at Rachel. "You're past due on your note. I've brought the sheriff here to enforce the law. That vicious animal bit Ida." He eased the hammer down on the heavy pistol and shoved it into his belt.

"If he did bite her, it was to protect Davy," Rachel defended. The gray horse snorted and tossed his head, and Rachel, still mounted, reined him in tightly and glanced at the sheriff. "You call taking my son enforcing the law?"

"No, Miss Rachel, I don't." John Voshell's sunburned face darkened to the color of new-washed beets. "But Isaac's within his rights to—"

"To get off my farm!" Rachel answered hotly. "Here's his money." She pulled the pouch from the bodice of her dress and threw it at Isaac's feet. The cloth bag burst open, spilling the crumpled bills and silver coins across the hard-packed dirt. "There's what you came for, Judas. Every last cent."

She urged her horse toward the buggy, but Isaac blocked her way. Deacon laid his ears back and pawed the ground. Rachel eased up on the leathers and let the horse move dangerously close to her father-in-law's feet.

"Not so fast, young woman," Isaac huffed as he backed up a few steps. "There's interest due on this month's—"

"I told you, it's all there." She gestured to Voshell. "Are you part of this outrage? Is it your job to terrorize war widows and steal their infants?"

"Isaac, I think you'd best give me your gun, pick up what's yours, and go," the sheriff advised. "It's clear you're not wanted here." He nodded to Rachel. "I'm sorry for the trouble, ma'am. But the note was overdue, and Miss Ida claimed that you'd abandoned the boy and run off God-knows-where with a half-wit farmhand."

Rachel scoffed. "I went to Philadelphia to secure an inheritance. That's where I got the money. You can contact Benjamin Gordon of London Bank and substantiate my story, if you like. And the hired man Ida mentioned ran off back to New Castle. His name was Abner Potts, and he was homesick for his mother." She grimaced. "You know I will receive a widow's pension from the war office. I have no need to marry—especially not a mute fieldhand."

"But the baby is our James's child," Ida whined as she pushed out of the door. Her bonnet was askew, and Rachel noticed a large rip in her skirt that could have been caused by a dog bite.

Bear snarled at Ida, and she shrank back.

"That beast is clearly dangerous!" the woman sputtered. "He attacked me once. Look at my dress."

Rachel maneuvered Deacon close to the buggy, dismounted, and picked up her son. He had ceased wailing and now was sobbing loudly. "There, there, sweetheart, Mama's here," she soothed. "It's all right, darling."

Nothing had ever felt so right in her life as holding Davy close to her heart. Tears of joy spilled down her cheeks to mingle with his.

"I'd never leave my child unattended, Sheriff," she said as she wiped her eyes and covered Davy with kisses. "Philadelphia is a filthy city, no place for a country-bred infant."

Davy's lips puckered into a half smile and he waved chubby, starfish hands at her.

"He's wet and hungry," Rachel declared as she laid her son against her shoulder and patted his back. "Cora Wright is a respected midwife. She delivered your daughter's babe last spring, didn't she? Would you consider Cora to be incapable of caring for a baby?"

"Rachel's an unfit mother," Ida insisted through the

partially opened door. "She didn't even notify us when he was born."

"That's not against any law I know of, Mrs. Irons," the sheriff said patiently.

"But she promised to tell us when the baby was born. You did!" she reminded Rachel. "This is our grandchild and you—"

"Have never been what you and Isaac wanted in a daughter-in-law," Rachel finished for her. "It's true that Davy has your blood as well as mine, but it's also true that James would turn over in his grave if he knew how you threatened me for the money he borrowed from you. Rachel's Choice will go to Davy when he's grown, and if you'd succeeded in robbing me of this farm, it's him you would have wronged most."

"We have rights," Isaac grated. "We'll see the boy, if we have to drag you before a judge to do it."

"You'll see Davy when you learn to act decently to me," Rachel answered. Her milk that she'd feared was drying up had leaked out as soon as she'd heard him cry. Now, as her fury evaporated, she wanted nothing more than to take him inside and nurse him, and she wanted Chance here.

Isaac gathered up his money and began to count it carefully. "There was no need to throw it on the ground."

"No?" Rachel eyed him warily. "And there was no need to load the back of your buggy with my personal belongings either." She looked at the sheriff. "My clock is here, and my jewelry chest."

"Merely for safekeeping, I'm sure," Isaac muttered.

"Thought you had succumbed to foul play," Ida supplied.

Rachel sniffed. "You hoped. Take it all back into the

house, or I'll spread it at Sunday service that James Irons's parents are nothing more than common thieves." She motioned Bear to her side. "Now, you'll be pleased to leave my home," she said to Ida. "And I trust that Sheriff Voshell will attend to the legal niceties, making sure that I receive James's note back, marked paid in full." She smiled at the sheriff. "I have all the money for last year's taxes and this, if you wouldn't mind settling that business as well."

"Not at all," Voshell replied, taking Deacon's reins and tying him securely to the metal ring on the corner of the brick well.

"Well, then." Ida flounced off the step and hastened to climb into the buggy. "Mr. Irons, I believe we are needed elsewhere."

"Indeed," Rachel agreed. "Anywhere else but Rachel's Choice."

"You will relent and let us see the child, won't you?" Isaac asked when he'd unloaded her things and taken them back into the kitchen. "It's the Christian thing to do."

"Perhaps," Rachel agreed as she rubbed Davy's back and nuzzled the nape of his neck. "Someday when I'm feeling particularly charitable."

Chance and Pharaoh arrived by boat only minutes after the Irons couple and John Voshell departed. Pharaoh stayed just long enough to make certain all was well with Rachel and then rode his gray horse home.

"You know, he's not as mean as he seems," Chance said to Rachel. "But he does pack a wicked punch."

"No, Pharaoh's not mean-hearted," Rachel agreed. "He's been a good friend to us."

"A wonderful friend," Chance said wryly as he rubbed his jaw.

"You're lucky he didn't shoot you and leave you in the swamp for the crabs."

He grinned, hugged her, and gave her a hasty kiss before scooping up Davy. The baby had been so exhausted by his crying that he'd fallen asleep in her arms as soon as she'd fed and changed him. Now, when Chance woke him, he began to fuss again.

"See what you've done," Rachel admonished. Secretly she was delighted that Chance wanted to hold the baby, but as Davy's mother, she had to keep up the appearance of being in charge of her son's care.

"He's put on weight," Chance said. "He wasn't this heavy when I left. You're going to be a big, strong boy, aren't you, Tiger?"

Davy grabbed two handfuls of Chance's hair and squealed.

"See that? He missed me." Chance glanced at Rachel. "Didn't he?"

"He did," she agreed. "We both did. You belong here with us." A lump rose in her throat, and she turned away. A few weeks more she'd have him, and then uncertainty would make her lie awake at night wondering if he was alive.

"Maybe I do," Chance replied. "Philadelphia's not far away. A smart young lawyer might make a living there."

Rachel felt a sudden chill. "I'm not a town woman," she said. "I don't know what fork to use if there are more than two, and I'll never learn to walk in a bustle. If you want the life you had before the war, it will have to be with someone else." She drew in a deep breath and plunged on. "My roots run deep in this land. As much as I love you, I could never be happy where the grass doesn't grow and the rain falls dirty from city soot. You'd be ashamed of my country ways, and I'd make you miserable."

His blue eyes dilated with affection. "I could never be ashamed of you, Rachel. And I still say you'd make a hell of a trial lawyer."

She reached for Davy, and he embraced them both. Then he put the baby in her arms. "This is where I should sweep you up into my arms and carry you both upstairs," he said. "But—"

"But . . ." She laughed and put her hand in his. "You can do it next month," she assured him, "when you've recovered from your trip to Pea Patch Island."

Together they walked up the steps to her four-poster, and they spent the afternoon laughing and talking and making love.

"Enjoy today," Rachel said. "Tomorrow the cow comes home, and life gets back to normal around here."

"I can't wait."

As Rachel had promised Chance, there was work aplenty to do on the farm before the fall harvest. There were tomatoes, beans, apples, and squash to dry, potatoes to dig, and fall spinach and turnips to plant. Rachel put the last of the season's cucumbers into pickling crocks and sliced cabbage to cure as sauerkraut. There were jams and jellies to make, grapes to press into wine, and fish to salt for the coming winter.

Cora Wright sent two of her granddaughters each day to help with the baby and the preparation of meals so that Rachel could work side by side with Chance in the garden, in the fields, and in the boat. Together they plowed a small field and planted winter wheat, netted fish, and dug clams and oysters.

The work was hard and dirty, but Rachel took such satisfaction in the completion of each task that Chance began to find a similar reward in the results. And at the end of each day they would bathe together in the creek or— when the weather turned cool—in the shower that Chance rigged in the barn with a barrel of sun-heated water. Evenings were for them and Davy alone.

Chance healed and grew strong, and Rachel stored up a chest of memories for the uncertain times ahead. Neither spoke again of marriage. She assumed that if he lived through the war and still loved her, he would come back and ask her to be his wife. But whether he believed the same thing, she didn't know and wouldn't ask. She was determined to save her tears and enjoy the time they had left together.

Somehow the days piled one upon another, as the green hues of summer turned to autumn reds and gold. Morning air was as crisp and tangy as the first sip of apple cider. Pumpkins ripened in the garden, and the branches of the gnarled old pear tree sagged under the weight of ripening fruit.

One silvery evening, after a light supper, Rachel walked hand in hand with Chance to the cornfield gate. Both were weary from the hours of cutting corn and stacking the stalks into rows of shocks. Neither spoke. Around them the silvery dusk vibrated with the mournful honking of great Vs of wild geese flying south to take shelter in the nearby marshes.

"Almost finished," he murmured.

She bit her lower lip and refused to weaken. She'd not beg him to stay. She knew before she opened her mouth that it would be useless. She could not shame them both by the attempt.

"I saw Pharaoh this morning," Chance continued in his honey-laced Southern tones. "He asked me if I wanted to buy his Deacon. I said I did, but that I didn't have the money. He said he'd trust me for it."

She felt all hollow inside as she leaned against him.

"He said it was best he sell the gray," Chance continued. "Your father-in-law was asking about the animal. It seems Deacon comes without a bill of sale, and Pharaoh thought we might suit each other because the horse was originally a Virginian. His wife's dowry, I believe he said."

Rachel squeezed his hand. "And if you don't come back to pay him?"

"I'll expect you to do it for me."

Tears stung her eyes. "Why is it the men I choose always leave me to pay their bills?"

He slipped an arm around her shoulder. "You'll be well provided for, Rachel. You and Davy. The truth is, in spite of the war, I'm filthy rich."

"You're what?" She stared at him.

"No, not just comfortable. More than that. Benjamin told me, when I was closeted with him at the bank. It seems that Mother's South African mining ventures have paid off. My share of the sale of a diamond mine is more than Davy is ever likely to spend. If . . . if anything happens to me, if you don't hear from me when the war is over, you're to contact Benjamin. The money's in trust, for me as well as you and Davy. There's American railroad stock, some South American cattle ranches—"

"No more," she said. "I don't want to know about it. I

don't care. I only want you, Chance. Just you, as I found you in my creek, stark naked and hungry."

He hugged her, then chuckled. "You want me naked and hungry?" He caressed her throat and ran his fingers over her lips. "Do you know how beautiful you are to me? How you walk through my dreams at night? How hearing you laugh warms my soul?"

"Then how can you leave me? Leave us?" She'd not expected it to hurt so bad. She'd prepared herself for his going, told herself that she was too tough to break down when the time came. And now that it had, she felt like corn mush inside.

"No tears tonight," he whispered, leaning close and kissing her eyebrows and each closed eyelid in turn. "Sweet, sweet Rachel. I kept my bargain. Now you must be strong for a few more hours. I can't go away and leave you weeping."

He stiffened and released her, and she heard the sound of a horse galloping across the meadow. She straightened, brushing the tears away. "Hide!" she urged him.

"No, no more," he answered. "I'm at an end of hiding."

The horse slowed and Pharaoh's deep voice rang out. "Miss Rachel? Chance? Is that you? I brought Deacon, and that other thing you asked me for."

Rachel saw that the blacksmith was carrying a large sack, but she was too upset to care what he'd brought. She murmured a greeting.

"He's a good horse," said Pharaoh. "Shame he's not a stallion. He'd sire fine colts."

"He's got good blood in him," Chance agreed. "I'll be proud to ride him."

"Into cannon fire?" Rachel cried.

"If I'm being shot at, I need a decent mount," Chance said.

"Naturally you'd need a fine horse to get yourself killed on," she answered. "So damned logical!" Without waiting for his reply, she ran back toward the house.

Upstairs, in her room, she paced the floor. She wanted to tear down the curtains, throw her jewelry box across the room, pitch Chance's clothing out the window. But Davy was resting peacefully in his cradle, and this was the last night she could sleep in Chance's arms, so she forced back her anger.

She removed her dress and underthings, let down her hair, and put on her best linen nightgown, the one with the Irish lace on the hem. She blew out all the lamps but one, then brushed her hair two hundred times and fortified herself with a glass of her grandmother's dandelion wine.

After what seemed an eternity, she heard Chance coming up the stairs. She rose, pulled back the bedspread, and extinguished the final light.

It was dark in the room, but not so dark that she couldn't make out his form in the doorway.

"I'm sorry, Rachel. Sorry we couldn't be married by now. Sorry I'm going to hurt you tomorrow by going away."

He waited.

"I'm sorry, too," she murmured.

"I'll go tonight if you want me to."

"Not tonight," she replied softly. "Tonight is mine."

She ran into his arms and tilted her face up for his kiss. And for a few brief hours, she did not think of tomorrow, only the bittersweet rapture, the giving and taking, and the glory of being loved by such a man.

And in the morning, when she woke to find the place beside her empty, she left Davy wailing in his cradle and ran down to the kitchen. The smell of fresh coffee drifted from the pot on the stove; the back door stood ajar.

"Chance!" she screamed as she ran out to the barn. Bear lumbered after her. "Chance!"

Susan raised her head over the edge of the stall and mooed. Blackie nickered. But the third stall was as empty as her bed had been.

Deacon was gone, and Chance with him. While she'd slept, they'd ridden away into the morning mist.

"No!" she cried. "No." Sobbing, she slipped to the floor and buried her face in her hands. "No, not yet," she said brokenly. "Not yet."

Bear uttered a strange *woof*. Something damp and scratchy brushed her bare ankle.

"Leave me alone."

Bear whined, and the odd sensation came again.

Rachel raised her head. Bear was sitting a few feet away from her on the straw, but something . . . She reached down and touched a squirming ball of fur.

"What is—"

Small sharp teeth nipped her shin.

Scooping up the squirming bundle, she carried it out into the morning light and discovered that she was holding a fluffy brown-and-white collie pup with a black nose, red tongue, and cinnamon-brown eyes. Tied around the puppy's neck was a red silk ribbon.

Her neck, Rachel corrected herself, and she tucked a hand under the warm, wiggling belly.

Tied to the ribbon was a note. Bear trotted after her as she took the puppy and the message into the kitchen. She poured a bowl of milk for the little collie, put her on the floor, and lit a lamp.

The note, written in bold, beautiful script, read

> *To keep you company until I come home.*
> *Love,*
> *Your devoted servant,*
> *William James Chancellor III, Esquire*

"William James Chancellor the Third!" she said in astonishment. "William James?" He hadn't named Davy after James Irons at all. He'd given the baby his own name. "You bastard! You good-for-nothing, fast-talking Richmond lawyer."

And then she laughed and hugged the puppy.

And then she cried.

Chapter 26

Rachel kept close to the farm as autumn leaves drifted down to skitter across the yard and gather into fragrant piles around the house. A fire crackled in the kitchen woodstove day and night, and by the time the first snowflakes frosted the landscape, Rachel was certain that her wish had come true. She was carrying Chance's child.

Knowing that it was futile to expect him so soon, Rachel watched the lane for a fair-haired, soft-talking man on a gray horse. Davy and the new pup, Merry, filled her days, but her nights were long and lonely without Chance beside her.

Her arms ached to hold him again, and the house seemed empty without the sound of his laughter.

She told herself that it was foolish to look for him at Christmas, but she did. And when she heard no word from him by midday, she choked back her tears and accepted Cora's invitation to join her family for the holiday dinner. Coming home through the twilight on horseback, Rachel fantasized that Chance would be sitting in her kitchen rocker waiting for her, but that, too, was only wishful thinking.

The house was dark and lifeless except for the two

dogs. Merry and Bear barked and wagged their tails when she opened the back door, but even that warm welcome didn't lift her spirits. And later, when Davy was tucked into his cradle, she wept as she packed away Chance's Christmas gifts with her ornaments.

Money continued to arrive monthly from Philadelphia, for both her and Davy. She hired a German couple, Dan and Betty, to help with the farmwork. And as the weather worsened, it seemed sensible to install them in the hired men's quarters in the barn. Rachel knew that when spring came, she would need full-time assistance on the farm if she hoped to get another year's crop in the ground.

In early February Rachel left Davy with Betty one morning and rode to the general store to buy nutmeg. To her surprise she found a letter waiting. Too nervous to read it in front of witnesses, she hurried outside and turned it over. The return address was Santa Fe, New Mexico.

With trembling hands, Rachel tore it open. To her disappointment, the handwriting was feminine.

Dear Mrs. Irons,

Words cannot thank you for your kindness. The package you sent arrived in poor condition, but I have faith that it may soon be restored. My family is presently residing in the Southwest, where the dry air has done wonders for a certain troubling chest condition. Each day I see real improvement. My daughter, husband, and I never fail to remember you and your brave friends in our prayers. May the Lord bless and keep you.

Yours, most sincerely,
Mrs. Travis Bowman

Another piece of paper fell to the ground. When she picked it up, she found that it was a note made out to her for the amount of two hundred dollars.

Numbly Rachel mounted Blackie and kicked him into a canter. She was glad that Chance's friend had made it home to his family, but it didn't make her own fears any easier to bear. And she certainly didn't want a reward for helping Travis escape. Her first thought was to return the money, but then she decided to cash it and give it to Cora. If anyone deserved to profit from the effort, it was the Wright family.

Rachel's own troubles couldn't be fixed with money. In weeks, perhaps two months at most, she would no longer be able to hide her advancing pregnancy. She knew she'd be able to support and care for both Davy and a new child, but her condition would place her outside the bounds of proper society. Who knew how long she would be welcome in the community? Worse, she wondered if James's mother might petition the courts for little Davy, claiming that she, Rachel, was morally unfit to raise him.

The baby that she and Chance had conceived with so much love would find the world an unforgiving place as one born outside the convention of marriage. She wanted this child very much, but she wondered if she'd been selfish.

For herself Rachel did not care about the scandal. She was strong enough to ignore the whispers and sly glances of the good townsfolk, but her children would suffer. She didn't regret what she and Chance had done, but for the first time she wondered if her decision not to marry him before he went away to war had been the right one.

February brought bitter cold and biting wind. And snuggled with Davy beneath the feather-tick comforter in her bed, Rachel wept for Chance and hoped that he was warm.

In March, Betty and Dan gave notice. "Poor, we may be," her hired man said in his broken English. "But we are good God-fearing people, and we cannot work for a whore."

Rachel sent them off down the lane with their belongings on their back, a week's pay in their pockets, and the cutting edge of her tongue to speed their departure.

"Good riddance to you both!" she called after them. "But be certain you tell the town gossips your juicy news. If any wish to know more, send them here. I'll give them a welcome they'll well remember."

In truth Rachel was happier to have the house to herself. Her morning sickness had passed and she felt good physically. Cora began to stop by every week and often sent her grandchildren with a loaf of fresh-baked bread or a jar of preserves. And when the ground was dry enough to plow, Pharaoh came to work up her garden plot.

"No word from your lawyer?" he asked.

Rachel shook her head. "No, but the war's still going on. He could be thousands of miles away." He could be dead, she thought, but she would not dwell on that possibility. She would only treasure her memories of Chance and hope that they might be together again someday.

"My mother gave Emma and me that two hundred dollars you gave her," he said. "You could have kept it, and none of us would be the wiser." He looked thoughtful. "You brought him out of the prison, Miss Rachel. Seems like that two hundred dollars should be yours."

"I brought Travis here, but you and your mother got

him home to Virginia. It's yours, Pharaoh. Without you, Chance would probably be dead as well as Travis."

"Don't remind me of it. Emma says I'm crazy. I've spent a lifetime struggling against his kind. She says I should have left him to rot behind those walls."

"I'm glad you didn't," Rachel said.

He grinned. "And I'm kind of glad I didn't either."

On the ninth of April, General Robert E. Lee surrendered to Grant at Appomattox Courthouse in Virginia, and the newspapers were heady with predictions of peace after so long a struggle.

Men who had fought for the South began to drift home to Milford and Lewes and Duck Creek. Each morning Rachel rose at dawn to watch for Chance's coming, and every night she hung a lit lantern by the well so that he could find the house if he came by night.

April days were filled with sunshine. Daffodils and tulips burst into blossom, the fruit trees flowered, and Carolina wrens began to build a nest in the eaves over the barn door. Rachel's cow, Susan, gave birth to a black heifer calf with a white spot over one eye.

But still there was no letter from Chance, no hint that he had survived the war, and Rachel's hopes faded.

One misty morning, early in May, she took Davy with her to the creek so that she could check her crab traps. Davy was a handful, constantly curious and willing to eat anything he could get into his mouth. Rachel knew she couldn't take him out in the rowboat; he didn't have the slightest fear of water and would be overboard in minutes.

Her only solution was to fasten a rope around the toddler's waist and tie him to a tree, leaving enough length between boy and willow so that Davy wouldn't feel

confined. Bear remained on the bank to guard him, and
Rachel took the collie in the boat. Leaving Davy and
Merry together, unsupervised, was an invitation to disaster, and her ever-thickening waist made it difficult for her
to move fast.

Even raising the crab traps seemed harder than when
she had been pregnant with Davy. "I must be getting
older," she grumbled. She opened the hatch at one end of
the dripping cage and dumped five fat jimmies into her
basket. "Crabcakes for dinner," she promised the pup.
Maybe she'd give Davy a little. She'd begun to wean him
when the calf was born, and Susan had plenty of milk to
spare.

"Good morning, ma'am," a familiar voice called from
the creek bank.

Rachel looked up, and her heart skipped a beat. Was
she dreaming? Or had she heard Chance's voice?

The gray form of a rider sat motionless on a gray
horse. Both were nearly concealed by a patch of fog lying in the hollow on the far side of the water.

"Chance?" she questioned. Was he ghost or solid
flesh?

"Rachel?"

She leaped out of the boat into the water.

"Rachel!" Man and horse plunged into the shallows
and splashed toward her.

"Chance!" she screamed. "Oh, Chance!"

And then he was pulling her up into his lap. His arms
were around her, and he was kissing her. Both dogs were
barking, and Davy was screaming, but Rachel had no
thought for anything but the man who held her as if he
would never let her go.

"Chance, Chance," she sobbed between kisses. She

locked her arms around his neck and squeezed him with all her might.

The big horse swam across the deepest part of the creek and waded out to the sandbar near the spot where Davy was tied. Somehow, without letting go of each other, both Rachel and Chance were out of the saddle and lifting the baby between them.

"You look different," he said, then grinned as he laid a hand tenderly on her swelling belly. "But you still have the craziest ideas about raising this boy that I've ever seen. You let the dogs run loose and rope the baby."

"You don't know Davy," she protested. "He's so . . ." She trailed off and shifted Davy to her shoulder. "I'm getting you all wet," she said.

"I don't mind."

He stared into her face, so intensely that she felt as if he meant to devour her with his eyes. "I've missed you, woman," he murmured.

"You've grown a beard." A small, neatly trimmed beard and mustache nearly hid a thin scar that ran from his lower lip across one cheek. Another healing wound showed at his wrist, just at the edge of his shirt cuff.

"You've gotten rounder."

Suddenly shy, she pulled away, aware of how she must look to him; barefoot, soaked to the skin, wearing her oldest skirt and a shirt of her father's.

This was her Chance, but not the ragged soldier she'd found here a year ago. This elegantly garbed gentleman wore boots that cost more than the price of an iron plow, and a fine gray frock coat with silver buttons.

"What's wrong, darling?" he asked.

She pointed to his hat, a flat-crowned, gray felt derby

adorned with a jaunty black plume. "You look like a Virginia lawyer," she stammered.

He grinned. "I'm a Philadelphia lawyer now, but if it bothers you . . ." He plucked it off and flung it into the current.

"You went to Philadelphia when I thought you were dead?"

He shrugged. "I didn't exactly go of my own choice. It was more in the line of duty. But it's over now, Rachel. I've come home to you and Davy . . ." He smiled even wider. "And it looks as if I've made it just in time. When are we having this new addition to our family?"

"June or July."

"The war's over for me, Rachel. I'm here to stay, if you'll have me."

A sweet sensation spiraled up through her chest at the warm-honey tones of his voice, and she felt so happy that she thought she'd burst with all the joy bubbling up inside her.

Deacon wandered away, reins trailing, and began to crop grass. Bear whined and licked Chance's hand, while Merry—soaking wet from swimming ashore—scampered round and round them, barking joyfully. Davy, in contrast, squirmed and hid his face.

"He's forgotten me," Chance said. "We can't have that, can we?"

"He'll come around soon. He needs a father, Chance. Can you be that father?"

"I brought him into the world, didn't I?" he reminded her.

She smiled at him. "I'd . . . I'd like that proposal now, sir," she smiled. "Officially, I'm not certain we're even betrothed."

"We'll remedy that." He dropped to one knee in the

fragrant red clover and clasped his hands together dramatically. "Mrs. Irons, ma'am," he said. "Would you do me the honor of becoming my bride?"

"I'm not going to live in Philadelphia."

"Your honor, the witness is avoiding the question," he teased.

"If I say yes, we have to live here, on Rachel's Choice, at least most of the time," she bargained. "And I'd like to be married by Preacher George. That might not be legal, because he's just a lay minister, but we could be married by Reverend Allen and renew our vows in front of Cora's congregation."

"Attempted bribery, your honor."

"You don't want Preacher George to—"

"A priest first, and then your choice. Rabbi, mullah, or judge, it makes no difference to me. It was the clause about where we live that—"

"You want me to leave Rachel's Choice?"

"I want you in my bed, woman. I can put the furniture anywhere. Unless you want to live in Richmond."

Tears of joy clouded her vision. "Overruled."

"Delaware. We'll live in Delaware, and I'll build you the biggest damned house this county has ever seen. Now, will you, or will you not, accept my proposal of matrimony?"

A dimple showed on his left cheek when he smiled, and she wondered if their child would have the same dimple. She hoped so.

"Yes, your honor," she replied softly.

Chance's eyes shone. "Yes, what?"

"Yes, I'll be your wife."

"I'm glad, otherwise I spent a lot of money on this for nothing," he said as he slid a large emerald ring on her finger. "I hope you like it, Rachel. This was my grand-mother's. But if you'd rather choose another, then—"

"Hush," she said, putting her fingertips over his lips. "The trouble with Southern lawyers is that they never know when to stop talking."

Laughing, he stood and swept her off her feet, swinging both her and Davy around until she cried out for mercy. Then he lowered her to the grass and pulled her into his arms. "I love you, Rachel," he murmured. "Love you, love you, love you."

"Forever and ever?" she asked him.

"Forever and ever."

"Case closed," she murmured just before he kissed her. And her heart whispered that this was one sweet-talking lawyer that she could trust to keep his word.

Epilogue

Rachel's Choice
May 1890

Rachel stood at the open window and looked down on the bustling activity below. The expanse of green lawn that ran down to Indian Creek was scattered with umbrella-covered tables, covered pavilions, and elegantly clad men and women. Balloons and bright-colored streamers fluttered gaily in the warm breeze, and the sounds of shouts and children's laughter drifted over the gathering of relatives and friends.

To the west, Rachel could see an endless line of horse-drawn carriages coming up the circular drive, and from the river on the northeast, she heard the wail of a steamer about to dock at their landing. Still more guests, she thought.

"You'd think you were the only baby ever christened in this county," she murmured lovingly to the red-haired infant girl in her arms. "I hope Cook has enough food for all these people."

"Mother Chancellor, have you got Victoria?" Mary called from the hall.

"I do," Rachel answered. "If you can find her in all these ruffles."

"And her bonnet? Do you have her bonnet?"

Rachel chuckled. "On the bed, but she doesn't like it. Do you, darlin'?" she whispered to the baby. "The lace scratches, doesn't it?" Rachel glanced at her daughter-in-law. "As warm as it is today, she'd be more comfortable in a cotton sacque and diaper."

"On her christening day?" Mary scooped the baby out of Rachel's arms. "Oh, you're teasing me, aren't you, Mother Chancellor."

Victoria waved her arms and hiccuped.

"She probably needs burping," Rachel advised. She gave the sweet-smelling little girl one more kiss on the forehead before her mother whisked her away to show her off to the guests.

Travis Bowman's daughter was a good match for Davy, or rather J.D. as she reminded herself he preferred to be called nowadays. But Rachel thought that Mary was a tad too fussy with Victoria. "Wait until she has two more," she murmured to no one in particular.

"Is it safe to come out?"

Rachel smiled at the sound of Chance's voice. "I wondered where you were hiding."

Grinning, finger on his lips, he strolled out of the small dressing room that adjoined their bedchamber. "You were the prettiest woman in Saint Anne's this morning," he whispered.

"Go on with you, Chance Chancellor. None of your soft-talking lawyer tricks with me."

"Wouldn't think of it."

A flood of happiness washed over Rachel as she studied her husband. Few people would guess his age; he looked more like a bridegroom than a grandfather, as slim and handsome as ever. And the fancy attire Chance had worn to church was perfect on him.

The silver streaks in his hair made him even more distinguished-looking, she decided, although with typical male vanity, he insisted they were from the sun. But best of all she loved his blue eyes, still as vivid as the day she'd found him. Chance's eyes could darken to steel when his temper was up, but just now they danced with mischief.

"What are you up to?" she demanded. "You look altogether too pleased with yourself, sir. Has Davy—"

"J.D.," he corrected her impishly. "Our eldest is too successful a counselor to be known as Davy to his associates." Chance slipped the lock on the bedroom door.

Pretending not to notice, Rachel glanced out the window again. "You should be downstairs," she said. "That looks like the governor's team of Cleveland bays pulling that vis-à-vis. He'd expect you to welcome him."

Chance came up behind her and put his arms around her waist. "J.D. can take care of him," he murmured as he kissed the nape of her neck. "Personally, I'm glad to have this time alone with my wife."

She sighed with contentment, wondering how many women who'd celebrated twenty-five years of marriage still thrilled to their husband's touch as she did. Her marriage to Chance had been truly blessed, and a day like this one brought enough joy to last two lifetimes.

They had bright, loving children, all beautiful and clever. Chance always claimed that it was the Lord's special gift that no parent ever knew when they had homely or dull offspring. But she didn't let his teasing get to her; she had the sense to know her four were special.

Davy had followed the law; he was a senior partner in Chance's firm and would become the head man when Chance retired. Virginia, born only a few months after she and Chance were married, had studied at a fine college in Dublin and was now an educator, overseeing black schools in New Castle County. She'd become engaged at Christmas to a neighbor's son and would return home to be married in the fall.

Gavin, at fifteen, talked of nothing but attending the Naval Academy, but his sister Cora Jean, two years younger, was a farmer born and bred. It was Cora Jean who'd suggested they plant apples when the whole state was crazy for peach orchards, and Cora Jean who filled Rachel's Choice with other people's stray dogs and aging ponies.

Chance kissed Rachel's neck again, sending sweet sensations through her. When he nibbled on her left ear, familiar stirrings made Rachel squirm. "I should be down there with our children and grandchild," she said, "not upstairs playing hanky-panky with a grandfather."

It pleased her immensely that she still fit perfectly in his arms when she turned to snuggle against him. "I love you," she whispered. "You've given me a fairy-tale life."

She moistened her lips, and he kissed them tenderly.

"Why shouldn't I? It was you who taught me what real happiness was. Giving you the biggest mansion house in the state seems little enough to do for you."

Rachel chuckled softly. "Not exactly the largest in Delaware," she corrected him. "Maybe in Kent County."

"Shall we put an addition on the south wing?"

"No, thank you, sir. This house is quite adequate. Any larger, and it would be taking up valuable farmland."

"As long as you're satisfied."

She pulled back a little and regarded him with suspicion. "What are you up to, husband? You're not running for Congress again, are you? You promised that one term would be all—"

He smiled at her. "I am not running for senator. I leave that to younger and more desperate men."

"Governor? They've convinced you to—"

"Not state office either. I've decided to open a branch office in Dover and leave Philadelphia to J.D. and Solomon."

"Solomon? Pharaoh and Emma's Solomon? He's coming to work at the firm?"

He nodded. "Graduated with honors. He'll be an asset to the company. I think he's going to make a brilliant lawyer, maybe even keep J.D. from getting too sure of himself. As for me, I think it would be nice to come home to my own front porch every night, drink iced tea, and watch the lightning bugs blink on and off."

"Oh, Chance!" She gave a little squeal and hugged him. "For real? I won't have to spend four months a year in Philadelphia anymore? We can live on the farm all the time?"

He plucked a hairpin from her elaborately coiled chignon. She sighed and traced his bottom lip with the tip of her tongue.

"You've followed me to Washington and back," he whispered. "And you've put up with spending weeks in that town house in the city. The least I can do for you is to find a courtroom closer to home. The governor has hinted that he needs honest judges. What would you think of that?"

She threaded her fingers through his hair. "If you'll be

in my bed on Rachel's Choice every night, you can go back to milking cows for all I care."

He broke from their embrace long enough to shed his coat and loosen his collar. "This is where you're supposed to complain that I'm mussing your hairdo," he said.

She laughed and began to undo the pearl buttons on the bodice of her silk polonaise gown. "I warned you when you married me that you weren't getting a lady."

"Oh, but I did," he replied. "The finest lady of all." He caught her around the waist and pulled her toward the bed. "Race you," he dared. "First one naked gets to be on top."

"Objection," she whispered. "Unfair. I've got more clothes than you, and you know I can't get out of this damned corset without—"

"Overruled."

She tugged at the buttons on her high black leather shoes, and one button flew off and shot across the room. "Now you've done it!" she cried.

"Me? What did I do?"

Giggling, they shed their clothing and dived into the high feather bed that would have dwarfed Rachel's bedroom in the old farmhouse.

Chance pulled another three pins from her hair, and the heavy braid fell forward over her shoulder. "I like it loose," he said as he began to undo it.

Someone rapped loudly on the door, and Rachel yanked the sheets over her bare breasts and giggled.

"Mother! Mother, are you in there?" Cora Jean called. "Gavin says my dogs have to be locked up. They don't have to, do they?" The doorknob rattled. "Mother? The door's locked!"

Another youthful feminine voice, one that Rachel recognized as belonging to a friend of her daughter's, echoed from the stair landing. "Cora Jean! Come on! Randy's here, and he's riding the most beautiful blood bay!"

Rachel buried her head under a pillow.

"This is a dereliction of duty on your part, madam," Chance teased as he ran appraising fingers over her bare bottom. "You are frolicking with a gentleman instead of entertaining the governor. Surely, a capital offense."

"Guilty, your honor," she whispered. "You matter more to me than all the governors in the country."

"What about all the crops?" he countered. "Do I matter more than your damned apples?"

"Hard choice." She gently massaged the old scar on his shoulder. "But . . ." She sighed. "If I had to choose, it would be you."

"I'm glad to hear that." He kissed her so soundly that she flushed to the tips of her toes.

"Mother! Are you in there?" That was Gavin, his voice cracking slightly. "People are asking for you. Have you seen Papa?"

She tried to answer, but Chance clamped a hand over her mouth. She squirmed and tried to get away, but he yanked the covers over their heads.

"Have you looked for your mother by the creek landing?" Chance asked. "Tell your brother that I'm in an important conference. I shouldn't be long."

"Yes, sir."

Gavin's footsteps faded as he hurried down the hall.

"Liar," she accused.

"Did I say you were there?"

"You led our son to believe that I was at the landing."

"I told the truth," Chance replied between kisses. "I . . . am . . . in . . . an . . . important conference." He cupped her breast. "They can wait," he murmured huskily. "They can all wait."

And then she kissed him, and for a precious hour they shut out children, friends, and responsibilities to renew a love affair that she knew with all her heart and soul would never, never end.

ON SALE NOW

MIDNIGHT RIDER
By Diana Palmer
The *New York Times* bestselling author of
The Long, Tall Texan series

To Bernadette Barron, Eduardo Cortes is the enemy. A noble count with a sprawling ranch in the grand state of Texas, Cortes challenges her with dark, penetrating eyes that seem to pierce her very soul. For theirs is a marriage of convenience—he needs a rich wife to save his land; she needs a titled husband. But can't he see the burning truth: that she loves him?

It is a secret Bernadette vows to keep until desire turns their marriage bargain into a passionate battle of wills. For it is love's fiery initiation that will make Bernadette aware of her own capacity for pleasure, and it is the sheer force of her own love that will give her newfound strength to battle against the odds to claim a man she will not be denied. . . .

LOOK FOR THESE TWO DELIGHTFUL REGENCY ROMANCES

MARRY IN HASTE
By Lynn Kerstan

While trespassing on a lavish estate, Diana Whitney strikes Colonel Alex Valliant squarely on the head with a frying pan. Rather than see the pretty interloper fall into disgrace, the love-struck soldier asks for her hand. But Diana refuses to march quietly to the altar and—much to the colonel's surprise and dismay—rejects his offer.

But when Diana's uncle threatens to marry her off to a man she finds completely intolerable, she accepts Alex's hasty proposal. However, Diana soon must make a bold gamble based on the calling of her heart—and engage in a battle for a future founded on love. . . .

THE HOMECOMING
By Marion Chesney

In this final volume to the ever-popular Daughters of Mannerling series, the Beverley sisters have one last chance to regain their ancestral home: Lizzie, the precocious, youngest sister, who would rather die an old maid than marry for anything but love.

And how could she ever love Mannerling's new owner, the stuffy Duke of Severnshire? Suddenly, it appears that no one, including the duke, is what he or she seems, and for the first time, saucy and canny Lizzie is at a loss for words. But is a homecoming really what she wants?

ON SALE NOW

DON'T MISS

the long-awaited paperback edition of the
New York Times bestselling petite hardcover

BETRAYED
By Bertrice Small

When Fiona Hay offers Angus Gordon her
virtue in exchange for a dowry for her sisters, she
so intrigues the rogue that he demands a higher
payment: She will be his mistress. Thus begins a
battle of wills and sensual delights. Destiny soon
draws the ardent lovers into the turbulent court
of King James. But the king's political schemes
force Fiona away from the man she loves . . . and
into the arms of a wild and passionate
Highlander, The MacDonald of Nairn. Will this
coldhearted and callous betrayal forever destroy
Fiona's chance at happiness?

ON SALE NOVEMBER 3